Poker without Cards

A Consciousness Thriller

by

Ben Mack

www.pokerwithoutcards.com

For information on eXe Active Media Group, contact the marketing
department at 27 West Anapamu Suite #166, Santa Barbara, CA 93101.
Phone: 805-490-2741
Email: press@exe-active.com

First published in March 2005 by eXe Active Media Group.

Forward

By Joseph Matheny

Dear Reader,

I am, I must admit, somewhat reticent to publish this manuscript as was requested of me. Since there are no copyright or confidentiality barriers, I am obliging this request with a modicum of effort and liability on my part. At least that much is easy. However, I must forewarn you; the book that you have open before you is not your typical transcription.

These are the facts as I know them: The "author" or compiler of this work, Ben Mack, did in fact work as a professional transcriber for The Transcription Company. That much is verifiable. I have contacted Kane'ohe Hospital and they state that Dr. Fink no longer works there. They would not verify having ever had a patient named Richard Brenneman Wilson. I have halted my investigation into this facet of the story at this time since I am unable to invest any more time tracking this down.

During the course of transcribing this piece from tapes, Ben did much due diligence and extensive research into many of the ideas discussed in the enclosed conversations. He tried to ensure the accuracy of these transcriptions and the ideas expressed by following up on most of the thought threads espoused herein. When he sent me the original, raw transcription it included minimal transcriber's notations. The bulk of these were later added since there was nowhere to send the completed project. This notwithstanding he continued to work on the transcription. You see, although he was paid for his work in advance through The Transcription Company, there was no client contact information attached to the tapes, therefore there was no place or person to send in the work to once it was completed. After obviously being too "assertive" with The Transcription Company, they began to refuse to return his calls, and eventually stopped giving him additional projects. This is when he contacted me. He wasn't able to set the project aside and be done with it. He doggedly continued the project on his own and continued researching ideas to improve the accuracy of his transcription. Some would say he acted as a man possessed or *infected*.

Here is some of what I now know: During the process of preparing a transcription of a peculiar hospital meeting (one may argue meta-liaison is a more fitting term) for hire, Ben was inspired to contact me. In part due to my public involvement with reporting the details of Ong's Hat and other fringe ephemera, Ben believed that I would find this information tantalizing. Being that I am a bit reclusive, due to the collective, unstable nature of the denizens dimwit brigades that shuffle the halls of paranormal and occult subcultures, I am not easy to find. However, Ben made a correct guess that one Dr. Christopher Hyatt*, an associate of mine, could at least get a message passed to me. Ben is a graduate of Dr. Hyatt's **Extreme Individual Institute**, which he stumbled across in the process of preparing this transcription. His journey to and through the EII is another story altogether and not one I'll go into here.

* (A note to Dr. Hyatt for that wonderful referral: Va te faire foutre!)

The final files that I received from him included "A Fecundity," a glossary that he asked me *not* to publish. I was confused as to why he would send me the glossary and then ask me not to include it. After much deliberation, I have decided not to honor that request. To say that Ben's behavior borders on the eccentric or bizarre at times is to understate the case. However, the protocols of politeness and brevity (not to mention journalistic objectivity) dictate that I leave my personal judgments in the closet, at least for now. If the contents of these conversations are as important as Ben seems to feel, then his comments on these events that are represented in the Glossary also warrant consideration. Do they not?

I would go one step further and propose that Ben's comments in fact demonstrate the effect that the recordings of these "conversations" may have on certain types of individuals under certain circumstances. I have left intact a rather rambling, disjointed and paranoid rant that was attached to this glossary, as way of introduction or explanation, so that you the reader may get a small taste of what I have had to endure during the course of this "correspondence" if one were so inclined to classify our interaction as such. I should have seen it coming. I should have ignored his first email of introduction. Read this paragraph and judge for yourself:

"It occurs to me that the primary agenda of the powers that be is to induce FAITH.

Faith means you are obligated to not think stuff through—whatever they tell you not to think through. And, the thoughts they find really threatening they label as insane. But, if you can't have real faith, at minimum, you are required to take the system seriously. I take the system seriously. In ten years, they may imprison me for my ideas. Is this a paranoid fear or a realistic concern? I would fear it less if our Homeland Security didn't monitor what books I buy or check out from the library. Please bear in mind that this transcription may be hazardous to your status."

During the course of our correspondence, Ben had asked that if I gave the work a title at all, that it be called *The Longer Line.* Having read the transcription, as you undoubtedly are about to do also, I disagreed. Since Ben is indisposed and has left me holding the bag so to speak, I wish upon him an encounter involving aerial intercourse on an oscillating pastry, if he has any problem with my decision! After more careful deliberation, I arrived at the title; *Poker Without Cards*, a label that was originally created by Mike Caro for a book he never published (or did he?), yet is for sale on Amazon. Since it appears to me that Ben is overwhelmed with the contemplation of ambiguous power structures, I found this title fitting. Since Mr. Caro never published said book (or did he?) I did not feel as if the title were being 'borrowed". If anything, it is shared.

If it seems like I'm bitter about this responsibility, I am. Ben sent me a modest sum of money, with the request that I publish the transcription as I saw fit. Since there is nowhere for me to return the fee, I feel obliged. However, let me add that I feel obliged the way a person who is being squeezed by the Mafia to do a contract hit or have his family whacked feels obliged. So, this is how I see fit, Baiseur De Mère!

I have also taken the liberty of setting up a forwarding email address to address all correspondence regarding this work, since I personally do not want to be contacted about it, in any way. The aforementioned account forwards to the last known working email address that I have for Ben. The last time I heard from him, he said he was heading to the New Jersey Pine Barrens. Why he would do such a thing is beyond me since there is nothing left there but history.

Now let me take a moment to make something perfectly clear: I do not want to be bothered, contacted, harangued or otherwise harassed in any way, in part or in whole, regarding this document and the contents therein. *This is NOT a game.* Those who persevere and transgress my declared boundaries on this will be hunted down and trampled like the small child on the street in RLR's *Dr. Jekyll and Mr. Hyde.* If you do not know what I am referring to, I suggest you read that book or at least consult the cliff notes. Maybe you could "Google" it.

Since you have gotten this far, I suppose you are going to read the transcript. Far be it from me to try and stop you.

That is all.

Joseph.Matheny.Com

2004

The Transcription

"The basic tool for the manipulation of reality is the
manipulation of words. If you can control the meaning of
words, you can control the people who must use the words."

Philip K. Dick

Media: WAV file 1 of 1
Source: PANELREVIEW062303.WAV

KZZXLQERDEG.UGR

Mechanical Considerations: Notations of sound shall appear in ALL CAPS and are intended to make the transcript easier to read and follow. [PAUSE] indicates three to five seconds of non-speech. [SILENCE] indicates five or more seconds of non-speech. Music and other sounds are similarly notated. Punctuation choices between commas and periods were made to reflect the cadence of the speaker—periods represent a full stop where commas suggest one sentiment: (e.g., [No, I won't. // No. I won't.]). Additional notations are cited parenthetically, such as unconventional spelling when the speaker has indicated a non-standard spelling. This transcription is broken into seven sessions, each corresponding to one session between Psychiatrist Dr. William Fink and the interviewee. As per request, attendee comments during playback have been omitted from this record.

[BEGIN TRANSCRIPT]

PSYCHIATRIST 1:

You will be given a transcript of the seven tapes I am about to play. We are recording and transcribing this meeting. Each tape contains an interview between Dr. William Fink and a man who identifies himself as Howard Campbell. However, no records have been discovered to indicate that a man named Howard Campbell exists who held the jobs this man describes. We have two documents this man gave to Dr. Fink. We do not have the journals or manifestos discussed, which the patient, Richard Wilson, reportedly read. You are aware of the problems surrounding Mr. Wilson's time here. Dr. Fink's license to practice medicine has been indefinitely suspended. Our task is to assess if the situation is contained, or if additional liabilities to the hospital may arise.

[SOUND: PSYCHIATRIST PRESSES PLAY. THE DRONE OF AUDIO PLAYBACK.]

SESSION 1

DR. WILLIAM FINK:

January 31, 2003, Howard Campbell giving oral background on Ward 3 patient Richard Wilson.

[PAUSE]

Tell me about Richard inviting you to Hawaii. When did you get here?

HOWARD CAMPBELL:

I arrived in Hawaii on December 23rd. I've been here since. I've been studying everything he left me in his room. A week earlier, at my home in Atlanta, I got a certified letter with a first class ticket to Hawaii. Richard had included a note, "Let's spend Christmas together." I wasn't expecting the kind of together he had prepared for me.

DR. WILLIAM FINK:

What do you mean?

HOWARD CAMPBELL:

Nobody answered when I rang his room at the Sheraton Moana Surfrider hotel. The front desk said Richard had registered me as a second guest, so they could give me a key, but that there wasn't a message for me or anything.

On his door hung a "Do Not Disturb" sign. Intricately bizarre barely begins to describe what I found inside.

His room had books everywhere, some neatly stacked, others spread out over an area of carpeting. On his bedside table he made a card-castle out of books on economics. There were hundreds of books—conspiracy novels, Sufi poetry, books on philosophy and books on everything from saltwater aquariums to quantum psychology. There were over a hundred and fifty DVDs interspersed with the books, along with papers and pictures. Each grouping of material formed mini-constellations, and they were all over his hotel suite. If you didn't see the order, the room looked like a royal mess.

Centered on the dining table, on top of a neatly stacked tower of papers I found a note from Richard addressed to me, "Howard, I hope you will find the accommodations amenable. If you are reading this, I have either escaped or am being held captive. Back Men found me."

DR. WILLIAM FINK:

Oglethorpe didn't put any of this in her report.

HOWARD CAMPBELL:

I didn't get a chance to tell her. I'm glad I'm getting the chance to tell you this now because his room was way peculiar. I mean I had seen his art installations at Bennington, but this was a new kind of art. It was an intellectual sculpture. The dining room table was center stage. Within the chaos of all his books and notes and DVDs, the dining room table was an uncharacteristically neat work area. I knew him well enough to know that. If you could have seen his dorm in college, it looked like a cyclone hit it but he knew where everything was. No. The note on the manuscript was meant for me to read. Bucky had created an event for me to experience. He imagined me reading all of his words and they were more carefully chosen than a casual glance would glean. He was...

DR. WILLIAM FINK:

Bucky?

HOWARD CAMPBELL:

Oh. We never called him Richard. We called him Bucky. We thought of him as a misunderstood genius. Bucky wasn't his middle name or anything, just a nickname that stuck, because he built geodesic domes out of straws in his dorm room at Bennington.

DR. WILLIAM FINK:

Bucky, as in Buckminster Fuller, the engineer who designed geodesic domes?

HOWARD CAMPBELL:

Exactly. The guy who made-up the word synergy. Fuller's first book was called: *Nine Chains To The Moon, An Adventure In Thought*. That's what it was like interacting with our Bucky, Richard Wilson. It was an adventure in thought.

I know Bucky about as well as I know anybody. Better probably. We had lived together for a number of years. I knew his eccentricities. I had tasted the luxuries his inheritance had provided. I didn't think twice about ordering room service. I ordered a crab salad for each of us, thinking he would be back soon. I scarfed [sic] one down, and then the next, waiting for him on the patio. I wasn't peeved. I stared out at the ocean. I figured Bucky was just fucking with me, with the note and all, and that he was out surfing or something. I figured he would be back soon. After lunch, I checked my email, and found the one from you. Well, you know what I spoke to Nurse Oglethorpe about, and I saw Bucky when we had arranged two days after that. And, I was expecting to meet you before I saw Bucky the next day at Kane'ohe Hospital. Bucky didn't seem alive.

[SOUND: PAPERS BEING SORTED]

DR. WILLIAM FINK:

None of this is in Nurse Oglethorpe's report.

HOWARD CAMPBELL:

Oglethorpe said she needed to know Bucky's history of mental illness and went through a list of yes and no questions. I tried to ask her questions about Richard, but she said she wasn't authorized to tell me anything. I was in a bit of a state of shock, and I didn't seem to be able to get any of this out, but she said you wanted to speak with me. So, I knew I could tell you all the details now.

How did Bucky actually get here? He didn't admit himself, did he?

DR. WILLIAM FINK:

No, he didn't. He's here in the custody of the state of Hawaii. Richard Wilson was picked up by police when tourists found him sitting cross-legged on the sand at Oahu. He had defecated on himself. He was unresponsive to questions. The paramedics brought him here.

HOWARD CAMPBELL:

Did he break any laws? Have there been any changes?

DR. WILLIAM FINK:

No.

[PAUSE]

When was the last time you spoke with him?

HOWARD CAMPBELL:

Last November. He was explaining to me how our federal reserve was a private corporation and that England's royal family actually owned controlling interest. He said that this was how the evil Sufis had created their own money machine. He kept saying that he was running out of cigarettes. I kept telling him to go buy some, but that didn't seem to be the point. The last thing Bucky said to me was "Is this the most likely means to effect my safety and happiness?"

DR. WILLIAM FINK:

What does that mean?

HOWARD CAMPBELL:

I assumed he was talking about his job. He'd been having some trouble, some design and execution difficulties. He said he felt uneasy and dispassionate. Either that or the fact that we live in a patrist society filled with too many fnords. He said he was reading Kurt Vonnegut's *Mother Night*. He had muttered something about Ulysses, but I can't follow when he talks like that.

(TRANSCRIBER'S NOTATION ON VERNACULAR: HOWARD CAMPBELL USES MANY NON-STANDARD ENGLISH WORDS. TO REFLECT THE SPEAKER'S VOCABULARY, NON-STANDARD WORDS HAVE BEEN GOOGLE'D TO ENSURE ACCURACY. JOE, THE RESULTS OF THIS INTERNET SEARCH ARE ATTACHED TO THIS DOCUMENT IN THE FORM OF A GLOSSARY OF PROPER NOUNS AND NON-STANDARD ENGLISH. A DEFINITION OF "FNORD(S)" AND OTHER NON-STANDARD ENGLISH WORDS CAN

DR. WILLIAM FINK:

Talks like what?

HOWARD CAMPBELL:

All philosophical. Referencing stuff I haven't read. It makes me feel disconnected. Like I should go online and Google the words I don't know. I probably would learn something new if I did that, but I'm essentially lazy.

[PAUSE]

Anyway, his talking all-philosophical doesn't make me feel as disconnected as I felt visiting him, however. Is he the same?

DR. WILLIAM FINK:

Richard is still in a catatonic stupor. Orderlies can get him to walk, but it's almost like pushing him because he'll stop walking after three or four steps. He is still completely unresponsive to audio stimulus.

HOWARD CAMPBELL:

I tried making sudden noises and got no reaction.

DR. WILLIAM FINK:

Yes, you could pop a balloon behind him while he ate and he wouldn't flinch. This is not uncommon. I am an expert in catatonia, specifically catatonia as an onset to schizophrenia.

[PAUSE]

I couldn't meet you then because I had a personal emergency.

HOWARD CAMPBELL:

The nurse on duty told me you had a personal emergency.

[PAUSE]

Why did you want to meet me?

DR. WILLIAM FINK:

Nurse Oglethorpe's report said you and Richard have done drugs together. I'm trying to ascertain if his state may have been drug induced. Any drugs or drug paraphernalia in his hotel room?

HOWARD CAMPBELL:

I brought cigarettes and a couple of lighters, but nothing illegal. Bucky has done drugs, but there was no evidence of recent drug use in the hotel room. Is that all you wanted to know?

DR. WILLIAM FINK:

His blood work came back clean, but some drugs don't show up on these tests. I want to rule out drug induced catatonia.

HOWARD CAMPBELL:

I don't think he was on acid, but I can't state that with certainty. He has a history of drug use. I wasn't close with him recently. I spelled out what I could with Nurse Oglethorpe.

DR. WILLIAM FINK:

Richard Wilson is at the upper range for the onset of adult schizophrenia. He had paintings in his backpack, suggesting an artistic temperament, a trait often strong among those who develop schizophrenia in their twenties. I'm hoping to identify and more accurately articulate cues that precede this sickness. That's why I have invited you here, because in the absence of family and current friends, you are the most likely conduit for me to uncover these cues. I want to know as much as you can share about Richard Wilson. The more intimate the details the better. I'm observing some subtle similarities not previously noted in schizophrenic publications. I hope that if I publish these observations, we may help alleviate, or at least delay, others from suffering this horrible sickness.

[SILENCE]

HOWARD CAMPBELL:

I take exception to your precepts of sickness and health. I hear your objectivity as a form of disdain. I am here to help Richard Wilson.

DR. WILLIAM FINK:

We are allies to that end.

HOWARD CAMPBELL:

Good. I should mention, however, that I am suspicious of your methods. And, to the extent anybody brings harm to Bucky, either directly or through neglect, I will hold you personally responsible.

DR. WILLIAM FINK:

Fair enough.

HOWARD CAMPBELL:

I will share what I know to be true. I will talk with you for so long as it feels productive for both of us. You want background; I want Richard back from whatever plane of existence Richard is visiting. Neither of us can immediately give the other what he wants. I suspect we'll get along fine so long as our hopes are respected, they may not be fulfilled, but our expectations must be treated with honor.

DR. WILLIAM FINK:

What do you expect of me?

HOWARD CAMPBELL:

I expect you to actively listen. To remember that this is a real person we are talking about. That you put aside your notions of crazy and try to see an intelligence in the motivations and actions of Richard Wilson. The stories of real people don't fit neatly into three or five act structures. I hope you will bear with me as I try to give you what I think is relevant.

DR. WILLIAM FINK:

I just ask that you be candid and truthful.

HOWARD CAMPBELL:

I will be candid. Maybe more candid than you are prepared for. I can tell you what I know and what I don't know. However, truth is a funny word. I don't mean to get into semantics or linguistics. You are seeking insight about the mind of a schizophrenic or you wouldn't have invited me here. I will tell you about a man on whom the label schizophrenic may be appropriate. You occur to me as having a fragile cosmography, overcompensated for in your need for deference from others. Maintaining your confidence is on your plate. By truly understanding schizophrenia, you will become somewhat schizophrenic yourself.

DR. WILLIAM FINK:

Schizophrenia doesn't work like that. It isn't something that you catch. Schizophrenia has biological roots.

HOWARD CAMPBELL:

You're right. I've never seen a schizophrenic rock.
[PAUSE]
That was a joke.

DR. WILLIAM FINK:

Right.
Would you tell me more about Richard's hotel room?

HOWARD CAMPBELL:

So we begin. His room was more like an art installation than the mess it appeared to be. I brought pictures in my backpack.

[SOUND: CHAIR SCREECHING. BACKPACK UNZIPPED.]

This was the most interactive assemblage probably ever created. Bucky had prepared an intellectual journey for me. Look at this picture, this is the card-castle of books I mentioned earlier. And this one.

[PAUSE]

DR. WILLIAM FINK:

This is astounding.

HOWARD CAMPBELL:

He intended for me to read everything he'd prepared and left behind.

DR. WILLIAM FINK:

What's this? A mountain?

HOWARD CAMPBELL:

That is the Sphinx? You know, in Giza.

DR. WILLIAM FINK:

It is? I visited it on vacation with my family.

[PAUSE]

I don't see it. How do you know that's what it is supposed to be?

HOWARD CAMPBELL:

Look at the profile and you might see it. But, that aside, this group of books was all on conspiracy theories and ancient cultures. But you see that book there? That book is *Finger Prints of The Gods*. It is the very topmost book on the torso. It has a picture of the Sphinx on the cover.

[PAUSE]

DR. WILLIAM FINK:

Fascinating.

HOWARD CAMPBELL:

He ordered the sequence specifically for my edification. Attached to the note on the table, he had this map.

[PAUSE]

See. It says Giza right there. That refers to this group of books and DVDs in the shape of the Sphinx.

[PAUSE]

In hindsight, I don't know if this was the nicest thing anybody had ever done for me, or the single cruelest gesture.

[PAUSE]

I should've known it was coming.

DR. WILLIAM FINK:

What was coming?

HOWARD CAMPBELL:

The last time I saw Bucky, we saw the movie *Adaptation* together. Bucky said, "You think *that's* self-referential, wait till I write you a book." I thought that was just a comment, I hadn't expected him to leave me his writings. After I emailed you back, I sat in his hotel room over Christmas and read his manifesto. When you e-mailed me the text of the note found in his pocket and asked me to meet with you, I knew he had intended this. "My dearest friend Howard, please explain." It was all premeditated. He included my e-mail address. Bucky invited me here to interact with you.

DR. WILLIAM FINK:

He had his driver's license in one pocket, and the note with your e-mail address in the other. And, a backpack with a few books. May I hold onto these pictures?

HOWARD CAMPBELL:

Yes, I brought them for you.

DR. WILLIAM FINK:

Thank you. May I go see the room?

HOWARD CAMPBELL:

I couldn't afford to keep that suite. That's why I took all these pictures. I also made this bibliography of sorts, a complete list of all the books and DVDs in the room.

[PAPER BEING UNFOLDED]

DR. WILLIAM FINK:

This is great. Thank you.

HOWARD CAMPBELL:

When we are finished, I hope you will still feel this way.

DR. WILLIAM FINK:

What does that mean?

HOWARD CAMPBELL:

[COUGHING]

I was not expecting this responsibility.

DR. WILLIAM FINK:

What do you think he wanted you to explain?

HOWARD CAMPBELL:

I've meditated on this. I waded through Bucky's materials. He had one sentence that he posted with yellow stickies all around the room, "Whoever holds the media, owns the world."

DR. WILLIAM FINK:

This sheds light on the kind of patient I have. Richard was probably suffering from paranoid schizophrenia before he developed a catatonic stupor.

HOWARD CAMPBELL:

Bucky wasn't suffering from schizophrenia. To live is to suffer. Bucky's primary pain sourced from the isolation of being an intellectual pioneer.

He had a definite point of view he was communicating, a point of view some in business would find threatening. There are certain experiences in life from which you can never go back. Not like a loss of your virginity kind of transformation, which is more like the gaining of experience, but like finding out that your wife is cheating on you when you had no suspicions. From that moment on, you will see her differently. Having sex for the first time rarely affects one's perception like that.

Having read his manifesto, I am changed. It started with a question, "That Voight Comm Test of yours, ever take that test yourself?" Of course I recognized the question from *Blade Runner*.

DR. WILLIAM FINK:

From what?

HOWARD CAMPBELL:

Blade Runner, the film adaptation of *Do Androids Dream of Electric Sheep*, by Philip K. Dick.

DR. WILLIAM FINK:

No. You mentioned a manifesto.

HOWARD CAMPBELL:

Yes. Bucky's exegesis.

DR. WILLIAM FINK:

I would like to read this.

HOWARD CAMPBELL:

I can't give it to you. Bucky was afraid you might hold it against him. He forbade me from letting anybody see it. He left a note that said I can tell you about it. He even said I could transcribe part of it for you if I thought it necessary, but the original was not to be shared.

Bucky held Philip K. Dick in the highest regard. Bucky read all his books, and he's the only person I know who made it through Dick's *Exegesis*, a book Dick wrote about his religious experiences. Bucky had some similar experiences. The goal of his manifesto was to make experiences more accessible. He left it for me as the manifesto he forbade me to share with you.

DR. WILLIAM FINK:

What kind of religious experiences?

HOWARD CAMPBELL:

The kind where you don't know if what you're experiencing is real or not. The kind of experience that makes you question your sanity. He saw a pink that had no source and he heard a voice that he heard as coming from outside himself.

DR. WILLIAM FINK:

In concert with other symptoms, this would indicate a schizophrenic break from reality.

HOWARD CAMPBELL:

Whose reality? It may be a break from your precept of reality, from your cosmography, but a psychologist with a background in phenomenology might not have such discrete realities.

One of the reasons I find the Bible incredulous is that when god speaks to people, nobody ever really freaks out and questions their sanity. I find that awfully convenient. Or, when these preachers on TV say god spoke to them, what the fuck? Shouldn't this be front-page news? Either god is speaking to them and we have a modern day prophet and the newfound words of God should be published everywhere, or they are criminals for swindling their donations. Or, are they insane?

DR. WILLIAM FINK:

Let's keep this focused on Bucky. Richard Wilson would question his sanity?

HOWARD CAMPBELL:

Well, yes. My point is that while Philip K. Dick could be viewed as schizophrenic, Bucky would hold that this label shouldn't discount his ideas.

[PAUSE]

DR. WILLIAM FINK:

But a schizophrenic will say things that don't make sense.

HOWARD CAMPBELL:

Not to your intelligence. Not even to the schizophrenic's quote-en-quote sane mind. And, Philip found this most troubling. However, that voice in his head and the light that he saw, gave him information he couldn't ever have had otherwise and it saved his daughter's life. How come a Christian can have a similar experience and it is okay, not insane for them, to frame the experience as Jesus speaking to them?

[PAUSE]

DR. WILLIAM FINK:

Do you think Wilson's breakdown was contributed to by this kind of speculation, the questioning of his sanity?

HOWARD CAMPBELL:

Of course. Dick asked how we know what is our free will, and not a program of prefabricated values with synthetic histories engineered to create the veneer of choice and free will. He suggested that this was the state of our republic, guised as a democracy, but where we vote between choices determined by a mechanism whose is known but its causes obscurred.

DR. WILLIAM FINK:

Would Richard obsess on these ideas?

HOWARD CAMPBELL:

No. He wasn't so single-mindedly driven to be *clinically* diagnosed with obsession.

[PAUSE]

Bucky would dwell on the idea that he was not a capitalist. I like capitalism. What other form of economy allows a person to leverage their common sense for great rewards? More than any economic system I've seen, capitalism allows for the individual to stand on his own merits. One is still pushed or pulled by social advantages and political influence, but your own merits contribute more than any alternative systems I've seen. Money, connections, and charisma open doors, but it's your character and wits that take you to the top. Knowledge is the application of character and intelligence. Character is the greater part of knowledge.

DR. WILLIAM FINK:

Those are deep ideas.

HOWARD CAMPBELL:

You think that's deep? It's just barely below the surface. Some of his ideas take focus and pondering to follow, but once internalized, these ideas changed the way I see the world. Once I grasped that character is the greater part of knowledge, I saw it everywhere I looked. Many really smart men can't make it past lower management. Relying too heavily on intelligence is a sign of immaturity. Young people are eager to show off. They flaunt what they know and what they think. They can't resist. While brilliant observations may help get the attention you need for early opportunities, the urge to share these observations must be tempered to rise to a higher level of management. I don't mean to preach. At 35, I'm a senior vice president at an international advertising agency. Sometimes I'm proud of myself. I engineer corporate storylines. This is what I do for a living. I'm an account planner on a $400,000,000 piece of business, a national wireless carrier with a personified inanimate doo-dad as its *spokesthing*. One lesson I've learned in advertising is that consensus breeds reality. Garnering and stewarding consensus is powerful.

[PAUSE]

I'm taking the first quarter off from work. But, I'm talking about myself and not about Bucky.

DR. WILLIAM FINK:

The two of you were very close friends. And, as you've said, your worldview has been expanded by the ideas he shared with you.

HOWARD CAMPBELL:

That's right, and we were as close as they come. It's hard to separate the two. Bucky's ideas have saturated me, as I'm sure I have influenced him.

DR. WILLIAM FINK:

Yes, the two of you were very close. You exchanged ideas as best friends do.

HOWARD CAMPBELL:

We were closer than you're probably imagining. We had sex together.

DR. WILLIAM FINK:

The two of you were lovers?

HOWARD CAMPBELL:

Yes, but, not the way you're imaging. We had sex with the same girl at the same time. So, we had sex together. Bucky was better than anyone I have met at talking a woman into going to bed with him. And, once in bed, talking women into doing things sexually that they had never considered.

[PAUSE]

Personally, I've never been good at talking a girl into bed. I live vicariously through Bucky.

DR. WILLIAM FINK:

How did the two of you meet?

HOWARD CAMPBELL:

I was walking by a bench, on the first day of classes at Bennington College, when he said to me, "Are you a magician or a civilian?" I said magician.

He asked if sometimes the whole world occurred to me as superficial. I said, "Yes." He thanked me for being honest. I said, "You're welcome." He commented on how the world occurred to him as lacking the civility I had demonstrated by saying, *you're welcome.*

DR. WILLIAM FINK:

That was how he introduced himself to you?

HOWARD CAMPBELL:

He is an unabashed mystic. He made comments like that to everybody. He alienated himself by making these kinds of comments. His comments seem peculiar if you aren't familiar with his use of language, and eerie when he's right about an insight. People don't know how to respond, so they usually retreat.

When I first met him, at the bench, I was carrying *Zen and The Art of Motorcycle Maintenance.* He said that for somebody at my age to be reading a new copy of that book meant that I was finally reading, and that I was a latter day enlightenee. He invited me to watch and learn. He asked me to sit on the bench as he went to talk with a young woman named Angie. When he came back, he asked what happened. I said I couldn't hear much of what he said. He laughed, and said that he didn't mean about Angie, whom he was probably going to sleep with that night, but about starting to read. He asked what got me finally reading. I explained that work and school had started occurring to me as pointless and I was...

[PAUSE]

DR. WILLIAM FINK:

Let's keep this focused on Richard's history.

HOWARD CAMPBELL:

I don't mind.

[LAUGHTER]

But, about Richard, the whole Angie thing, though, might give you the wrong impression. Angie turned out to be a vindictive fuck. He wasn't making love to her; he was trying to psychically kill her.

DR. WILLIAM FINK:

Psychically kill her?

HOWARD CAMPBELL:

Yeah, but all he accomplished was embarrassing her. You see, Angie had traumatized an emotionally unstable girl. Bucky explained that she did this without just cause, simply as a blind exertion of power. Bucky took exception to people who wielded real power without concern for its repercussions.

[PAUSE]

DR. WILLIAM FINK:

How did he attempt to *psychically* kill Angie? I don't know what that means exactly, to psychically kill somebody.

HOWARD CAMPBELL:

To psychically kill somebody is to immobilize their psyche. Immobilizing somebody's psyche is accomplished by illuminating the dichotomy of their values in such a permanent way that they can no longer live in denial, yet they see no viable action other than inaction. A psychic kill generates substantive social withdrawal, ranging from clinical depression, on the low end of the psychic kill scale, to suicide, at the high end.

When Bucky spoke with Angie, he explained to her that he knew she was going through a hard time. That she was raised with rules that were no longer relevant to *her* world, and that she had made choices with which she wasn't fully reconciled. She said she wanted to talk with him more. He went over that night, and they talked for hours, and had sex in ways she had never imagined herself doing and enjoying. She told Bucky that nobody had ever made her feel that special.

[PAUSE]

When she woke in the morning, she found a book and an audio CD. The book was *Metamagical Themas* by Douglas Hoffstadter, earmarked to a page on cold readings with a paragraph highlighted on what most people view as peculiar to themselves, yet are actually emotions and strong sentiments felt by many people. The CD had a script that psychics use, covering the exact same type of material. Bucky's talk with her was largely lifted verbatim from these two sources. Angie went from feeling touched and special, to feeling foolish, exposed and manipulated.

[PAUSE]

DR. WILLIAM FINK:

What happened to her?

HOWARD CAMPBELL:

Bucky told her, in no uncertain terms, that she was ordinary. That she wasn't special, and that Bucky had played her for a fool in a manner he was probably willing to share publicly, at least in story—something Angie would find humiliating.

DR. WILLIAM FINK:

You said he didn't succeed in his attempt to psychically kill her. That he only embarrassed her. How did she react?

HOWARD CAMPBELL:

She was hurt, angry, embarrassed...so much so that the following week Angie withdrew from Bennington College.

DR. WILLIAM FINK:

Richard sounds like a sexual predator.

HOWARD CAMPBELL:

No, nor was he a sex addict. Richard would sometimes go weeks or even months without having sex, or thinking about getting laid. He enjoyed sex, but he wasn't a sexual predator. Bucky was a righteous man, many times taking on the responsibility to create justice. He was judge, jury and executioner. He had sex with Angie because that was something she held as sacred, and Bucky had deemed her as nasty and sentenced her to be expunged from our school. He carried out the execution as quickly and neatly as he knew how. She needed to be run out of town.

DR. WILLIAM FINK:

He sounds like a volatile man.

HOWARD CAMPBELL:

Not often. Richard is one of the most peaceful men I've ever met. When he wasn't peaceful, he was standing up for the little guy, the downtrodden, under-represented or misunderstood. That's what he thought he was doing in getting back at Angie. He saw his thoughts as real as a Catholic sees the wafer in communion as the body of Christ. Richard was proud of his thoughts. A good deal of what I can share with you is from my personal experience with him, the ideas are from the manifesto he left me to read, *The Longer Line.*

[SILENCE]

DR. WILLIAM FINK:

He wrote a *manifesto?*

HOWARD CAMPBELL:

Yes, I mentioned that earlier.

DR. WILLIAM FINK:

I wasn't thinking of a manifesto as a specific book, I was thinking of it more as the collection of writings in his hotel room, on all the slips of paper and everything.

HOWARD CAMPBELL:

It was an actual book. Not published by traditional means. Actually, it was just three-hole-punched paper held together by brads. It's an obtuse account of his first visit to a mental hospital, and Bucky's commentary about life on Earth. If it sounds grandiose, it is. Bucky thought that the downfall of contemporary America was a failure to understand the implications of the works of Gödel, Einstein and Kuhn. Kuhn was the first to put the power of consensus over the power of fact in *The Structure of Scientific Revolutions.* To the scientific community that prided itself on its objectivity, Kuhn's treatise was a huge blow to their ego, yet the objective facts it presented made argument against it futile. Kuhn had used the language and structure of science to hold the category in contempt, and the scientific community had little choice but to admit that they'd acted in such ways and cry "Uncle."

DR. WILLIAM FINK:

Was Richard's, [STUTTERING] *Bucky's* manifesto in the hotel room?

HOWARD CAMPBELL:

Yeah. I knew Bucky was working on some sort of master book. He left it for me, in his hotel room.

DR. WILLIAM FINK:

Go on.

HOWARD CAMPBELL:

Bucky was fucking with me. The hotel suite's fridge had a case of a dry white wine we both liked. How he fucked with me was by placing a printed cardboard sign in the drawer next to the fridge that said, "Check under your pillow." The cardboard he'd written on was old and smudged. I didn't think it was written to me. You see, when I saw the wine, I was looking for a corkscrew. First, I opened the drawer and saw the sign, but I didn't think that the sign related to my search for a corkscrew. I checked the entire kitchen, gave up, and called room service to bring me a corkscrew. When I went to sleep that night, I felt something uncomfortable under my pillow: the corkscrew with a note attached that asked if I'd called room service, and if I was having fun yet.

DR. WILLIAM FINK:

[LAUGHING]

I'm sorry to interrupt. That is really funny.

HOWARD CAMPBELL:

I found it funny, too, but I didn't laugh. I spent the evening on the hotel patio, eating crab salad, drinking wine and reading Bucky's manifesto, which is way too dry to be funny. He went on, ad nauseam, about the historical value of consensus. Bucky claimed that valuing consensus was a prerequisite to the acceptance of democracy as a legitimate form of government, and yet, he was convinced that the greatest conspiracy was a confederacy of dunces that had no formal association. The Catholic Church was the first organization to recognize that garnering consensus was an effective path to ruling people. The church was the first to employ this tactic. Using this tactic means that they recognized that if you seize the mind, the body will follow.

Bucky loved the Oxford English Dictionary because of its effort to find the first known usage of each entry. Bucky pointed out that the word "propaganda" is cited as first used in 1622 within the Sacra Congregatio de Propaganda Fide, which was commissioned by Pope Gregory XV. Here, look at this photograph—these books and Internet print outs are in the form of a Roman numeral fifteen.

DR. WILLIAM FINK:

I was wondering if the X and V were meant to represent something.

HOWARD CAMPBELL:

You don't see intentionality. When an artist, or a team of artists, creates something, there is a sensitivity and focus that makes each choice, every element, with a consideration for the consumer of the medium. At minimum, the consumer feels respected or addressed. They feel the medium is speaking to them, or at least to their concerns and values. They may feel attacked, cared for or exalted, but they sense that the medium was speaking to them. In a culture of anonymity, being spoken to makes one feel alive.

[PAUSE]

Yes, each constellation of books and mixed media was in the form of something it represented. In this other photo, it is in the shape of an infinity sign. These were the books on philosophy. There is a self-referential quality to the work that will be lost on most consumers. Just because they don't see the intentionality doesn't mean they don't feel at least some of it.

DR. WILLIAM FINK:

I thought the infinity sign was the number eight. Back up a second. The Catholic Church coined the word *propaganda*?

HOWARD CAMPBELL:

Yes. One of Pope Gregory's accountants observed that it was more cost effective to teach Catholicism than to invade and force conversion. The accountant had the insight to recognize that a territory could be acquired by converting people's minds. If you convert the minds, the bodies will follow. And, converting minds is less expensive than physically enforcing new sovereignty.

[PAUSE]

To the Catholics of the time, the word propaganda was synonymous with education; to the Protestants of the time, propaganda was an evil word. But it took the capitalistic agenda of the United States during World War I to popularize the word propaganda. Back in 1622, Pope Gregory saw that his regime's utilization of Holy Wars to ignite faith in The Church wasn't a cost effective tactic. Bucky held that as the birth of capitalism. That's what he held to be true.

DR. WILLIAM FINK:

Richard was an intelligent man.

HOWARD CAMPBELL:

Richard *is* an intelligent man.

DR. WILLIAM FINK:

I stand corrected. Richard *is* an intelligent man. However, his intelligence is not very evident now.

HOWARD CAMPBELL:

Unless he's making a statement that's beyond our comprehension.

DR. WILLIAM FINK:

Like he has some hidden message that his admission to my hospital is supposed to solve?

HOWARD CAMPBELL:

I guess that would be a logical extension of him making a statement that's beyond our comprehension. But, that doesn't make sense.

DR. WILLIAM FINK:

You're defending your buddy. That's quite admirable, actually. I brought up his intelligence because paranoid schizophrenics tend to be inordinately intelligent and extraordinarily knowledgeable about government and corporate structures.

HOWARD CAMPBELL:

So are some academics, corporate honchos, financial wizards, political strategists, and the list goes on.

DR. WILLIAM FINK:

Okay, point well taken. Did Richard ever appear unstable to you?

HOWARD CAMPBELL:

Yeah. As I mentioned before, he went into a mental hospital once before when we were at Bennington. He writes about that in *The Longer Line*. I read about his perspective while I was at the hotel between Christmas and New Year's. I'd been there, at Bennington, but it was a trip reading about what it had been like for him.

I remember first suspecting that Bucky was thinking peculiarly when he began capitalizing the "i" in "It." I saw this in notes he left for me on my door in the dorm. Then, as he walked around campus you could sometimes hear him chanting, "It is important that you believe in *It*." And he would emphasize the *It*.

(TRANSCRIBER'S NOTATION ON CAPITALIZATION: IN AN EFFORT TO CONFORM TO THE CONTENT OF THE TRANSCRIPTION, "IT" WILL APPEAR CAPITALIZED WHEN EMPHASIZED IN SPEECH BY CAMPBELL.)

You might be on to something about his interest in structure leading to his hospitalization. Bucky loved Foucault. He was reading Foucault before his first hospitalization.

DR. WILLIAM FINK:

The philosopher who wrote *The Order of Things*?

HOWARD CAMPBELL:

That's the one. Foucault was also fascinated by mental illness. When society says that insanity is bad, citizens won't think in uncharted patterns because that kind of thinking would mean that you are crazy. Foucault asked if the legal ramifications of insanity was just a device that a society could use to discredit and invalidate minds that didn't think according to the society's ordained patterns. Is there much of a difference between a jail and a hospital if they won't let you leave?

DR. WILLIAM FINK:

Well, we've stopped using straight jackets, but prisons still use that form of restraint.

HOWARD CAMPBELL:

It was a rhetorical question. Bucky said that a society was defined not by its culture but by its enforced laws. The discrepancy between their laws on the books, and their enforced laws, was a manifestation of their repression. But, he hated criminology. Bucky explained that criminology as a subject, is a joke, because of the existence of competent criminals.

DR. WILLIAM FINK:

How did we get from Foucault to criminology?

HOWARD CAMPBELL:

Because Foucault studied the application of laws, and criminology studies the enforcement of laws. The link is law enforcement. The problem with criminology is that criminologists only study failed criminals. A criminal is a person who broke the law in such a way that a prosecution system, as cumbersome and full of restrictions as ours, could prove their guilt beyond a reasonable doubt. Bucky maintained that our nation hosts a caste of outlaws that consistently break the law without repercussions. While criminology may have internal consistency, it is intellishit, something imaginary with beautiful construction and absolutely no relevance to the physical world.

Can you imagine a mind like Bucky's creating an alternative reality?

DR. WILLIAM FINK:

Another rhetorical question.

HOWARD CAMPBELL:

Yes.

By the time Bucky went to the hospital near Bennington College, he had manufactured a world ruled by magicians. Bucky thought the Illuminati were real, and that he'd discovered portals into their ranks and proof of their existence. He was hunting the Knights Templar. What set him over the edge was all the reading he did. You know you can't find stuff like this, including stuff that destroys criminology, as a subject, in traditional textbooks. You've got to go to the fringe. No matter how hard government tries, when you go to the fringe, you don't impose your order, you adopt the energy of the fringe. Also, when you come from the fringe, and enter an economic system, you bring some chaos, street smarts, wisdom or some kind of non-system thinking with you. And to a certain extent, this energy can help the system grow and evolve, and compete more efficiently. But once it owns this new energy, and can generate it on its own, you, as its carrier, are no longer needed, unless you have become integrated into the system. This new system you have entered must saturate your way of being, or you will be rejected by that system, like an organism killing a cancerous cell. You can't just fake it, because acting a specific way to fit in actually becomes part of who you are. Your actions affect your thoughts just as your thoughts have an effect on your actions.

DR. WILLIAM FINK:

Kurt Vonnegut shows this in *Mother Night*. His lead character worked as if he *was* a Nazi, and that ultimately *made* him a Nazi, even though he was a subversive Nazi.

HOWARD CAMPBELL:

Yes. Vonnegut covers these intricacies well. But, Buckminster Fuller took it to another level, and really fleshed it out, calling it "pattern integrity." But, I was talking about criminology.

Traditionally, criminology explores what's contained within one set of laws, and what's outside the law isn't within criminology's scope of inspection. "History is written by the victors" also means that the victors create the laws. If Hitler had won World War II, the biggest post-war crime would have been being a Jew, or a homosexual, or holding just about any non-government-sanctioned belief or perception.

It's not the act that jeopardizes the government, it's the thought crime. Bucky asked whether you'd prefer to live in a country where you could act however you wanted, but were required to think a certain way, or in a country where you could think however you wanted, but were required to act in a certain way. Before you think about your decision, let me tell you that Bucky held that these were the same, that your thoughts create unavoidable actions, and either scenario was totalitarian. Bucky's cosmography held that thoughts generated action. But there are very different kinds of thoughts. Some thoughts are useful, some are fun, and some are dominant. Dominant thoughts have evolved for tens-of-thousands of years, and when unleashed on a brain, they can take it over.

A dominant thought can take over a brain, and change the person, reframing the person's entire operational system. Kind of like how a computer can get a virus that changes how it operates. A meme could do this to a person. Can a fucked-up thought fuck somebody up?

Bucky explained that this happened to him, and that it was what led him to go into the hospital Back at Bennington. He saw idea viruses as what organize people. Politics then becomes a competition of ideas. Bucky thought ideology should be spelled *idea-ology*. Dominant thoughts are thoughts that present themselves as reality and are extraordinarily good at spawning with fidelity and recruiting additional brains. He referred to dominant thoughts as religions, sciences, or economies.

DR. WILLIAM FINK:

You're suggesting that thoughts are alive and humans are merely their host?

HOWARD CAMPBELL:

Humans are DNA and meme repositories. We exist because of DNA and memes. We cannot exist outside of them. Just as an ocean wave is the materialization of the energy force of a wave, Bucky saw humanity as the manifestation of ideas vying for supremacy as they exert their power. Power is a slippery field to explore. Bucky saw poker as an inquiry into the structure of power.

DR. WILLIAM FINK:

Why poker?

HOWARD CAMPBELL:

Because, the goal of poker is sustainable increases in money. Money is power. The study of poker includes risk assessment, assaults, and retreats, but a professional's goal is long term sustainability. Survival is their ultimate ideology. Poker strategy begins with desired results and goes backwards. Academia works the opposite way: it builds up hypotheses from theorems, or develops theorems from observed phenomena, both of which are included in poker, but academia focuses on process, while poker focuses on the outcome. Poker includes playing on emotions and social motivators usually discounted in other inquiries into power or disciplines, such as sociology, which include mass social motivators, but lack the tactics to create desired outcomes.

You see, economists study the microcosm of specific systems and the relative strength of the systems of monetary exchange that order society, but perpetual sustainability is not an objective. Besides, forces far greater than currency determine social order. Otherwise, a penniless carpenter wouldn't be the best known name in the world, better known than The Beatles or Michael Jordan. The spread of Jesus' name has reorganized more families, countries and wealth than the invention of gunpowder.

Besides, gunpowder only fends off invaders or facilitates invasion. Jesus holds groups together.

DR. WILLIAM FINK:

The family that prays together stays together.

HOWARD CAMPBELL:

Exactly. Bucky explored memetics, a new kind of science that examines the spread of ideas. Memetics looks at the structure of communicability and analyzes the relative strength of mental bonding. But memetics can only examine *how* the idea of gunpowder spread, not the effect of using gunpowder with projectiles.

A common misunderstanding about memetics is that something memetic is spreading like crazy. No. That would be an epidemic. However, by *leveraging* memetics, one can create an *idea* that is more communicable.

DR. WILLIAM FINK:

I read about memetics once in *The New York Times*. Something about how a drug was being abused and the idea of getting high off this drug was a meme and spreading memetically, via the Internet. I didn't understand. What is a meme?

HOWARD CAMPBELL:

They said it was spreading memetically because the idea of taking the drug was spreading without physical contact. In the past, the idea of using a new recreational drug was spread from physical contact: a person takes a new substance because somebody physically offers it to them. And, the use spreads by physical demonstration, or physical solicitation, of the drug. The drug mentioned in the *New York Times* article was being used throughout the country without being introduced to each person via physical demonstration. Historically, new drug habits have only been replicated when they're seen in the flesh. The idea of using *that* drug was being transmitted from mind to mind without physical contact.

A meme is any word, title or slang expression. For instance, the word "Internet" is a new meme, while the word "blue" is a much older meme. The saying "The family that prays together, stays together" is a meme. But a meme can also be a physical gesture, a habit or a selection of color or fashion. For instance, Americanism has been a hot meme since 9-11, and is evident in the increased usage of American flags, and the colors red, white and blue in clothing, stickers and even tattoos. A meme is anything that takes hold in the mind.

Memes that take hold might strike an emotional chord, like the pride in Americanism or something nostalgic like the Jolly Green Giant. Memes that take hold often fit an unmet need for expression, like, "Where's the beef?" or "Would you *Xerox* this?" Remember when everybody would sing versions of:

[SINGING:]

"I'm too sexy for my shirt. Too sexy for my shirt…"

[PAUSE]

[RESUME NORMAL VOICE:]

I guess not.

I don't know how much of this is useful.

DR. WILLIAM FINK:

I don't know either. This is not what I expected. Usually, friends or family of the schizophrenic tell me about how the patient grew increasingly incomprehensible. You seem to be defending his perspective, as if creating a bizarre hotel room full of clues is the mark of superior intellect.

HOWARD CAMPBELL:

Yes.

[SILENCE]

DR. WILLIAM FINK:

I'm having trouble fathoming that the catatonic man upstairs created this work of immense depth. Yes, I have interviewed paranoid schizophrenics who have elaborate theories of world deception and conspiracies, but the theories unravel and their minds tend to focus on minute details of their own work.

[PAUSE]

HOWARD CAMPBELL:

I understand how you feel.

[PAUSE]

I felt the same way when I first saw him. I had seen him around campus, just kind of being by himself and writing in his journal. I thought he was a passive, innocuous being. I figured he was just introspective. What I found was that once he engaged me, I was captivated by his ideas. However, when I first met Bucky, I lacked the argot to follow his train of thought. We have a lot of work to do if you want to understand the intellectual dilemmas that might have shut down his mind. If you meet a Christian, it would be impossible to see the world through their eyes without a concept of a holy ghost...

DR. WILLIAM FINK:

The Holy Ghost.

[*PAUSE*]

HOWARD CAMPBELL:

Yes, without knowing *The* Holy Ghost.

[*PAUSE*]

How is Richard? I don't know what to ask in terms of his health.

DR. WILLIAM FINK:

His health is stable.

HOWARD CAMPBELL:

Has he come out of this at all?

DR. WILLIAM FINK:

Once. He started talking word salad and turned violent when he was approached.

HOWARD CAMPBELL:

Then what?

DR. WILLIAM FINK:

We gave him Haldol to get him through it, but he relapsed into catatonia.

HOWARD CAMPBELL:

He has really strong associations with Haldol.

DR. WILLIAM FINK:

We saw that. He got violent and needed to be restrained when he heard me order a Haldol injection. He seemed to be almost chanting, "This is politics. This is *all* politics."

HOWARD CAMPBELL:

Politics to Bucky is a loaded word.

DR. WILLIAM FINK:

How so?

HOWARD CAMPBELL:

[COUGHING]

I'm sorry. May I have some water?

[SOUND: CHAIR PULLS BACK]

[SOUND: FOOTSTEPS]

[SOUND: DOOR OPENS]

DR. WILLIAM FINK:

Virginia, may I have a cup of water from the cooler?

[INAUDIBLE: PUBLIC ADDRESS PAGING]

[PAUSE]

[INAUDIBLE: PUBLIC ADDRESS PAGING]

[PAUSE]

FEMALE VOICE:

Here you go, Doctor.

DR. WILLIAM FINK:

Thank you, Virginia.

[SOUND: DOOR CLOSES]

DR. WILLIAM FINK:

Here.

HOWARD CAMPBELL:

Thank you.

[SOUND: DRINKING]

Bucky used the word "politics" as a biological force, or as a verb meaning "to oppress." Politics is to biology what gravity is to physical objects: that which binds things together. And, as a verb, Bucky would say, "Don't politic me." In biology, politics is consensus, like the direction a school of fish swims as a group. When the school of fish swims in different directions, there is a force greater than consensus. Like when a hillside is exploded by TNT, there is a force greater than gravity acting on the dirt. But fish that school are compelled to swim together, just as the dirt that exploded up is still being pulled back to earth by gravity.

[PAUSE]

When he talked to you, he probably meant more of the oppressive use of the word politics.

[PAUSE]

DR. WILLIAM FINK:

When you spoke with him in November, did Richard seem depressed?

HOWARD CAMPBELL:

No, he wasn't depressed. In fact, he seemed amped.

DR. WILLIAM FINK:

Did he see himself as oppressed?

HOWARD CAMPBELL:

Yes. Not relative to many, but, overall, yes. Bucky felt he was compelled to play a game he never signed up for. In that way he felt oppressed. He also was extraordinarily grateful he was born an American white male. Bucky's fascination with Foucault was at the heart of his perception of being oppressed.

DR. WILLIAM FINK:

Go on.

HOWARD CAMPBELL:

Bucky looked down on political science as a byproduct of academia that's blind to the power that created it. Bucky wanted you to have a *Fuller* understanding.

(TRANSCRIBER'S NOTATION: CAMPBELL EMPHASIZES THE WORD FULLER. IN REVIEWING THIS MANUSCRIPT, IT IS APPARENT CAMPBELL WAS CITING A SOURCE, BUCKMINSTER FULLER. THEREFORE, FULLER IS TYPED WITH A CAPITAL "F".)

[PAUSE]

Political science is a field studied at universities, entities that only exist because of their endowments. Did you know that before corporations, sovereign governments were standing endowments? And that monarchs weren't the actual source of power? The great pirates, the traders and sea dwellers who needed men organized on land to expedite their trading created monarchies.

Pirates were inherently outlaws.

DR. WILLIAM FINK:

Okay. You lost me. We were talking about Foucault and now we're talking about pirates.

HOWARD CAMPBELL:

Doctor Fink, you think I am talking, which I am, but these aren't my ideas. I'm using Bucky's ideas to give you a *Fuller* explanation. Bucky was interested in systems. In order to understand a system, you have to get outside the system to see other possibilities. Bucky felt oppressed because there aren't options to live outside the system. Pirates lived outside the system. The only laws that could, and did, rule them were natural laws. Pirates battled with one another to see who was going to control the vast sea routes and, eventually, the world. Their battles took place out of sight of land dwellers and the keepers of written history. The losers generally went to the bottom of the sea. Those who stayed on top of the waters, and prospered, did so because of their comprehensive abilities. They were the antithesis of specialists.

DR. WILLIAM FINK:

Running a ship means knowing about navigation, weather and managing people.

HOWARD CAMPBELL:

Yes. Pirates were applied scientists. The wider and more long-distanced their anticipatory strategy, the more successful they usually were. Experience proved that multiple ships could outmaneuver one ship. So pirates created navies.

DR. WILLIAM FINK:

No. Countries created navies.

HOWARD CAMPBELL:

No. That's what our *history* tells us. But, history is simply a story agreed upon.

DR. WILLIAM FINK:

No, wait. Only countries had the infrastructure to build and sustain navies.

HOWARD CAMPBELL:

Therein lies the rub.

DR. WILLIAM FINK:

What?

HOWARD CAMPBELL:

The rub. The catch. The cost of doing business.

DR. WILLIAM FINK:

I'm not following.

HOWARD CAMPBELL:

Pirates created countries.

DR. WILLIAM FINK:

How do you figure?

HOWARD CAMPBELL:

You think Western civilization just sprung up simultaneously along different coasts?

DR. WILLIAM FINK:

People were trading via shipping routes. Businessmen.

HOWARD CAMPBELL:

Pirates. Pirates created foci of power. These powers expanded until they overlapped with other powers. Wars require immense resources. Boundaries emerged as means to focus resources on their ports of trade. The pirates, or businessmen, were constantly demanding output. Defending takes less energy than attacking. Boundaries allow for the proper focus of energy. When one has excess resources, you can expand and attack. But I'm getting ahead of myself.

To consistently sustain a navy, pirates had to control mines, forests, and lands to build the ships and establish the industries essential to building, supplying, and maintaining their navy. The pirates went to the various lands where they either acquired or sold goods, and picked the strongest man there to be the pirate's local headman. The chosen man became the pirate's general manager of the local realm.

If the chosen man in a given land had not already done so, the pirate told him to proclaim himself king. But this king was a stooge to commerce. His sole job was to maintain order on behalf of the pirates. Order was most easily maintained by having the local king proclaim that he was the headman of all men, the god-ordained ruler on earth. The locals weren't traveling, so they saw no disparity. The pirates gave their stooge-kings secret lines of supplies that provided everything they needed to enforce their sovereign claim. The more massively bejeweled the king's gold crown, and the more visible his court and castle, the less visible was his pirate master.

Masters had to sleep occasionally, and therefore found it necessary to surround themselves with super-loyal, muscular, but dumb-as-shit, illiterates, who couldn't see, nor savvy, their masters' strategies. There was great safety in the stupidity of these henchmen. The great pirates realized that the only people who could possibly contrive to displace them were the truly bright people.

Secrecy was the pirate's strongest defense. If the other powerful pirates didn't know where you were going, when you'd gone, or when you were coming back, they wouldn't know how to waylay you. If anyone knew when you were coming home, small-timers could come out in small boats and waylay you in the dark and take you over, just before you got home tiredly after a two-year treasure-harvesting voyage. Hijacking and second-rate piracy became a popular activity around the world's shores and harbors. So, secrecy became the essence of the lives of the successful pirates. That's why so little is known of these pirates. This secrecy was at the heart of Bucky's obsessive search through literature. Bucky held that secret knowledge was real. Furthermore, Bucky sought It. A book like Buckminster Fuller's *Operating Manual Spaceship Earth* was named too peculiarly to be normal. After reading that book, he studied topology for four months. But back to Bucky's pirate story.

These great pirates said to all their kings, statesmen who were functionally only lieutenants, "Any time bright young people show up, I'd like to know about it, because we need bright men." So, each time the pirate came into port, the local king would mention that he had some bright, young men whose capabilities and thinking shone out in the community. The great pirates would say to the king, "All right, you summon them and deal with them as follows: As each young man is brought forward you say to him, 'Young man, you are very bright. I'm going to assign you to a great history tutor, and, in due course, if you study well and learn enough, I'm going to make you my Royal Historian, but you've got to pass many examinations given to you by me and your teacher.'" And when the next bright boy was brought before him, the king was to say, "I'm going to make you my Royal Treasurer," and so forth. Then the pirate said to the king, "You will finally say to all of them: 'But each of you must mind your own business or off go your heads. I'm the only one who minds everybody's business.'"

And this is the way schools began, as royal tutorial schools. And, it's the way specialization began. It is our current form of education. Academic education equals specialization. Exclusively, the great pirates retain comprehensive knowledge. Exclusively the great pirates, known today as businessmen, enjoy knowledge of the world through its resources.

DR. WILLIAM FINK:

Is this just a metaphor or some kind of syllogism?

HOWARD CAMPBELL:

In his journal, Bucky emphasized that he was not being facetious. He meant the pirate story to be literal history. Bucky stressed that this was not a metaphor, but the way he saw where our current world order came from. This was the beginning of schools and colleges, and the beginning of intellectual specialization. The development of the bright ones into specialists gave the king very great brain power, and made him and his kingdom the most powerful in the land and, therefore, secretly and greatly advantaged his patron pirate in world competition with the other great pirates.

The power rested not with the power figureheads, the kings, but with the men behind the kings, the great pirates. Just as today, a corporate president may be the king, but the power is in the hands of the board of directors.

DR. WILLIAM FINK:

There are some interesting points in Bucky's argument. What was he getting at?

HOWARD CAMPBELL:

That the story makes the reality. Remember how I said that Bucky's hotel room was like an art installation?

DR. WILLIAM FINK:

Yeah.

HOWARD CAMPBELL:

Look at this photograph. I found a set of billiard balls in one of those plastic trays that they use at billiard halls. This may be hard to imagine. I should have brought the actual balls. These were not a normal set of balls numbered one to fifteen and a cue ball. Instead, this was a set of one cue ball, fourteen black and white balls and one eight-ball. The black and white balls were arranged to have increasing amounts of black, from a dime-sized black spot to a larger spot and a larger spot, to one that was exactly half black, and then the balls where the black area got larger and larger until one had a black area almost as large as the black area of an eight ball, then the eight ball.

There was a note attached: "For a full explanation, see Allan Carse's *Finite and Infinite Games*. You can never draw one circle. Any specification is actually a division of 2. Is an eight-ball a black ball with a small white circle, or a white ball with a black circle that almost covers the entire ball?"

DR. WILLIAM FINK:

That's clever. Let me look at this again.

[PAUSE]

That's really clever.

HOWARD CAMPBELL:

Bucky was much too serious to try and be clever just for the sake of entertainment.

DR. WILLIAM FINK:

So, what's the big picture here?

HOWARD CAMPBELL:

That schools are blinding us to the concept of "one." I know Bucky was extremely irked when *scientists* asked what was outside the universe.

DR. WILLIAM FINK:

Nobody knows what's outside of the universe.

HOWARD CAMPBELL:

Nothing. No thing. Every *thing* is included in universe. There is only one-one. God, Universe? Same difference.

DR. WILLIAM FINK:

We are getting off track. You are making semantic distinctions.

[PAUSE]

It would be helpful for me to know more about his religious experience and his religious orientations.

HOWARD CAMPBELL:

Perspective and religion to Bucky were virtually interchangeable words. Our precepts of Universe affect the way we see our world. You believe that Heaven and Hell are real places and in transubstantiation.

DR. WILLIAM FINK:

Communion?

HOWARD CAMPBELL:

Not just communion, an acceptance of matter changing, albeit undetectably, but in a means that is never to be defined by our science. I don't think you are an appropriate psychiatrist to treat Richard Wilson.

DR. WILLIAM FINK:

I don't think you are in a position to make that call.

HOWARD CAMPBELL:

Richard invited me here...

DR. WILLIAM FINK:

To explain his perspective. I am the best doctor in Hawaii for treating schizophrenia. I have several success cases of patients who have returned to productive lives.

HOWARD CAMPBELL:

Productive to what end? You say things that you don't even hear containing precepts that are not only off-putting to Bucky, but threatening. Especially since you are in such a position of authority here. And, here is not limited to the hospital, but on this whole planet. You will make comments that Bucky will see as an attempt to sculpt his mind, to wash his brain into submission, into a pillar of support for transubstantiation, an irrational world view. I think that is what Bucky wanted me to explain to you and his family, why he just couldn't take it anymore.

DR. WILLIAM FINK:

You told Olgelthorpe that Richard doesn't have any living family.

HOWARD CAMPBELL:

Not that I know of.

You hold that Heaven and Hell are real places. How do souls get there? About transubstantiation, Bucky would say, "it's just fucking bread." And, that those people who see the wafer as the literal body of Christ should be hospitalized, labeled as delusional or at least as irrational and not the mindset to be a scientist or a doctor. Yet, these minds are the umpires of reality?

[SILENCE]

When he was only twelve, John Kennedy Toole stated: "Whether human equality and economic freedom can coexist is yet to be proven."

DR. WILLIAM FINK:

Who is John Kennedy Toole?

HOWARD CAMPBELL:

One of Bucky's favorite authors, a voice he found empathizing, and a really good author who killed himself young and was only published posthumously. His second novel, *A Confederacy of Dunces*, won a Pulitzer. Toole questioned capitalism, and, in the essay that I drew the quote from, he ends by suggesting that economic freedom will lead to unimaginable fiefdoms. At least, unimaginable to his mind in 1958.

Bucky held that neither human equality nor economic freedom could ever exist. Both concepts, equality and economics, are comparative by nature and thus are never absolutely equal nor free from the rules of their systems. This isn't semantics. It's structural analysis. Bucky held that the popular ken equates freedom with capitalism. Bucky once asked President Bush The First if democracy could exist without capitalism. Bush said absolutely not. This confirmed Bucky's suspicion of Bush's cosmography. Look, the corporation is the keystone of American capitalism. America was the first government to imbue an organization with legal rights comparable to humans, and to divorce liability from the actual human owners.

Bucky was a capitalist by practice, trade, and passion. But, capitalism does not require removing personal liability from the owners of corporations. He argued that there was a parallel with slavery. Similar to corporations, slaves were viewed as property and given some rights. A major difference between owning a slave and owning a corporation, though, is that a slave could generate a liability greater than their market value. Corporations can not. If the corporation creates a liability greater than its worth, the corporation just disappears. Bucky advocated the re-implementation of ownership liability.

DR. WILLIAM FINK:

Was Bucky active in any political groups?

HOWARD CAMPBELL:

No. Not active. He would write the occasional opinion article, or a letter to the editor. Generally, he was just very opinionated. Bucky liked looking at structure and projecting where a momentum would lead. A single dandelion suggested a field of dandelions the following season. Bucky held that our current system of capitalism has a negative end game. While there isn't a calculus of large systems to show if, when, and how they terminate, Bucky understood people. There are evil people, actually evil. They are called sociopaths.

DR. WILLIAM FINK:

Actually, they are called anti-social. What is colloquially called sociopathic is actually an aggressive anti-social disorder.

HOWARD CAMPBELL:

Exactly. These people's only evolutionary worth is to cull the herd. Fortunately, these evil people are few and far between. Their agenda is self-fulfillment with no regard for their impact on others.

DR. WILLIAM FINK:

Okay.

HOWARD CAMPBELL:

What do you know about sociopaths?

DR. WILLIAM FINK:

The DSM describes hyper-anti-socials as intelligent and manipulative, viewing others primarily as objects to be manipulated for personal gain. They are charismatic, performing attention-getting displays to woo new people to exploit. They're hyperbolic, telling grossly exaggerated accounts of the past and present to hold the attention of their prospective exploits. These people usually blame the system and complain that if they have transgressions, the system created the need to act the way they did. They are devoid of tension and anxiety, and a polygraph examination can not discern their lies from truth. They are genuinely devoid of guilt with a complete absence of shame, self-adherence or "conscience." And they're path dependent, developing a lifestyle in which no other way of being seems possible.

HOWARD CAMPBELL:

Bucky saw leaders of political parties as sociopaths.

[PAUSE]

DR. WILLIAM FINK:

Was Bucky involved in any fringe organizations?

HOWARD CAMPBELL:

Bucky *was* a fringe organization.

DR. WILLIAM FINK:

What do you mean?

HOWARD CAMPBELL:

Nothing. I was trying to make a joke. Maybe Bucky would see himself as an ecological socialist. But, no, he wasn't involved in any fringe groups. His paternal grandparents had been card-carrying communists, but Bucky was a capitalist, and he argued that capitalism has fended off more atrocities than it has created.

[PAUSE]

But, Bucky also thought that capitalism wasn't capitalism, anymore.

DR. WILLIAM FINK:

What do you mean *capitalism isn't capitalism, anymore?*

HOWARD CAMPBELL:

Today, if you say *trunk,* you think of the rear of a car and not wooden luggage. The word has remained the same, but its meaning is different. Only, nobody is noticing this happening to the word "capitalism" because it has happened gradually, imperceptibly slowly to the popular ken.

[PAUSE]

Before corporations, we had sovereign governments. America was the first break from this. Now, corporations are a means to garner the resources to powerfully engage sovereign control. Monarchies no longer comprise the ruling power of Spaceship Earth. But monarchies weren't the real source of power, because, remember, the great pirates created monarchies.

Mind if I smoke? I'm presenting his story in much the same way he would have, conversationally. Bucky often cited his favorite comedian Bill Hicks, "I try and talk to my audience the same way I talk to my friends."

[SOUND: RAPID LIGHT THUD AND STRIKE OF A CIGARETTE LIGHTER]

DR. WILLIAM FINK:

I'm sorry. You can't smoke in here.

HOWARD CAMPBELL:

Yeah, okay.

[PAUSE]

I have Nicorette. I didn't really want a cigarette. I forget that I'm not addicted to cigarettes, I'm addicted to nicotine. Cigarettes are just a nicotine delivery mechanism.

[SOUND: WRAPPER OPENING]

[PAUSE]

DR. WILLIAM FINK:

How much do you know about Richard Wilson's medical record?

HOWARD CAMPBELL:

Quite a bit, actually. I told Nurse Ogelthorpe as much as I knew, and I'll tell it to you, too. Bucky's first hospitalization was when we were in college together in 1993.

DR. WILLIAM FINK:

Did Bucky have more than one hospitalization?

HOWARD CAMPBELL:

Not that I know of.

DR. WILLIAM FINK:

What was his diagnosis?

HOWARD CAMPBELL:

Most people would ask, "What was he diagnosed *with*?"

DR. WILLIAM FINK:

Huh?

HOWARD CAMPBELL:

Most people would ask, "What was he diagnosed *with*?" I listen to how people speak. You speak extraordinarily literally. It just made me laugh. I didn't mean anything by it.

DR. WILLIAM FINK:

Oh.

HOWARD CAMPBELL:

I interrupted you.

[PAUSE]

I extrapolate temperaments and habits, and habits from nuances. I don't always mean to say those things out loud. I guess I'm just accustomed to being behind a one-way mirror at focus groups.

DR. WILLIAM FINK:

In our roles here, I'll ask you to limit your observations to Richard Wilson.

[SILENCE]

HOWARD CAMPBELL:

You rarely swear.

[PAUSE]

DR. WILLIAM FINK:

Almost never. You're right. I am more exacting than most. My exactitude developed from years of reading science and medical books. Can you tell me what Bucky was diagnosed with?

HOWARD CAMPBELL:

Bucky was initially diagnosed as a paranoid schizophrenic. His exit diagnosis was bipolar. The notes stated that while he appeared schizophrenic, he could not have regained his equilibrium so quickly if he had actually been schizoid. They concluded, then, that he must have entered the hospital in a state of rapid cycling mania.

DR. WILLIAM FINK:

How do you know this?

HOWARD CAMPBELL:

I read his medical records.

DR. WILLIAM FINK:

In the hotel? In all the papers?

HOWARD CAMPBELL:

Yes, they were there, but I'd read them back at Bennington. I read his journal for the first time at the hotel. His medical records were something he just left around in his dorm room. I read it. So did most of his friends.

DR. WILLIAM FINK:

The first time you read his journal was in the hotel room?

HOWARD CAMPBELL:

Yes.

[PAUSE]

DR. WILLIAM FINK:

What did his journal say about his hospitalization at Bennington?

HOWARD CAMPBELL:

Bucky explained that people had started appearing strange to him. He said that most people always appeared strange to him, but that his newfound strangeness shifted his focus, and each person he encountered seemed stranger than the next. In truth, he was the stranger. He had manufactured an image of America that didn't jive with those around him, and they outnumbered him, and he couldn't hang. This was the premise behind the title of his manifesto, *The Longer Line*. There was a study by a Dr. Ash…

DR. WILLIAM FINK:

I want to stick to Richard's history of mental illness for now. Was Bucky ever diagnosed as paranoid?

HOWARD CAMPBELL:

No, but he had a similar profile to a paranoid schizophrenic, including above average intelligence, and an emotionally unavailable parent.

DR. WILLIAM FINK:

You know a lot about abnormal psychological profiles.

HOWARD CAMPBELL:

I've done my reading. Bennington has a history of students checking into mental hospitals and so when a friend gets admitted a bunch of us would read up on what they had. Kids will sit around talking about how Pokemon characters would act; we'd sit around talking about how specific psychoses made people act. Bucky describes the onset of his mental illness in the first entry of *The Longer Line*, dated *April 6, 1993, sometime after noon*.

DR. WILLIAM FINK:

Was that literally the date of the entry: "sometime after noon"?

HOWARD CAMPBELL:

Yes, it was. He begins by explaining how he was playing Cosmic Wipeout, a dice game similar to Yahtzee. Cosmic Wipeout's verbiage and rules are supposed to reward you for your psychic abilities to affect the dice. The prize is always a bong hit. Bucky won this particular game. Instead of dice with spots on each side, Cosmic Wipeout dice have pictograms. He called to the heavens for the power of the sun and then rolled; four of the six dice came up sunspots. He repeated his petition to the heavens and his remaining two dice rolled as sunspots.

After a few rounds and several bong hits of killer ganj, he was feeling trapped by the game. He had been enjoying calling his shots, but the pot fucked with him, and he asked how the game would end. Stephan told him he had to win it. He found himself muttering that he wanted to stop playing the game. He repeated the mantra, "I want to stop playing the game," and he kept winning points.

When he found himself proud from collecting points, he would have a cosmic train wreck and crap out. He wanted to win, not for the sake of winning, but because winning would mean he could quit playing the game. While he wanted to win, he found that if his energies were distracted by the joy of approaching the win, he would lose his luck. He created a distinction between winning so he could regain his liberty, and winning for the sake of victory, which would be to understand and support the game, to feel obligated to pay attention. He focused his energy and emerged victorious.

Two of the doctors at the hospital concurred that this incident of getting stoned acted as a catalyst for a loosening of his associations that led him to place himself into their care. They explained that the pot made the experience seem mystical. This explanation discredits the perceptions of the other people in the room—presumably because they were also smoking pot.

Bucky wrote, "My head was not well integrated back then. Trying to reconstruct these events is like a farsighted man assembling a jigsaw puzzle of a familiar visage. I'm not able to see the contours of the edges, but I know what the final picture looks like. Things get blurry when I strain for the detail of the moment, so I overcompensate by describing some of the thoughts that I know surrounded the event." I'm drawing from his journals, some written in present tense, some after the fact.

DR. WILLIAM FINK:

What happened after Cosmic Wipeout?

HOWARD CAMPBELL:

When he'd won, we decided to go shoot pool. Emily Kischell asked him if he used magic to roll the dice. He explained that it wasn't magic, it was somehow real. He talked about finding the power we all have in us. When I asked him about the event, he didn't remember much of what was said. Anyone else present would probably have a better recollection. But, we were all really stoned. Best way to stump a stoner? Ask them: "What were we just talking about?"

Bucky was talking about breaking the boundaries of convention. He talked about them forming a brain trust or a corporation to do some sort of big business, the specifics were unknown to him, but he was confident we could figure something out. Stephan asked what kind of boundaries and Bucky lunged over and kissed him. He wasn't accustomed to kissing men and neither was Stephan. Stephan went with the flow and waited to see what Bucky was getting at. Bucky talked about how we were blind because we saw life through our parents' veils. He said that with a new perception, the world was ours for the building.

Later, Emily said she felt like she had witnessed a manifestation of newborn madness that was so viscous in the room that day that it could've been bottled. She said she was both worried and in awe, but more than anything, it was incredibly interesting to her. Emily stressed that the vibes in the room were in disturbance. She was convinced Bucky was suddenly seeing the world as it really was, that he'd snapped into a different dimension, and that she and her friends were still as confused as cavemen in a solar eclipse. She wanted to know if it was magic.

DR. WILLIAM FINK:

What did she mean by magic?

HOWARD CAMPBELL:

Bucky had paid his way through UCLA as a magician. Emily was asking if he was using sleight of hand to control the dice. He wasn't using prestidigitation. He was certain he was somehow influencing the outcome of the dice. He viewed this skill as a science, a science rooted in the heart of our current world order. He knew the power to be real. He feared better practitioners would be invisible to him. He felt excited by the prospect of learning, yet vulnerable to those with mastery. I'm adding a lot of commentary. I'm synthesizing from his notes.

Bucky saw the world as imbued with spirits. This was his first dose of the spiritual world manifested real. It was bound to happen. His mother is a mystic, having had a deep, active spiritual bent.

This period in Bucky's life was filled with deep exploration. He had more notes on his interactions with Brian than any other college friend. Brian was kicked out of Bennington College for assaulting another student, having released saliva from his mouth onto another student who was taunting him. The guy he spat on was Justin Theroux, the character actor playing the producer in the Lynch movie *Mullhuland Drive*, and from *Charlie's Angels*. Justin was very well liked. The act of spitting is an act of assault. Bullshit if you ask me, but I imagine the law was created for a reason. Brian wouldn't have been expelled if he hadn't been so disliked. He creeped most people out. But, Bucky liked him. A couple of months before the Cosmic Wipeout incident, Brian was expelled. A friend gave Bucky a play to read that Brian had written. Bucky thought it was great and wanted to meet him. The first couple of times Bucky tried to talk to him, he scurried away. On a whim, Bucky asked Brian if colors had meaning. The two talked for almost two days straight. Bucky wrote that he couldn't remember most of their conversation, except that they talked colors, number theory, and about the functional meaning of grammar. On the second day, Bucky made a comment about the effect of hierarchy on learning. Brian responded, "So, you know Kaiser." Bucky said, "Huh?" Bucky noted that Brian looked pissed. Brian said, "You're shitting me." Bucky assured him he didn't know who Kaiser was. Brian looked spooked and wandered away. Bucky would see Brian and ask him, "Kaiser who?" and Brian would say something about Kaiser having been a great man in history. Bucky compiled a long list of Kaisers and showed them to Brian, who just laughed. Bucky wrote that they never really talked after that, between that conversation and Brian being expelled.

There is no date on these notes, but all of this evidently happened before April 6, 1993. Bucky interspersed these notes with the notes about the events that led up to his incarceration. That's what Bucky called his stay in the Southern Vermont Mental Hospital, an incarceration. When I asked him about this, he asked, "What do you call it when the people in a building have the legal right to forcibly hold you captive?" This is plain weird considering he admitted himself into their care. But, Bucky had a different relationship with the idea of incarceration than most. He thought that when a person found themselves unable to act, that their actions were arrested. The physical means to this "incarceration" would have been cultural. In this way, people are prisoners of their own thoughts, but the bars are invisible, the bars are what we understand or hold to be true, the assumptions of their cosmographies.

DR. WILLIAM FINK:

I want to spend less time on his ideas. Can you describe more of the tangible events that preceded his hospitalization?

HOWARD CAMPBELL:

Yes.

His journal reads, "April 6th, I made it back to my dorm with little incident."

DR. WILLIAM FINK:

This was after playing pool?

HOWARD CAMPBELL:

No. They decided to play pool, but a lot happened between playing Cosmic Wipeout and playing pool. Bucky describes that, on the way to his dorm room before playing pool, his head was clear and that he had extreme focus because he was on a mission. He had found the Sufis. In the privacy of his dorm room, he rolled a die as he reshaped words in his head. He thought hard.

He decided he needed to pack. He surmised he needed gear that was versatile and traveled light. He filled a fanny pack with a credit card, a passport, what cash he had around, a toothbrush, a lighter, Chapstick, the key to his dorm, three packs of cigarettes and a comb. He was ready.

Sufism was relatively new to Bucky. He'd been introduced to the idea, the meme, at Mildred's parents' house. Mildred was a girlfriend he never fully let go of. Maybe not even now. It's hard to tell since he's catatonic. Although self-proclaimed Sufis had their own definition, Bucky said that Hank, a warrior of the newly found recycling initiative of the late '80s, described it to him best. Hank surmised Sufism was derived from Sophism and was the art of seeing things more clearly, more simply. Hank was wrong about the name being derived from Sophism. But, he understood Sufism. Bucky used to tell Hank stories on his morning route collecting aluminum cans. Hank would tell him stories of his own.

Sufis refer to themselves as idiots, and refer to their teachings as the wisdom of the idiots. The underlying principle of Sufism is to not take one's self too seriously. Sufis call themselves idiots in a loving way. Idiot refers to acknowledging when one's perception has been off and one has been an "idiot." This appreciation, as opposed to resistance, leads to clearer sight, allowing one to appreciate having had a misperception as opposed to resenting having been wrong. Sufis teach through stories. Many of the stories have the same lead character, Nasrudin, a fool. For example, Nasrudin was sitting on his porch getting wet in the rain. A passerby asked why he didn't go inside the house. Nasrudin explained that his roof was leaking and he would get wet either way. The passerby asked why he didn't fix the leak. Nasrudin explained that when it was raining he couldn't do work on his house, and that when it was sunny, it didn't leak, so it didn't seem like it needed fixing. This story amused Bucky enough for him to repeat it to me several times.

DR. WILLIAM FINK:

Would Bucky regularly repeat many things he said?

HOWARD CAMPBELL:

Bucky collected stories like some people collect jokes, and similarly, he would tell them often. At school, I don't know how many times I heard his story of Great Sphinx of Giza.

I didn't know where he got the story from until I began reading *Fingerprints of the Gods.*

DR. WILLIAM FINK:

The book on the back of the Sphinx in the photo?

HOWARD CAMPBELL:

Yeah. Egyptologists date the Sphinx at approximately 2,500 years old. Many have invested a lifetime deciphering a story based on artifacts collected seen as relating to the Sphinx. It wasn't until a geologist looked at the Sphinx that a new piece of evidence was submitted for evaluation on the age of the Sphinx. Geologist Robert Schoch explained that the Sphinx showed evidence of rainfall erosion. Such erosion could only mean that the Sphinx was carved during or before the rains that marked the transition of northern Africa from the last Ice Age to the present interglacial epoch, a transition that occurred in the millennia from 10,000 to 5,000 BC.

Many Egyptologists maintain that the Sphinx is only 2,500 years old. Bucky would add that many people still believe the Earth is flat.

DR. WILLIAM FINK:

But the Sphinx was built 2,500 years ago.

HOWARD CAMPBELL:

[LAUGHTER]

Did you not hear what Bucky was saying?!

DR. WILLIAM FINK:

Huh?

[PAUSE]

HOWARD CAMPBELL:

Egyptologists date the Sphinx at approximately 2,500 years old. A geologist named Schoch explained that the Sphinx has rainfall erosion which could only mean that the Sphinx was carved during or before the rains that marked the transition from the last Ice Age, a transition that occurred 10,000 to 5,000 BC.

You saying that our model of geology is wrong? That Schoch mistook something for rain erosion that wasn't? Or, that there have been heavy rains on the scale of ice age transitions since 500 BC?

[PAUSE]

DR. WILLIAM FINK:

I guess I wasn't listening.

[PAUSE]

HOWARD CAMPBELL:

I think you're getting tired. We should stop.

DR. WILLIAM FINK:

But we aren't scheduled to meet for another three weeks.

[PAUSE]

HOWARD CAMPBELL:

That's your schedule. But, that's a minor point. I think what lead Bucky to come here is precisely what you just demonstrated.

DR. WILLIAM FINK:

What?

HOWARD CAMPBELL:

I present you with one of Bucky's observations about how a whole field of study appears as ludicrous, as superficial, because it is based on incomplete information, information subdivided and kept separate by the specialization of academia, and you weren't listening closely enough to get it.

[SILENCE]

DR. WILLIAM FINK:

You're saying that Bucky had observations that he viewed as revolutionary, but that hadn't made their way to mainstream consciousness.

HOWARD CAMPBELL:

I think the key to breaking through his catatonia may be to empathize with some of his ideas.

DR. WILLIAM FINK:

Are you suggesting I tell him I know the Sphinx is over 10,000 years old?

HOWARD CAMPBELL:

I'm not telling you how to do your job.

[PAUSE]

DR. WILLIAM FINK:

I'd like to see you sooner than we'd scheduled.

HOWARD CAMPBELL:

I can come back tomorrow, but then I'm traveling to Maui for a couple weeks.

DR. WILLIAM FINK:

I'll clear my schedule for tomorrow morning. Can you come in at 10?

[PAUSE]

HOWARD CAMPBELL:

Yes.

DR. WILLIAM FINK:

Okay, I'll see you then. Oh, one more thing. I know Nurse Ogelthorpe asked you, and I know you told her he was an only child and raised by his grandmother and all, but Richard has no living relatives?

HOWARD CAMPBELL:

None that I know of.

DR. WILLIAM FINK:

No cousins?

HOWARD CAMPBELL:

I went with him to his grandmother's funeral. Friends of hers were in attendance, but no relatives. If he had *any* living family, he never mentioned them and they weren't close enough to attend.

She had been really sick. Actually his grandmother was more old and frail than specifically sick, the doctors called her different ailments sicknesses, as if she wasn't supposed to have stuff stop working at age 88. She couldn't speak much, and her hearing was essentially non-existent, but she was very aware and apparently read voraciously until a month before she died. Anyway, the hospital called Bucky at Bennington and said she might die any day.

That night, Bucky sent her a fax. It had one sentence on it, "When I tell your story, I'll tell a love story." She passed that night.

I went with Bucky back to his grandmother's.

DR. WILLIAM FINK:

For the funeral?

HOWARD CAMPBELL:

The funeral, and to help take care of her personal effects.

[PAUSE]

DR. WILLIAM FINK:

I'm sorry. Thank you. I just needed to ask for myself.

HOWARD CAMPBELL:

I imagined so.

DR. WILLIAM FINK:

Very well. I'll see you tomorrow.

[SOUND: RECORDER SWITCHING OFF]

(DISCUSSION OMITTED)

[SOUND: RECORDER SWITCHING ON]

SESSION 2

VOICE OF DR. WILLIAM FINK:

February 1, 2003, session two with Howard Campbell.

HOWARD CAMPBELL:

Hi.

DR. WILLIAM FINK:

What else can you tell me about April 6th? We still haven't gotten to the pool hall yet.

HOWARD CAMPBELL:

I have grave concerns about continuing this conversation.

DR. WILLIAM FINK:

Grave concerns? Aren't you being hyperbolic?

HOWARD CAMPBELL:

No. I'm telling you the internal thoughts of somebody who went insane. It would be healthier for you to stop right now. These ideas are communicable.

DR. WILLIAM FINK:

You mean these ideas are contagious?

HOWARD CAMPBELL:

Yes. By sharing these ideas with you, I am implanting live meme viruses in your head. By continuing this conversation, I'm putting you at risk of destabilizing your precept of reality, and I don't know if you can handle it.

[PAUSE]

DR. WILLIAM FINK:

I've worked in mental health for years. I don't seem to have caught any insanity viruses, yet. I'm willing to risk it. Besides, you've been exposed to these ideas. You seem relatively well adjusted. I can handle whatever you tell me.

[PAUSE]

HOWARD CAMPBELL:

Okay. I may be painfully self-aware and sensitive. You are cardboard and too detached to feel me. I suspect if you really tried on Bucky's your defensive walls may come tumbling down. Americans like their righteousness and contorted definition of freedom.

Try this on for size: America's democracy ended with the assassination of John F. Kennedy. His murder was a coup de tat. Lyndon Johnson, aided by the Central Intelligence Agency, stacked the deck for the game of politics we've been playing ever since.

DR. WILLIAM FINK:

You sound like some of the paranoids who come through here. I don't suffer fools lightly. I'm interested in what happened to Richard "Bucky" Wilson, not your theories about politics. Tell me more about what happened on April 6th, 1993, please.

HOWARD CAMPBELL:

Bucky had been researching the assassination just prior to April 6th. Bucky was a student of the events surrounding JFK's assassination, or as he would call it, the Johnson Coup. You can go to Bennington College's library and find what he checked out over this period. It should be easy enough to find out, and his books became overdue because of his hospital stay. I bring this up because these ideas could've been a catalyst. A sudden realization that the world was not as he knew it. A realization that affected the way he saw reality. In his journal, on April 6th, Bucky stated that...

[SOUND: GULPING LIQUID. CLINK OF GLASS ON TABLE.]

…everything occurred to him as superficial.

DR. WILLIAM FINK:

Did he give specifics?

[PAPER BEING UNFOLDED]

HOWARD CAMPBELL:

His journal simply stated, "Everything is superficial."

I assume he was reading *Man's Search for Meaning.* Because he also wrote, "Compared to a psychiatrist held captive in a Nazi concentration camp, nothing in my life is significant." On the morning of April 6th, he had come up to me, ranting, "Everything is fake, manufactured, synthetic and dirty." He ran off as quickly as he had approached.

DR. WILLIAM FINK:

You knew he was losing it?

HOWARD CAMPBELL:

No. I just thought he was being dramatic. None of us really knew the extent of his thoughts and how debilitating they were until he was hospitalized. While he was hospitalized, we were in the dark. I didn't start reading his journal until I got here and found it in his hotel room.

DR. WILLIAM FINK:

Why do you think he left his journal for you now?

HOWARD CAMPBELL:

Now, you're asking me to speculate. I don't think Bucky could give you a rational answer. He explains in his journal that the events of April 6th are obscured. His notes don't seem to be from that day—like he revisited his notes from that day and made comments on top of them. One of these comments reads, "sometime this afternoon is the last point I was connected with time." *Speculatively*, this is about the time he headed to the campus poolroom.

[SOUND: PAPER BEING UNFOLDED]

Allow me to read to you from his journal,

> "Halfway there, I stopped walking and looked at a tree. I felt a breeze and anticipated the tree's movement. When I was surprised by the tree's movement, somehow it was noted, not in words, but a thought nonetheless. After a bit, I stopped noticing any discrepancy. I stood there and observed the tree. I felt what the tree felt. The spring air had a bite to it. The sun offered a warm reprieve from the Arctic gusts. I empathized with the tree for budding, and felt its resistance to release its flowers. Any way I try to put this experience into words is only a metaphor. At the time, I had no words in my head. I know I was content to stand there looking at the tree."

[SOUND: PAPER BEING FOLDED]

Bucky was speaking about human-plant entrainment. Bucky had always been fascinated by entrainment.

DR. WILLIAM FINK:

What is entrainment?

HOWARD CAMPBELL:

Centuries ago, Christian Huygen noticed how separate entities will fall into rhythm with one another. Specifically two pendulum clocks placed in close proximity that began to keep the same time. In 1665, he coined the word "entrainment" to describe this phenomenon.

Huygen noticed that the clock in his study ran about a minute slower each day from the clock in his living room. He moved the two clocks side-by-side. When they were side-by-side, the discrepancy disappeared. They kept the same time. When he separated the two clocks, the discrepancy reappeared. Christian Huygen saw that the clocks had formed a compromise. The clocks together ran at the same time, but they ran 30 seconds slower than his pocket watch.

These observations lead to his discovery, or labeling of entrainment: the tendency of cyclical objects to meld into a common rhythm. Bucky would give examples of entrainment, such as women in college dorms whose menstrual cycles become one, and electric generators across a field that develop a common rhythm.

As I said, he collected stories and facts—and he didn't discriminate between the two—and put them in his notes. I'm telling you about his entries in the approximate order he left them for me to find.

DR. WILLIAM FINK:

I derailed you from Bucky's experience with the tree.

HOWARD CAMPBELL:

Bucky entrained with the tree. He slowed down his rhythm and softened his assertiveness to feel the rhythm of the tree. Gihan, the scruffiest student on campus, came by and stood with him for a bit before asking what he was doing. Bucky told him he was standing with the tree. Gihan asked Bucky if he was okay. Bucky said yes. Together, they stood with the tree. After a while, Gihan said "okay" and wandered away.

Then, Bucky made his way to the poolroom. He hadn't realized he'd spent over three hours with the tree. This was the beginning of a tweaked perception that would last for four days. When he got to the pool hall, people there appeared to him as automatons. They didn't seem human. He couldn't feel them. They told him that his friends had been there, and played pool for a couple hours, and had left. Bucky headed to Darrin Barschdorf's room.

Bucky wrote that when he left the poolroom, Bennington's campus seemed empty. He wrote that he did not see a single person on his way to Darrin's room. This was odd. The campus was silent. When he got to Darrin's room, there was a sign on the door written in crayon that said: "Welcome."

In Bucky's state, this played nicely into his idea that he was being admitted into the Brotherhood of Sufi warriors. Bucky took the sign as an invitation to enter without knocking. He found an empty room with an uncharacteristically made bed. On Darrin's bed was a hexagonal white board with a black border. It occurred to Bucky first as a puzzle, and then as a test, a component of an elaborate ritual which he saw himself having to pass before being initiated. There were 23 pieces on this six-sided board. Bucky had spent too much time in numerology and too much time reading *The Illuminatus! Trilogy* to let 23 pieces on a six-sided board go unnoticed. He meditated on the pieces, which looked like Escher building blocks, in that the puzzle pieces fit together to build 3D objects on a 2D board that could never be built, because these Escher pieces visually bent rules of any known physical plane. He constructed the rules of his vision quest as he went along. At the time, this invention of rules occurred to him as akin to discovering the laws of physics. He saw Sufis as real magicians, practicing magick. Magick was the science of being effective. Bucky cited Aleister Crowley, "That which we do not understand, we attribute to magick."

(TRANSCRIBER'S NOTATION: MAGICK WITH A "K" REFERS TO THE WORD COINDED BY ALEISTER CROWLEY, THE PRACTICE OF INTENTIONAL EFFECTIVENESS.)

DR. WILLIAM FINK:

Crowley? The Satanist?

HOWARD CAMPBELL:

I'll come back to that, but yes, Crowley was a self-proclaimed Satanist. He intentionally wanted to address that which the church forbade. He attacked the church built in Jesus' name.

In the dorm room, Bucky examined the board, trying to understand his mission. He noticed a design on the back that could be created with the magnetic pieces on the front. This felt too easy. But for all he knew, the challenges leading to initiation may start easy. This could make sense, as a means to ensure that a new player recognizes that there's a game to be played. The design was a box inverted on itself. Bucky started trying to arrange the pieces on the front to mirror the image on the back. He quickly found this to be impossible with the pieces at hand. He was foiled. He thought about drawing the required image on the face of the board, but that didn't feel right. The solution would make itself known to him. He relaxed. He started playing with the pieces he had. He found that he could create the inverse image minus one piece. This was the answer. He expected the Sufis to easily see things two different ways, and his solution was inline with his expectations that a Sufi puzzle would test his ability to loosen his associations and re-associate objects. Bucky went further. He saw the puzzle and himself as part of the solution.

You see, there were five of the six pieces required to make the inverse object. Once assembled, he saw:

First—the six-sided board with

Second—the picture on the back that Bucky deduced to be six pieces and

Third—the picture on the front consisted of five pieces plus one inferred object for six pieces.

Thee-elements of six: 6-6-6. His initiation had begun.

DR. WILLIAM FINK:

Was the board part of an elaborate hoax somebody was playing on Bucky?

HOWARD CAMPBELL:

Nobody had orchestrated Bucky finding these objects. In hindsight, it appears as a series of bizarre coincidences, bizarre in their overlap with what Bucky was focusing on.

[PAUSE]

DR. WILLIAM FINK:

Did Bucky occur to you as delusional?

HOWARD CAMPBELL:

No, delusional people aren't grounded in reality. Delusional people seem to overlook obvious schisms between their ideas and reality. Bucky was incredulous about what was happening. He tested his realities, but the schema he was testing his experiences against may have been delusional.

DR. WILLIAM FINK:

The schema of a schizophrenic is delusional.

HOWARD CAMPBELL:

Our Bucky was labeled as bipolar. So, please curb your judgment.

I was with Bucky, five years earlier, when he discovered *Magick*, by Aleister Crowley, at a bookstore. He had gone there to buy something else, and the title *Magick* caught his eye, so he bought it. The book suggested that he lived a perfunctory life, not taking responsibility for his actions. While the book was old, and not written in our modern self-help vein, he interpreted it as a guide to a possible way of life. *Magick* begins with the premise that to know anything, you must approach life in a scientific manner. Crowley borrowed Plato's premise that to know others, you must first get to know yourself. Bucky took this as an instruction, that he must know his *self*. Crowley suggests that without self-knowledge, we're just following a pattern we constructed earlier in life that fit our earlier needs. Crowley suggested that by knowing yourself, you would discover your true will. Crowley proposes one all-binding, unifying code of conduct: "Do what thou Wilt shall be the whole of the law."

DR. WILLIAM FINK:

Do what you want shall be the whole of the law sounds anti-social—sociopathic, to use your loose term.

HOWARD CAMPBELL:

The line doesn't say *want*, it says *wilt*—your true will. Crowley would argue that an anti-social hasn't quieted himself down enough to be in touch with himself.

DR. WILLIAM FINK:

How do you know you aren't anti-social?

HOWARD CAMPBELL:

The same way you know you aren't Jesus Christ. You just know. I'll go one step further. Anybody who thinks they *are* Jesus Christ should check themselves into a hospital like this.

Crowley told Bucky, via his book, that Bucky hadn't learned anything for himself because he hadn't recognized which values he'd accepted from his parents and culture, as opposed to deciding for his Self. Crowley accused him of being a robot, programmed by his society. Crowley was out to prove this to him. Crowley mocked him for entertaining the notion that he was agnostic. Crowley chastised him for trying to compartmentalize an all-powerful unifying power under the label of God. He challenged Bucky, stating that he mistook labels for actual energy. He accused him of being a Christian without knowing it. Once Crowley hooked Bucky with His logic, Crowley told Bucky that he was the Beast 666, Satan. Crowley said that if Bucky weren't a Christian, these labels wouldn't have an impact on him. Crowley promised that if Bucky could let go of his prejudices towards these labels, he could teach him to be happier through increased effectiveness. Bucky studied Crowley's teachings.

[SILENCE]

DR. WILLIAM FINK:

Can you keep going?

HOWARD CAMPBELL:

Sure.

[PAUSE]

Another thing that bugged Bucky was the way that The Church has a tendency to report ideas as facts. For Bucky, Christmas is an occasion to give and receive gifts. For others, December 25th is the day to honor the birth of Jesus. During the first two centuries after Jesus' death, Christmas was not celebrated. Biblical scholars came up with multiple dates: January 1, January 6, March 25, and May 20.

The May date makes the most sense for Christmas. Luke 2:8 reports that the shepherds were watching their sheep by night when they heard about Jesus' birth. Shepherds guarded their flocks day *and* night only during lambing time, which was in the spring. However, in 349 A.D., Pope Julius formally selected December 25 as Christmas, a date no biblical scholar was suggesting. You see, this date was already widely celebrated by Romans in honor of the sun god, Mithras. It was easier to reframe a celebration, usurping its meaning than to create a new celebration and get villagers to abandon another.

DR. WILLIAM FINK:

I'm more interested in what happened at Bennington, before Bucky went to the hospital.

HOWARD CAMPBELL:

Bucky wrote about the Pope's selection of Christmas Day in his journal, when he was at Bennington, just before he went to the hospital. He thought these were important details. He praised the church for helping villagers not throw away their money on charlatans who presented themselves as having supernatural powers. That part was good. The burning people at the stake part rather sucked. But, Bucky put this shit in his journal. This is the essence of what he was thinking about then: those in charge of labeling labeled the unexplained negatively, as supernatural, in the interest of preserving their larger power structures, what Bucky called super-meme-plexes.

[PAUSE]

DR. WILLIAM FINK:

Yeah, okay, go on.

HOWARD CAMPBELL:

Okay, back to the puzzle in Darrin's room. Bucky placed the solved puzzle back where he'd found it. He emptied the ashtray and left. Outside, people appeared peculiar to him. His manifesto depicts him asking himself if everyone at Bennington was in on *it?* Was he the only non-initiated here? He didn't think so, but the idea haunted him. Bucky thought of Bennington College as a modern day *Witch Mountain* monastery where…

DR. WILLIAM FINK:

Witch Mountain?

HOWARD CAMPBELL:

Yeah, like in the Disney movie *Escape To Witch Mountain*, where all the kids with special powers go for training.

DR. WILLIAM FINK:

My kids love Harry Potter. Maybe it's like Hogwartz.

HOWARD CAMPBELL:

Yes, like Hogwartz, but instead of where the kids naturally knew they had tangible powers, kids at Bennington were assimilated into the way of Sufism through the ordeal of a testing mechanism. Bucky speculated in his journal that if one wasn't assimilated, they might be discredited, banished or abandoned. Bucky didn't know. And this scared him.

Outside Darrin's room, Bucky stood still, watching as people passed in small groups or alone. Gihan emerged and smiled at him. He said, "You going to dinner?" Bucky nodded and they joined the direction of the general flow. They walked in silence.

Once upstairs, they said their student ID numbers and were admitted to an all-you-can-eat buffet that catered to Bennington's students, children of some of the wealthiest families in the world.

Bucky followed Gihan into the smoking room and they joined friends at a back table against the wall. I was among them, but these details are more from his journal than my recollection. I wouldn't have remembered the details of the conversation. From my perspective, nothing special was going on.

Bucky wrote in his journal about how Bill Scully was ranting about an article he'd come across. Bill smoked Natural Spirits to avoid chemicals, but Bill looks more like a Marlboro Man than a granola boy—he was a tough kid raised in El Centro and notorious for wearing steel-tipped boots, even with shorts.

DR. WILLIAM FINK:

Let's stay on task. What was the article about?

HOWARD CAMPBELL:

Yes, sir.

Apparently the Pope had decreed some new sins for the first time in some 80 years. Primarily, Scully was going off on how it was now a sin to evade taxes. Scully was preaching how this was irrefutable proof that the church was sucking-up to local governments, a/k/a nations, since its fall from prominence with what started as the Church of England, but spread like a virus to the new world as Protestantism.

Bucky heard what Bill was saying, but he was enchanted and distracted by what he saw in the room. He wasn't looking at the people, although they were interesting enough. Ginger Parker and the glamour set had decided it was formal night, so she and her friends were dressed in formal cocktail attire. Three guys were in black tie, and the women wore cocktail dresses with breast popping necklines and feather boas. Very Roaring Twenties, but in modern garb.

If stereotyped from a distance, our table looked pretty Goth. Scully's best friend Jim was in town. Jim always brought abundant alcohol, which warranted some to suit his fancy by adorning themselves in black outfits with spiked jewelry and heavy mascara.

Instead of looking at the people, Bucky was staring at the colors around most everybody, primarily blue and green. Then he saw somebody shift from blue into green, through yellow, and intensify into orange, at which point this person lit a cigarette and settled back down to green. His eyes settled on another person who repeated this cycle. As he scanned the room, virtually everybody was aglow; some shifted in color while others remained relatively stable. From this account, you might think Bucky was tripping on acid, but he wasn't.

Bill was yapping away. He shifted from yellow into orange, and back to yellow, but never calmed down to green or blue. He was incited.

DR. WILLIAM FINK:

Could you tell he was taking a break from reality? How did Bucky occur to you?

HOWARD CAMPBELL:

When somebody takes a break from something, I think of them as resting. Bucky wasn't resting in any sense of the word. He didn't sleep for four days and he was always quietly engaged in something is all I can recollect. I don't rightly know. I wasn't focusing on him. When Bucky told me about his experiences, after getting out of the hospital, I was shocked. I remembered Bill's rant, but I hadn't remembered anything unusual about Bucky. Kind of scary to have somebody having such a peculiar experience and not be able to sense anything out of the ordinary was going on.

DR. WILLIAM FINK:

Did Bucky explain how he kept it a secret in his journal?

HOWARD CAMPBELL:

He said that he thought he was being tested, that his task back then was to see if he could get Bobby to finally shut-up.

DR. WILLIAM FINK:

Bobby?

HOWARD CAMPBELL:

Bucky wrote that ever since he could remember, Bobby had been talking. Bobby is the voice in his head, not the problem solving one, but the chatterbox. They both have the same voice, just one is intentional and one feels passive. Bucky named this passive voice "Bobby" at some point during the four days before he entered the hospital. He didn't specify the situation in his journal where he named Bobby, but he does write:

[SOUND: PAPER BEING UNFOLDED]

"I remember being 12 years old and very aware of Bobby. Of course I hadn't begun personifying my voice, so I just thought of that voice in my head as me. Imposing my current perspective on a younger me, I wanted to know if Bobby was always talking, or if sometimes he was silent and I just didn't notice the silence. To test this, I used one of those newfangled digital watches and I would randomly set the alarm so that I didn't know when it would go off. I found that every time the alarm went off, Bobby was talking. The only exception was when the alarm woke me. After a while, I concluded that when I was awake, Bobby was talking. I view this as symptomatic of a nervous mind. Then, it occurred to me as normal."

[SOUND: PAPER BEING FOLDED]

DR. WILLIAM FINK:

The stuff before what you just read, that was *all* in his journal?

HOWARD CAMPBELL:

Yeah. All except for the characterizations like "goth" and "very roaring twenties."

DR. WILLIAM FINK:

Please, stick to what you know Bucky was commenting on. At least let me know when you are commenting as opposed to reporting Bucky's observations from his journal.

HOWARD CAMPBELL:

Yeah, okay. But this next part is from his journal *but not about Bennington.*

[PAUSE]

DR. WILLIAM FINK:

Go on.

HOWARD CAMPBELL:

In 1991, Bucky began his first mind experiments. He knew his mind was capable of far more than he was using it for. His initial interest was to do complicated mathematics in his head. He figured that if he could visualize numbers, he could do complex algebraic equations in his head. He never accomplished this, at least not through these means.

Bucky goes on to describe that it wasn't until 1992 that he actively worked at silencing Bobby. This was not a violent move, but an active interest in what his mind could do if it didn't need to exert the energy to follow Bobby's train of thought. Bucky wrote: "Never whistle while you piss" and credited this to Robert Anton Wilson author of *The Illuminatus! Trilogy.* Wilson said that the two biggest fallacies of the twentieth century were that politicians weren't that smart, and that they mean well.

Anyway, Bucky saw Bobby as a deterrent to seeing clearly and hearing with acuity. He found that as he got a better look at a sculpture, he saw it more clearly as Bobby slowed down. He particularly found that he heard people better. He didn't have this already running commentary on their conversation. This commentary interpreted their comments through his veil of prejudices, anything he'd decided before this conversation. These prejudged notions manifested in the form of the voice, Bobby, and was triggered by their comments.

Bucky's main objective, with his early experimentation, was to mess with his visual field. He wanted to hold images of numbers in his sight, and, play with them the way a child rearranges building blocks. He started by trying to visualize geometric shapes imposed on what he was naturally seeing. He talked to people who say they can do this. He had conversations where friends claimed to be able to visualize others in different clothes. Bucky didn't doubt they could do as they claimed. He just never attained this skill.

Bucky said that his greatest results came from being extraordinarily accurate with his word. He said that when he intentionally became verbally accurate, and adamant about keeping his word, his life became fuller. He noted that when he became an extremist about keeping his word, he was much more guarded against promising anything, and much more likely to generate that which he spoke. But, this was a later experiment. At this point in time, he was working on mental experimentation with his visual field.

Visually, Bucky was able to create waves in patterns. In 1992, he spent about one-and-a-half hours waiting for Mildred to get home, and with few interruptions, he watched wave after wave roll across her front lawn. In order to do this, he had to be still and Bobby needed to be quiet. On that day, Bobby obliged him. Following this anecdote, Bucky wrote, "When he lost all his money gambling, he started making mental bets. That's how he lost his mind. -author unknown." Obviously, I don't know where he got this from.

His journal continues....

DR. WILLIAM FINK:

Is his journal and the manifesto, *The Longer Line*, the same document?

HOWARD CAMPBELL:

Yes. His journal continues with Bucky sitting in the Bennington cafeteria and "flowing with the scenery." Bobby was nowhere to be heard. Gihan turned to him and asked what he was spacing on. Bucky explained the colors to him. Gihan told him that he sometimes saw colors around people, too. Bucky knew he was among magicians, producers of magick. Gihan was helping Bucky feel comfortable with his new powers, his psi.

DR. WILLIAM FINK:

Sigh? As in an exhale?

HOWARD CAMPBELL:

No. Psi. P-S-I, the 23rd letter of the Greek alphabet, a word commonly used by some psychologists to represent phenomena outside their understanding, otherwise known as ESP.

[PAUSE]

When Bucky left the cafeteria and made his way back to his dorm, he wanted a nap. He was used to taking naps. When he settled into bed, Bobby appeared and questioned Bucky's self-perceived magick. Bobby questioned the discrepancy between what he'd known as real and what he'd been experiencing.

[PAUSE]

Bucky wrote about a dream. He was flying over hills and mountains. He dreamt of a transparent plane powered by tourists who were pedaling to keep their plane aloft. As he flew beneath them, their tour guide announced, "Ladies and gentlemen, Benjamin Garth." *Benjamin Garth* had been Bucky's stage name as a performer of magic. The dream continued and he glided over a hill and saw Bennington College. In the middle of the central lawn he saw about 30 women, all wearing skirts. As he flew overhead, the women waved and lifted their skirts—no panties. Bucky glided back around, and headed for Ginger Parker, a beautiful young woman with the charisma of a queen. She was one of the girls that had been all dressed up at the cafeteria earlier. Ginger leaned back and spread her legs open. He started to go down on her. She was enjoying it. Bucky was enjoying it. The other women disappeared. Bucky and Ginger were suddenly in a room without edges, enveloped by an endless, soft, flowing comforter. Bucky wrote that it felt "gloriously good." Then, Bucky heard Bill Scully's voice through his dream. Scully said, "Bucky, if you need me, I am here." Bucky looked up and out into the whiteness and told him to go away. Bucky looked down. Ginger Parker was gone. Bummer. Scully's voice resumed, "You need me. I am coming."

Bucky woke up saying, *"Fuck you!* I don't need you." But the image was gone and Bobby was awake. Bobby asked, "What do you make of that?" Bucky wrote that he wasn't accustomed to Bobby asking questions. Bobby had tended to be more of a commentator than an inquisitor. Bobby went silent. Bucky got out his die and started talking while rolling the die until he landed on the notion that Bill Scully was coming over.

Bucky was journaling while all this was happening. His notes are very exacting. He also wrote, "Am I being ridiculous, worthy of ridicule?" He notes that Bobby chided him. With Bill's friend Jim in town, Bill was hosting a party. No way Bill would come. Bucky smoked a cigarette while Bobby chastised him for entertaining the expectation of Bill's arrival. There was silence. Bobby and he weren't talking. Bucky sat on the edge of his bed, feeling dumb but nonetheless expecting Bill to show up. Then the front door to his dorm house opened. Bucky heard the unmistakable clank of steel-tipped boots on the stairs. Bill was there. Twisp.

DR. WILLIAM FINK:

What does Twisp mean?

HOWARD CAMPBELL:

Oh. Twisp is just an expression. Like "Oh, shit." Before I continue with what happened after Bucky's nap, I have to fill you in on the previous spring. The night before graduation, Bucky, Bill Scully, their friend Dave Williamson, and another 120 students all dosed on liquid a.

DR. WILLIAM FINK:

Liquid a?

HOWARD CAMPBELL:

Liquid acid.

DR. WILLIAM FINK:

Oh, wow. 120 students all hallucinating en mass. No good can come from that.

HOWARD CAMPBELL:

I won't argue. On this night, of a campus of 430, 180 students stayed for graduation, and two-thirds of these students were tripping their asses off. During that night, Bucky found Stephan Fowlkes playing with fire. Stephan is an artist, and he was playing with words as he sparked the fire, stoking the flame to create a blizzard of red and orange flying sparks. He talked about feeling magical and empowered. He kept repeating "Flutter by, butterfly" as Bucky and a circle of onlookers watched the sparks, flying bugs of glowing amber, "Flutter by, butterfly." Stephan talked about how if he did become famous and published, then after his death, people would know him through select words. He didn't know which of his words would represent his spirit. "Flutter by, butterfly." He just hoped that enough of them would be captured to communicate his spirit. "Butterfly flutter. Bye."

It was then that Bucky first had the vision of the world as primarily controlled by the powerful few, the meme generals—that the power to garner consensus was more powerful than money. Granted, in many ways money can buy consensus. However, money is not powerful when people won't accept your currency. Bucky noted, "If people won't accept your currency, is it still money?"

A meme general is one who controls vast influence. His or her army shapes the messages consumed by the masses, enchanting the listeners to understand their message. For countries this is called propaganda, for churches this is now called a sermon, for companies it is called marketing or communications.

Bucky figured that the Dalai Lama must be a meme general. Our president was questionable. He viewed him more as a puppet. Bucky reasoned that some chairmen of insurance companies were part of this set. He didn't know. He tried to derive rules of engagement from which he sought to appeal an entry. Whether or not Einstein had been a member, he wasn't sure. He was growing to suspect that Buckminster Fuller definitely was not a member, but that Fuller knew of the club and had attempted to let the rest of us know. Perhaps this last notion was the seed idea that led to Bucky's newfound worldview and eventual hospital incarceration.

DR. WILLIAM FINK:

How so?

HOWARD CAMPBELL:

A seed idea is an aggressive meme, a meme that seeks to take possession of a mind.

DR. WILLIAM FINK:

Why do you think this seed idea, the notion that Fuller attempted to tell the general public about this set of meme generals, was a catalyst to psychosis for Richard Wilson?

HOWARD CAMPBELL:

Hoffstadter's *Gödel Escher Bach* toys with phrases like "I am not the subject of this sentence." Bucky described *Gödel Escher Bach* as the most self-referential book he'd ever read. The book presented the idea of self-unfolding codes that featured a flag to their existence and included the decoding structure within its nature. Bucky projected this structure on Fuller's work, searching for an encoded meaning. Why do I think this was a seed idea? Because it seems to be the central theme that lead to his first hospitalization. If an idea is self-unfolding, it requires little external validity, because the idea is meant to be hidden to begin with.

Bucky had been reading about how a scientist in the fifties had sketched out a doomsday device, utilizing huge speakers in the desert, enabling the controller to throw the Earth off its axis. Einstein went out of his way to discredit this scientist. Later in life, Einstein said that the theory was viable, but that he'd discredited the young man because of his lack of discretion.

Bucky figured other meme generals would discredit those who did not hold a great enough respect for discretion. He took this notion a step further. He figured that the meme generals would contrive a system to discredit those who might divulge their existence. He figured mental hospitals would be useful to this end.

DR. WILLIAM FINK:

Memes are the same as thoughts?

HOWARD CAMPBELL:

Thoughts would limit memes to conscious ideas.

A meme is anything a mind replicates, from a song to the notion that *Ford puts quality first*, but it could also be a gesture or even seen in shifting proclivities. Memetics is the study of memes as living organisms, primarily by applying the laws of genetics to ideas. In genetics, it is recognized that isolation breeds mutation. In cultures, it was evident that separate societies developed separate languages.

Now add entrainment. Memes placed near each other have a tendency to meld. The Southern accent is an amalgamation between a British rhythm of speaking and an African rhythm. Funny. Despite the bigotry of many Caucasian Southerners, and their pride in distinguishing themselves from African Americans, a defining quality of a Southerner, their accent, was adopted from extended close proximity to Africans.

Anyway, back to April 6th, 1993. After Bucky woke up from his dream about flying and Ginger Parker, Bill Scully came in and asked Bucky if he was sleeping. Bucky said yes, but that he was awake now, and asked him to turn on the light. Bill offered him a smoke and they lit up. Bill asked Bucky if he was doing okay. Bucky said yes. Bucky told him about the dream. Bill said that he hadn't seen him at the party, so he figured he would come by and see if Bucky was okay. Bucky told Bill that if he had waited fifteen minutes, the dream would have had him fucking Ginger Parker. Bucky told Bill he was fine, he'd just had a long day and that if he didn't fall back to sleep, he'd come over. Bill left.

Bobby chided Bucky for not telling Bill that he'd expected him to come over. Bucky got irritably bored with Bobby saying that if he was so confident in his intuition, that he'd have told Bill exactly what he'd been thinking. Bucky fell back asleep.

The previous summer, Bucky spent two months in Richmond Virginia with Bill Scully and Dave Williamson—Dave grew up in Richmond. That trip to Richmond tweaked Bucky's perception and probably contributed to Bucky's hospitalization.

Bucky began noticing fnords. He saw that many establishments near an area called The Bend had the word "Truth" with a capital "T" someplace, somewhere. Bucky didn't know what this meant or where it came from. Dave didn't know what he was talking about.

DR. WILLIAM FINK:

We call this patter recognition, seeing patterns in chaos. This leads to the creation of conspiracy theories.

HOWARD CAMPBELL:

There are patterns in mathematical chaos. Since they are ephermeral, only existing within ranges of space, time or other conditions, scientists were blind to them up until recently.

Truth with a capital "T" exists among other public symbolism. It is a conspiracy. And, if you are black and live in Richmond, it is dangerous to test this theory. The force is well known by local non-whites.

Bucky's journal explains how Bucky explored the city's museums and took a self-guided tour of Monument Boulevard, a beautiful tree-lined street with statues commemorating what, in the South, they call the War Between the States, which he'd been taught to call the Civil War. Each statue was embedded with hidden codes. If the warrior was looking north, they fought for the North and vice versa. They were all on horseback, and if the horse had his front hoof up, he'd been wounded in battle. If it was rearing, the rider had died in battle. At the very end of the boulevard was a monument to the whole war. This was a huge monument, the size of a small house. On its base these words appear: "We have lost a battle, but the war continues. Eventually, Truth will prevail." Bucky saw, "Eventually, 'Truth' will prevail. That's where it came from. This is the tag line for the KKK." Truth with a capital "T" was a racist slur warning blacks to stay out.

DR. WILLIAM FINK:

You can still see this in Richmond?

HOWARD CAMPBELL:

To the best of my knowledge. But, Bucky started looking for secret symbols. His journal shows an increasing suspicion with the word *welcome*.

DR. WILLIAM FINK:

Why *welcome*?

HOWARD CAMPBELL:

Because the word welcome is usually posted or painted outside of churches and retail shops, places where professionals attempt to alter your perceptions for their profits. He looked for the number 23 and Masonic symbols. He looked for repeating patterns to see if there was meaning behind those images he found frequent or peculiar.

DR. WILLIAM FINK:

Did he find anything?

HOWARD CAMPBELL:

Bucky found *Cosmography*, a new book by Buckminster Fuller. Fuller died in 1983. This was 1992. It turned out that Fuller finished *Cosmography* in '83, on the day he left for the hospital to attend to his dying wife. Fuller was on the cover of *Time Magazine* in 1980 as one of the century's greatest thinkers, then died three years later and they couldn't get his last book published! The preface to the book explains that when the manuscript had been discovered after Fuller's death, it was found on an uncharacteristically neat desk, with a note on top that seemed to intuit both his death and this problem: "If something happens to me and I die suddenly, I want you to know of the extraordinary importance of my now being written book *Cosmography*."

DR. WILLIAM FINK:

Fuller sounds like he was paranoid, "If something happens to me, and I die suddenly…"

HOWARD CAMPBELL:

He was 88 years old. Thinking he may die suddenly is fairly reasonable for an octogenarian.

[PAUSE]

But, Fuller was a bit self-aggrandizing. And, he was a modern day Cassandra, blessed with foresight and cursed with incredibility. He talked about wealth as a system's ability to sustain itself into the future. This works for a person, a species, or any living organism. Look at the way capitalism is set up. Fuller cautioned that year after year, less and less "money" is available to the average person. The rich are getting richer. At a certain point, this system will fall apart. You don't hear politicians discussing this. Politics is the Potemkin village of corporations. It is a mathematical certainty that if our economy continues this trajectory, it will implode. Fuller talked about the need to find a statically indeterminate societal system, outside of lords and peasants. He talked about this being the promise of America.

Fuller talks about us living under a false assumption of scarcity. This perception is propagated by those currently supported at the Lord level by the toils of the masses. The resources of this spaceship are being disproportionately distributed under the veil that there isn't enough to go around, so we each need to grab what we can.

Cosmography begins: "The dark ages still reign over all humanity, and the depth and persistence of this domination are only now becoming clear. This Dark Age's prison has no steel bars, chains, or locks. Instead, it is locked by disorientation and built from misinformation. Caught up in a plethora of conditioned reflexes and driven by the human ego, both warden and prisoner attempt meagerly to compete with God. All are intractably skeptical of what they do not understand. We are powerfully imprisoned in these Dark Ages simply by the terms in which we have been conditioned to think."

Bucky read *Cosmography.* Realize that just before he left Bennington for that summer in Richmond, he'd had the acid trip where he saw the warriors of Magick ruling the planet. He thought there was value in being recognized by these powers. He was really tripped up when he found himself named in *Cosmography.* Fuller literally pointed to Bucky: "In 1979 a newspaperman in Los Angeles, Richard Brenneman, arranged for me to meet with a group of very young people to discuss the subjects I have dealt with in this book. After six months of reading my books, each had prepared a set of questions about my thoughts and statements. They had lively interest in what I had to say. I asked them their ages. The oldest, a boy, was twelve. He said he was interested in the tricks of magicians." That was Bucky. Bucky interviewed Fuller and was the twelve-year-old interested in the tricks of magicians.

DR. WILLIAM FINK:

This is real?

HOWARD CAMPBELL:

You can buy the book and find the reference. Yes, it's real. Anyway, Bucky reread *Cosmography.*

[SILENCE]

Did you know that Buckminster Fuller died two days after entering the hospital?

DR. WILLIAM FINK:

No.

HOWARD CAMPBELL:

His wife took him there. While there, she faded into a coma. Both died within one day of each other. Neither consciously knew the other died. They were a Duprass, paired souls that melded together, performing a celestial dance where neither object is orbiting around the other. Duprass was one of the cosmological vocabulary words Bucky adopted from Vonnegut's *Cat's Cradle*.

[PAUSE]

You characterized Bucky's grave premonition as paranoid. Just because somebody is labeled paranoid doesn't mean the patterns they recognize aren't real.

DR. WILLIAM FINK:

What else do you know happened before Bucky went to the hospital at Bennington?

HOWARD CAMPBELL:

He wrote about a second dream. Sometime after Bucky fell back asleep, he had another dream. He may have had more. This is the one he woke up to. Bucky dreamt that he was in the country outside of Richmond, Virginia. He was spying on self-help guru Anthony Robbins, who was dressed in black with a long leather coat, and he was standing next to a large fire and surrounded by naked women who were circling him while chanting, "Whether you know you can or you believe you can't, you're right." Then Anthony Robbins spotted him. Robbins pointed to him, and the naked women ran through the forest to surround Bucky. They started chanting in tongues while some circled him. Two of the women pulled Bucky prone by his hands and his feet. He couldn't move. Knowing Dave Williamson lived close by, he started calling for him.

Bucky explained to me that he woke up and couldn't move. He opened his eyes okay, but it took him some time to regain mobility in the rest of his body. He was sweaty and rather freaked. He was staring thoughtlessly when Bobby woke up and said, "So, you really expect Dave Williamson to show up?" Bucky just lay there. Bobby and he were silent, but his question echoed in his system. Then, he came to a realization that he'd just had a bad day. He said to himself, "When I wake up tomorrow, everything will be normal." He decided to close his eyes and try to drift back to sleep. He lay there for a while.

Bucky heard Dave Williamson's voice. Dave was singing, "What time is it? *4:30!*" Dave kept singing as he entered Bucky's dorm house and made his way to his door and knocked. Bucky invited him in and told him about the dream and about his notion that everything would be fine tomorrow. Dave told Bucky he was tripping. Dave offered him some Boone Farm wine. They laughed about Anthony Robbins being in Bucky's dream. They drank. Dave said to find him if Bucky needed him and he left.

In Bucky's manifesto, *The Longer Line*, I read that at age 14, Bucky had met Anthony Robbins. Robbins introduced him to Neuro-Linguistic Programming and the power of thought pattern mimicking. Robbins cited *As A Man Thinketh*, a book written by a devout Christian who believed that if we aligned our thoughts with God, we could do whatever we believed we could do. Similarly, if you believed you could not do something, that thought alone was an unbreakable barrier. The book states, "whether you believe you can or you can't, you're right."

I hold this to be true: *We create what we focus on.* It you focus on the difficulty of getting rich, you will probably be frustrated and thwarted in the attainment of wealth.

DR. WILLIAM FINK:

Attitude affects outcome has been proven to be true, but simply focusing on something can't create something out of nothing.

HOWARD CAMPBELL:

It's not nothing; your focus is something. In the 1950's, the government was focusing on *communists*. My grandfather was fired for being a communist. After being fired, he couldn't get a job. Nobody wanted to talk to him. Guess what? He became a communist. The government actually created a large group of communists opposed to their form of government by focusing on this idea. There wasn't a large population of people identifying themselves as communists until after the government focused so much energy on disseminating this idea.

But, Anthony Robbins went a step further and suggested that by using Neuro-Linguistic Programming, we could get other people to do things. And, that you could train humans to have physical reactions to specific words. This is something that psychologists are beginning to embrace more fully.

DR. WILLIAM FINK:

I know it to be true. I mean, outside of the growing popularity and credibility of hypnosis. My mom would say to me, "Sleep, my angel" and I would fall asleep.

[PAUSE]

HOWARD CAMPBELL:

Really?

[PAUSE]

That is very trusting of you to share.

DR. WILLIAM FINK:

Thank you. I mean if I didn't fall asleep, I would at least feel drowsy. It works to this day. If I'm having trouble falling asleep, my wife will say to me, "Sleep my angel" and I will get drowsy and she may repeat it and, at any rate, I will eventually fall asleep.

HOWARD CAMPBELL:

Your wife does what your mom created as a trained response?

DR. WILLIAM FINK:

I'd never thought about it like that.

This isn't about me. Please continue.

HOWARD CAMPBELL:

Right, back to the story. Bucky went back to sleep for a while. When he woke next, it was 4:20 AM. He had just had a dream about his old roommate, Marc Maiman, and a good friend, David Gleiberman, coming to see him.

Bobby had a field day with this, "Yeah, right, Marc and David are coming. They are in L.A." Bobby went on for a while about how he was being ridiculous, chiding Bucky hard and saying that if they showed up, he had won. Then Bobby went silent. Bucky sat there feeling awkward. Out loud, he cursed himself for thinking this way. He was sitting there, not feeling tired, not feeling good. He felt like his mental equilibrium had been snapped, and he was sitting up straight but not knowing which way was up.

Then the phone rang at 4:23. It was 1:23 in Los Angeles. It couldn't be Marc and David, and yet he thought it was. He answered the phone. It was Marc and David. Bobby said, "You win." For the next three days, Bucky didn't sleep.

DR. WILLIAM FINK:

How do you know this?

HOWARD CAMPBELL:

I was there and he wrote about it. Bucky was excited and scared, and he didn't sleep because of that combination. He was excited at having tapped into a new energy; he was scared because he feared those who had mastered this energy may try to recruit him as their subordinate or banish him from The Game.

[PAUSE]

Bucky walked around chanting, "Those who are bound by desire will only see the outward container." This was a central theme of a spoken word show he was producing discussing two frames of mind, Attacca and

Nacirema. Don't bother looking these words up, Bucky invented them. They're similar to the left brain/right brain distinctions. Bucky defined Attacca as the frame of mind where he was playing in symbols. Nacirema was the frame of mind where he was playing with aesthetics and the senses. Another way of looking at it would be closed and open systems. Attacca could grapple with finite systems, while Nacirema danced with cosmic order.

The show, which eventually toured to Martha's Vineyard, was entitled *Magick: Modern Persuasion In Advertising and Politics*. The show opened with drumming and a single light illuminating a 2D statue of a box. The shadow on a scrim looked like how one might draw a simple cube. Four drummers filled the stage behind him, led by Mohammed, the eldest son of a king in Africa. Mohammed was raised with a father who played a talking drum, where two people can have complete conversations with drums, a language sophisticated enough to discuss philosophy.

[PAUSE]

Bennington school officials thought that the pressure of giving the show helped push him over the edge. I agree that there was a connection, but pressure in the traditional sense wasn't a motivator. Bucky had been working very hard on *Magick: Modern Persuasion In Advertising and Politics* during the week before he lost his shit.

[PAUSE]

DR. WILLIAM FINK:

Did Richard think of himself as a magician?

HOWARD CAMPBELL:

Just in terms of being a performer. He loved how Phil Goldstein would present himself as a *real* magician.

DR. WILLIAM FINK:

What do you mean?

HOWARD CAMPBELL:

Richard presented himself with the confidence of a magician—and air of invincibility that is only achieved by knowing you know something that others don't and this gives you calm prowess. He would sometimes recite lines from movies that helped him capture that energy.

DR. WILLIAM FINK:

Can you give me an example?

HOWARD CAMPBELL:

Sure. I heard him say it enough that I practically have it memorized. It's from *Pulp Fiction*: "Ezekiel 25:17. The path of the righteous man is beset on all sides by the iniquities of the selfish and the tyranny of evil men. Blessed is he who in the name of charity and goodwill shepherds the weak through the valley of darkness, for he is truly his brother's keeper and the finder of lost children."

Remember? It was when Samuel Jackson and John Trovolta are about to shoot the shit out of some incompetent, wannabe gangster. The quote goes on about striking down with great vengeance those who harm his brothers.

DR. WILLIAM FINK:

Interesting. Yeah, I know the scene. I was distracted that the combination to the briefcase was 6-6-6.

HOWARD CAMPBELL:

Richard's air of magician was very different than Phil Goldstein who presented himself as having supernatural powers. Phil did an act as Max Maven, mentalist, capable of reading minds. When he called himself Max Maven, he presented his magic tricks as reality. When he was Phil Goldstein, he wrote articles on the tricks of prestidigitators. When Richard Wilson did his stage shows, he was a different persona.

DR. WILLIAM FINK:

What were his stage shows like?

HOWARD CAMPBELL:

The premise of his show was that by unconsciously accepting mass communications, we are adopting alien thought patterns. These thought patterns are viruses engineered to run specific programs. They have an agenda to trigger a buzz-whir effect in our brains when presented with certain situations. At best, these Manchurian triggers feel like self-expression, at worst they feel bothersome.

DR. WILLIAM FINK:

How did Bucky relate to being a magician when he was offstage?

HOWARD CAMPBELL:

In real life, Richard would sometimes frame himself as a magician.

DR. WILLIAM FINK:

What would Richard do to present himself as a magician?

[PAUSE]

HOWARD CAMPBELL:

Once, when I was here in Hawaii, and I was about to get on the plane to go home, he gave me one of those cardboard box Dole carry-ons with two pineapples in it. He told me that no matter what, I wasn't to open the pineapples until I got back to my house. I thought, "Yeah right, I was planning on breaking out a machete on the plane and cracking these bad boys open." This was way before nine-eleven. Anyway, I got home and didn't think anything about them. I just had two pineapples. My girlfriend Beth came over, and the next morning she was excited to have Hawaiian pineapple. So, I cut the crown off the top of one in preparation to serve it up.

[PAUSE]

There was a hole inside the pineapple, like it had a cavity in it.

DR. WILLIAM FINK:

Cavity, like it was rotted out?

HOWARD CAMPBELL:

No. A cavity like a compartment or non-filled space, a cache. I cut down the side, and inside the pineapple was a QP of Hawaiian kind.

DR. WILLIAM FINK:

QP? Hawaiian kind of what?

HOWARD CAMPBELL:

Chronic. Quarter pound of pot, really good marijuana. They call it *kind* because it's very kind to you. You know, like somebody saying *that's really kind.*

Beth wanted to open the other pineapple. I wanted to wait. I couldn't figure out how Bucky got the pot in the pineapple. I couldn't see any incisions or anything. I figured that if I let the other pineapple rot, I could see where the incision was, but nothing emerged. It just rotted and eventually the bag of pot oozed through the decomposing skin of the pineapple. I couldn't see any glue, or grafting, or anything.

[PAUSE]

I have no idea how he got the pot in the pineapples. It was probably five months before I saw him again. I asked him, "Bucky, how did you get the pot in the pineapples?"

Bucky shook his head, and in a faux disappointed voice said, "Howard, I never ask how you do your tricks."

DR. WILLIAM FINK:

[LAUGHING]

That's a great story.

HOWARD CAMPBELL:

I didn't think you would like it, because of the pot.

DR. WILLIAM FINK:

Howard, I was in college during the sixties.

102

[COUGHING]

Did Richard have any developmental problems that you knew of?

HOWARD CAMPBELL:

He was diagnosed as being dyslexic when he was in elementary school, but he claimed he wasn't dyslexic. However, Bucky did fall from a tree house and landed on his head when he was five. That had a substantive impact on his development.

DR. WILLIAM FINK:

A concussion doesn't usually have a long-term effect.

HOWARD CAMPBELL:

It does if he had Proper Noun Anomia. In terms of over-compensating for not remembering names.

DR. WILLIAM FINK:

Where did you learn about that? Proper Noun Anomia wasn't written up in journals of abnormal psychology until the *late* eighties. He couldn't have been diagnosed with PNA when he was five. One can't even detect the symptoms in young kids.

HOWARD CAMPBELL:

I read about it in *Seven Sins of Memory*. I read a lot. Anyway, just because something doesn't have a proper label doesn't mean it doesn't have a substantive impact. Gravity still held us in when we thought towards Earth was uniformly down and we didn't have the word gravity. We humans think we are so smart and yet it took us until the *late* nineties to figure out how to put wheels on a suitcase and invent a working roller bag.

[PAUSE]

I got distracted from Bucky's trip at Bennington, and what led him to the hospital in Vermont. Remember where I left off? Marc and David were calling; Bucky asked Marc and David why they called. They told him they had just gotten back from a concert and had called each other and were thinking of him, so they figured they would give him a call. Bucky asked David if he was a magician. David said yes, but he was joking. David was stoned and just rolling with the flow of the conversation. It didn't matter. Twisp. Bucky took David's confirmation that he was a magician as a revelation. Bucky knew his initiation had begun.

Hanging up the phone, he went back to his room to throw his die. Bucky's description of this series of events is rather incomprehensible. Bucky would say a thought while rolling the die, and the die would tell him the structure of the thought. A one referred to a thought that was either a part of a bigger idea or a unifying principal. A two represented a duplicity, like calling a circle on the eight ball "one" circle. A three was a base to an idea, like how a triangle is the base to a tetrahedron. A triangle can not exist in nature; it is a surface of a bigger structure. Two-dimensional shapes only exist in our minds, not nature. A four was a solid structure of a thought. Five was an idea that was prone to influence, either being influenced or influencing others, and six was a working system or a restructured thought, synthetics in motion, intellishit. These meanings from numbers were derived from his numerology. One either was one element of something else, or was the grand idea that there is only one one, all, infinity. Two was either the idea of one idea rotating around another, or two ideas circulating around each other in a celestial dance.

I brought with me what he actually noted in his journal.

[SOUND: CHAIR SCREECHING BACK, PAPER UNFOLDING AND CHAIR BEING REPOSITIONED]

DR. WILLIAM FINK:

Is that the original?

HOWARD CAMPBELL:

No. It's a Xerox. There is no way I could remember this sequence. I brought it because I thought it might help.

DR. WILLIAM FINK:

I'm glad you brought it.

HOWARD CAMPBELL:

Reportedly, Bucky rolled a die as he spoke. He explained in the previous page that he internalized the answer as he said the statement aloud. Which is weird because he actually notates the answer for each role.

He said aloud, "This is weird." Then he rolled the die, which landed on five.

5—A thought prone to persuasion.

Then he said, "I am weird." And rolled a five again.

5—A thought prone to persuasion.

"I have power."

3—A solid thought.

"There is power."

[NOTE: CAMPBELL SPEAKS MUCH FASTER]

4—A complete thought.

"I have power."

3—A solid thought.

"I am the power."

5—A thought prone to persuasion.

"I am him."

5—A thought prone to persuasion.

"This is It."

1—An ambiguous answer. Either a duplicitous thought with 2 disguised as a 1 or one-one.

"This is it?"

6—A restructured thought.

"It is it."

4—A complete thought.

"I am it."

2—A duplicitous thought.

"This is normal."

3—A solid thought.

"This is it."

1—An ambiguous answer. Either a duplicitous thought with 2 disguised as a 1 or one-one.

[NOTE: CAMPBELL RESUMES NORMAL SPEED OF SPEECH]

Should I keep going?

[PAUSE]

DR. WILLIAM FINK:

How much longer is it?

HOWARD CAMPBELL:

Another page.

DR. WILLIAM FINK:

Yeah, maybe I'll hear a rhythm.

HOWARD CAMPBELL:

All right. But he stopped notating the meaning of each number.

[NOTE: CAMPBELL SPEAKS MUCH FASTER]

"Who are you?"

6.

"The devil?"

5.

"God?"

5.

"I am God."

3.

"You are God."

2.

"You are It."

2.

"You are all."

4.

"There is only one one."

1.

"One."

1.

"One."

1.

"One."

1.

"Yes."

5.

"One."

1.

[NOTE: CAMPBELL RESUMES NORMAL SPEED OF SPEECH]

"One?"

5.

"One."

1.

"There is only one one."

4.

That's it. That's all he included.

DR. WILLIAM FINK:

That was exhaustive. I'm going to need to review it. May I keep these sheets?

HOWARD CAMPBELL:

[COUGHING]

Sure.

DR. WILLIAM FINK:

What happened next?

♪♪ *[ROCK MUSIC: DIGITIZED VERSION OF Satisfaction]* ♪♪

What's that?

HOWARD CAMPBELL:

My cell phone. Excuse me.

[SOUND: CHAIR SCREACHING]

[END MUSIC]

This is…Hello.

Hey.

[PAUSE]

Yes.

[PAUSE]

Uh huh… Yup…

Okay… Uh huh…

What?

[PAUSE]

Why would he say that?

[PAUSE]

No. He isn't getting it. We can't be superlative and specific on a national basis.

[PAUSE]

We're eleven individual wireless companies joined into one. We don't have a national attribute to hang our hat on.

[PAUSE]

Fits you best is superlative and ambiguous enough to allow for our regional advantages.

[PAUSE]

Yes. Okay. Tell him I'll be there in the afternoon.

[PAUSE]

This is important to me. I scheduled these as vacation days.

[PAUSE]

This isn't the type of thing I can reschedule.

[PAUSE]

When I get on the plane this afternoon, I won't get in to Hartsford until after 2, tomorrow. I lose almost a full day flying from Hawaii.

[PAUSE]

No. It's afternoon here now.

[PAUSE]

Can I call you on your cell in half an hour?

Okay good. I'm sorry to rush you... Yeah, I'm still in a meeting.

[PAUSE]

Yeah... Okay. I'll call you soon.

[SOUND: CELL PHONE FLIPPED SHUT]

I'm sorry. Where were we?

DR. WILLIAM FINK:

That's quite all right.

[PAUSE]

What did Richard write happened next?

HOWARD CAMPBELL:

Bucky headed to VAPA, Bennington's Visual And Performing Arts Center. VAPAC sounded funny so they left off the "C."

He found one kid working up there, an Asian kid he'd talked to before, but Bucky wasn't sure of the name because he wrote "Wayne" followed by a question mark. He watched him for a while. He nodded an approval of Bucky's company and painted undisturbed. After a while, he turned to him and asked, "Bucky, do you believe there is one right way to do something?"

Even in retrospect, it's freaky how much of what happened over this time shared a synchronicity. At the time, Bucky projected this theme as relating to a Sufi moral value system, and this question felt like part of an initiation, a Socratic conversation to lead him to their ways.

Bucky said that he thought at times there were multiple right ways. Wayne said yes, but for each one from one perspective it was the right way. Bucky agreed. Wayne talked about how Dave Williamson eats a cheeseburger. The whole process is in preparation for the last bite. Williamson eats around the edge. Williamson designs it so that the last bite has a bit of everything, some tomato, some lettuce, cheese, burger and the right combination of sauce. This way, the last bite, the experience that lingers in your mind, is a great bite of cheeseburger.

Williamson and Bucky talked about the merits of rolling toothpaste tubes and paint tubes from the bottom. They talked about avoiding taking unnecessary physical risks without being restrained by the idea of physical harm. They talked about the value of altered states of consciousness, and wound up on the idea that there is no such thing as an altered state of consciousness since neither believed in an empirically normal state of consciousness.

Bucky got up to go, and another student named Craig wandered in, and asked Bucky where he was going. Bucky said outside. Craig asked him what he was doing up, and Bucky told him he couldn't sleep. Craig said not sleeping was dangerous and then Craig sped off. Once outside, Bucky saw the lightness of blue that indicates dawn is not far off.

Buckminster Fuller hated the word sunrise. He suggested that it disorients people. Intellectually, we are taught that Earth rotates, which controls the visibility and non-visibility of the sun. The term sunrise suggests that we are still and the sun is rising. Fuller thought that terms like this should be replaced by something that better resembles our phenomenological experience, and he suggested "sunsight" for sunrise, and "sunclipse" for sunset. Fuller argued that for 500 years we have known that the Earth is revolving on its own axis, but our vocabulary hasn't caught up with our knowledge.

Bucky dwelt on Fuller's ideas. I know this because his journal has an essay at this point looking at synergy from a psychological perspective.

I added the previous stuff about Fuller and sunsight. Bucky's journal only has the previous encounter with Wayne and Craig, and then says "When I left VAPA, it was a beautiful sunsight. The oranges were intense. Afterwards, I headed to the cafeteria for breakfast."

Then the word "synergy." Fuller coined the words "synergy" and "sunsight." I figured it was appropriate to go off on what I speculate Bucky may have been thinking about. Bucky's later notes also had additions to the concept of four. He held that four could be a complete thought or it could be duplicitous, representing a square, the ultimate syntheticizing of unnaturalness, presented as natural.

[SILENCE]

HOWARD CAMPBELL:

Is this okay?

DR. WILLIAM FINK:

It's great. I appreciate your perspective. You're doing great. It's really helpful for me to understand this much about Richard Wilson. I would like to spend some time with his journal.

HOWARD CAMPBELL:

I'm getting tired.

DR. WILLIAM FINK:

Maybe we should take a break. It would help if you brought Bucky's journals in and let me read them for myself.

At any rate, I have to get to The Children's School, an elementary school here in Kane'ohe. I volunteer there one afternoon a week.

[PAUSE]

HOWARD CAMPBELL:

Donating my time makes me appreciative that I'm in a position to give. Donating my time allows me to count my blessings.

DR. WILLIAM FINK:

Me, too.

HOWARD CAMPBELL:

I'm not always sure where to focus my positional advantage.

DR. WILLIAM FINK:

I was introduced to the school because my nephew goes to The Children's School. I didn't like the way they were handling the children with special needs. They were trying behavioral counseling, but they just didn't have the resources. My nephew was falling behind in his grade, along with a number of other children. When appropriate, I prescribe medications that help them in class and in school.

HOWARD CAMPBELL:

How have you helped them?

DR. WILLIAM FINK:

I have diagnosed many children, and the behavioral problems have diminished.

HOWARD CAMPBELL:

How do you treat them?

DR. WILLIAM FINK:

Many remain in counseling, but many, like my nephew, are fine with just meds, so long as they stay on them. This frees up the counselors to work with the kids that really need the counseling. Kids that come from hostile homes and need immediate coping skills.

[PAUSE]

But, we got off track. I was asking about Bucky's journals.

[PAUSE]

HOWARD CAMPBELL:

I can't let you have his journals.

[COUGHING]

Bucky told me not to. I can share what I have read verbally, but I am not to release his original materials to anybody.

DR. WILLIAM FINK:

Surely this is an extenuating circumstance.

HOWARD CAMPBELL:

I'm telling you everything I can. I cannot give the journals to you. I gave my word.

DR. WILLIAM FINK:

Fair enough.

HOWARD CAMPBELL:

We'll meet again in three weeks then.

DR. WILLIAM FINK:

Yes. February 23rd.

HOWARD CAMPBELL:

Until then.

DR. WILLIAM FINK:

Yes. Until then. Thank you again.

HOWARD CAMPBELL:

You're welcome.

[SOUND: CHAIRS SCREECHING]
[SOUND: FOOTSTEPS]
[SOUND: RECORDER SWITCHING OFF]
(DISCUSSION OMITTED)
[SOUND: RECORDER SWITCHING ON]

SESSION 3

VOICE OF DR. WILLIAM FINK:

February 23, 2003, session three with Howard Campbell. Southern Vermont Mental Hospital has no record of a Richard Wilson being admitted on April 6th, 1993.

[PAUSE]

HOWARD CAMPBELL:

And?

DR. WILLIAM FINK:

And, that's the Hospital you said Richard went to. They have no record of ever having a patient named Richard Wilson.

HOWARD CAMPBELL:

Maybe there is another hospital near Bennington. I'm sorry. I remembered that being the name. I must have been wrong. What other hospitals are in that area.

DR. WILLIAM FINK:

We didn't check.

[PAUSE]

What was Richard like? You've told me a lot about his ideas, but what was he like as a person?

[PAUSE]

HOWARD CAMPBELL:

I'm sorry. Two things. First, it felt like you were accusing me of something just then. Second, I'm having trouble concentrating. Yesterday, my boss asked me, "Do you want to be employed by CCEO?" My boss was asking if I was dedicated to my job. He was telling me I needed to be more of a team player.

[PAUSE]

DR. WILLIAM FINK:

I'm sorry. I'm very sorry. From my private practice, I know how much an unstable work environment can weigh down on somebody. That's why I came to work at this hospital.

HOWARD CAMPBELL:

That's the advantage of working for a large corporation as opposed to hanging your own shingle, the security of a paycheck. But, it looks like my security is less grounded than I imagined. Obviously my boss was frustrated with me. I didn't know when and where a meeting was, and I was supposed to give a presentation.

DR. WILLIAM FINK:

Was this your fault?

HOWARD CAMPBELL:

No, but I took the responsibility for it.

DR. WILLIAM FINK:

Would you call your place of employment a hostile work environment?

HOWARD CAMPBELL:

Of course. It's advertising. We're the meme generals fighting the most publicized war ever fought.

DR. WILLIAM FINK:

What war?

HOWARD CAMPBELL:

I don't mean to burden you with this.

DR. WILLIAM FINK:

It's okay. But, I don't know if you are being hyperbolic when you say *the most publicized war ever fought*.

HOWARD CAMPBELL:

Marketing is the war of brands. I mean that literally. For some, fighting helps them feel alive and rejuvenated. For me, I just get tired. And I'm almost always tense, and it comes from being in battle day-in and day-out.

[PAUSE]

Of course it is a hostile work environment. We are waging war. We are trying to be the dominant brand in the wireless category. War tactics are manifested on the battlefield of media and on the battlefield called office or corporateland.

These war tactics are akin to moves in poker.

In poker, one seeks to exploit positional advantages. Information is powerful, so, you have an advantage over the players to your immediate right, because you always play after them. You play after you know what they have done and before they know what you will do. Less than one-quarter of the time the cards will decide who wins, you always act with more knowledge than the players to your right, unless you are first to act. Meanwhile, the players to your immediate left have an advantage over you. It is like an M.C. Escher painting where the steps go in a circle and every step to the left is up, only the figurines are real and they are carrying loaded guns. More often than not, a player surrenders their hand when a shot is fired over the bow in the form of a bet or a raise. I just mixed metaphors.

DR. WILLIAM FINK:

Yeah, you had figurines on steps and then suddenly there were bows of boats.

HOWARD CAMPBELL:

I'm glad you are following. We forget that figures of speech often have embedded imagery.

In poker, I might move seats to position myself to the left of a loose player, exploiting their tendency to overplay; in marketing, we might adjust our positioning to exploit another company's weaknesses—such as their hyping a product with inferior qualities.

Both marketing and poker are games of money that are won by exploiting weaker players. Most weak poker players bluff too much. Most weak marketers over-promise and hype their products: over promising in marketing is bluffing the consumer because you don't have the goods you purport to have. Bluffing garners a lack of respect. In essence, bluffing is utilizing resources for a short-term gain. While short-term gain is a viable part of business, if utilized too often, bluffing is a form of unduly exposing yourself to liability.

DR. WILLIAM FINK:

Where does cheating fit into this?

HOWARD CAMPBELL:

Cheating is being an outlaw, or a pirate. It is taking money in a way that the casino won't support your entitlement. But you aren't a criminal unless you are successfully prosecuted. But the concept of cheating versus not cheating is a legal distinction. These divisions are synthetic. They don't occur in Nature. We get trapped in our own systems, mistaking our systems for *Reality*. Anybody who tries to undermine the power of the system is quickly labeled a criminal. Their biggest crime is not respecting the power of the system, they point out the systems logical inconsistencies.

Larry Beinhart addresses the contemporary implications of this premise in *American Hero*. Larry explains that this is the function of Propaganda, and begins with the premise that propaganda that *looks* like propaganda is third-rate propaganda: We are innocent, while they are guilty; We tell the truth and inform through news, while they lie and use propaganda; We defend ourselves, while they are aggressors; We are law-abiding, while they are criminals; We respect our agreements and treaties and abide by international law, while they are liars, cheaters, thieves and opportunists who break treaties. Historically, white men have been the best at generating propaganda.   Perhaps that's the reason we call content-less sounds white noise.

[PAUSE]

Anybody who doesn't have an inkling as to how the United States of America honored their agreements with the native people who lived here prior to our arrival should stop whatever they're doing and get an education. I guarantee you these people have never heard Columbus Day called *Homeland Invasion Day*. Its even doubtful they've heard of the Fourth of July referred to as *Good Riddance Day* by Brits, that's less germane—but it makes the point that history is produced by the victors.   Anyone who sees the logic of *defensively* attacking another country because they may eventually attack us, probably wouldn't make a good drinking buddy for me.   The majority of our aggression as a nation is done under the guise of *defending our way of life*. America often defends *our way of life* by killing individuals or large groups. But we are not alone in this modus operandi.

Larry goes on to say that in each opposing country, the home country, through propaganda, says that we stand for justice and civil rights while they brutalize, repress and tyrannize their own and their neighbors.   All in all, our leaders govern with the consent of the people, while their leaders are usurpers of power with no popular support and will eventually be overthrown.

More elements of propaganda: The enemy commits torture, atrocity, and murder because he is a sadist who enjoys killing. We use surgical or strategic violence only because the enemy forces us to. Killing is justified so long as one does not take pleasure in it, and it's done in a clean manner, preferably from an antiseptic distance—the saturation bombing and the free-fire zones in Vietnam were legitimate; the face-to-face slaughter in My Lai was a war crime.

Larry asks if there are companies in America, whose business is generally non-criminal, tied to the government or not, that kill people and then go on about their business? High-profile prosecutions—Boesky, Milken, Watergate, Iran-contra—tend to convince us that crime never pays, and that even the high and mighty are dragged down when they stray, that the system works. But this is just a form of propaganda.

Larry reminds us, "It is very important to the system that we believe in it."

He explains that when movies were subject to censorship, which they were in a very formal way from 1934 to 1968, by the Hays Office, one of the strictest rules—as strictly enforced as not letting ten-year-olds view close-ups of oral copulation–was that crime must not profit. If someone committed a crime on-screen, they had to be punished. Later, when TV came around, network codes of standards and practices had much the same requirement. For dramatic reasons, we always see stories about independent-minded cops who defy all institutional resistance to bring down the biggest of corrupt bigwigs.

But, this is a round about discourse on cheating. In academia, the study of cheating is criminology. As long as criminology has been a field of study, it has always been haunted by what Beinhart calls "the theory of the competent criminal." For obvious reasons, criminologists and psychologists and sociologists only study failed criminals–that is, those persons whose criminal acts led to their conviction and to punishment. If there's a group of people out there who commit crimes and are not caught, and live happily ever after, then criminology is not a study of criminals, but of incompetents, bumblers, and fuckups and should instead be called fuckupology.

[PAUSE]

If you are a poker player, the benefit of the casino is that if you play by their rules, they ensure you get the money you are entitled to—they promise to protect you from cheaters. The risk of opening your own small business, your own casino, is that you become responsible for collections and security.

DR. WILLIAM FINK:

Who is the casino in marketing?

HOWARD CAMPBELL:

In some regards the government is relied on to make sure companies don't cheat. Put in a more tangible way, each retailer is its own casino for consumer brands that are sold on their shelves. Wal-Mart, Kmart, Target, Barnes & Noble and a local bar are all casinos. But we advertise for players on mass media, so to a certain extent, America becomes the meta-casino. Look, this metaphor will break down if scrutinized too closely.

DR. WILLIAM FINK:

Then is poker a valid model for society?

HOWARD CAMPBELL:

Absolutely, at least in terms of money. Look, no model is going to accurately replicate the real system. Chaos theory teaches us that a model may be valid within a specific range, but not on another scale. I want to focus on the part of the model that works. In the poker game of marketing, consumers are so saturated by paid media that they can't see the game, they just migrate from one image tribe to another as their emotions deliver their loyalties in the form of dollars.

[PAUSE]

DR. WILLIAM FINK:

You see this as bad?

HOWARD CAMPBELL:

Most niche account planners don't see the game. They just see themselves on a directive to get representation for their special interest group or client. But, it's the niche appeal that perpetuates distinct image tribes, that divides the audience. Most ethnic media are not created to better *serve* their audience, but to better *exploit* their target audience, to more efficiently *extract money from this group* and, to maintain a need for specialized media. The media perpetuates ethnic distinctions because they have a vested interest in producing discrete messages. That's how they make money, by consumers demanding their own messages. But, it's not just a division of ethnicity, it can be age or any psychographic. Adolescence is a marketing tool, teaching kids they have special needs, which means they buy special products. The average twelve-year-old today buys 20 times the constant dollar value compared with 30 years ago, yet the dollar itself has only gone up seven to twelve times in value, depending on the measurement.

[PAUSE]

But, we're not here to talk about me. You asked me what Richard was like as a person, as opposed to his ideas. Frankly, it's hard to separate the two. He was always going on about one notion or another. Going to the movies with Bucky was a trip.

DR. WILLIAM FINK:

A *trip* how?

HOWARD CAMPBELL:

We could be in mid-conversation when the movie started and we would stop talking. We might say one or two things during the movie, like if we saw somebody we knew, or saw some place we had lived, or if the continuity was messed up, but then when the movie was over, Bucky would pick right back up where we'd left off, just assuming you were right there with him on the same page. It was as if he was waiting to resume the pre-movie conversation. But he wasn't really waiting. He could do that at will. He could often recite conversations we had had several weeks ago, and it seemed as if it was verbatim.

DR. WILLIAM FINK:

He sounds almost autistic.

HOWARD CAMPBELL:

Well, he was never diagnosed as such, but it was almost an idiot savant type of behavior. The mind can do amazing things. People used to recite *The Illiad* from memory. That is a several-thousand-line poem.

[PAUSE]

Another thing trippy about Bucky: what he would say would often make me see things differently. For instance, I ended a sentence a several sentences ago, before you interjected, with "assuming you were on the same page." Bucky would call this *second-person-speak*. I could have said "assuming I was on the same page" because I was talking about my experience.

Bucky held that when people can't talk in the first person, it's a symptom of an inferiority complex or mild duplicity. Bucky thought about thinking. I rarely say the word, believe. Bucky held that believing was inefficient thinking. You should *know* things or *not know* things, but what benefit has believing?

DR. WILLIAM FINK:

I believe Jesus is the only begotten son of God. I can't prove it, so, I believe it.

HOWARD CAMPBELL:

Bucky would argue that you know Jesus is the only begotten son of God, because you have faith that it is so. Structurally, it's the same as knowledge because you treat this notion as fact. Then, Bucky would be likely to go off on a Bill Hicks rant asking how his father's Bible could be the literal word of God if it is the King James' version.

DR. WILLIAM FINK:

My Bible isn't King James'.

HOWARD CAMPBELL:

I know. You're Catholic. We established that with your acceptance of transubstantiation. Bill Hicks was razzing *his* father.

It doesn't matter how you generate your confidence, just that life is easier when you act from confidence. Having one's faith shattered is one of the most disorienting things that can happen to a person. Most people never know the existential trauma of having their faith shattered, whatever that faith may be—it takes confidence to know. Bucky held that the reverse was also true, knowing generates confidence.

Bucky held that people trapped in second-person-speak lacked confidence. Bucky defined neurotic as being incapable of saying what you mean and incapable of meaning what you say. When somebody does second-person-speak, they're incapable of talking about themselves. Something is going on there.

Once I learned this idea, my ear started picking up on second-person-speak, both in others and in myself. I started all this by saying that some of what Bucky said changed how I saw the world. That is just one example.

[PAUSE]

DR. WILLIAM FINK:

What other ideas were core to Richard's philosophy?

HOWARD CAMPBELL:

Bucky's notes show that he looked at the definition of synergy: "The behavior of the whole system is unpredicted by the behavior of any parts of the system when considered only separately." And: "The whole is greater than the sum of its parts." Buckminster Fuller wrote an 800-page book defining synergy, so it's hard to nail him down to one sentence. Fuller used those two definitions. Bucky examined what happens psychologically when synergy is noticed. Generally, we have a new label that defines a system. Graphite-steel. Steel is strong, graphite is a joke from a tensile perspective, but you put the two together and you get super steel. The molecules take on a new shape that makes it super strong. Chemists look at graphite-steel as a different animal from graphite or steel, hence the word alloy. Having this label enables a chemist to look at these individual elements as a whole system. Synergy, from a psychological perspective, is the gaining of a new paradigm to look at a system's interaction differently. However, both the words "synergy" and "paradigm" are overused and improperly used, so most people hear "paradigm shift" as an adaptation of a new fad and not a comprehensively discrete perspective. Most people are relatively blind to the indivisibility between thinking, seeing and acting, so they attribute thinking to what we do in words. Learning a word rarely alters how you frame entire situations, but it can, and synergy and paradigm are words that should be reserved to describe those phenomenon.

Since we organize meaning through words, when our understanding of a situation changes but we maintain our original vocabulary, we are retaining our original meanings. Our mind is slow to adopt new versions of reality, new cosmographies. We have evolved to trust what we know over new hypotheses. Despite logic, if we have conflicting ideas, humans have a tendency to cling to original notions.

DR. WILLIAM FINK:

You're talking about cognitive psychology.

HOWARD CAMPBELL:

I'm talking about Buckminster Fuller's ideas and what they meant to Richard Wilson.

Fuller says that the word synergy gives a label to the phenomenal experience of seeing a system differently. By having this label, it allows us to learn faster. The word synergy can allow us to recognize when we're learning.

Sufis have talked about the value of recognizing when we are learning. However, Sufism comes at it from the other direction: when you feel like an are an Idiot because you are stronger for now having a clearer of what's going on around you.

have an outdated label in your head that's messing with your , how do you get rid of it? First, you need a label that recognizes this mental condition. Bucky proposed "twisp." Twisp can also be used for the process of releasing this false label, or it can be used as an imperative when somebody is stuck on an idea that isn't working anymore. You can say, "twisp." Like, "Let it go."

DR. WILLIAM FINK:

Earlier, you said *twisp* was like "Oh, shit."

HOWARD CAMPBELL:

I wasn't ready to explain it. We hadn't developed a common realm of understanding or vocabulary.

DR. WILLIAM FINK:

Why did you tell me something that wasn't true?

HOWARD CAMPBELL:

I didn't, really. Emotionally, twisp is like saying, "Oh, shit." It is recognizing a disjunction between an expectation and a realization. That's when I say "Oh, shit." The faster the old framing can be let go of, the easier I find life to be. The outmoded idea must be left behind.

[SOUND: DRINKING WATER]

Anyway, getting back to what led Bucky to the hospital. A peculiar thing happened the day before he went to the hospital.

Bucky entered the cafeteria's smoking room and saw a large painting of a bat. Bats were the secret symbol of the Sufis, just as a fish was the clandestine symbol of the Christians, when Christians vs. lions was a popular betting proposition.

He was waved over to a table below the bat by Maggie Shaw, a woman commonly called "the chicken" because of her gaunt frame. Maggie was sitting with Trudy, the school psychologist, a person Bucky had speculated to be a leader of the Sufi admission board. Maggie had been a good thought

126

partner in Bucky's understanding of numerology. She's a mystic. b began speculating that Maggie was an initiate posing as a candidate. May, everybody at Bennington was an initiate. He didn't know.

When Bucky got to their table, he noticed Trudy was wearing a bat brooch and bat earrings. He said hi and sat down. Maggie asked how things were going. Bucky was having trouble not staring at the bats. The previous day, Bucky had an epiphany that he was truly among Sufis, and *now*, there were Sufi symbols everywhere he looked. To Bucky, the bats were confirmation of Bennington as a *Magic Mountain*. Sufis wouldn't say, "Welcome to sufi-land." But, plastering the campus with bats, the secret Sufi symbol, now *that* made sense for how they would confirm his speculation. Confirmation. Bucky perceived himself as at step two of an initiation, acknowledgement that the game was on.

So, when Maggie asked how things were going, Bucky replied that he was working on understanding if there was an ultimate value system. Trudy said that that sounded pretty heavy. He asked her if she was a Sufi. She said she didn't know what a Sufi was, but she was pretty sure she wasn't one. To Bucky, this was like calling the FBI to verify a secret operative—of course they're going to say there is no affiliation. Bucky flinched. In his head he criticized himself for bad form. He was pretty sure it was bad form for one undercover FBI person to ask another undercover FBI person if they are FBI. Shit. Fuck-up. Of course she would say "No." In his head, he must have been saying, "Who are you sons of bitches?" Bucky was amongst people he thought he knew, but who were now appearing very differently to him. Bucky imagined himself as the only outsider, surrounded by the most powerful people in the entire world. How else could you explain how well known Bennington College is, yet how few students and teachers are actually there?

Illuminatus Trilogy by Robert Anton Wilson should bear the warning that it contains a live meme virus. Then again, so should *The Bible* and *Magick*. It's a joke that an album should be forced to contain a warning because it has the word "fuck" somewhere in its lyrics, and yet these mind-altering books can be sold to any eight-year-old with enough change at a used book store. Just about every kid in the United States has heard the word fuck. Saying the word fuck may change the biochemistry of a grandmother, but it's not a seed crystal to restructure a teenager's cosmography. The Bible, though, has done this to billions of minds.

ucky
re

...ou switched subjects very abruptly? What *are* you talking about?

.ARD CAMPBELL:

Sorry. Bucky was reading *The Illuminatus! Trilogy*. He used it as source book from which he might glean Sufi etiquette. *The Illuminatus! Trilogy* presented Bucky with a new idea for a structure of world order. The counter establishment consisted of people who were united by cause, yet un-linkable, unthinkably connected because there was no label under which to associate them. He viewed this to be the code of the Sufi. The irony is that by this dictum, they wouldn't call themselves Sufis. Whatever. He viewed the Sufis as united by a common value system. It was a similar structure to what he imagined a secret agent must work within. If you ask a secret agent if they're a secret agent, they say no. Having Trudy say "no" felt like proof that she was a Sufi. This is flawed logic. But, at the time, it made perfect sense to Bucky. Robert Anton Wilson suggests that part of the code of the intellectual warrior is to write. Deny any association, and write about your observations and values; describe your visions.

[PAUSE]

> For although in a certain sense and for light-minded persons, non-existent things can be more easily and irresponsibly represented in words than existing things, for the serious and conscientious historian it is just the reverse. Nothing is harder, yet nothing is more necessary, than to speak of certain things whose existence is neither demonstrable nor probable. The very fact that serious and conscientious men treat them as existing things, brings them a step closer to existence and to the possibility of being born.

DR. WILLIAM FINK:

Who said that?

HOWARD CAMPBELL:

Hesse wrote it. Don't know if he ever said it.

Bucky was craving a life more intense than he was experiencing. He wanted a *fuller* experience on this planet.

He was viewing the world as comprised primarily of people with a herd mentality, people who took culturized patterns of thinking as free will. He saw himself as having risen above the herd. To this extent, he felt righteous. He didn't blame the herd; they were doing the best their psychology allows them. He viewed the herd as not seeing the forest for the trees, not seeing outside their personal space. The opening poem of the Tao Te Ching reads, "Those who are bound by desire see only the outward container." Bucky viewed the herd, at least what he knew of the "American" herd, as in a constant state of desire, denying them the ability to loosen their associations, to see things two ways simultaneously, constantly weakening their resolve. *The mind of the weak is easily influenced.* (Transcriber's notation on italycs: Campbell is citing George Lucas line from *Star Wars*.)

Bucky saw the Sufis as holding themselves to a higher standard, having a code of ethics above the common law of the land, or law of the jungle, as waiting to step in and take control before the world order spun into tyranny, or the health of the planet spun into rapid change. Bucky was an optimist. He saw the powerful, in terms of money, as being pawns of the meme generals, forcing a culture on the masses, insisting that an ultimate respect for money replace the previous ultimate respect for God.

[PAUSE]

DR. WILLIAM FINK:

Then what is finance? The politics of money?

HOWARD CAMPBELL:

Not at all. Politics deals with consensus. Money deals with that which is quantifiable. Money is an energy delivery mechanism.

DR. WILLIAM FINK:

An energy delivery mechanism?

HOWARD CAMPBELL:

Yes. Money entitles the bearer to goods and services. Money is the lowest common denominator. Money is the symbolic representation of the quantification of barter-able energy. Money is potential energy. In the process of purchasing something, money is kinetic energy. I present money and I am entitled to your goods and energy, which required energy to produce.

DR. WILLIAM FINK:

Okay.

HOWARD CAMPBELL:

Bucky was more interested in politics, the garnering of consensus, than he was in finance, the garnering of monetary energy. Monetary wealth is the accumulation of barter-able energy; Consensus is knowledge agreed upon. Both are potential energy, transferable into kinetic energy—dynamic action.

[PAUSE]

DR. WILLIAM FINK:

What if the knowledge is wrong?

HOWARD CAMPBELL:

Agreed upon wrong knowledge is still consensus, and thus, potential energy. Consensus is structure. Physics teaches us that structure is stored energy. Just look at how an atomic bomb extracts the energy from the structure of an atom. For consensus, the power is in the accumulation of agreement, and has nothing to do with the truth of the perception.

DR. WILLIAM FINK:

So Sufis were experts at garnering consensus?

HOWARD CAMPBELL:

No. Sufis are students of truth. Bucky imagined that the Sufis were spotting individuals who had begun absorbing their knowledge. He envisioned that these individuals were either nurtured by the Sufis, or judged evil, and discredited, thus discarded by the system. Deep inside, Bucky feared this would happen to him, that he'd be discredited and discarded. Bucky lacked self-confidence in his moral weight. He felt accountable for perpetuating moral iniquities. He was proud that he'd broken free of the constraints of his upbringing. But, he feared he wouldn't measure up to his newfound standards. Pride and shame are two sides of the same coin. Yet, his head was still in the Western mentality of binary perceptions of black and white. As opposed to seeing a Ying-Yang perception that everybody was both good and evil, he was striving to impose a binary perception on the world around him.

I was with Bucky in the cafeteria when Trudy said she was concerned about him. She'd heard that some unusual things had happened to him. Bucky acknowledged that he'd had some unusual experiences, but assured her that he was fine. We left the cafeteria.

I don't remember what happened next. I know that he spent a lot of time in the library. He was trying to find what he was supposed to be doing. He felt he needed to study. He was expecting to be tested, or more accurately, he imagined that the testing had begun, so he wanted to get his head into it. When I would visit him, Bucky was reading books like *Thought Control In Totalitarian China*, *Critical Path* and *Time, Space and Knowledge*. If it were today, he would probably be reading Dr. Edward O. Wilson, but I'm pretty certain he hadn't come across the doctor. Bucky had this theory that the Sufis had placed hints in popular literature. These hints to their existence could be seen by those looking, but invisible to the unaware. Kind of like how if you show a schizophrenic authentic "word salad" interspersed with similar lines by poets, schizophrenics can distinguish between the two, but others can't. Bucky thought that books entitled *Operating Manual Spaceship Earth*, *Diary of a Schizophrenic Woman*, or *Psychology of Religious Experiences* were written in Sufi word salad. He even analyzed the Dewey Decimal system for clues.

This secret code, if it existed, would look similar to the mathematics we sent to outer space for alien life to find. We included a series of zeros and ones that had embedded in it a decoding mechanism. There was a series of numbers that was meant to act as a red flag to let intelligent life know we had a message. The red flag also contained the method to decode our message. He thought there might be something similar in the Dewey Decimal system.

DR. WILLIAM FINK:
What did he find in the Dewey Decimal system? Anything?

HOWARD CAMPBELL:
Not that he shared with me.

I spotted him outside the commons building reading *Whiz Mob*, a book about how pickpockets communicate so that they understand each other, but anything overheard by a passerby wouldn't trigger alertness—a coding technique similar to calling marijuana "V-8" and acid "Santa Barbara"—it sounds like English, but the words have different meanings. *Whiz Mob* focuses on the pickpocket's language, and how it was designed to be very specific in terms of instruction, yet unintelligible and unnoticeable to the general public.

I overheard a woman ask what he was reading. He told her, and she asked what it was about, and he told her, and she said, "Bucky, you always read books that are really interesting." Bucky replied, "Why would you read anything else?"

[PAUSE]

Specifics from his second day of tripping are few. His journaling shows he was dwelling on wordplay. "Pay attention" was written and rewritten as "Pay a tension," followed by "What gives one person the right to demand tension from another?" Another entry: "disgruntled" followed by "Have I ever felt gruntled?" He wondered if the root of *official* was the same as the root of *superficial*. In which case, was *ficial* reality?

DR. WILLIAM FINK:

[LAUGHTER]

That's funny.

HOWARD CAMPBELL:

It wasn't meant to be. But, you'll probably like this one, "Have you ever felt combobulated?"

DR. WILLIAM FINK:

I don't get it.

HOWARD CAMPBELL:

It is another entry from Bucky's Journal. He was playing with the word "*dis*-combobulated."

DR. WILLIAM FINK:

Oh, okay.

HOWARD CAMPBELL:

Bucky liked playing with words and inventing words. He journaled about a connection between *taught* and *taut*. He circled back to the notion that when teachers said, "Pay attention" they were actually saying, "Pay a tension." He reasoned that this was provable. He looked at how tension was only manifested in conjunction with compression. You can not have tension without compression. Concave can only exist with convex. A concave lens is concave to the macrocosm, but convex to the microcosm. Inside the glass, if he were a glass molecule, he would be experiencing a convex barrier. Similarly, *up* can not exist without the concept of *down*, *in* without *out*, or *pride* without *shame*. Likewise, in physics, you can not have tension without compression. Think of a rope. If you pull on the ends, exerting tension, the center compresses. Bucky was looking at the word he invented, Attacca, as being linear thought. Our education system tends to focus on linear learning. Our education builds the roads of thought in our heads. Our formal education is primarily Attaccan, dealing with knowledge as it is notate-able.

Being taught literally means having a thought in my head pulled thin, made linear. This is when in his journal he started capitalizing the word *It*. He noted that tensions compressed his thoughts into the molds of our societal education, making his perception more linear. Being taught was literally having his head pulled taut.

DR. WILLIAM FINK:

He was focusing on phonics.

HOWARD CAMPBELL:

Some. But, he was also focusing on non-word intelligence. I know he had a Xerox of two magazine articles: A group of six chimpanzees are placed in a room with a ladder. Above the ladder is a banana hung from a string. When one of the chimpanzees climbs the ladder, the remaining monkeys are sprayed with frigid water. They clamor, and the climbing monkey gets down. A while later, a second monkey climbs the ladder, and again the rest are sprayed with frigid water. When a third monkey climbs the ladder, one in the group begins to beat him and pulls him off the ladder. Then, a monkey is replaced with another chimp. This chimp tries to climb the ladder, but is stopped and beaten by the remaining monkeys. The water is now turned off. They replace another chimp, and when this chimp climbs, the remaining monkeys beat it up, with the other recent monkey joining in. They switch out more monkeys and this pattern continues until none of the monkeys in the cage have experienced the water. However, when they replace a chimp, and that chimp climbs the ladder, the ritual beating takes place. Societies are slow to let go of customs, even when the rational for the behavior is no longer present.

The second article was about a monkey trap in Costa Rica that was constructed by putting some food in a coconut that was chained to a tree. The opening to the coconut was big enough for a monkey to put his hand in, but not large enough to take it out as a fist. The monkey will find the food, but not be able to get it out. A human nearby can go up and capture the monkey because the monkey won't let go of the food—"Those who are bound by desire see only the outward container."

DR. WILLIAM FINK:

From phonics to animal behavior, truly disparate ideas. It sounds like he was really loose associating.

How unusual was Bucky acting from the time he wrote this in his journal?

HOWARD CAMPBELL:

I didn't see him during this time. It is difficult to tell if these were notes from April 7th, 8th or 9th. Heck, I don't know if he wrote sequentially after the first day. He was reading a lot and jumping from one idea to another. There were blank pages. He might have just been picking a page for an idea and filling-in details as he came across them, rather than recording his ideas in sequence.

He was speculating about how he might structure the world. Next I saw him was the night of April 7th at a rehearsal for his spoken word show. He flowed. He interspersed magic tricks with real life examples of similar persuasions and Sufi stories. He taught a magic trick through introducing a vocabulary word, and explained that since he taught them a word they could now see the apparatus that had been invisible to them before. He suggested that language affects how we see the world. Without certain words, some things are invisible. He explained how we use the words "snow" and "sleet," but that the Eskimos have 28 words for various types of snow or ice or other kinds of grounded frozen waterand an additional 13 words for the falling varieties. These subtleties are invisible to our minds' eyes. He introduced the audience to the word, fnord. The main vein of his talk that night was on "Attacca" and "Nacirema." Attacca is the backbone of science; Nacirema is the absence of Attacca. He explored the internal validity of mathematics, and how rules are developed when discrepancies are noticed between math and nature. He talked about how Gödel said that validity comes from outside a system, like how in grade school they don't let students use a form of the word they are defining in their definition. Gödel says the opposite can also be the case, something can be true and not contained within a system. Just because we can't articulate an idea doesn't mean it doesn't exist.

DR. WILLIAM FINK:

That's a double negative.

HOWARD CAMPBELL:

Yes. Allowing for ambiguity—maybe logic.

Bucky went on to explain that when the church waged a war on science in words, science was bound to win. Religion is outside of Attacca. Attacca is the product of science. He explained how Attacca cannot stand on its own. In science, we generally learn something new by organizing labels that describe this new thing. For each new thing we learn, we usually have to create new labels. Then, the cycle repeats itself and the new-new thing requires new labels, each of which requires a new, new label. So, the number of new things we don't really know expands faster than what we do know. If what we know is a numerator, and what we don't know is the denominator, you'd get a fraction or a percentage of what we know. However, if taken to infinity, the fraction is equivalent to zero. In essence, we know nothing.

DR. WILLIAM FINK:

Knowledge doesn't accumulate like that. The model doesn't work.

HOWARD CAMPBELL:

I know that…Bucky knew that. But, it exposes how Attaccan thought can be twisted. It is sort of like how you can prove that one equals negative one, if you are allowed to divide by zero.

DR. WILLIAM FINK:

That's why we have a rule that you can't divide by zero.

HOWARD CAMPBELL:

Yeah, but I bet we didn't have that rule until somebody showed how to exploit the system.

DR. WILLIAM FINK:

So?

HOWARD CAMPBELL:

I guess we have to be wary of people that exploit systems to their own advantage.

DR. WILLIAM FINK:

So?

HOWARD CAMPBELL:

Look, it wasn't my show. Why don't you ask Bucky?

[PAUSE]

Never mind. That was mean of me.

When the show ended, I went to sleep. Apparently Bucky did not go to sleep. Perhaps reading *The Bible* at this time wasn't the strongest move for his mental stability. But, Bucky's journal shows him drawing a connection between the story of Genesis and the origins of intelligence. It begins with the idea of a void, which gets filled with light. Bucky took light to be a metaphor for consciousness. The story rang of similarities to Helen Keller's story of gaining language. Before she had language, she had no memory, because our brain's sorting mechanism doesn't work like that. It doesn't mean she didn't learn things, she just couldn't recollect them. Language began creating distinctions in her head that were sortable. In her head appeared a world that had not been there before. It wasn't that nothing existed before she had language, but it took language to codify the experiences, so that an external world appeared as if it was materializing around her. Similarly, with the appearance of light, came the distinctions of our surroundings.

Then his journal entries become indecipherable. I assume he hallucinated his name being called. He notes that he heard his name being called, but there was nobody there. What followed were patterns and shapes and poor drawing skills mixed in with the words "show your self" and "stop It". Then the word "Normal" written several times. Sometimes with a question mark and sometimes without. Then, "Normal=modern psychology definition of healthy, but if the mass of humans are sick, then what is normal? If the majority of people feel a certain way, that doesn't make it good."

Bucky was reading a George Beard book entitled: *American Nervousness: Its Causes and Consequences.* Beard introduces a word, *neurasthenic*, the physical condition he attributes to "modern civilization," a wealthy disease, afflicting those with delicate temperaments or highly charged brains. Neurasthenic doesn't afflict people who primarily worked with their hands. Theodore Roosevelt was diagnosed with this disease. He was told to get fresh air and plenty of physical activity. He went to a dude ranch.

Bucky wrote: "Neurasthenic is Attacca, playing in symbols too much." Roosevelt's cure suggests this. Get away from your books and symbolic representations, and get to another state of mind. Get physical. Explore Nacirema.

DR. WILLIAM FINK:
Freud suggested exerting our domination over nature.
[SOUND: THUD; SPLASH; CHAIR SCREECH]

HOWARD CAMPBELL:
Ah, shit.

DR. WILLIAM FINK:
Not to worry.
[SOUND: CHAIR SCREECH]
[SOUND: FOOTSTEPS]

HOWARD CAMPBELL:

I'm sorry.

DR. WILLIAM FINK:

Not a problem.

This is cleaned-up in a jiffy.

[PAUSE]

Would you like more water?

HOWARD CAMPBELL:

No. I'm fine.

Thank you.

Modern society created modern ailments. Corporations were there to provide remedies. Another cure for neurasthenic was Coca-Cola, which at the time contained cocaine. The stimulation would raise you out of the funk you were experiencing. This is the same as taking an aspirin for a headache. You don't cure the headache by taking aspirin. Your body doesn't have an aspirin deficiency. What is the most common employee benefit offered by corporations? Free coffee.

Our economic base has shifted from the majority of people doing physical work in the United States, to the majority of people spending the majority of their time manipulating symbols. Our heads are reeling. Caffeine makes it so we can sustain this mode of thought with less effort. This may be mainstream, but it hardly feels normal. Bucky and I reject the notion that average equals normal. The mental health of the average American is going down the crapper, and virtually nobody in psychology seems to be aware of it, let alone alarmed. Bucky wrote something I mentioned before, but I hadn't thought of it in terms of us humans: "If you drop a frog in boiling water, it will jump out. However, if you place a frog in a double boiler and slowly turn up the heat, the frog will sit there until it dies of heat and the water boils around him."

Sleep isn't physically needed, but psychologically needed. Sleep and dreaming are necessary to process the stimulus we have absorbed during the previous waking spell. But Bucky didn't sleep.

[SOUND: PAPER UNFOLDED]

Here's a note from his journal: "Day 3: It is morning. I have my first waking hallucination. My previous 3 episodes of sleep ended approximately 54 hours earlier and could hardly have been classified as restive. My body begins to generate sleep deprivation hallucinations. I have internalized too much stimulus."

I'll continue to read: "I am in the administration building, called The Barn. I see Hank pulling two plastic trash bags. He turns the corner. Somehow, I know he isn't real, but I see him clear as day, like the other people passing him in the hallway. He hustles around the corner, but he is nowhere to be seen...I see him twice more in the course of the morning and twice again that early afternoon. It occurs to me that Hank pulling the trash bags is a metaphor for me pulling all my issues and baggage around with me."

Bokonon appeared as an emerging reality. He was trying on the religion to see how things would appear, like a Jew trying to see how the world would appear differently to him if Jesus of Nazareth was the only begotten son of God.

Another journal entry: "Everybody on San Lorenzo is a devout Bokonist, the hy-u-ook-kuh not withstanding—Satan is Christian. If I left his Christian mindset, Satan would disappear as I know him."

When I saw Bucky next, he was at the snack counter asking for Camel flavored nicotine. Then he went back to a blanket where he was selling books. As a salesman, Bucky was too generous. He was more interested in unloading his books to good homes than he was in making money. Phoenix, a large woman interested in the tricks of magicians, was disappointed she had missed some of his books on magic. He sold her books on something else. In parting, she said to him "Magic is only as powerful as the magician. You are a great one."

Before I wandered away, Nikki and Chrissy came by his book sale and asked if he wanted to go for a drive. Bucky replied, "Dancing with our celestial partner means going on excursions when they are offered." He got up and left his books. He also left a hat and placed a five dollar bill in the hat. There is an entry in his journal, "Revenue from hat $18".

Nikki and Chrissy told me that Bucky was way peculiar during the ride. Not surprising since he saw them as Sufi Warriors and the ride as a test. He wanted this car ride to be the beginning of his brethren telling him he was safely home. As they drove, he looked for signs. They asked him where he wanted to go. He said wherever. They suggested Route 14. He saw one plus four equals five, a state of easy influence and suggested Route 11, one-one. They said okay. Nikki asked him what was up. He said, "Most things that aren't down." He wasn't trying to be funny.

They drove and talked, and Nikki asked him what he'd been working on. He talked about the show and his ideas. He wasn't bringing up the secret order of the Sufi brotherhood. He had decided that the etiquette of the order mandated not confronting a member about their membership. He talked about the encroaching corporate meme he saw enveloping America. Nikki and Chrissy tried to follow. Please realize that these notions of memes were new to him, so he wasn't as succinct in his descriptions. He was impossible to follow. This was his biggest psychological challenge. He found he couldn't communicate the way things were appearing to him. They asked him why he seemed troubled. He talked about It. He talked about a sense of righteousness he felt in most people, a sense he didn't pick up from either of them. They were more like Brahmins. A Brahmin is not a Brahmin because he is born a Brahmin, but because his body is an arrow and his soul is a bow and with all his might he is aiming his soul at being Brahmin. At least that's what Hesse says. The righteousness he was feeling from most people was a sense that they saw themselves as better than other people. A sense that deep down inside these people are stuck up. He was beginning to see neurasthenic as being a plague over America that nobody else seemed to be noticing. It was like neurasthenia had become accepted as the norm. If neurasthenia was once a stress related sickness, then being sick was not only now normal, but expected.

It's like when you're sick, and you see the doctor, and the doctor tells you that you have a virus. Like a drug, It affects the way you feel. It is an invisible thought pattern. It is the corporate meme. When your body is invaded by It, you are more rigid. You have an alien life form in your system, a meme virus. Symptoms of this possession are righteousness, irritability, inflexibility in seeing other's perspective, defensiveness, the urge to cut people off, background thinking that gives you a monologue in your head while others are speaking, and nervousness, a general sense that everything is not okay. I imagine the root of Bucky's frustration at the time was an inability to communicate the phenomena he was experiencing. Not having access to the words also meant he wasn't able to make his experience tangible. Not being able to share his experience with others made him feel disenfranchised.

DR. WILLIAM FINK:

He felt alienated.

HOWARD CAMPBELL:

Yes, and this alienation left him feeling disoriented. Bucky was disoriented because his expectations were at odds with his phenomenal experience. Bucky was mostly concerned that he was failing his test, and he wasn't going to be initiated. The brotherhood hadn't deemed him worthy. In which case, he wasn't safe. He didn't know where to look or how to act. He felt wrong. He wanted to be something else. This extreme desire, of course, limited the way he saw things. Just as any addiction takes an invisible hold on your perception. Bucky was on It. He was trapped in an Attaccan maze and couldn't see over the hedges. He felt like there was a problem to be solved if only the decoder would make itself known to him. Everywhere he looked, he saw red flags, but he felt inadequate because he couldn't discern the symbol's meaning.

DR. WILLIAM FINK:

Were there literally red flags around campus?

HOWARD CAMPBELL:

Yes. They were there for the visiting trustees' and board of directors.

DR. WILLIAM FINK:

And Bucky mistook the trustees' arrival as some sort of initiation committee?

HOWARD CAMPBELL:

Exactly.

I asked Nikki what he sounded like when we went for the ride. She said that he was saying a lot of things that made perfect sense to her in terms of the way people would interact. At a certain point, she would stop following his train of thought, and she said she could see his pain as he tried to find a way to help her see it, but then his speech would go from making perfect sense to nonsensical, but she wasn't quite sure where the shift happened.

When Bucky got out of the car, they said they were all hooking up in Lori's room later, and that he should come by. The idea of "all" was an invitation he couldn't resist. He thought that maybe this would be the initiation ritual.

I found some Grateful Dead lyrics in his journal that appear around this time: "I don't know who put it there; believe it if you need it or leave it if you dare. And it is just a box of rain or a ribbon for your hair. Such a long, long time to be gone and a short time to be there."

Bucky knew he'd spent too much time recently in Attacca to be ready for initiation. When they got back, it was nearly sunclipse and he wanted to feel more. He wanted to feel the Earth moving. He stood on the grass, at The Edge of the World, and felt the sun. He thought of the sun as a heat source 96 million miles away, although he couldn't conceptualize 96,000,000 miles. He closed his eyes and tried to feel the Earth spinning on its axis. He opened his eyes to watch the sun being clipsed from his view and feel the world turning. He stood there and tried to feel the sense of movement within the rotation, to feel the Earth hurtling through space at 140,000 miles an hour as we spin on our axis. It got dark and he got cold, so he headed to Lori's room.

In route to Lori's room, Bucky passed Phoenix. She was watching him. At a party, while thoroughly trashed, he had danced with her in a grinding fashion. Mistake. Now he couldn't shake her energy. Later on, when he got back from the hospital, he asked why she'd said certain things. She said she didn't know. She said she'd just said random things to him as they occurred to her. She said she just needed to say them. Well, when he passed her this time, she said, "Once you've entered, you can not leave."

Bucky describes that outside of Lori's dorm house, he felt weird. The building seemed to be a separate energy from the rest of the campus. He wrote that the other dorms were stark white. This dorm was gray.

As he entered, he heard the chattering voices of kids running down the other flight of stairs, but as they exited, one said, "Let's get out of here." The dorm was silent. He walked to Lori's door, and on the door was the book jacket of a Bible. He looked outside. The sun had broken through, so there was bright light basking the grass and cherry trees. This dorm still felt dark. He went back to the door. He knocked. No answer. He listened, silence. The whole dorm and campus felt silent. He knocked again. He did the secret knock from his fraternity. Still, silence. Bucky opened the door. What he saw was unworldly. He saw a vast expanse. He stared and saw the

142

edge of doom. No fire, no creatures, but this was Hell to him. The notion in his head was that if he stepped inside, he couldn't come out. He stood there for a minute, staring down, and out, and up, and in all directions. It was a hazy abyss of nothingness. He closed the door, and knew that by going out through the door marked "Exit", he was forfeiting some power that he was scared to accept. About fifteen feet outside the dorm, he started to see people again. He went back in the dorm house and to Lori's door. The Bible cover was not there. He knocked. Nobody answered, so he opened the door to see the dorm room with a bed and four walls as he had expected to see earlier. Later that evening, when he saw Lori, he asked her if she'd had a Bible dust cover on her door. She said no.

I often wonder what would've happened had he stepped inside the first time, if the physical reality not meshing with his mental picture would have snapped him back to "reality," if his hallucination would have mutated to incorporate what he was sensing, or if his mind would have crumbled at the discrepancy and maybe he would have passed out. Or maybe he would have entered another dimension. I'm only joking. We both know that never happens.

DR. WILLIAM FINK:

Do you think people enter other dimensions?

HOWARD CAMPBELL:

I try not to think. I see Bucky's experience as akin to what Pirsig describes in his second book, *Lila.* He talks about having a map of one port, navigating into shelter, and in the morning finding out that he was in a completely different port. You see, in the dark he had greater faith in the map than his vision, and so he skewed what he actually saw, in order to accommodate what he was looking for on the map. Projecting the symbols from the map on to the surrounding terrain didn't exactly work, yet Pirsig thought it *was* working. In fact, it worked well enough to guide him into a slip to tie-up for the night. To the best of his hindsight, this is what Bucky was doing. He had a concept of a world order in his head, which made sense to him. He projected this map on the physical world around him. He was searching for vin-dits. The vin-dit was his search, but he was looking for something else. He didn't see that *This* was part of *It.*

Packers fans? A granfalloon, a group that exists because people hold a heuristic distinction. These football enthusiasts' false wompeter is the premise that "Packers winning is good." Everyone within this group can rally behind anything that helps the Packers win. They may have different notions as to the best methods, but they are united in their desire. This entity, however, does not correlate to the physical world. It has complete internal validity, but you can remove this group from our presence and the world would basically continue as we know it. The Packers existence or lack there of, does not alter The Universe.

DR. WILLIAM FINK:

Is this semiotics?

HOWARD CAMPBELL:

Yes, but I want to take it metaphysical. And, to that end, I'm going to talk very Attacan for a while. Christianity is another example of a granfalloon. You need to not be a Christian to get this next point. An axiom of Christianity is: "Christianity is not provable." If the statement is false, then Christianity is provable, so Christianity exists. If the statement is true, then Christianity is not provable, but it is also true. Win-win. Either outcome makes Christianity exist. Neat mental trick. From a mathematical perspective, we can remove Christianity from The Universe and all the laws of Nature as science knows them still function.

Bucky's problem was that he had gotten so into the internal workings of his newfound religion, which kept emerging as having internal validity, that he began projecting this cosmography onto reality, as opposed to creating his reality from his interaction with Nature. A lot of Christians do this, too.

I feel bad for the followers of that freak who committed suicide to join the alien spacecraft behind the comet. He was searching for vin-dits. He was desirous. You can't search for vin-dits. Vin-dits just happen. He can not induce a vin-dit. You deduce a vin-dit after your perception has changed. Religion is not inductive. When you induce religion, you make false magic and pray to false idols. What is the difference between spending 30 minutes praying to a cow of gold and spending the same amount of time reading a prospectus? Structurally, how is focus with future aspiration not a form of petitioning the universe? Don't answer that. My bad.

Bucky's point is that a religious experience happens in Nacirema. Any explanation in words is an Attaccan metaphor. Talking about dancing is like tap dancing about architecture.

Bucky was having some sort of religious experience. I am probably using a broader definition of religion than most people commonly allow. I view a religious experience as connecting with oneness, as that which catapults one's mind into this connectedness. An art object is that which catapults one into an altered state of consciousness; art induces a sense of the sublime. Sometimes there is little difference between art and religion except that formal religion tends to hold clusters of people together while art tends to break through current groupings and develop new clusters. Christianity is not bogus. It affords many an opportunity of connectedness, to feel enfranchised. God bless them.

DR. WILLIAM FINK:

You are not a Christian.

HOWARD CAMPBELL:

No more than I am a psychologist. But I feel that I am a better Christian than many who attend church regularly, and that I am a better psychologist than many of those who have a degree in psychology.

Bucky feared mental hospitals. He thought that the best way to systematically discredit somebody was to legally label them insane. He looked at what was supposed to be a madman: hearing voices, hallucinating, and thinking one had powers not recognized by conventional physics. Yet all of these attributes fit into his world order of magicians as healthy. He thought to himself that the only difference between himself and a madman was that he wasn't mad. He was wrong about that, but it occurred to him that maybe the hospital is where the initiation begins, and that maybe he wasn't fit to be a Sufi until he had faced his ultimate fear, the possibility of being systematically, legally discredited.

DR. WILLIAM FINK:

How did he decide to go?

HOWARD CAMPBELL:

Trudy, Bill Scully and Maggie Shaw decided it was best for Bucky to get outside help, at a mental hospital. Bill led the charge, in terms of the conversation, when the three found him. Bucky asked how he would go about going to the hospital, and Trudy said she'd take him. She said he should pack some things. He asked what. She said that he might be there a couple days, so to bring whatever he might want for the next couple days.

At some point, Bucky had stopped carrying his fanny pack. He had it in his room, but just wasn't carrying it with him. When he went back to his room, in the hallway outside his door was a duffel bag with a jean jacket on top. He saw this as what he needed to bring. The duffel bag had some shirts his size and six dollars in it. The jacket had a pack and a half of his brand of cigarettes and $17 in its pockets. He saw the $6 and the $17 as being in sync with the Sufi vision of an incipient initiation: 17+6=23, after all.

When they got to the hospital, Bucky was hyper-literal. Bill told me that at the admissions desk, the nurse needed to ask Bucky almost every question two, three or several times. She was very patient. Bucky was in a rare frame of mind, being hyper-literal and yet free-associating at the same time. The nurse was seeing his logic, though, so they both found humor in the conversation. When all the paperwork was said and done, Bill escorted Bucky to his new residence for the next eight days.

Perhaps it was just an unfortunate coincidence that the mental ward was on the 6th floor. The nurse there escorted him into ROOM 623, and he laughed. She asked why. He told her 623 was the sign of the Illuminati. She asked him to hold on a sec, and she consulted with the head nurse before assigning him to room 624.

DR. WILLIAM FINK:

This really happened?

HOWARD CAMPBELL:

Yes.

DR. WILLIAM FINK:

Shit. That must've messed with him.

HOWARD CAMPBELL:

Yes, it did. His notes on the hospital stay are very sketchy and obtuse. Some of it is clear, but not much. The big idea that he came to was that the name

Illuminati was like the label UFO, a catchall label for the unidentifiable. When the church found resistance to its domination, those unseen resistors were labeled Illuminati, just like how America labeled people as communists in the '50s. But this wasn't an immediate revelation.

When Bucky entered room 624 he thought the doctors might be Illuminati or, they were automatons controlled by the Illuminati. He just didn't know. His biggest sickness might have been that he was extraordinarily open to either reality. Eventually, he would realize that neither of these cosmographies were sustainable.

He got set up in his room with the help of a compassionate orderly who gave him toiletries, supplies Bucky hadn't found in the duffel bag, and a pair of green slippers. A doctor came in. She asked him a bunch of questions about his hallucinations and about his family's medical history. She asked him if he did drugs. He pointed to his Coke and said that he primarily did caffeine and nicotine. She asked him if he did any harder drugs. He told her that he was under the impression that next to heroin, nicotine was one of the hardest drugs to kick. She asked him if he smoked marijuana. He said yes. She asked if he smoked a lot. He asked, "What kind of lot?" She asked about the last time he smoked marijuana. He found it funny that she was not as interested in what he experienced in the previous four days, as what happened in the previous few months. She was looking for posttraumatic stress disorder.

DR. WILLIAM FINK:

Of course she was. The first thing we try to ascertain when a new patient comes in is if something happened recently.

HOWARD CAMPBELL:

Things happen all the time—it's just that most people are only interested in what's happening on TV. This nurse wasn't interested in talking about how thoughts were living organisms or even creatures. She was interested in the idea that he could stare at the wall and see faces. He made some sort of god reference. She wanted to see if he had religious delusions. She asked him what he thought about God. He said, "First of all, She's black." It's an old joke. He noted that she probably took that as a sign he was delusional, but maybe not in a religious way. Bucky wrote, "I got the sense she didn't take me to have a Jesus complex, but that I definitely wasn't stable." Then she left. Bucky holds that an interviewee can learn more about an interviewer than the interviewer generally learns about the interviewee.

Bucky was invited to use the phone. He thought the phone may be connected to this overarching organization. He knew this was a trite idea, but just because it was trite didn't mean it couldn't be true. If there was such a coordinated group, of course they would control the communications. He called his friend Larry, his mentor in magic.

When he filled out a menu for his week's food, he saw it as part of an initiation test. He ordered vegetarian and tried to create variety while maintaining balanced meals. He asked for a book on nutrition, but they said none was available. He walked out a couple times, but they gently steered him back in, escorted him back into his room, closed the door and left him alone. He found a paper airplane. He began labeling it. He put the name Bobby on each side of the plane's nose. He put the words "my values" on the trim tabs, the small wings that come out of the tail that allow the plane to fly steadily. He labeled each of the plane's wings as "my feelings." This was how he saw himself traveling through time: his values kept him stable, and his feelings created directional volatility.

Nurse Ratchet came in—that's what he called her, yet I'm confident she had another name. She walked in abruptly and stepped into his room, and apparently stood with her arms crossed and tapped her foot. Bucky said, "Where I come from, people knock before coming through a closed door." She stood there and continued to tap. He added, "Sometimes they even wait for a 'Hello' or even a 'Come in'." She continued to tap her foot. Bucky tried a different approach. He waited for her energy to calm and he said, "Hi." This only incited her tapping. He asked, "Did you want to talk about something?" She continued to tap. She was trying his patience. He went back to playing with his airplane. She kept tapping. Realize that he had extraordinarily keen perception at this time. He saw the run in her stockings. He saw the chip in the polish on her left ring finger. He saw a woman with too much respect for authority. Unfortunately, he didn't process what this meant to him. He said to her, "If you don't act more socially, I'm going to hurt you psychically."

I noted several important safety tips that will come in handy, if I ever find myself incarcerated in a mental hospital. Bucky suggested that never, under any circumstance, even as a joke, say anything that can be misconstrued as a threat. I should treat this situation like security questions at the airport. Your people have strict rules enforced on them, which severely mitigate their sense of humor.

DR. WILLIAM FINK:

I don't like the sound of "my people."

HOWARD CAMPBELL:

Be that as it may, hospital employees are very good at following orders. Some are even called orderlies. Based on Bucky's experience, I'd tell them I'm allergic to Haldol. That's probably why he had the violent reaction he did here.

One of the last things I want to experience is a Haldol injection. Bucky made notes to himself for future stays: order a lot of food. They'll give you whatever you want from the menu. Sometimes what he imagined and what arrived seemed difficult to classify under the same rubric. He wasn't allowed to order two entrees, but he could order all the side dishes he wanted. It's easy to order a lot of food, but very difficult to get snacks. Bring smokes if you're an addict. They don't sell them. A mental ward is probably not the environment in which you want to get used to the taste of nicotine gum.

About Haldol...Nurse Ratchet sighed with an inhale after he said he would hurt her psychically. She turned and briskly exited. Bucky wasn't alarmed, but he should have been. She came back and stood in the doorway, expectantly. Two orderlies entered his room. Bucky was sitting in a chair. One was black, the other Hispanic. They were both large men. The black guy told him, "We're going to hold you down." Bucky nodded and asked what was happening. Nobody responded. He repeated the question. It was as if he wasn't talking. A third orderly came in, a white guy, with a syringe loaded with some clear liquid. Bucky asked, rather calmly, "What is that?" The guy said Haldol. Bucky asked what it was going to do to him, but again it was as if he hadn't said anything. As the white guy brought the syringe to his arm, he saw an air bubble. I can't be certain there was an air bubble, but that's what he saw. Bucky said something to this extent, but the white orderly kept bringing the syringe towards him. Bucky pleaded that the orderly squirt a little out to get rid of the air bubble as it kept getting nearer. Bucky started to resist and immediately realized it was futile to fight. Then he said, "Let the wookie win. Let the wookie win. Jabberwockies abound."

At this point, he reasoned that he was hallucinating the air bubble. Either way, he didn't want to be tense, so he just relaxed. The two orderlies holding him down eased off. Bucky asked what they gave him. The black guy said Haldol. The white guy scowled. He asked what it was going to do. The black guy said, "Shhh. Just relax." Bucky relaxed. He looked around. He was fine till he began to feel the Haldol. He asked, "What is this doing to me?" They didn't answer. He kept asking the question, or at least talking. At first it was to try and learn what to expect, but as the Haldol kicked in, it became a battle of wills. He was resisting the drug's effect. He began to loose control of his faculties. It became more and more difficult to talk. It took immense effort to move his mouth. He could still do it, but it was like being partially paralyzed in the face and trying to sound normal. He fell off the chair and formed a fetal position trying to urk out the sounds of his words, the sounds of his will. He slowly had less and less control of his physical self. He was still aware and thinking, he was just trapped in a body he couldn't control. His tongue hung out, touching the floor, but he couldn't taste it. Nurse Ratchet watched. Bucky blacked out shortly thereafter.

Psychologists in England originally referred to themselves as alienists. This never would have flown in the United States. It didn't work well there either, because they no longer go by that label. The idea of alienists was that they treated people who were alienated, somehow disenfranchised. The problem with this label is denial: most people who see a shrink don't see themselves as alienated. The head shrinkers who started this were hyper-literal people. Being hyper-literal has a tendency to alienate. Most psychiatrists don't see themselves as alienated.

Am I offending you?

[SILENCE]

DR. WILLIAM FINK:
No. No. Please go on.

HOWARD CAMPBELL:
I see most psychiatrists as disconnected from others on a "human" level. They don't feel and empathize with the energies of healthy humans. It is similar to how most doctors that circumcise boys report that after a few times they don't really hear the baby crying. Being mad is a symptom of being on It. Being hurt is a symptom of being on It. Think of It as a drug, an odorless, tasteless and weightless drug, but It is real. If you are on It, you may not think of yourself as mad. If you are mad, you are definitely on It. If you are on It, you are less sensitive to those around you. Bucky journaled

150

that he would get hurt, but not "mad." He was denying himself madness. And, that which we resist, persists. Being "hurt" is a passive state of anger. Being angry requires feeling enough moral weight to entitle madness.

If somebody is on It, and they don't know about It, can they be held accountable for their actions? I think so. Can you blame them for acting the way they do? I think not. Maybe I'm reading too much into it, but I see It in *The X-Files.*

DR. WILLIAM FINK:

I know the show.

HOWARD CAMPBELL:

Flow with me: Imagine the aliens in *The X-Files* as a metaphor for the corporate meme, It. First of all, the government supported by It is conspiring to keep It a secret. Secondly, those who do see It are often discredited as insane or a felon. Finally, they talk about It as a living entity. Here's a quote from *The X-Files Movie* I brought with me.

[SOUND: CHAIR SCREECHING BACK, PAPER UNFOLDING AND CHAIR BEING REPOSITIONED]

> "A plague to end all plagues. A silent weapon for a quiet war. The systematic release of an indiscriminate organism for which the men who bring It on have no cure…The virus is extraterrestrial. We know very little about It, except that It was the original inhabitant of this planet. What is a virus, but a colonizing force? Until it mutates and attacks….AIDS, the Ebola viruses, on the evolutionary scale are newborns. This walked the planet long before the dinosaurs. We believed the virus would simply control us, that mass infection would make us a slave race…Survival is the ultimate ideology…Without a vaccination, the only true survivors of the viral holocaust will be those immune to It…Trust no one. Chose hope over selfishness."

What do you think?

DR. WILLIAM FINK:

You're saying that functionally, viruses colonize?

HOWARD CAMPBELL:

At least propagate. Some say there is a built-in structure to our language that creates automatic reactions in us. It's been proven that in sales, responding to a question with "because" is better received then just answering the question. Our brains are expecting a structure in response to the structure presented.

When I sold cars, we were taught many mental tricks like this. If the prospect has a major objection, such as a negative reaction to a $900 destination fee. We were taught to approach any objection with this type of response: "I understand how you feel. I felt the same way the first time I heard the destination cost was $900." You validate them, then you take them down another path. "What I learned is that there is a lot involved in getting the car here…" And you just list off costs and set-ups, and just make up stuff if you can't remember specifics.

I think these manipulation tools should be taught in school, so that Joe consumer is not blindly manipulated by those educated in persuasion. I recommend reading: *Influence; The Psychology of Persuasion* by Cialdini. You haven't read that either, have you?

DR. WILLIAM FINK:

Where are you going with all this?

HOWARD CAMPBELL:

Have you read *Influence*?

DR. WILLIAM FINK:

No.

HOWARD CAMPBELL:

And you pride yourself a free thinker.

DR. WILLIAM FINK:

I never said that.

HOWARD CAMPBELL:

Point taken. I took that for granted.

DR. WILLIAM FINK:

No, you're right. I think of myself as a free thinker.

HOWARD CAMPBELL:

You can't be a free thinker if you can't divorce yourself from others' agendas.

DR. WILLIAM FINK:

I don't think I'm easily duped.

HOWARD CAMPBELL:

That statement suggests you are highly susceptible.

DR. WILLIAM FINK:

Can you prove it?

HOWARD CAMPBELL:

I'm drawing on studies that show that people who claim they are not susceptible to hypnosis are actually as susceptible as those who state that they're highly susceptible to hypnotism.

DR. WILLIAM FINK:

I've read studies that present that conclusion.

HOWARD CAMPBELL:

Well, media is not as straight forward as it presents itself to be.

DR. WILLIAM FINK:

I think everybody knows that.

HOWARD CAMPBELL:

Yes, but by not comprehending the depth to which it is fabricated blinds them from seeing its impact on their visions of reality.

Have you seen the movie *Wag the Dog*?

DR. WILLIAM FINK:

No.

HOWARD CAMPBELL:

It's a documentary. It's about the first Bush administration. How Bush created the *Persian Gulf War* to increase his approval ratings.

DR. WILLIAM FINK:

It wasn't a documentary.

HOWARD CAMPBELL:

Might as well have been. It's probably a more accurate depiction than *The War Room*, covering similar ground. *Wag The Dog* accurately depicts American media and politics. I further hold that all the basics of marketing and perception can be learned from *Wag The Dog*.

My favorite part of the movie is when, at the beginning, DeNiro is brought in as a spin doctor. He's taken to a special, secret room in the White House. He is told about the president's transgressions with a Firefly Girl. He almost immediately says that he needs a ticket to Los Angeles and some cash.

DR. WILLIAM FINK:

Why did he do that?

HOWARD CAMPBELL:

He needed to ask a Hollywood producer to help him produce a war.

DR. WILLIAM FINK:

That doesn't really happen.

HOWARD CAMPBELL:

Yes, it does. You just aren't ready to hear the truth. That's the point I was making about you being susceptible. Your confidence is blinding.

DR. WILLIAM FINK:

I guess saying, "No, it's not" would just demonstrate my denial.

HOWARD CAMPBELL:

Yes, it would.

My favorite part of *Wag The Dog* is when DeNiro is asked what he's going to do and he says, "I'm working on it."

DR. WILLIAM FINK:

Why is that so important?

HOWARD CAMPBELL:

He already has the war idea. That's why he asked for the tickets and the money. But, he knows these colleagues are not ready to hear his idea yet. So, he says he's working on it to maintain the project's momentum without jarring his coconspirators.

DR. WILLIAM FINK:

That's interesting.

[PAUSE]

HOWARD CAMPBELL:

Can you detect when an alien meme broaches your mind? I don't think you can. You didn't follow when I discussed the concept of *understand*.

[PAUSE]

This gets back to the insight that prompted the Sacra Congregatio de Propaganda Fide. If you get people to understand something, their actions will follow. What a person accepts as fact, affects how they act. Understanding is the act of *standing under a precept*. Are you following?

DR. WILLIAM FINK:

No.

HOWARD CAMPBELL:

Yes, you are. You're following because I am leading the conversation. You just aren't tracking. That's okay. Enough is penetrating to effect a change. These ideas will bubble up in your thoughts over the next few days, or maybe longer, and it won't occur to you that they're connected. It will seem to you like a random thought. This is a fallacy. Our mind doesn't present random ideas. Our mind projects related concepts. Most people don't seek the connections. Some do through dream analysis, but most don't see the parallel of fleeting thoughts while awake. These fleeting thoughts are similar to waking dreams: the subconscious has deemed something worthy of focus.

DR. WILLIAM FINK:

You are so confident in your interpretations.

HOWARD CAMPBELL:

As you are confident in your diagnoses.

DR. WILLIAM FINK:

Yes, but I've trained for years with very respectable doctors.

HOWARD CAMPBELL:

And I've apprenticed top practitioners.

DR. WILLIAM FINK:

You are arrogant.

[PAUSE]

HOWARD CAMPBELL:

How long have you been having an affair with Virginia?

DR. WILLIAM FINK:

I beg your pardon?

HOWARD CAMPBELL:

How long have you been having an affair with Virginia?

DR. WILLIAM FINK:

What makes you think I've had an affair with Nurse Prynne?

HOWARD CAMPBELL:

So the affair is over?

DR. WILLIAM FINK:

What makes you think I've had an affair with Nurse Prynne?

HOWARD CAMPBELL:

I don't think. I know. Until this conversation, I didn't know if it was a mutual attraction, or if either of you had acted on your passions.

DR. WILLIAM FINK:

What makes you think I've had an affair with Nurse Prynne?

HOWARD CAMPBELL:

Primarily your defensiveness.

[PAUSE]

DR. WILLIAM FINK:

I had an affair with Nurse Prynne.

[PAUSE]

HOWARD CAMPBELL:

You want to talk about it?

DR. WILLIAM FINK:

I do not want to talk about it.

[PAUSE]

HOWARD CAMPBELL:

I think of myself as confident. I'm sorry I came across as arrogant. I was making distinctions in our education, trying to maintain an equal footing. I felt like you were putting me down. I over compensated by demonstrating my power of perception.

[PAUSE]

DR. WILLIAM FINK:

How did you know I had an affair?

HOWARD CAMPBELL:

It was obvious. As I'm sure it is to everybody here.

[PAUSE]

You called her Virginia. You call everybody else Nurse so-and-so.

[PAUSE]

Does your wife work here?

[PAUSE]

DR. WILLIAM FINK:

No.

[PAUSE]

HOWARD CAMPBELL:

Should we stop? Do you need to take some time?

DR. WILLIAM FINK:

No.

[COUGHING]

I can keep going. You were talking about Richard's experience with Haldol.

HOWARD CAMPBELL:

Bucky regained consciousness from the Haldol on a mattress in a small room, dazed and confused. He remembered what he could of the time before he lost consciousness. He very consciously said, "Hi." He moved his legs. He had regained his mobility. He sat up. His room had a viewing window for the nurses' station. The clock said 6:25. The sky was sparsely lit, so he didn't know if it was early morning or evening. He knocked on the glass, but the nurse close to him just shook her head. After studying the sky, Bucky realized it was getting lighter. The sun would soon crack the sky. It was early morning. He looked around the room, an 8x8 box with two windows. He found a jagged piece of plastic on the floor next to his mattress. He noted thinking, "This is odd." Bucky knocked on the glass again. The nurse shook her head again. The older nurse behind her reprimanded her for acknowledging him. He knocked more insistently. No reaction. He knocked and said, "If I'm in here for my own protection, should this be in here with me?" He was pointing to the jagged plastic. The closer nurse couldn't help herself, and looked. She gasped and turned and said something to the older nurse that Bucky couldn't hear, and he couldn't read their lips. The older nurse said something and the younger nurse left the room. But she didn't come in.

About two minutes later, an orderly opened the door and Bucky handed him the plastic. Bucky asked how long he was going to be in there. The orderly said a while longer. Bucky asked if that was a couple of hours or a couple of days. The orderly left without answering. Bucky looked outside. He pondered what the healing objective is in keeping a man in a small room, and then realized that he couldn't blame the nurses. They were just the monkeys who got switched on when the ritual of the ladder was already in place.

Emily, the woman I mentioned earlier as having been there for the game of Cosmic Wipeout, and her boyfriend Blaine, visited Bucky in the hospital, but I know that from them, not Bucky's journals or notes. His journal just skips two of the days he spent in the hospital. Bucky was heavily drugged. His notes pick up with his decision that he didn't like it at the hospital anymore. He wrote, "These medical professionals are not enlightened." There were four days from this decision to his release.

Bucky wrote that he asked how he could stop playing the hospital game. That didn't work. He realized he had to speak their vocabulary. That was the primary rule for almost any club: speak their vocabulary. Mental hospitals are like anti-clubs; they keep you in *unless* you speak their vocabulary.

He asked when he might return to school. They replied, when *they* said he was okay. He asked if they could legally hold him if he wanted to go, since he was a voluntary patient. They said no. The kind nurse was listening, but not speaking up. Later, the kind nurse suggested he check with his school to see what kind of conditions needed to be met for him to return for the rest of that semester. This was important. Had he decided to check himself out as opposed to being discharged, Bennington would not let him come back to finish the semester. His school would only let him come back on the conditions that he was discharged by the hospital, agreed to regularly see a psychologist and a psychiatrist, and that he stay on any and all meds that his psychiatrist prescribed.

Bucky participated in all hospital activities. He wrote his résumé in the career seminar. He went to arts and crafts. He made a Pegasus that looked like it was flying in the middle of a translucent box. He did what was asked of him. He ate all his meals. He read in his spare time. He was there a total of eight days. He started playing along on day three. By day five, the doctors reevaluated him as being manic-depressive on the assumption that if he was schizophrenic, he couldn't have recovered to this level of "normality" this quickly. They then shifted their diagnosis to include the idea that when he entered the hospital, he was in a state of mania. They told him that the clinical name for what he had was called bipolar disorder.

You okay?

[PAUSE]

DR. WILLIAM FINK:

Yeah, why?

HOWARD CAMPBELL:

You don't seem very engaged. You aren't nodding along like you're tracking.

DR. WILLIAM FINK:

I guess I'm distracted by being told that I am much more transparent than I imagined myself to be.

HOWARD CAMPBELL:

Maybe we should call it a day.

DR. WILLIAM FINK:

I don't want to lose our time together. Both of our schedules are tight.

HOWARD CAMPBELL:

Okay.

[PAUSE]

DR. WILLIAM FINK:

What else is obvious about me?

HOWARD CAMPBELL:

You don't want me to answer that.

DR. WILLIAM FINK:

No, I do.

[PAUSE]

HOWARD CAMPBELL:

You are gay.

DR. WILLIAM FINK:

That, I am not.

HOWARD CAMPBELL:

Okay.

DR. WILLIAM FINK:

I may not know many things about myself, but I know I'm not gay.

HOWARD CAMPBELL:

You are regularly impotent with your wife.

DR. WILLIAM FINK:

That doesn't make me gay.

HOWARD CAMPBELL:

Okay.

[PAUSE]

DR. WILLIAM FINK:

Why do you think I'm gay?

HOWARD CAMPBELL:

You can only get off when you're doing something taboo. That's why you are addicted to having affairs. You only have an affair for a couple months at a time. Then, the taboo is gone and you return to your legal spouse.

DR. WILLIAM FINK:

That has nothing to do with being gay.

[PAUSE]

HOWARD CAMPBELL:

I'm sorry.

[PAUSE]

DR. WILLIAM FINK:

Let's get back to Bucky.

[SILENCE]

HOWARD CAMPBELL:

I don't know if there's anything else I can tell you about Richard.

[PAUSE]

Maybe this is goodbye.

DR. WILLIAM FINK:

No. You need to come back.

HOWARD CAMPBELL:

Look, I'm stressed-out. My boss is coming down on me, he expects me to keep on top of the account executives. I expect them to manage themselves. I'm not sure I can handle everything and keep working with you.

DR. WILLIAM FINK:

I never asked what prompted him to blow-up at you.

[PAUSE]

HOWARD CAMPBELL:

I never said he blew-up at me.

DR. WILLIAM FINK:

It's rare that a boss asks an employee if they want to remain employed in a calm fashion. If he were calm, he would have simply said that he was frustrated with you, but ultimatum questions suggest a mind that flares up.

HOWARD CAMPBELL:

You read him right.

DR. WILLIAM FINK:

What happened that made your boss lose his cool? What was the catalyst?

HOWARD CAMPBELL:

He was already frustrated with me. Probably because I said I wasn't comfortable consistently putting in sixty to seventy hour weeks. Well, I had been traveling the previous week and I didn't know where and when a presentation was that I was presenting.

DR. WILLIAM FINK:

That seems like a reasonable thing to be angry with you about.

HOWARD CAMPBELL:

I did take full accountability for not knowing. However, if either he or the account director had told me any of these facts, or invited me through the office calendar system, it would have been more likely that I would have known the details of the meeting, rather than expecting me to ask and figure out my own role and then having it be appropriate for me to be unnaturally humble when I failed to meet their expectation. My job would be easier if they issue me a crystal ball so I could know to ask what they hadn't told me, but expected me to know.

[PAUSE]

But, you are not my psychiatrist. Our work here is about Richard. And, I don't know if I have any more to contribute.

[PAUSE]

DR. WILLIAM FINK:

I'll have specific questions next time. You've given me so much information about Bucky that I couldn't have learned about otherwise. It makes me hopeful that therapy may work with him.

HOWARD CAMPBELL:

Why?

DR. WILLIAM FINK:

I just need to help him organize his ideas.

[PAUSE]

HOWARD CAMPBELL:

That reminds me of a story. Mephistopheles is out with a trainee demon. They see a young boy pick up a piece of Truth and put it in his pocket. The young demon demands, "We have to do something." But Mephistopheles ignores him. The young boy continues walking and sees another Truth. He picks up this piece of Truth and also puts it in his pocket.

The young demon looks expectantly at Mephistopheles. Nothing happens. The boy continues walking and puts another piece of Truth in his pocket.

The young demon is beside himself with anxiety. He blurts out, "Aren't we going to do something?"

Mephistopheles says, "Yes, we'll wait until he has a few more pieces of Truth. Then, we'll help him organize them."

DR. WILLIAM FINK:

You said Sufis taught through jokes. Is that a Sufi story? It's not exactly a joke.

HOWARD CAMPBELL:

Jokes are a type of story. Just like comedies are the plays that end in a union or marriage. Tragedies are the plays that end in death or separation. A joke is the type of story that, at some point, creates an image in your mind, and then asks you to reframe your perception. That's when we laugh, in the process of reframing.

DR. WILLIAM FINK:

What are love stories?

HOWARD CAMPBELL:

Love stories are tales of passion. A love story can be a comedy or a tragedy. Some stories might be a comedy in one regard and a tragedy in another. These distinctions aren't mutually exclusive and completely exhaustive. It isn't like the DSMR Four or the Dewey Decimal System. This isn't technology of that sort.

DR. WILLIAM FINK:

The Dewey Decimal System is a technology? Yeah, I see it is.

HOWARD CAMPBELL:

Any system is a technology.

DR. WILLIAM FINK:

But then fish swimming in a school is a technology.

HOWARD CAMPBELL:

Exactly. There is a shared meme that keeps the fish together.

DR. WILLIAM FINK:

What is the shared meme?

HOWARD CAMPBELL:

To stay together.

[SILENCE]

DR. WILLIAM FINK:

Yes.

[SILENCE]

DR. WILLIAM FINK:

Systems are intelligence.

HOWARD CAMPBELL:

We were so fucking close. You kill me. No. Systems are a *form* of intelligence. There are at least two forms of intelligence, systems and non-systems. And, any system that says there are more than two systems, is a form of intelligence, called a system, otherwise known as a finite game. That's the Howard Campbell corollary to Alan Carse's theory of *Finite and Infinite Games*. Carse is the Gödel of intelligence. Gödel proved that there are mathematical proofs that can not be proven. Carse proved that there is intelligence that can not be defined.

I'm sorry. I gotta go.

[SOUND: CHAIR SCREECHING BACK]
[SOUND: RECORDER SWITCHING OFF]
(DISCUSSION OMITTED)
[SOUND: RECORDER SWITCHING ON]

SESSION 4

VOICE OF DR. WILLIAM FINK:

March 18, 2003, session four with Howard Campbell.

HOWARD CAMPBELL:

You look spry.

DR. WILLIAM FINK:

[RAISED VOICE]

Shut up!

[SILENCE]

Bucky never went to Bennington. Bennington College has never had a Richard Wilson as a student. There is no other hospital near Bennington other than SVH where we checked.

[PAUSE]

Why did you do this? What are you doing here? Bucky doesn't exist.

[SILENCE]

HOWARD CAMPBELL:

The greatest trick the devil pulled is to prove that he doesn't exist.

DR. WILLIAM FINK:

What is that supposed to mean? What's anything you've said supposed to mean?

[PAUSE]

Everything you have said, at least so far, is an artifice. Where did you get those photographs?

HOWARD CAMPBELL:

I was trying to graphically depict the content of a book of mine I knew Richard read. That's why he emailed me. He read my book, *The Longer Line*. That's where he got my email address from.

DR. WILLIAM FINK:

You are a complete fraud.

[PAUSE]

Why are you here? What are you doing?

HOWARD CAMPBELL:

I got an e-mail asking me to contact you. I found it to be an extraordinary coincidence that I was here in Hawaii on vacation when you asked me to contact you, and you were where I was. But then, there are no coincidences. Look, I wouldn't be a Bokononist had I turned down your invitation. Bucky asked me....

DR. WILLIAM FINK:

His name is Richard Wilson.

HOWARD CAMPBELL:

Richard asked me to explain.

DR. WILLIAM FINK:

Explain what?

HOWARD CAMPBELL:

I don't know. But he said, "My dearest friend Howard, please explain." I could not deny that invitation. What I have told you is the best of my ability to figure out what he wanted me to explain.

DR. WILLIAM FINK:

You could have told me the truth.

HOWARD CAMPBELL:

You could've observed me visiting Richard as we'd scheduled. I hadn't thought up this ruse then.

[PAUSE]

DR. WILLIAM FINK:

I was unavoidably detained.

[PAUSE]

HOWARD CAMPBELL:

The last time I was contacted about a reader being hospitalized, the supervising psychiatrist did not value the perceptions I saw as leading to his hospitalization.

DR. WILLIAM FINK:

This has happened before?

HOWARD CAMPBELL:

Yes. I was planning on coming clean, but only after I was confident you understood the dichotomy Richard was facing. As a Bokonist, I don't have the same relationship with truth as you do. "Anybody who doesn't see the value of a book based on lies won't see the value of this book either" begins *The Book of Bokonon*. I told you, I tell stories for a living.

DR. WILLIAM FINK:

You've been lying to me for your own pleasure. I'm beginning to think *you* are a sociopath.

HOWARD CAMPBELL:

Intelligent and manipulative? Yeah, I am that. Hyperbolic? Sure, I exaggerate. Who doesn't? But I don't blame the system. If I were so devoid of tension, I wouldn't be taking Neurontin. Free of anxiety and guilt? I've worked hard on reducing my sense of guilt and the anxiety of perceived possible guilt.

I'm not a sociopath. I was riffing. I wrote the bit about the letter before our first exchange, but the rest was riffing. You invite me to tell you what I knew about a guy named Richard. I know he was reading my ideas. I figured I would share my ideas, so you could see some of what Richard was contemplating. My ideas are derivative of Buckminster Fuller. To personify these ideas, I said that Richard was called Bucky so I could more easily organize my thoughts on the fly. As a kid, I interviewed Buckminster Fuller, whose nickname was Bucky. Everything I said about Richard is basically true, at least to his spirit. I wasn't speaking about the Bucky that you were thinking of as Richard. I was thinking of him more like James Joyce's Finnegan. I call it the Bucky Virus.

DR. WILLIAM FINK:

A virus?

HOWARD CAMPBELL:

Yes. Richard adopted a mind virus, a system of thought that altered his perception to the point that he could not function in modern America, except as he is coping, in your care, with his physical safety assured, as he works through whatever mental dichotomies are conflicting him.

DR. WILLIAM FINK:

You call it a virus?

HOWARD CAMPBELL:

Yes, a virus. Viruses can get people sick. You see Richard as sick. A thought virus is what lead him to be hospitalized here.

DR. WILLIAM FINK:

Thoughts aren't really a virus.

HOWARD CAMPBELL:

Why not?

DR. WILLIAM FINK:

Viruses have DNA.

HOWARD CAMPBELL:

And?

DR. WILLIAM FINK:

No DNA, no virus. You can say it is *like* a virus, but you can't say it *is* a virus without showing me the DNA.

HOWARD CAMPBELL:

I can show you the DNA. Thoughts have DNA.

DR. WILLIAM FINK:

Don't give me some crap about memes and memetics being the DNA of a thought.

HOWARD CAMPBELL:

Okay.

DR. WILLIAM FINK:

You are telling me you can show me the DNA of a thought. The type of DNA I can see under a microscope?

HOWARD CAMPBELL:

Yes.

[PAUSE]

DR. WILLIAM FINK:

Well?

[SILENCE]

Are you going to share this with me?

[PAUSE]

HOWARD CAMPBELL:

You're looking at it.

[PAUSE]

I am thought DNA.

[PAUSE]

Thoughts can not exist where there is no DNA.

[PAUSE]

DR. WILLIAM FINK:

Humans are the host for thought viruses?

HOWARD CAMPBELL:

Not just humans. I can teach a bird to speak.

DR. WILLIAM FINK:

But the bird doesn't know the meaning of the word.

HOWARD CAMPBELL:

What if meaning is an illusion? What if replication is intelligence? What if intentional replication is consciousness?

DR. WILLIAM FINK:

It is not that simple.

HOWARD CAMPBELL:

I never said it was simple. I just said it was so.

[PAUSE]

We're beginning to understand replication with new found clarity. In art, Duchamp presents ideas as sculptures.

DR. WILLIAM FINK:

Clarity does not equal science. There is no field of science called memetics.

HOWARD CAMPBELL:

Kuhn would argue that that is yet to be seen.

[PAUSE]

I keep forgetting you never read Kuhn's *Structure of Scientific Revolution.* Time will tell what the politics, the consensus, of Science, will deem *real.*

We are on the cusp of a new understanding of consciousness. Perhaps the biggest social breakthrough ever, a redefining of the mass values to praise sustainability. Anything else is worshiping false idols.

DR. WILLIAM FINK:

You know how many schizophrenics I've heard say stuff like that? False idols? Age of Aquarius shit. It ain't happening. We already learned that the earth is round and then that it travels around the sun. End of story.

There aren't any major paradigm shifts left.

HOWARD CAMPBELL:

[VOICE RAISED]

How arrogant!

[RESUME NORMAL VOICE]

But you're not alone. Every generation thinks they have all the answers. Or, I should say, the least imaginative people of every generation thinks that.

[PAUSE]

I told you stories about events Richard had internalized because he read about these events in my book, *The Longer Line*. That is the only way I can figure he had my email address. I had never met this man before.

DR. WILLIAM FINK:

Go on.

HOWARD CAMPBELL:

Reading is powerful like that. It irks me when elementary school libraries have a pizza party to celebrate reading. At the end of the day, reading isn't a party. It's you and the book. It isn't an extroverted event. Reading is living art in the palm of your hands. Hegel says that an art object is that which catapults your mind to an altered state of consciousness that you never fully return from. Isn't that the acquisition of new perceptions? Some knowledge you can never go back from. It's a seed that crystallizes, and your mind is never the same thereafter. *That* is memetic propagation. Then if they tell somebody, it happens again. Memes in books are like viruses suspended in resin. If given appropriate carbon, they can grow or fester again. What's important about reading is that you can discover that other people have had similar experiences to yours, and hearing how they approached the scenario is like reading about poker, you become more apt to gauge where you stand and what your options actually are. But, you gotta keep pursuing the type of information or experiences that are very dear to your heart. And, that takes a persistence that few people have. And to write one's experiences of these endeavors is even rarer.

Those who do have this persistence, and have written, usually have been raised in the means to expect many liberties. They were raised with money and an expectation that they would go to college. This expectation gives them direction and perseverance. Yet their objective is usually not the pursuit of the idea, but the pursuit of a degree. Tracking the ideas is just a means to that reward. Others have a glimpse of muse and write down their experiences, but lack the discipline to give it clarity and see their thoughts to their ends. Both of these types of writings sometimes just offer validation of another having had similar experiences, or ideas, and that is enough. Sometimes they contain a brilliant insight embedded within a string of other notions. And, that is well worth the read. But those authors who fought for their minds, and carved out the space to think freely, and then describe their path—these works are extraordinary to me. They feel like a gift addressed to me.

[SILENCE]

I'm sorry for rambling. I've been concerned, no, preoccupied with when this would happen, when you would accuse me of being full of shit.

[PAUSE]

And here it is, and I have extra energy.

[PAUSE]

DR. WILLIAM FINK:

We found Richard's family. At first, we thought we had the wrong family because none of their facts matched what we thought we knew—what you told us—about Richard Wilson.

[SILENCE]

Your lies jeopardized Richard.

[PAUSE]

Have you no respect for Richard's life and family?

HOWARD CAMPBELL:

Family? Family is a biological granfalloon. Memetic similarities override biologic relations. In the War Between the States, brothers fought for opposing ideologies. I have grave respect for life. I love life. In fact, I'll go a step further and say that love *is* life. Life is not always love, but it works the other way. Matter is energy. Energy is matter. Energy materializes. Love is that which binds. Fuller says that love is metaphysical gravity. Love is the antonym of Entropy.

DR. WILLIAM FINK:

You should be one of my patients.

[PAUSE]

HOWARD CAMPBELL:

Did you learn anything valuable from Richard's family?

DR. WILLIAM FINK:

I got real background. I learned his *real* family history.

[PAUSE]

HOWARD CAMPBELL:

He is an only child, his parents divorced when he was young. He lived with his mother. He dropped out of college. He surfs. She doesn't know any of his friends. She hasn't seen him in over two years. She reported that Richard was heavily involved with drugs. He spent time traveling with the band Phish.

[PAUSE]

DR. WILLIAM FINK:

How do you know this?

HOWARD CAMPBELL:

I saw him.

[PAUSE]

DR. WILLIAM FINK:

Did he talk with you?

HOWARD CAMPBELL:

No. He was catatonic.

DR. WILLIAM FINK:

Then, how do you know this?

HOWARD CAMPBELL:

This is what I do for a living. I listen. I listen to what people say, but I learn more by listening to how people present themselves.

DR. WILLIAM FINK:

How could you possible have gotten anything from a catatonic man? He presented himself as wearing hospital garb.

HOWARD CAMPBELL:

I've been meaning to talk to you about the hospital garb. Those clothes are so dreary, and frankly, humiliating. I imagine patients would feel better if they could wear happier clothes. There is a correlation between what people wear and how people feel. Look at the Allman Brothers.

DR. WILLIAM FINK:

I know dressing well gives people confidence, but the Allman Brothers?

HOWARD CAMPBELL:

Yeah. Their first record label gave them outfits that made them feel icky. Their music sounds squelched. It sucked. They weren't comfortable in their own skin because they weren't comfortable in their clothes.

The garb you have Richard wearing is demeaning. His hairy ass hanging out and all. Why can't you have him wear the clothes he came in wearing, or some other civies? You know, GAP khakis or something. Or, better yet, jeans and a T-shirt.

The robe does show his tanned legs, one with a white band near the ankle, the type of un-tanned area that only a regular surfer gets from where they Velcro the tether to their board.

Also, he was all Guatted-out.

DR. WILLIAM FINK:

Guatted-out?

HOWARD CAMPBELL:

Had Guatemalan clothing. He had a Guat shirt, a Guat hat, Guat shorts. I saw his clothes that he came-in wearing. The orderlies wouldn't let me see his personal effects, but his clothes were in his room.

DR. WILLIAM FINK:

What does Guatemalan clothing have to do with anything you said, being an only child of divorced parents, living with his mother, dropping out of college, and his mom not seeing him in over two years. And I don't know what it means to travel with fish.

HOWARD CAMPBELL:

Phish is a band. He traveled with them and sold Guatemalan clothing at their shows. No surfer wears that much Guat. Core surfers wear Guat because it's cheap. But Richard had all Guat, which means it was real cheap. So he was a Guat vender. Phish was in Hawaii the week before Richard was brought here to the hospital.

DR. WILLIAM FINK:

That might explain the twelve hundred dollars we found on him.

[PAUSE]

His mom thought he was probably selling drugs.

HOWARD CAMPBELL:

How did his parents find him?

DR. WILLIAM FINK:

They hired a private detective when he had been out of contact for his second birthday. It took the detective eight months to track him down to here.

HOWARD CAMPBELL:

But he's only been here less than four months.

DR. WILLIAM FINK:

His mom hadn't heard from him in nearly two years. She didn't know if he was dead or alive. And, we didn't do any of the things we normally do to try and find relatives of catatonic patients. She could have found him sooner.

[PAUSE]

HOWARD CAMPBELL:

You didn't tell me about the money.

DR. WILLIAM FINK:

It didn't seem relevant. Plus, with your story, he had money, and it made sense. It's part of why I believed you.

I first saw Richard and thought it was odd that such a well-groomed kid looked like a beach rat who sold drugs. I thought it was drug money until I met you. Then after speaking to Mrs. Wilson, I thought it was drug money again.

HOWARD CAMPBELL:

And now?

DR. WILLIAM FINK:

Now, I don't know.

HOWARD CAMPBELL:

His mom doesn't know shit. He didn't make his money selling drugs. At least not much, if he did at all. But not for the moral reasons you hold as dear. Like I said, he was smart enough to see the liabilities of getting busted.

DR. WILLIAM FINK:

What about the other stuff?

HOWARD CAMPBELL:

The single mom *stuff* was straight out of *Drama of a Gifted Child*. Richard read a lot. How old is Bucky?

DR. WILLIAM FINK:

Richard is 23.

HOWARD CAMPBELL:

Yes, Richard. Well, that's about as far as I got. You didn't think it was odd that he was at Bennington at 13?

DR. WILLIAM FINK:

Interesting. No. It hadn't dawned on me that the two of you couldn't have been in school together until I learned that you weren't what you presented yourself as, a college friend of Richard's. Then I did the math.

HOWARD CAMPBELL:

Interesting? Fucking tragic, a kid with his brain feeling so disenfranchised that he is led to commits himself to a mental hospital. Since our first meeting, I've been waiting for you to ask me about that age discrepancy. Or, about how I had met him at Bennington College, yet had been with him five years earlier when he bought the book *Magick*.

DR. WILLIAM FINK:

Richard Wilson didn't commit himself to the hospital. He was brought here in a catatonic stupor.

HOWARD CAMPBELL:

Maybe a matter of semantics.

DR. WILLIAM FINK:

The police called an ambulance to bring him in.

HOWARD CAMPBELL:

If he hadn't anticipated being brought here, then why did he have the note asking for me to explain him?

[PAUSE]

DR. WILLIAM FINK:

I don't know.

[SILENCE]

HOWARD CAMPBELL:

You appear to me as unenlightened.

DR. WILLIAM FINK:

I beg your pardon.

HOWARD CAMPBELL:

No need.

DR. WILLIAM FINK:

What did you say?

HOWARD CAMPBELL:

That you didn't need to beg my pardon.

DR. WILLIAM FINK:

Before that.

[PAUSE]

HOWARD CAMPBELL:

You appear to me as unenlightened. So long as you want honesty.

DR. WILLIAM FINK:

Why would I want enlightenment?

[PAUSE]

HOWARD CAMPBELL:

A better question is, why do you *want?*

DR. WILLIAM FINK:

What?

[SILENCE]

Why do I want WHAT?

HOWARD CAMPBELL:

Not what.

DR. WILLIAM FINK:

What do you mean "not what"?

HOWARD CAMPBELL:

I mean the question was complete: Why do you *want*?

DR. WILLIAM FINK:

Oh, you're getting psychological on me.

HOWARD CAMPBELL:

I'm not getting fucking psychological on you. You are the objectivist. You can't see It. You are elitist scum without the presence to see your elitism, and that's what makes you scum, because you hold others down without seeing It. You never read *Emergency* did you?

[SILENCE]

That's my problem with you shrinks, you're so uneducated.

DR. WILLIAM FINK:

I graduated from Harvard.

HOWARD CAMPBELL:

Am I supposed to be impressed with that label? You don't know shit, and what's worse is that you don't *know* it. If you could drop your pretension, we might make some progress.

DR. WILLIAM FINK:

Progress towards what?

HOWARD CAMPBELL:

Away from what.

DR. WILLIAM FINK:

What is away from what?

HOWARD CAMPBELL:

Away from what is a multiplicity of experiences, some of which are often grouped as enlightenment. What is Attaccan. Non-what is Naceriman. But that description is completely Attaccan. So, it is meaningless since that which it describes is not of the description. Nacerima can't be shown; you must see it for yourself.

DR. WILLIAM FINK:

You've watched *The Matrix* too many times.

HOWARD CAMPBELL:

That piece of Hollywood phantasmagoria?

DR. WILLIAM FINK:

Who's the elitist?

HOWARD CAMPBELL:

I'm an elitist. But that's not the point. There is a difference between what can be done to you and what you must do for yourself if it should happen. You can't force somebody to see culture as matrix, or make somebody see a Zen koan. In fact, applying force or stress probably slows the process. Just like you can't make somebody relax, you can only help them.

But back to your point, I know I'm an elitist, which helps me not always be scum. Your agnosia makes you a slave to an unseen master. I try to serve myself. That makes me more human than you.

The Matrix is a great way to popularize the story of Socrates and his contemplative perspective. How do you know reality? How do you know you exist?

DR. WILLIAM FINK:

Cogito ergo sum. Descartes.

HOWARD CAMPBELL:

Thinking proves you exist, it doesn't prove external reality. *The Matrix* suggests that the mass of humanity does not live in reality, but in a virtual space. You are already in the looking glass, and have always lived in the looking glass, so the looking glass appears normal to you. *The Matrix* explores the impact of culture on individuals.

DR. WILLIAM FINK:

The matrix isn't real.

HOWARD CAMPBELL:

Culture is real. The matrix is Culture.

DR. WILLIAM FINK:

The matrix is a construct to get some philosophy into a teenage movie.

HOWARD CAMPBELL:

No metaphor. The matrix is real. Matrix equals *culture*.
[PAUSE]

The compacting of technological advancement has compacted our visible event horizon. Fuller talks about this. His point is that since technology is advancing so quickly now, we can't see the change. It is like the frog in the boiling water I mentioned the other day.
[PAUSE]

When most people think of the word "culture," they think of festivals, pageants, and languages they don't understand. Or, they have a vague image of Third World poverty. Or, something else equally limited.

[PAUSE]

Culture equals ideology. An ideology is a meme-plex, a complex organism of memes. Think of meme-plex as a group of people connected by their traveling as a tribe, or as Kurt Vonnegut termed "karass" in *Cat's Cradle*. Now, stop looking at the people, and just look at the idea that's the glue that holds them together.

[PAUSE]

Weapons are an integral part of an ideology, meme-plex, or karass. However, weapons are not permanently tied to specific ideologies. Memetics allows for mini-memes within a meme-plex to be adopted by a competitive meme-plex. So, weapons created by one meme-plex can be adopted by another. The predominate culture has historically been the ideology with the baddest bad-ass weapons. This idea has been made popular to the literati through *Guns, Germs and Steel*.

DR. WILLIAM FINK:

Where are you going? This feels like you are just spouting your philosophy. What does any of this have to do with Richard?

HOWARD CAMPBELL:

Richard had spent some time with The Peace Corps or some other heal-the-Earth non-profit, right?

DR. WILLIAM FINK:

Mr. Wilson spent time with The American Friends Service Committee about a year ago.

HOWARD CAMPBELL:

Richard might have realized what Neo does not.

DR. WILLIAM FINK:

Which is what exactly?

HOWARD CAMPBELL:

Zion was created for Neo, and everybody else who rejected the Matrix. But, Zion is also a construct; it is a matrix by another name. Did you know that Republicans run the Peace Corps?

DR. WILLIAM FINK:

What?

HOWARD CAMPBELL:

Yes, I've worked on their ad campaign. I felt funny when I learned that The Peace Corps is run by a director that is appointed by the current president. The Peace Corps exists for people who reject *the system*, and yet it's run by the same heads of state that run *the system*.

When Richard learned that, it could've freaked him out.

[PAUSE]

One of the main points I get from *The Matrix* is that Zionists want to make you aware of where you are. They call this knowledge, "freeing the mind." But the mind doesn't become free; it just knows where it is. So, freedom as defined in *The Matrix* is clearly seeing where you are within the larger system. There is only one matrix. Zion exists within the matrix, it's just the subset of matrix citizens who comprehend the matrix and wish to substantively alter its course.

War is show business, part of the props, pomp and circumstance of competing cultures.

More and more people are seeing this. I think Microsoft Windows helps to this end.

DR. WILLIAM FINK:

How can a software program help us see culture differently?

190

HOWARD CAMPBELL:

Windows demonstrates reality within a reality—people are learning fractal structure. People are beginning to see the cosmos as a Holographic Universe. Computer users are getting better at distinguishing realities, and meshing realities, because they are learning the distinction and interconnectedness of universes through Microsoft Windows. I hold that culture is on the brink of comprehending what Lucas stated in *Star Wars*, that corporations have become The Empire—Corporations are the new empire. Like the British Empire, same structure.

DR. WILLIAM FINK:

But you are co-mingling things that are real with ideas. And, treating ideas as if they are real, just because we have a word for something.

HOWARD CAMPBELL:

Gravity is real without a word. Packs of animals have culture without a word for their group dynamics. The Matrix is the contrivance of the culture. It's the structure that exists beyond any individual. It's where to hide secret knowledge if your audience isn't contemporary. The trick is to get commerce to perpetuate your secret knowledge. Either that or find a university or museum to preserve the ideas, which probably won't happen unless they have some commercial value. In *The Matrix*, the oracle is a program, the sentinels and Smiths are programs, but they have tangible impacts on the humans they encounter. Publishing is how we play in The Matrix. Publishing a contrarian's perspective lets future Neos know they are not alone. By publishing, one creates their own Oracle, embedded in *The Matrix*.

DR. WILLIAM FINK:

You are insane.

HOWARD CAMPBELL:

Certifiably. But that doesn't change the fact that I am better at what you do than you are. You don't even *know* what you do. What do you do?

DR. WILLIAM FINK:

I help patients change their behavior.   I heal people.

HOWARD CAMPBELL:

Bullshit.   How many people have you healed?   Give me one name and address. I'd like to meet a healed person. You assimilate people. You make people work within a machine you cannot see. German psychologists during the Holocaust helped Nazi officers process their input. You are dumb.

DR. WILLIAM FINK:

I have an IQ of 162.

HOWARD CAMPBELL:

IQ was invented during World War I and used en masse during World War II to ascertain proclivities towards success performing specific tasks. A tool invented by psychologists for a war effort. You are proud that a tool of domination has deemed you as good as it gets? You narcissistic, blind, little man. IQ stands for Intelligence Quotient, from tests created in 1905 by Alfred Binet to determine whether children were sufficiently intelligent to benefit from schooling. Although the tests are often referred to as intelligence tests, their results can only identify strengths and weaknesses in children's learning styles. You do not have an IQ. No one does. What you have is a score obtained from a test attempting to measure proclivity towards learning styles, which by the way has been revealed to test acclimation to dominant white culture.

Psychologists defined IQs over 140 "genius." The average IQ for those obtaining a Ph.D. degree is 141. A psychologist with a Ph.D. must reach the obvious conclusion.

[PAUSE]

Intelligence is a qualitative understanding, and attempting to quantify qualitative relationships is mixing metaphors. In fact, it occurs to me as arrogant to promote that there is only one intelligence, *one that labels the labeler as a genius.* The IQ system of labeling appears to me as a tool for a deformed culture to ratify its deformity as beautiful. It is a closed-loop system that feeds back to its elite that they are good. This is intellishit, internal validity without respect to external reality.

[PAUSE]

DR. WILLIAM FINK:

Most people don't have what it takes to be a psychologist.

HOWARD CAMPBELL:

Most people don't have what it takes to traverse a glacier and build an igloo, but you don't see Inuits calling people morons. Howard Gardner is promoting a new paradigm: multiple intelligences. My computer's spell check doesn't recognize intelligence as having a plural.

It seems obvious to me that people have different gifts. Most of psychology is still based on comparing an individual to the masses. If the person is not near the "center" of the common tested element, they are labeled abnormal. This illustrates a lack of understanding of the social ramifications of Einstein's relativity and separate universes. If average is normal, and America is depressed, is it so bad to be abnormal?

Our country has limited respect for intellectual diversity. A 1993 U. S. Department of Education investigation of the status of gifted American students, revealed the depth of anti-intellectualism in American schools. It's not surprising that gifted children are often called "nerd" and "dweeb," but the study found evidence that gifted African-Americans are often accused by their peers of "acting white."

[SILENCE]

DR. WILLIAM FINK:

I think you should go now.

HOWARD CAMPBELL:

A novice umpire, a seasoned umpire, and a journeyman umpire are asked how they tell the difference between balls and strikes: Novice umpire— some pitches are balls, some are strikes. I call them as they are. Seasoned umpire—some pitches are balls, some are strikes. I call them as I see them. Journeyman umpire—some pitches are balls, some are strikes...

[PAUSE]

…but they are nothing until I call them.

DR. WILLIAM FINK:

You should go now.

HOWARD CAMPBELL:

It would be useful for me to see the contents of Richard's backpack.

I may be able to see what has gotten him hung up. I'm expecting to find a copy of my manuscript, *Perpetual Motion,* and I'm hoping to find a journal.

DR. WILLIAM FINK:

I thought you had his journal.

HOWARD CAMPBELL:

I made that up. I staged the photographs and I wrote what I brought in and presented as his journal.

DR. WILLIAM FINK:

Shit.

[SOUND: POUND]

Fuck you. I can't take this. I'm still sorting out what is real and what is not.

[SOUND: SCREACH]

[PAUSE]

I am not inclined to humor you any longer. I do not suffer fools lightly. Will you leave right now, please?

[SILENCE]

HOWARD CAMPBELL:

Remember when I talked about sociopaths earlier? You defined them from DSM as charismatic and hyperbolic, blaming the system, saying that the system forces them to act the way they do, devoid of tension and anxiety, path dependent and genuinely without a *conscience*. A public corporation's doctrine of fiduciary responsibility combined with their legal status is a sociopath incubator. Corporations are incapable of doing anything other than what they do because they are driven by their fiduciary responsibility. There are many parallels between sociopaths and corporations. Intelligent and manipulative? Corporations hire the smartest and most persuasive. Charismatic? They advertise. Hyperbolic? Again, they advertise, but they also self promote stock prospectuses and public relations. Blames the system? *They are* the system. When companies are caught doing something wrong, the most common retort is, "But, this is the only way to be competitive." Devoid of tension, anxiety and guilt? It ain't alive. Path dependent? Laws and fiduciary responsibilities. If corporations are structurally sociopaths, can a world order comprised of such entities be our best possible choice?

[PAUSE]

The answer is no.

DR. WILLIAM FINK:

That is truly disturbing.

HOWARD CAMPBELL:

I didn't make that up. It is an observation from a California reporter named Richard Brenneman. But this be false and upon me proven, then I'm the one that belongs inside here.

[SILENCE]

Some filmmakers in Canada also came up with this idea, but I doubt they had the idea back in 1992. Just shows that credit goes to the first that promotes their idea.

DR. WILLIAM FINK:

I'm too busy to waste my time with your delusions about reality.

HOWARD CAMPBELL:

Delusions? It is the average American who is delusional because they mistake illusion as reality. Show me a naturally occurring phenomenon in humans today. We are so saturated by the influence of media that we can't see straight.

Maybe that's what Richard wanted me to explain to you. In *The Longer Line*, I discuss how the sprite.com launch party was entirely synthesized.

If you watched it on MTV, it looked like a bunch of very powerful hip hop stars so love Sprite that they are willing to perform at sprite.com's launch party. No way any corporation could afford to pay that kind of talent just for a party. Well, that's true. MTV had another show that Sprite sponsored. The sprite.com launch party show was aired a couple weeks prior to the other show, making it look like these talent stars just love Sprite. But it went another step into the unreal. The kids at the party, they were all paid fifty bucks to be there. The only way you can ensure the perfectly hip crowd is to invite the exact crowd you want. But kids watching this at home saw it as a *real* party.

[PAUSE]

Vonnegut suggests that the government has been assisted in its policies by television, stating: "Television is now our form of government."

Even in Vegas, they make proposition players announce that the house is paying them. But not in Corporateland. You never know who sponsors whom.

[PAUSE]

Broadway now allows product placement.

DR. WILLIAM FINK:

What do you mean that Broadway now has product placement?

HOWARD CAMPBELL:

You know how in *Wayne's World* they made fun of the casual use of products and pointed out that it was obviously product placements? Like how in *The Truman Show* the wife would say something obtuse and Jim Carrey would ask why she talked that way, because it felt fake to him. Movies have done this for years. Corporations pay for their products to be placed in movie scenes. It's just another form of advertising. The pointing it out for comedy won't last long. It will feel tired to see this device exploited too many times. Sprite did it with its spokesmen being presented as paid shills, but they couldn't maintain the gag for long. What felt fresh and real for a period of time, just becomes accepted as true and no longer funny as a revelation.

Well, now shows on Broadway will have actors drinking Pepsi.

[PAUSE]

DR. WILLIAM FINK:

How do you know this?

HOWARD CAMPBELL:

I work for Omniscient, the world's largest media conglomerate. Our goal is to create a full interactive experience with our client's products in the most rich and realistic environments possible. Omniscient sees its clients as a revenue delivery system. They aren't a communication company; they're a human interaction delivery mechanism, servicing everything from recruitment to health care to private investigation and security. They do population control, overseeing everything that relates to employees as depicted in George Orwell's *1984*. Omniscient companies interface with humans. They are beginning to comprehensively manage *human resources*. Humans are not souls, but energy to be extracted and managed.

DR. WILLIAM FINK:

You are being a little extreme.

HOWARD CAMPBELL:

Am I? Omniscient companies handle everything that relates to humans. From company culture to ascertaining if employees are doing what they are supposed to, all the way down to screening emails. When voice recognition software is privately available, they will screen phone calls also.

DR. WILLIAM FINK:

Privately available? You mean the government has this capability?

HOWARD CAMPBELL:

Yes. The word exploit literally means to use fully. We use the word exploited when people are being oppressed, because people are not supposed to be *used fully*. But employers feel entitled to fully use their employees in the work place.

[PAUSE]

DR. WILLIAM FINK:

Don't they have that right?

HOWARD CAMPBELL:

The question isn't whether they are legally entitled to do this. The question is about whether they should have this legal entitlement.

But the saturation is comprehensive and invisible in non-personal ways. A celebrity on *Oprah* talked about some great drug they were on, and afterwards, it turned out they were being paid by the pharmaceutical company. That's the kind of product placement that irks me. It is the invisibility that ruffles my feathers. Fortunately, now, guests must disclose who they receive compensation from, before they go on TV talk shows. But, the invasion of sponsored events becomes smaller and smaller and more and more invisible. Last night, a girl offered to buy me a Miller Lite. I thought I was getting lucky. It turns out she was hired by Miller. Think about that level of marketing saturation. Will they hire prostitutes to fuck me if I agree to drink Miller Lite exclusively for the next three years? If I put together a cost analysis, they might be willing to hire the hooker if they didn't fear a PR backlash.

[SILENCE]

How long before the news is purely an entertainment device?
[PAUSE]

DR. WILLIAM FINK:

The news is already entertainment...We're done. You're just ranting at this point. Stuff I hear in leftist literature.

I'm tired of you wasting my time. You will have to leave now.

HOWARD CAMPBELL:

How long were you a chef?

DR. WILLIAM FINK:

What does that have to do with anything? How did you know I was a chef?

HOWARD CAMPBELL:

When we shook hands the first time, I knew you were a chef, a sauté chef.

DR. WILLIAM FINK:

Did you hire a private eye on me? Or, did you dig that up on your own?

HOWARD CAMPBELL:

No. Neither. When we shook hands, I knew. Your hand is callused, in a place and way, which few things other than the repetitive use of a chef's knife can create.

DR. WILLIAM FINK:

But, how could you possibly know I was a sauté chef?

HOWARD CAMPBELL:

You had corrective surgery on your right forearm to get rid of the oil burns. What's fascinating to me is that you chose to get rid of those marks, through expensive surgery, while you chose to leave the callus, which is much less expensive and less painful to remove. I imagine it's a badge of honor, of how you paid your way through med school. You really pride yourself on your learning. You probably graduating from culinary school with honors, only to find that chefs don't garner the respect you imagined. That's part of why you became a psychiatrist. You got an MD then got a Ph.D. in psychology.

[PAUSE]

I'll bet you five dollars I can tell you something you know, that you once said nobody would ever ask you again.

[SILENCE]

Do you want to bet?

DR. WILLIAM FINK:

I'm not playing with you.

HOWARD CAMPBELL:

Oh, but you should. You'd have so much more fun.

DR. WILLIAM FINK:

Mr. Campbell, this isn't what I do for fun. I'm a doctor.

HOWARD CAMPBELL:

As you've mentioned. You can tell me I'm wrong and I'll give you the five dollars.

[SOUND: CHAIR SCREECHING]

[PAUSE]

Hell, let's make it a hundred.

[SOUND: THUD OF WALLET ON TABLE]

What are the 103 ways you can cook an egg?

[SILENCE]

DR. WILLIAM FINK:

I never bet.

HOWARD CAMPBELL:

That's ok. You can keep the money.

DR. WILLIAM FINK:

No. You are right.

Not only can I remember the 103, I can write them in order.

HOWARD CAMPBELL:

I know.

DR. WILLIAM FINK:

How can you know this?

HOWARD CAMPBELL:

I'm good at what I do.

[PAUSE]

DR. WILLIAM FINK:

Why have you been coming here?

HOWARD CAMPBELL:

Primarily, because I was invited.

DR. WILLIAM FINK:

This is too much of an effort to simply come because you were invited.

HOWARD CAMPBELL:

I'm a Bokonist. The invitation occurred to me as a religious obligation.

[PAUSE]

DR. WILLIAM FINK:

Am I supposed to take you seriously now?

HOWARD CAMPBELL:

I don't know.

DR. WILLIAM FINK:

What do you mean you don't know? This is your show. This is your stage. You orchestrated this whole scenario.

HOWARD CAMPBELL:

I didn't orchestrate Richard Wilson being catatonic.

[PAUSE]

You invited my ideas into your house. Whether you choose to take me seriously, or not, is up to you. I just ask that you don't mock me. I don't like to be mocked.

[PAUSE]

DR. WILLIAM FINK:

I'm angry.

HOWARD CAMPBELL:

Thank you for being honest.

DR. WILLIAM FINK:

That's more than I can thank you for.

HOWARD CAMPBELL:

True enough.

[PAUSE]

I'm sorry.

I do feel like I wronged you. That wasn't my intention.

DR. WILLIAM FINK:

How am I supposed to feel?

HOWARD CAMPBELL:

There is no proper way to feel.

DR. WILLIAM FINK:

Well, how am I supposed to feel since you duped me? Are you proud of your ruse?

HOWARD CAMPBELL:

No.

You can't breathe through your eyelids.

DR. WILLIAM FINK:

What's that supposed to mean?

HOWARD CAMPBELL:

Its from the movie *Bull Durham*. Susan Sarandon says that to the young baseball prodigy about the lessons she gave him. The coaching helped him be a better player. When he called bullshit on her, she replied, "Of course, silly. You can't breathe through your eyelids." It doesn't mean that the coaching didn't work, it just means that it might not make literal sense.

DR. WILLIAM FINK:

I do buy that.

HOWARD CAMPBELL:

You just took a big step into a much larger universe.

DR. WILLIAM FINK:

That's the part that irks me. You seem so condescendingly self-assured.

HOWARD CAMPBELL:

I don't feel self-assured.

DR. WILLIAM FINK:

Well, you come across like you know that there is a better, more advanced, way for me to live.

HOWARD CAMPBELL:

Isn't that the same tone you take with your patients?

DR. WILLIAM FINK:

Yes, but I'm a doctor. I have patients.

HOWARD CAMPBELL:

Okay.

DR. WILLIAM FINK:

I feel like you're being smug with me.

[SILENCE]

What do you do?

HOWARD CAMPBELL:

I work in advertising.

DR. WILLIAM FINK:

Why are you here?

HOWARD CAMPBELL:

I was invited.

DR. WILLIAM FINK:

No really, why are you here?

HOWARD CAMPBELL:

I told you. Because I was invited.

DR. WILLIAM FINK:

Are you a journalist?

HOWARD CAMPBELL:

No.

DR. WILLIAM FINK:

What are doing with your writing?

HOWARD CAMPBELL:

I'm working on a book.

DR. WILLIAM FINK:

Will you include our conversations in this book?

[SILENCE]

HOWARD CAMPBELL:

The book will reflect our conversations. I'm trying to explain…

DR. WILLIAM FINK:

Get the fuck out of here! GET THE FUCK OUT!!!

HOWARD CAMPBELL:

You asked me to be honest with you.
[SOUND: CHAIR SCREECHING]
It's a book about marketing.
[SOUND: PHONE BEING DIALED]

DR. WILLIAM FINK:

Hello, security? I have an intruder.
[SOUND: CHAIR SCREECHING. FOOT STEPS]
[SOUND: ZIPPER UNZIPPING. THUD OF BOOK ON TABLE]
What's this?
Hello? He's five foot ten. Brown hair. About 200 pounds.

HOWARD CAMPBELL:

It's the book I'm writing.

DR. WILLIAM FINK:

I don't want this.
Hello? I need you here now.
[SOUND: FOOTSTEPS]
Yes, it's an emergency.
[SOUND: DOOR OPENS AND CLOSES]
He's walking down the west corridor. Fuck. Hold on a sec.
[SOUND: RECORDER SWITCHING OFF]

(DISCUSSION OMITTED)
[SOUND: RECORDER SWITCHING ON]

SESSION 5

VOICE OF DR. WILLIAM FINK:

April 12, 2003, session five with Howard Campbell.

[PAUSE]

Thank you for coming back.

HOWARD CAMPBELL:

You're welcome.

I've thought a lot about what might have led to Richard's hospitalization, and I have an idea. I was rereading my own books. In *Perpetual Motion,* I explain a mental experiment I did back in 1992: I stopped being self-deprecating. I suggest to the reader that if they want to be more powerful, they should stop being self-deprecating, that being self-deprecating undermines your charisma. I think he may have tried it.

DR. WILLIAM FINK:

Why would that be a pivotal experience?

HOWARD CAMPBELL:

Because when you stop being self-deprecating, it can upset your standing in social circles, because people treat you differently. Transitioning into increased power can be very disorienting.

DR. WILLIAM FINK:

I'll take that into consideration.

[PAUSE]

HOWARD CAMPBELL:

I don't think you appreciate how different Richard is from his peers.

DR. WILLIAM FINK:

What do you mean?

HOWARD CAMPBELL:

Ever see the movie *Finding Forrester?*

DR. WILLIAM FINK:

No. Should I?

HOWARD CAMPBELL:

Well, the lead character is an inner-city black kid who is wicked smart. He hides his intelligence so he can fit in and hang with his set.

DR. WILLIAM FINK:

And?

HOWARD CAMPBELL:

And, I think this is also true of Richard Wilson. Most people are easily fascinated by demonstrations of stupidity, especially among men. That helps explain why so many men love *The Three Stooges*. Few men are engaged by sustained intelligence. Richard falls into this latter group.

DR. WILLIAM FINK:

I'll bear this in mind.

HOWARD CAMPBELL:

I guess I am a little nervous being back here. You were damn pissed at me when I was here last. I half-expected you wouldn't see me.

[PAUSE]

You were fucking livid.

DR. WILLIAM FINK:

I was. I'm sorry I yelled at you.

[PAUSE]

I'm embarrassed I called security on you. I want to get that out of the way.

HOWARD CAMPBELL:

It's all right. I appreciate the apology.

DR. WILLIAM FINK:

I need to know what might have sent Richard over the edge. You might be able to help. Richard had a copy of both of your manuscripts, *The Longer Line* and *Perpetual Motion* plus he had *Emergency*, which you reference in *The Longer Line*.

I listened to the tapes of the conversations you and I had.

[PAUSE]

Guess what? We found a Phish ticket used as a bookmark in Richard's journal.

HOWARD CAMPBELL:

Lucky guess.

DR. WILLIAM FINK:

Maybe so. But, a lot of thought went into that guess. It was a good guess.

HOWARD CAMPBELL:

Richard read *Perpetual Motion*.

DR. WILLIAM FINK:

Why did you figure that?

HOWARD CAMPBELL:

My e-mail address was in *Perpetual Motion*. I couldn't figure out any other way for Richard to have my e-mail address. I distributed about a hundred copies of *Perpetual Motion* and *The Longer Line*. Somehow he got copies. He probably knows somebody who went to Bennington or somebody who worked at Deutsch advertising. But those people gave them to others, so maybe he doesn't. Plenty of people I don't know have them now. May I take his copies of my books with me?

DR. WILLIAM FINK:

Yes. By the way, I Xeroxed his journal for you, so you can take that, too. I can make little of its entries.

HOWARD CAMPBELL:

I'm glad he had a journal. I'll start reading it tonight. That is a good sign, that he was journaling. It's also a good sign he had *Emergency*. Having *Emergency* suggests he was using my references as a means of creating his own reading list. In *Perpetual Motion*, I explained how I did that with *Zen And The Art Of Motorcycle Maintenance*. Did you read my manuscripts?

DR. WILLIAM FINK:

They're rather incomprehensible.

HOWARD CAMPBELL:

Not to Richard they weren't.

DR. WILLIAM FINK:

They're riddled with spelling and grammatical errors.

HOWARD CAMPBELL:

Yeah, but the content is good. There are ideas in there you've never seen before.

DR. WILLIAM FINK:

That's why I invited you back.

HOWARD CAMPBELL:

Thank you. I'll tell you about them as we go on. One of these ideas may have been the catalyst for Richard's lapse. Maybe first I should pick up where I left off, talking about when Bucky went back to school after he left the hospital.

DR. WILLIAM FINK:

You are Bucky.

HOWARD CAMPBELL:

Not exactly. I am Howard Campbell…

DR. WILLIAM FINK:

My patient is Richard Wilson, and in the story you've been telling me, *you* are Bucky. These experiences—Bennington, the hospital there, entraining with the tree, and everything else—they happened to you. It says so in your book.
[PAUSE]

HOWARD CAMPBELL:

Child psychologists will often use puppets so children can tell a story without having to first-person-speak. I would prefer to continue in the same voice I've been using. Besides, for me the term *Bucky* is similar to how you use "schizophrenic," a label for people who have knowledge that doesn't jive with what is accepted as okay by psychiatrists. But yes, as I talk about "Bucky" now, I am speaking about my own experiences.

DR. WILLIAM FINK:

Talking about your self as Bucky is third-person-speak. You present your self as an alter ego.

HOWARD CAMPBELL:

You're beginning to catch my language. Look, at Southern Vermont Hospital, your system at one point classified me, at my purest, as paranoid schizophrenic. As a schizophrenic, misplacing pronouns maybe the only way to communicate my ideas.

Richard adopted a debilitating memeplex while reading my manuscript.

You've invited me back to better understand why Richard checked-out. I wish Richard hadn't checked out. I wish he had become a self-sufficient freelance writer, as I had instructed. I tell every "Bucky" to be a freelance writer, in addition to their day job. Write what you see. Please. Sometimes I will speak in first person, sometimes in third person. It's a mind control technique. If I say *he*, meaning *me*, it's easier for you to transfer the *he* with *I* and then the meme is more deeply embedded in your psyche. Have you studied neuro-linguistic programming?

[SILENCE]

You've never read *Thought Control In Totalitarian China?*
[PAUSE]

I didn't think so. The book is a study of how the Chinese government converted people to their new regime, now labeled as communist. My point is that within this book, they outline the methods of thought conversion, also known as brainwashing, they employed, and to what extent each technique worked. Our current government uses many of these techniques in unusual ways. Commercial enterprises employ these techniques, too. Remember when companies had contests, and they asked for consumers to write that they 'prefer Tide' or write some slogan? You know why they asked consumers to write these sentiments? Because what we write becomes part of *who we are.* What we commit to words literally affects our future, even if we say we don't believe it when we write it. It seems like P&G read *Thought Control* in the '50s and had a huge edge up on other social engineers who called themselves marketers. Is it such a leap to hold that Proctor and Gamble marketers used the brainwashing techniques of cruelian China? Read *Soap Operas*, the book about the industry, not TV shows, and then you tell me. Write me an essay contrasting the two only after you've dug for similarities. If you want to change peoples' behavior, why not research the experts on behavior change who work in fields outside your own?

[SILENCE]

That was a question. Do you know why they want to change peoples' behavior? Because it helps them make money, *because it helps them make money.* I'm talking about business. Regardless of what I'm working on, if a client asks me: "Why are working on that?" the answer is always: "Because I'm trying to help you make more money."

I am a consumer profiler. Just as a police profiler can deduce the characteristics of a murderer, you can give me any product, in any category, and I can tell you subtleties about its buyers. At the Account Planning Group convention in 2000, they had a leading F.B.I. profiler speak. We are the same animal, but one set works for the government and the other for commerce. I'm not so certain these are separate entities. Given a budget to conduct consumer research, I can get damn accurate and predictive against specific criteria. Consumer profilers are skilled at identifying what qualitative differences may be leveraged to garner substantive results.

Consumer research grew out of polling. It was treated as a science, without garnering absolute results of the specific, long before chaos theory or quantum physics had shown the value of studying something that provided no definitive knowledge about a specific, but only a general, likelihood. Probability was the first modern science that did not study the specific, but sought to uncover incidence. Why? To help 17th century insurers consistently make money. You live within the system. The system cannot be shown to you; you must see it for yourself. Few people study the history of history. We fixate on the now, romancing the current as if it's significant. We treat the now as if it's Truth. When was the last time you looked at a history book from 1950? See if that looks like truth. It did to many in 1950. Now, look at a history from 1850. You get my point. My point is that we track events, but we rarely show the evolution of perspective. This creates a sense that now is truer than any previous truth. I hold that truth is what we are attempting to live into. To this end, we currently have no future.

DR. WILLIAM FINK:

I feel like you're lecturing me. I want to hear more about what in your manuscript might have affected Richard.

HOWARD CAMPBELL:

I'm telling you what's in my book. What we're discussing, and the content of my book, are the same.

[SOUND: KNOCK ON DOOR]

[SOUND: DOOR OPENS]

FEMALE VOICE:

Excuse me doctor. Your wife is on line-two. Do you want me to transfer it in here?

DR. WILLIAM FINK:

No. I'll take it in the corridor.

Howard, this'll just take a minute. My wife didn't want to buy a TV without speaking to me first.

HOWARD CAMPBELL:

Okay.

[SOUND: DOOR CLOSES]

♪♪ [ROCK MUSIC: DIGITIZED VERSION OF *Satisfaction*] ♪♪

This is Den... Uh, huh. Okay.

[PAUSE]

No. Listen, I don't care how great they think Rollover is. The study showed it is only worth a 9% premium. They're killing us on price. We're 30% more for the same number of minutes.

[PAUSE]

I need to discuss this tomorrow.

[PAUSE]

Because I'm busy right now. Listen, I gotta go.

[PAUSE]

Tomorrow.

[PAUSE]

Yeah. Bye.

[SOUND: CELL PHONE FLIPS CLOSED]

[SILENCE]

[SILENCE]

[SOUND: DOOR OPENS]

DR. WILLIAM FINK:

Sorry about that.

HOWARD CAMPBELL:

Not a problem.

DR. WILLIAM FINK:

Where were we?

HOWARD CAMPBELL:

I was talking about what Richard would've read about in *Perpetual Motion*. After the hospital, I was back at Bennington. At school, after a week, I felt like one of the bunch again. But, it took me probably three years to reach a comparable comfort level with my family.

Part of my conditional return to Bennington College was that I stay on the prescribed medications. This isn't something you can fake. I was having blood drawn once a day to monitor my Lithium blood levels. They gave me five different meds, one called Trilliphon. This is weird shit, but you know that. Not weird because it acted as the anti-hallucinogen it was designed to be, but because of a side-effect of distorting my vision. They didn't tell me about this because they didn't want to trigger a psychosomatic effect. On my third day back at school, I noticed I was having trouble seeing distant objects. Within three hours, my vision deteriorated to about 20/500, very disturbing. Before a friend rushed me to the hospital, a nurse at Bennington saw this as a possible side effect in the *Physician's Desk Reference*. It took two days for my sight to return to normal. I bought a copy of the *Physician's Desk*

Reference. Good book to have if you're on medications. A bad book to have if you're on medications and prone to psychosomatic symptoms you read about. I recommend getting it.

DR. WILLIAM FINK:

Psychosomatic ailments are always a problem.

HOWARD CAMPBELL:

I wouldn't always call the phenomenon a problem. It's the same mechanism that makes placebos work.

Anyway, I found my meds disturbing.

DR. WILLIAM FINK:

This is common. Two-thirds of the patients who are hospitalized and prescribed Lithium go off Lithium. Of these, 70% have a relapse and are re-hospitalized within a year of going off Lithium. There are many papers written addressing the issue of patients' compliance with Lithium prescriptions.

HOWARD CAMPBELL:

I think the issue isn't in keeping patients on Lithium, but finding a solution where these people experience a life they find works for them. If being on Lithium isn't working, maybe finding ways to keep people on Lithium isn't the solution. Maybe there is a better way than Lithium.

I found the effect of Lithium disconcerting. I thought differently. Lithium kept my ideas in Attacca. It didn't let my Nacireman self dance with my Attaccan self. I know Lithium was the drug that caused this effect, because after a few weeks this was the only drug I was on.

I found Lithium turned my head into a plodding machine. I never had runaway thoughts. I never thought weird tangents. I thought about one thought at a time. My mind was simple. It wasn't creative. I was less motivated. My sex drive was negligible.

I finished the semester on meds, and with no major discrepancies with what most people label as reality. After my "recovery," I performed my show for parents' weekend. One of the parents managed a theater on Martha's

Vineyard and invited me to perform there. The second night's show was the best performance I have ever given in my life. I flowed. The drumming worked. My speech made sense to both Attaccans and Naciremans. I explained both to each other. I talked about memes. I discussed how memetics played into politics and advertising. I talked about the importance of sound bites because they were easily replicated, and so they had the genetic advantage of being breeders. I talked about economics. I discussed Bucky's theory that wealth was the ability to sustain a pattern of living into the future. Two-thirds of the house gave us a standing ovation. Our team was charged.

DR. WILLIAM FINK:

You never met Richard Wilson.

HOWARD CAMPBELL:

Not that Bucky. I met Buckminster Fuller when I was 12 years old. I was talking about his theories in the show. And, that is who I was modeling myself after in our earlier conversations when I told you I was describing Bucky. It wasn't your Bucky—Richard Wilson—and it wasn't exactly me either.

"The Bucky virus" is what I call having Buckminster Fuller's perception. Bucky Fuller held that our mass education instills a blindness to comprehending the concept of Universe, one-one, a compartmentalization style of thinking that begs the question, "What's outside of the universe?" Fuller reiterated that Universe means absolutely everything.

[PAUSE]

Can you detect when an alien meme broaches your mind? I don't think you can. You didn't follow when I discussed the concept of *understand*.

Maybe you can't. Getting the Bucky virus increases your sensitivity. It is like a Christian saying they see the devil in anything challenging or a Scientologist saying something is obscuring their "clear" state of mind.

This gets back to the insight that prompted the Sacra Congregatio de Propaganda Fide. If you get people to understand something, their actions will follow. What a person accepts as fact, affects how they act. Understanding is the act of *standing under a precept*. Are you following?

DR. WILLIAM FINK:

No.

HOWARD CAMPBELL:

Yes, you are. You're following because I am leading the conversation. You just aren't tracking. That's okay. Enough is penetrating to effect a change. These ideas will bubble up in your thoughts over the next few days, or maybe longer, and it won't occur to you that they're connected. It will seem to you like a random thought. This is a fallacy. Our mind doesn't present random ideas. Our mind projects related concepts. Most people don't seek the connections. Some do through dream analysis, but most don't see the parallel of fleeting thoughts while awake. These fleeting thoughts are similar to waking dreams: the subconscious has deemed something worthy of focus.

Buckminster Fuller contended that Euclidean geometry messes with our heads. He suggested that if geometry is the study of space, it falls apart because it's not projectable to nature. What is real is that which has integrity. The Bucky Virus exists because it has pattern integrity. Bucky said a pattern has an integrity independent of its medium. The Bucky Virus is a meme. It exists outside of the perceiver. To quote Buckminster Fuller verbatim, "Pattern Integrity is when a pattern has integrity independent of the medium by virtue of which you have received the information that it exists." This is applicable to advertising.

DR. WILLIAM FINK:

How so?

HOWARD CAMPBELL:

If we replace the word "pattern" with the word "brand," we create the statement: "A brand has an integrity independent of the medium by which you have received the information that it exists." A brand has an integrity independent of the product, product name, product logo, advertisements, or any other brand accessory.

Fuller sees humans as evolutionary patterns. While interviewing him, he asked me to think of our mind, and the outside world, as akin to a rubber doughnut that you can continuously turn inside out. Fuller was illustrating the systemic affects of thoughts and experiences; we manifest what we think, as we internalize what we experience. The rotating doughnut has its inside becoming the outside, and, its outside becomes its inside, in an ongoing metamorphosis that never ends. This simultaneous recreation of inside and outside is constant and continuous, constant fluid movement. *Kind of like this conversation in some ways...*

[PAUSE]

This doughnut model is what inspired me to name my first manifesto, *Perpetual Motion.*

DR. WILLIAM FINK:

Why?

HOWARD CAMPBELL:

Because the Universe is the only known perpetual motion system. Because we have discovered perpetual motion, but most people just can't see it.

[PAUSE]

What's on the inside manifests the outside, and the outside saturates the inside. One's perception of a product affects your experience of the product, and your experience of a product affects your perception of it.

One can have many different interpretations of the same data points. As a marketer, I help people look for the stimulus that will help them have their best experience. It's kind of like a *Panic* song, "Why can't we know to see the things that make us happy?"

DR. WILLIAM FINK:

I'm not quite following. *Panic?*

HOWARD CAMPBELL:

Panic, as in Widespread Panic.

DR. WILLIAM FINK:

What is *Widespread Panic?*

HOWARD CAMPBELL:

Mass hysteria.

[PAUSE]

Just kidding. *Wide Spread Panic* is the name of a band, a band that checks out the psychology of modern Americana.

[PAUSE]

Take your home. You chose the contents, the colors and even the structure. Other minds may have designed the structure, and designed the furnishings, but your mind selected these things. If something has been with you your whole life, that means you have chosen to not eliminate this element. These elements are manifestations of your values. The essence of your mind has made all of these selections. Imagine a doughnut rotating toward its own hole. The part of it that was outside is now inside, and the part that was originally inside is now outside.

The mathematical name for this shape is a torus. The importance of the doughnut shape, or torus, is that it has an inside and an outside that can invert on itself. Bucky said that this is why humans and intelligence evolves. He said that each individual is a pattern integrity, claiming that the pattern integrity of the human individual is evolutionary and not static.

As a marketer, I work on finding a cool way of looking at a product, which the experience of the product will support. The brand essence you construct defines your brand's values.

DR. WILLIAM FINK:

A brand essence?

HOWARD CAMPBELL:

In the '70s, a premiere game show was launched called *The $20,000 Pyramid*, offering the largest payoff of a game show up until then. The show gained popularity. Soon, other evening game shows were offering large payouts. The "premiere" status of $20,000 was eroding. In order to remain true to their essence, the show became *The $100,000 Pyramid*. The marketplace changed the meaning of $20,000. The brand's values and essence remained the same. The show had to change to reflect the constant values. A changing marketplace effects consumer's perceptions of your brand. Their shift in perception will shift their relationship with your brand. The cycle never stops.

DR. WILLIAM FINK:

They pay you well for this?

HOWARD CAMPBELL:

Yes.

[PAUSE]

DR. WILLIAM FINK:

Why?

HOWARD CAMPBELL:

Because it helps them make money.

[PAUSE]

If you want to discover what idea of mine may have incited Richard to go over the edge, you have to hear my story, and when you understand me and my ideas, you will clearly see how a mind can dis-integrate.

[PAUSE]

(TRANSCRIBER'S NOTATION ON HYPHENATION: "DIS-INTEGRATE" IS BEING PRONOUNCED AS TWO WORDS.)

And to do that, I have to educate you.

DR. WILLIAM FINK:

Okay. Go on.

HOWARD CAMPBELL:

Let's begin.

About 700,000 years ago, Homo Erectus was beginning to master fire. Homo Erectus was on the verge of metamorphosing into homo sapiens. Over the next 100,000 years, the size of our brain would double. Mastering fire manipulation taxed the mental power of Homo Erectus.

Survival favored big brains; those packs of Homo Erectus monkeys able to master fire were often the packs with slightly more brain space. Survival favoritism can be seen as having two intertwined components: genetic and memetic. Genetic evolution is traceable in body changes; Memetic evolution is traceable through cognitive changes. Genetic and memetic evolution are indelibly intertwined and manifest themselves physically.

Trying to understand favoritism in evolution is like guessing the mechanism of a closed watch. Although we'll never be able to open this watch, knowing the outcome we can try and infer the inner workings.

DR. WILLIAM FINK:

Is that analogy taken from Albert Einstein?

HOWARD CAMPBELL:

Yes, but he used the watch analogy to describe god and understanding the Universe.

If current humans only use a set percentage of our brains, it can be surmised that a slightly larger brain would access greater capacity to assimilate, if the percentage of one's brain utilized remained constant. Presently, it appears that there is little opportunity for our brains to grow in size. An increased cranium may throw off our physical balance and balancing hardwiring.

But 700,000 years ago, there was an opportunity for brain size to increase while imparting minimal affects on our body. Fire's affect on food is malleability. Cooked food requires less effort to chew, allowing for smaller teeth and smaller muscles, therefore increasing the cranium space available for the brain. Also, it was during this time that Homo Erectus began pounding grains, also relieving the need for exceptionally strong biting and grinding abilities. The effect of Homo Erectus' food preparation technology was an accelerated big brain favoritism. Don't mistake this for surviving because they were smarter. Survival favored those monkeys who maximized this opportunity. As Darwin says, "It is not the strongest of the species that survive, nor the most intelligent, but the one most responsive to change."

Approximately 20,000 years ago, humans began to record on what are called "batons" the celestial observations known to repeat themselves with the seasons. This technology of reading and writing preceded regional settling. This notation was essential in terms of feeling safe. As humans, we needed a sense of stability before we were ready as a tribe to settle down. In fact, settling down didn't even occur as a possibility since we were still chasing our food sources.

Early man was lead by shamans, those who were more closely in tune with nature than the rest of the tribe. In essence, shamans were scientists. However, their science encompassed both nature and spirituality. An increased ability to understand the history of nature lead to an increased ability to forecast nature, and that proved to have a direct correlation to the probability of survival. My point is that the same holds true today. But there is another point here: knowledge surpassed physical strength in proclivity to survive. Knowledge became power.

When humans began to record celestial observations known to repeat themselves with the seasons on those "batons," the tribe's shaman likely used them to predict the events of nature. Knowing when to fish or hunt for certain animals brought great advantage to tribes that incorporated this technology.

Batons are the first known deliberate and detailed use of a device to extend the memory, notating sequences of nature outside of the brain. Previously, it has been speculated that many of these sequenced observations were passed through the generations via ritual. While we'd used pictures before this time to depict scenes from hunts and recurring seasons, people didn't have records of the details of events noted to repeat themselves cyclically.

Batons were made of carved bone or antler horn. Several thousand have survived, and they appear in most cultures of the period. The baton is covered with markings that correspond to events in nature. Some of the marks are simple lines, others are curved lines, and some are a grouping of dots. Some historians speculate that the baton is the root of the image of the magic wand in folklore.

About 9,000 BC, we started domesticating animals to. This was the beginning of Man not just using nature, but feeling like he owned living things. A couple thousand years later, man began to plant seeds. Around 5,000 BC, communities emerged, as man stayed in one location and created food around him.

Accumulating stuff requires different efforts than finding stuff. If your tribe is nomadic, there is little need for property rights—you have *your* animal and some stuff, but all *your* stuff is on you, or in very close proximity. But when you're stationary, you can accumulate stuff, and you can have stuff nearby that you expect to be there when you go to it. So you need to know what you own and have others know that even though you aren't guarding something, it's still yours. Tokens were established to represent physical items. A new level of abstraction emerged. If you had one cow and one token for a cow, then the token of the cow now equaled your cow. There was a direct representation between a symbol and something else. In addition, tokens began appearing with a symbol of the leader, so names were developing.

Improved ability in farming lead to abundance. Not having an immediate need for what has been produced requires accounting of what's on hand. Originally, a cross tick equaled one. However, many cross ticks was incomprehensible. And, as communities grew larger, comprehending their resources required new ways of looking at the data. Tremendous surplus lead to mathematics. The use of numbers other than one tick equaling one item seems to have developed circa 3,000 BC.

[PAUSE]

I have another story.

DR. WILLIAM FINK:
Go ahead.

HOWARD CAMPBELL:
There is a story of a kid at UCLA who was taking an exam when the professor called out, "I will accept no late papers. You have two minutes to complete your exam. If you do not have your exam to me at precisely 3p.m., you have failed this final." This one kid was working away, writing furiously. He was finished as the teacher began to count from ten to zero. He was fighting his way past exiting students. The student made it to the teacher just seconds after the teacher said, "Okay, it's 3 o'clock. I will accept no more exams." The kid handed his exam to the teacher. The teacher gave it back and said he would accept no late exams. The student tried to argue with the teacher. He complained about the exiting students getting in his way. He pleaded that the teacher saw him coming. He argued that if he'd known this rule prior to the exam, he would've sat up-front. It was all to no avail. Then, he asked the professor, "Do you have any idea who I am?" The teacher said

no. The student lifted up the stack of exams and put his in the middle of the stack and ran out.

DR. WILLIAM FINK:

That sounds like something you might do.

[PAUSE]

You go from 3,000 years ago to a modern story, what are you getting at?

HOWARD CAMPBELL:

I'm exploring the role of perception in power. The best way to do that is to examine the leaps in consciousness we've made over the past few hundred millennia. The words "psychology" and "consciousness" are brand new to our vernacular and understanding. Looking at how concepts of self and ownership and righteousness emerged is helpful in understanding what might trigger a disintegration of the self.

Until the 20th century, the "unconscious" was unknown. Thought is mostly unconscious, and abstract thoughts are largely metaphorical. I take gravity for granted, but at an earlier age it was a revolutionary idea.

Let's look at consciousness. William James said that the greatest discovery of his generation was that a human being can alter his life by altering his attitudes. I hold that we tend to create that which we focus on. So, what we look at is what we create. When you choose your perception, you are creating your future.

DR. WILLIAM FINK:

I'm not surprised. That's a little further out on a limb than I'm willing to go.

HOWARD CAMPBELL:

I'm not surprised. Psychology has grown to adopt an evolutionary perspective based on blind adaptation. This means that our skills have evolved not because they were good for an individual, but because the effect of that adaptation was good for the survival of our species.

Depression does not necessarily benefit the individual, but it may have helped maintain tight knit tribes. A depressed person is more likely to be picked-off by a predator than a healthy human. Evolutionary psychology

228

seeks to see if there is an evolutionary benefit to this mechanism. For instance, if going contrary to a group triggers depressive chemicals in our body.

DR. WILLIAM FINK:

We know that separating from a group that we have grown accustomed to often precedes depression. But then, so does any major change. But an evolutionary benefit?

HOWARD CAMPBELL:

Genes haven't evolved for the individual. The individual human or animal or plant is happenstance. Genes that exist now made it because their gene pool was best suited to sustain that particular gene. Memes that exist now made it because their meme pool was best suited to sustain that particular meme. Memes organize humans.

DR. WILLIAM FINK:

Specific please.

HOWARD CAMPBELL:

Government. It's a memeplex, but our form of government was an idea that didn't exist 300 years ago.

DR. WILLIAM FINK:

Good point.

HOWARD CAMPBELL:

I got off track from my time at Bennington. Bennington allows students to create their own major. I choose ontology, the study of being. My work at Bennington examined generalized patterns of thought. I saw some people as predominately what I labeled Attaccans, and some people primarily as what I labeled Naciremans. I've discussed those distinctions in our previous conversations.

I saw Attaccans as people who are good at playing with representations, whether in words or equations. I saw these people as comfortable in the realm of the abstract. They primarily function and process information in "facts." They remember facts. These people often appear "grounded." They tend to be good at noticing the actual. They tend to be literal and accurate at remembering details. Sometimes they complain that Naciremans "can't be trusted." Attaccans are slower to arrive at judgments. However, evidence can quickly change their perception.

Nacerimans are more comfortable in aesthetics. They tend to intuit ideas and flow with what "feels" right. Complex notions can appear to these people as a whole. They lack an attention to detail, so many times they appear flighty because for them arriving at 8:05 AM is the "same difference" as 8 AM, they're both *early*. They are prone to complaining that Attaccans "get hung up on things." Naciremans have immediate reactions to situations. When presented with "evidence," they may hear it, but cling to a gut reaction. Myers-Briggs labels similar distinctions as *Judgers* and *Perceivers*. Physiologically, our skin will register reactions to negative situations before we consciously know to avoid them. This chick gave people four decks of cards and hooked them up to electrodes, and had them play a game for cash, but all the decks were rigged, two good and two bad. These subjects' skin could discern the bad decks before the subject would avoid them to make more money. Perceivers are more in touch with their skin than judgers.

The truth is that we are all perceivers and judgers, with a dominant proclivity. Strong integration is one's ability to swim in both realms. Historically, I'm an Attaccan. However, I'm very intuitive. Notions of new constructs, of looking at scenarios, will come to me in a flash. It will feel right, and thereafter, I will see things differently.

DR. WILLIAM FINK:

Isn't this just an artistic temperament?

HOWARD CAMPBELL:

I don't know. I do hold that men tend to live in Attacca, while women tend to live in Nacirema. MIT is 70% male. Bennington College is 60% female. Anthropologists vs. Chameleons. I find Attaccans tend to take a scientific approach to their environment, while Naciremans tend to flow with their environments. Anthropologists study their environments; Chameleons entrain with the rhythms of their environment.

An amusing note on gender mixes. I've read that to keep primates in the zoo, a good mix is one male to every three females. If they have too many males, they fight. A majority of women helps keep the peace. I found that at a college like Bennington, 60% female/40% male was a good mixture. It was this way when I got there. When I left, it was 70% female. Bennington is laden with Naciremans, both male and female. Gay men, I have found, tend to be Naciremans. Roughly half the guys at Bennington are gay. While many women may have slept with other women, there were comparatively few lesbians. If half the guys of a 40% male college population aren't available for sex with women, then there are only 20% available. 60% available women to 20% available men, this is the same 3 to 1 ratio that works well in zoos. Bennington is a zoo of adolescent humans. When I left, the ratio was 70% women to 30% men, so with only half of those guys sexually available, we were looking at an available female to male ratio of 70% to 15%. That's nearly 5 to 1. The freshman girls got angry when they didn't get any. Some guys think this ratio would have been heaven. They have never lived in a sea of women who think they should be getting what they aren't.

DR. WILLIAM FINK:

I'm willing to try.

HOWARD CAMPBELL:

That was a joke. You made a funny.

DR. WILLIAM FINK:

You're teasing me.

HOWARD CAMPBELL:

Yes, I am.

Think about gatherings. Men gather and talk about football, something external that revolves around points and other symbols. Women used to, and still do in many parts of this country, gather around church groups, entraining into a universal energy. You find both in both. I'm stereotyping.

I see people who are diagnosed as bipolar slipping from being Attaccan-based to being Nacireman-based. Most people are generally grounded in one or the other, and while they might have experiences in the foreign realm, they are still attached to their native land. Bipolars, I see, as switching bases, literally changing their orientation. Disorientation then follows, because rapid cycling creates great disorientation.

DR. WILLIAM FINK:

Psychology recognizes rapid cycling.

HOWARD CAMPBELL:

Yes, but then you don't do anything with this knowledge. For the bipolar, not recognizing what is occurring can feel like different spirits possessing one's body. I literally see the spirits as changing. I see it as the same spirits we always have with us, but different spirits are leading my moods.

Bipolar disorder used to be called manic depression. I see mania as highflying Nacirema and depression as deep-dwelling Attacca.

Psychologists describe manic patients as impulsive. It's characteristic for these patients to disregard the rules of Attacca, spending on whatever they like or having extramarital affairs. I know that in a "manic" state, I am sexually charged. I attract women. I must give off pheromones that attract and excite women. Buzz whir. At the heights of manic Nacirema, I'm going with the flow and flowing with the curves. I'm dancing with the energies and giving off extraordinary vibes. I've become the quintessential chameleon, which is odd for me because I tend towards being an Attaccan. Chameleons meld, and manics are the ultimate melders; this is contagious and inviting to Naciremans. Nacirema in its purest sense is seeking to entrain with oneness. Nacirema is connectedness. Connectedness is part of love.

Manics flow with a Universal vibe. It's no wonder to me that some bipolars report having religious experiences. I believe them. The words may sound crazy, but trying to describe Nacirema in English, which is a territory within Attacca, is back to tap dancing about architecture. Shrinks who ask patients to describe these experiences are often creating a greater disintegration of the patient's mind rather than helping to heal.

DR. WILLIAM FINK:

We do the best we can.

HOWARD CAMPBELL:

Psychologists describe depressive patients as being withdrawn, with a lowered sex drive. Attacca spirals inward. It's not being present, but instead in Its own world. Attaccans have a tendency to study, to bring external ideas into one's head in a static way. Sex drive is lowered because the depressive person is inwardly focused, so there's no desire to meld with others. One's thoughts are an island. I become an anthropologist of myself. When I'm depressive, I feel like I'm wearing girl repellant. Nobody wants to be studied during sex.

The thing is, slipping into the inward spiral also feels wrong. I reach for somebody, something to pull me out. But it doesn't happen because I'm not able to entrain. Love knows no boundaries. The reverse is also true, boundaries preclude connection and love.

Manic-Depressive: It's the same person, but with different spirits leading the pack. It's the same person wearing a different spiritual face.

Ever seen a two-dimensional cube that when you stare at it you can see it two different ways? It's the same cube, just oriented differently. Same difference.

DR. WILLIAM FINK:

I'm more interested in what you wrote about, and what happened in school, than your theories in my area of expertise.

HOWARD CAMPBELL:

They're one in the same. My book is about what happened to me at school and my theories about what happened. Being back at school afforded me contact with kids and teachers who knew about the stuff I was grappling with. I was looking at thoughts as living organisms. I went to Alex, the guy who tortured plants, for lessons in genetics. Alex turned me onto Dawkins. Alex talked about isolation breeding mutation. How gene pools separated, become distinct. If you have a large group of insects that get separated by, let's say a fire, they grow distinctions. If they're separated long enough, they become different enough so that they can no longer breed with each other. If they become reunited, whichever one has the better-suited distinctions becomes the predominant critter.

Alex talked about survival of the fit. Fit had many different meanings. An individual animal could be very fit, and survive well. A hawk, who makes it through adolescence generally lives to breed. This type of species can be thought of as survivors. Or, a species may be fit enough to continue living, but there's very little chance of any individual animal surviving, like a rabbit. Most rabbits become food before they have a chance to reproduce. They continue as a species because rabbits reproduce in huge quantities. This type of species can be thought of as a breeder. Alex talked about the difference of temperaments between these animals. Breeders tend to be schitzy while survivors tend to be calmer.

Of course, there are exceptions or combinations of these two types. There is a theory that everybody can be divided into two groups: those who can be divided into two groups, and those who can't.

[LAUGHTER FROM DR. WILLIAM FINK.]

Companies use this type of groupings to help them make money. It's called segmenting—you group like animals together. In a questionnaire, a market research firm may spend 25 minutes asking a consumer to rate how accurately 70 statements describe their lifestyle, attitudes, or habits, on a scale of 1 to 10.

A computer then compares all of the answers from all of the participants, looking for patterns and possible groupings. Ideally, you wind up with five to nine groupings of rather similar customers. That is, within each grouping, customers share fairly similar values, attitudes or habits or some combination thereof. Then, you can identify the target with the greatest profit potential.

A sick consumer is one who is not loyal.

DR. WILLIAM FINK:

That's a funny way to define health.

HOWARD CAMPBELL:

Is it? Prosperity is the chief divining rod of success from the company's perspective. Structurally, it is quite similar to how my therapist Joey segmented people into four quirky styles: Obsessive-Compulsive, Paranoid, Hysterical and Impulsive. There isn't much of a difference, except that Joey viewed everybody as sick, and segmentation studies at least see loyal customers as healthy.

John Nash is a Nobel Prize winning mathematician, physicist and game theoretician. At the age of thirty he had a mental breakdown and thought that aliens were contacting him.

When people ask me how I thought that there could be a secret order of magicians ruling this planet, how a logical person could live this perception, I like to point to Nash's explanation, "The ideas just came to me. They came to me just like a solution to a problem. How was I to distinguish these notions as being any different than the ones that helped explain how the universe works?" When I was a contrarian, I would ask if it were ludicrous for the Greeks to have had a God named Fred, who created everything, and was in control of everything, and that they knew Fred knocked-up this chick, who had a god-baby who was murdered, but came back to life, but for only three days, and that now the god-baby in spirit, but as a grown man, and his daddy watch us from heaven, and make stuff happen, and will damn us if we don't acknowledge and thank them, regularly. Most Christians reject the fact that Jesus was black.

DR. WILLIAM FINK:

You can't deny somebody their religion.

HOWARD CAMPBELL:

At what cost? I'm with you, but then it gets complicated. The line-length study shows that people often go insane when they conform to a societal standard with which they disagree.

DR. WILLIAM FINK:

What line-length study?

HOWARD CAMPBELL:

The one by Dr. Ash.

DR. WILLIAM FINK:

I'm not familiar with it.

HOWARD CAMPBELL:

I'll come back to it. It is important, but let me finish this thought first.

[PAUSE]

One-hundred years ago, people saw spirits in everything. With the onset of the industrial revolution, we have discredited this mystical perception. Today, there's a stigma attached to saying that you're a mystic. It's almost as bad as being called a liberal.

I am a mystic. I know there are things beyond my comprehension. I know that there is more between heaven and Earth than my philosophies allow.

I see Truth in the description, "He's not in good spirits." I see that multiple spirits will war when in close proximity, if agitated. I hear: "He's not in good spirits" as, "He is not filled with integrated memes." When I hear the word spirit, I find I can often use the word meme. I think this helps me be spiritual.

DR. WILLIAM FINK:

That's interesting.

HOWARD CAMPBELL:

I see many people around me scoffing at others' religions. I only tend to scoff when I feel those religions being pushed down my throat. I have deep respect for people entraining to energy greater than themselves. I see fewer and fewer people doing this. This makes them linger in Attacca longer and longer. Lingering in Attacca doesn't feel good. Attacca should be entered and exited, but lingering there has a similar effect to watching infomercials for too long, one feels suddenly compelled to do something inane, like order and maybe even use a Flowbie.

As a culture, we're spending more and more time in Attaccan waters. Attacca has a tendency to heat things up. I see us swimming in hot waters; I see that the temperature has been turned up so slowly that as a culture, we are like the frog that doesn't know to jump before the heat of the water boils him, permanently debilitating his ability to jump.

DR. WILLIAM FINK:

This is what you were getting at, about us not having a future? Is this what helped lead to Richard's breakdown?

HOWARD CAMPBELL:

Not a communal future that we promote, as a society. It's all about the individual. How something relates to individual prosperity, whether individual be a person, a family, or a nation, but not one-one.

Everything in Attacca is relative. Symbols only exist in relation to something else. Breaking out of Attacca is removing yourself from perceived relativity. It doesn't mean anything, until It is applied to something real.

My hesitation towards advertising is similar to my qualms about working in quantitative research; they're both intrusions into peoples' personal space.

As citizens in our market economy, we trade our attention for services. Free TV is free because we agree to ingest commercials.

Advertising and marketing research is an ongoing experiment on public perceptions. We live in a meme pool. We should start fining those companies that are peeing in the pool. If we define infractions, we could start doing this. I feel some advertisements should be illegal because they spread negative memes. There was an Excedrin commercial out several years ago that threw out a vibe that was akin to having a headache. I feel there should be a council set up to ticket companies for inflicting this pain on us, similar to how they set up a council to monitor experiments on humans.

What makes me hesitant about our whole economic system is that the system seems to be in place purely to perpetuate itself without regard to quality. We humans are supposed to bring quality with our votes, but the majority of us are voting against our monetary position and not for a greater good. And the game keeps mutating. We're playing financial musical chairs with fewer and fewer people able to find a chair.

My dad asked me if it was truly more competitive now than before. I stared at a frog not realizing the water was warming. I told him that in 1970, there were 380 banks that had 10 or more branches. In 2000, there were less than 40. That is 340 fewer ad agencies with a bank as a client. Okay, that's a personal perspective of how my career is more competitive than it may have been, but I know it's also true for executives at banks; there are fewer places for them to be bank executives. Aren't we recreating a feudal system of power justified by an imaginary force? Is this not religion but with agreed upon rules? On this theatrical stage, I'm a monkey who stepped-in when there were already rules in place that I can't stand on certain ladders.

DR. WILLIAM FINK:

You resent not being higher on the ladder?

HOWARD CAMPBELL:

No! Not that kind of ladder! The ladder refers to the story of the monkeys I told you earlier. The increased competitiveness is just a fact. Resenting increased competitiveness is like begrudging water for getting hot. It just happens. But the world is a substantively more competitive place, partially because there are more people, partially because information is so much more accessible.

Regardless of competition, sometimes just knowing something is possible is enough to replicate action. Look at the four-minute mile.

DR. WILLIAM FINK:

Once one person did it then a slew of others soon followed?

HOWARD CAMPBELL:

Exactly. Pirsig's *Zen and the Art of Motorcycle Maintenance* is an exploration of quality. The process of working this through is the structure of the book. It's amazing to me how unpopular *Lila*, Pirsig's second book, was compared to his first. *Zen* provided a means to overcoming gumption. *Lila* talked about choices one makes once they find themselves productive. *Lila* was an inquiry into morals. If *Zen* was intellectual caffeine, *Lila* was intellectual valium.

Ahh fuck. I'm losing you again.

DR. WILLIAM FINK:

I'm getting tired.

HOWARD CAMPBELL:

Why don't you take a nap and we'll start again tomorrow. Then, I have to get back home tomorrow night. I want to leave you today with a quote.

[SOUND: CHAIR ADJUSTING AND PAPER UNFOLDING]

Pirsig from his *Zen* book: "Technology is blamed for a lot of loneliness, since the loneliness is certainly associated with the newer technological devices...TV, jets, freeways and so on...but I hope it's been made plain that the real evil isn't the objects of technology, but the tendency of technology to isolate people into lonely attitudes of objectivity. It's the objectivity, the dualistic way of looking at things underlying technology that produces the evil. That's why I went to so much trouble to show how technology could be used to destroy the evil. A person who knows how to fix motorcycles...with Quality...is less likely to run short of friends than one who doesn't. And they aren't going to see him as some kind of object either. Quality destroys objectivity every time."

DR. WILLIAM FINK:

I know people feel more alienated today than they used to. I've ascribed it to not having the threat of death over us the way people used to have death as a bigger part of their lives. I'm really tired. We're done.

HOWARD CAMPBELL:

A short story before we split: a kid at UCLA who was taking an exam on the philosophy of existence. The teacher said, "Prove that this chair exists." Students began writing furiously as students often do taking a final. One kid didn't lift his pen for more than a half-hour. He just thought about the problem for a while. After long pondering, he'd turned in his one-sentence response: "What chair?" He received the only A.

A similar story speaks of a teacher who said that a double negative in many cultures equaled a positive, but that in no culture did a double positive equal a negative. A kid in the back spoke out, "Yeah, right."

DR. WILLIAM FINK:

Okay, goodnight.

HOWARD CAMPBELL:

Yeah, I'm gonna go read Richard's novel. See you in the morning.

[SOUND: RECORDER SWITCHING OFF]
(DISCUSSION OMITTED)
[SOUND: RECORDER SWITCHING ON]

SESSION 6

DR. WILLIAM FINK:

April 13, 2003, session six with Howard Campbell.

Howard, I don't know how to say this. I have some bad news...

HOWARD CAMPBELL:

I'm sorry to cut you off. Actually, I have some bad news, too. But I've got something more important than any bad news. Richard's been faking it. He has journal entries cryptically written over previous entries that reference news events that have happened since he has been in the hospital. I don't know if he has been faking it all along, he doesn't say that I could find, but he's definitely not catatonic now...

DR. WILLIAM FINK:

We know.

HOWARD CAMPBELL:

You know? How come you didn't tell me?

[PAUSE]

What the fuck?!

DR. WILLIAM FINK:

Richard Wilson took his life late last night.

HOWARD CAMPBELL:

Ahh FUCK!

FUCK, FUCK, FUCK! FUCKING, FUCK FUCK!

[CRYING]

Why the fuck would he do that? Why the fuck couldn't he have come down and talked to me?

DR. WILLIAM FINK:

We thought he was in a catatonic stupor.

[PAUSE]

Obviously, he wasn't.

HOWARD CAMPBELL:

[SOBBING SUSTAINED]

[BLOWS NOSE]

[CRYING]

That's a *no-shit*.

[CRYING AND SNIFFLING]

Ah shit. I'm an asshole.

[SNIFFLING]

I could have insisted on spending more time. At least on seeing him one more time.

God damn it!

DR. WILLIAM FINK:

Maybe we should cancel today's session?

HOWARD CAMPBELL:

[SNIFFLING]

Fuck it.

[SNIFFLING]

We're here.

DR. WILLIAM FINK:

I'm going to turn this off and give you a few minutes.

HOWARD CAMPBELL:

Fuck that. Why should you stop recording?

DR. WILLIAM FINK:

I was going to leave the room and give you a few minutes to compose yourself.

HOWARD CAMPBELL:

I am making you uncomfortable.

DR. WILLIAM FINK:

I thought you might want some time. That's why I suggested we cancel today's session.

HOWARD CAMPBELL:

Today's session? Why meet at all? Richard is dead. I warned you I would hold you accountable.

[SNIFLING]

This isn't about Richard anymore.

[PAUSE]

DR. WILLIAM FINK:

I know.

[PAUSE]

HOWARD CAMPBELL:

Why do you want to meet?

[PAUSE]

DR. WILLIAM FINK:

I don't know if it's still appropriate.

HOWARD CAMPBELL:

Fuck appropriate. Why do you want to continue our conversation? Whether it be today, or any other day? Why are we here? What do you want?

[PAUSE]

DR. WILLIAM FINK:

I want to better understand you. I'm learning from you.

[PAUSE]

HOWARD CAMPBELL:

Then, listen to our old tapes. Revisit the material we've covered so far. Then, well meet again.

[PAUSE]

DR. WILLIAM FINK:

Fair enough.

[PAUSE]

You said you had some bad news.

HOWARD CAMPBELL:

I guess everything is relative. It doesn't seem very bad in the face of a suicide. But, I got fired last night.

DR. WILLIAM FINK:

On the telephone?

HOWARD CAMPBELL:

Yes.

DR. WILLIAM FINK:

I'm sorry.

HOWARD CAMPBELL:

Thank you.

DR. WILLIAM FINK:

You're welcome.

[PAUSE]

HOWARD CAMPBELL:

They were right to do it. I was pissed, but right now, I just feel numb. Fuck the job. Let's make this real. What do you really want to know?

DR. WILLIAM FINK:

Maybe we should continue this the next time you're in town?

HOWARD CAMPBELL:

Next time I'm in town? This is Hawaii. It's not like I travel through here to get to Cincinnati. Next time I'm in town? I live in Atlanta. I've been coming here to have these conversations with you. It's not like you go through Hawaii to get to Phoenix, Arizona from Atlanta, Georgia.

DR. WILLIAM FINK:

And, you're going back tonight.

[PAUSE]

HOWARD CAMPBELL:

Fuck that. I don't need to go back tonight. I don't have work tomorrow. But don't fucking change the subject. What do you really want to know? What aren't you asking me?

[PAUSE]

246

Come on.

[PAUSE]

What do you want to talk about?

[PAUSE]

DR. WILLIAM FINK:

Tell me about Dr. Ash's longer line experiment.

HOWARD CAMPBELL:

Fuck the Ash study. What do you really want to know? You can fucking look it up on Google. Is there anything you want to know from me, that only I can tell you?

DR. WILLIAM FINK:

What did you find in Richard's journal?

HOWARD CAMPBELL:

Two very short entries, there may be more, but the two I found reference Bush's war on terrorism. One is dated March 19, and is followed by the words, "Damn Freedom theatre." The other had the date April 9 and says, "Baghdad's father is the son."

[PAUSE]

DR. WILLIAM FINK:

Nothing substantive?

HOWARD CAMPBELL:

Nothing substantive? Huh. It certainly suggests his presence here was more willful than either of us imagined; I'd call them substantive. And, that's just what I found last night. There may be more.

[PAUSE]

If you really wanted to know Richard, why didn't you read his journal?

DR. WILLIAM FINK:

You're right. Honestly, I didn't even know he had a journal. I never checked his personal belongings.

[PAUSE]

HOWARD CAMPBELL:

Well, one of the wardens told me there wasn't anything but clothes, even *in* his backpack. I asked. So, don't hold yourself too responsible.

[PAUSE]

DR. WILLIAM FINK:

How much of what you told me is really about *you*?

HOWARD CAMPBELL:

Every single thing that I said happened to Richard at Bennington, actually happened to me.

[PAUSE]

DR. WILLIAM FINK:

You hallucinated walking into hell?

HOWARD CAMPBELL:

Yes.

[PAUSE]

DR. WILLIAM FINK:

Have you had any other episodes other than what happened at Bennington?

HOWARD CAMPBELL:

Yes.

DR. WILLIAM FINK:

What happened?

HOWARD CAMPBELL:

Ah fuck. I guess I brought this on. I have a hard time talking about these episodes in the first person, because people have a tendency to look at me like I'm crazy when I explain what I experienced.

DR. WILLIAM FINK:

We don't have to, if you don't feel up to it.

HOWARD CAMPBELL:

Damn. It is amazing how much you avoid tense situations, and yet you are a psychiatrist.

[PAUSE]

Okay, I'll tell you what happened. I felt it coming. This time, I was determined to ride it out, not to fight, not to go back to a hospital. This experience didn't come on as suddenly, nor was most of this experience as emotionally isolated. As opposed to four straight days of weirdness, I had a number of bizarre experiences spread out over three months. The details of this experience are hazier for me than the previous trip. I didn't journal the experiences, and there wasn't a definitive moment when they started or when the trip ended. Yet, while I was tripping, I was very aware that reality had taken a detour into the far side, but I wasn't tripping on the fact I was tripping. I'll try and track my experience.

It was January, 1999. I had recently quit my job at Deutsch advertising. I'm sure that was a stressor. And then, I was also in the process of doing a spoken-word magic show. I guess that is a striking similarity to what happened at Bennington.

[PAUSE]

I was driving to the airport to pick up my mentor in magic, Larry Clark and his fiancé, Sandra. I was taking the back way to LAX, by Marina Del Rey. I was coming over a dark hill and my car stalled. It didn't just stall. Al the electricity went out. Everything kaput.

[SILENCE]

DR. WILLIAM FINK:

Then what?

HOWARD CAMPBELL:

Then, I saw lights in the car. The tape in the tape player went back and forth playing snippets of the songs on the tape.

DR. WILLIAM FINK:

What do you mean you saw lights?

HOWARD CAMPBELL:

Lights. Floating points of light. Mostly white, but many colors.

[SILENCE]

DR. WILLIAM FINK:

How did this make you feel?

HOWARD CAMPBELL:

Very present.

DR. WILLIAM FINK:

Were you freaked out?

HOWARD CAMPBELL:

I wasn't panicked, but I can't say that I felt comfortable. I was hyper aware. I had pulled the car over to the side of the road. I didn't know anything peculiar was happening at first. My first thought was: "Ah, shit. How am I going to get to the airport?" I was just sitting there when the lights appeared. They floated around the car, then the tape thing happened. I mellowed out and just absorbed. The tape went back and forth. Sometimes the radio came on. The radio flipped through different stations. I told this to somebody once. They responded by saying, "Yeah, I had a car with a fucked-up electrical system like that once." Maybe. But I was ascribing meaning to what I heard. I was feeling it as a communication directly to me. This event ended with the radio on some AM program where the announcer said, "First, you must love your mom. Life won't be good until you love your mom. Love your mom for all she could do." I can't recall this event without saying, "I love you, Mom."

[SILENCE]

DR. WILLIAM FINK:

Was that the entire experience?

HOWARD CAMPBELL:

No. Immediately following the "Love your mom for all she could do" message, my radio went off, my interior car lights came on and I was able to restart my car.

DR. WILLIAM FINK:

Then things were back to normal?

HOWARD CAMPBELL:

No. Well, I mean, sort of. I was extremely aware that I had just had a non-normal experience. I continued on to the airport, driving extremely carefully. I was replaying what had happened to me in my head again and again. Some more weird stuff happened at the airport. Most notably, the car radio started acting up again. I started asking the radio questions, like if I should go back to Bennington. A radio program came on that discussed property values and ended with the advice to stay put right now. That now was not the time to move from Los Angeles. Even though I wasn't a homeowner, I took that as a "No." I asked a few other questions I don't recall. Finally, I asked if this woman that I was fixated on at work, Jennifer, was whom I would marry.

This time, when the radio came to rest the announcer said, "First of all, her name is Heather." And the radio went off again, fully broken. Would not work. Would not go on, would not play the tape.

DR. WILLIAM FINK:

Other than quitting your job and doing the show, had anything else significant happened in your life?

HOWARD CAMPBELL:

Sort of. A pedophile I had known as an adolescent had just died. Draw your own conclusions from that. I won't talk about that.

DR. WILLIAM FINK:

Why did you bring it up?

HOWARD CAMPBELL:

You asked. And talking about Peter's death may be important. Get this— I've played poker the night before both of my maternal grandparents' funerals. Each time I had extraordinary luck. I even won a bad-beat jackpot with one of them. It felt like I had an angel on my shoulder.

DR. WILLIAM FINK:

Do you believe in an afterlife?

HOWARD CAMPBELL:

No. But I did in my last life.
[PAUSE]

DR. WILLIAM FINK:

[LAUGHTER]

I wasn't expecting a joke.

HOWARD CAMPBELL:

Maybe it was inappropriate.

DR. WILLIAM FINK:

No. It was funny. It is the only death joke I've heard that isn't morbid. Why might Peter's death have been important?

HOWARD CAMPBELL:

Well, if there is an afterlife or angels or something else I can't fathom that we can access or feel from this dimension, maybe Peter was affecting the car.

DR. WILLIAM FINK:

Is that what you think happened, Peter was talking to you through the radio?

HOWARD CAMPBELL:

No. But I don't rule it out either.

DR. WILLIAM FINK:

How'd the car work after that?

HOWARD CAMPBELL:

Worked fine. No problems all the way through when I eventually sold it. When I picked up Larry and Sandra, Sandra said we needed music, and she turned on the radio, and it worked like nothing had been wrong with it.

You know, I met Peter through Larry. Peter was a great mentor to me in many ways. A year before he died, I was with Larry who was having coffee with Peter. Peter asked about me. Larry called me and I came by. Before we left, Peter asked me how I was. I said fine. He held my gaze. He asked again. I paused. I calmed down a notch. I said that life was more complicated than I expected but that I was doing okay. He nodded, adding, "Good." It's weird to speak soul to soul when the vast majority of our conversations in life are more like protocol than real. I think he was asking for forgiveness in this conversation, and I granted it.

DR. WILLIAM FINK:

Did anything else ever happen with the car? Was that the end of the episode?

HOWARD CAMPBELL:

I had thought so. Nothing more happened with the car. I thought that phase of the episode was over. I mean over the three months I had a number of unusual experiences, mostly precognitious stuff. But the day after the car experience, I took a yoga class. After the class, a woman in the class came up to speak with me. She was compelled to share her surprise that a yoga novice had the focus I showed in that class. We spoke for a while. I asked her name. She said, "Heather." Twisp. Of course it was. Fuck, fuck, fuck. Just when I thought I wasn't living in weirdville, there is a callback. I wondered if she was who I was supposed to marry and a bunch of other stuff. I hope she isn't who I am supposed to marry because I never saw her again.

DR. WILLIAM FINK:

What else happened during these three months?

HOWARD CAMPBELL:

Nothing nearly as noteworthy. Stuff like I would concentrate on my father and he would call. I did this twice that week. As scientifically as I could, with unmistakable intention and both times it worked.

DR. WILLIAM FINK:

Did you try it with anybody else or other times?

HOWARD CAMPBELL:

No.

DR. WILLIAM FINK:

Why not?

HOWARD CAMPBELL:

I don't know.

[PAUSE]

DR. WILLIAM FINK:

Do you miss the mania?

HOWARD CAMPBELL:

Fuck yeah.

[PAUSE]

DR. WILLIAM FINK:

May I ask you some more questions?

HOWARD CAMPBELL:

Shoot.

DR. WILLIAM FINK:

Do you do anything ritualistic?

HOWARD CAMPBELL:

Yes.

[PAUSE]

DR. WILLIAM FINK:

Will you share?

HOWARD CAMPBELL:

Before I write each day, I chant a little ditty:

> "Now as I write, plots unfold.
> Language is magic;
> A story is told.
> What I envision:
> Sights, sounds and smell,
> Will flow onto the page,
> In the story I tell."

DR. WILLIAM FINK:

Does it work?

HOWARD CAMPBELL:

I'm still writing. Does it work? I don't know. It is just something I do. Does praying work for you?

DR. WILLIAM FINK:

It makes me feel more settled.

HOWARD CAMPBELL:

Same thing with my poem.
[PAUSE]
What else do you want to know?

DR. WILLIAM FINK:

What happens in the play, *Emergency*?

HOWARD CAMPBELL:

A psychologist was in a state of despair to the point of depression. His wife encouraged him to see a psychologist, but he wouldn't go. The play begins with her getting around this by asking another psychologist to take on her husband as a patient, but to see him in the guise of being her husband's patient. Her husband would think he was seeing a psychologist as a patient, when actually the intended curative powers were intended to go the other way. By the end of the play, these two shrinks have in some way cured each other.

DR. WILLIAM FINK:

Why is *Emergency* so important to you?

HOWARD CAMPBELL:

It was written by Hellmoth Kaiser. I think this is the Kaiser that Brian at Bennington was referring to. The play got Kaiser kicked out of the psychiatrists' association he was a member of. His play states that we don't know why analysis works, like in the Garfinkle studies.

DR. WILLIAM FINK:

What about the Ash study?

HOWARD CAMPBELL:

What are you doing, going down your list?

DR. WILLIAM FINK:

Basically, yes.

[PAUSE]

I'm trying to understand what's important to you.

HOWARD CAMPBELL:

Okay, the Ash study is what was the syllogism I was drawing on by titling my manifesto, *The Longer Line*. Dr. Ash had a person come into a test room, ostensibly to be one of six subjects in an experiment on eyesight and perception, but the study was actually designed to ascertain levels of compliance. The person was actually the only subject. The other five people were actors, students pretending to be subjects. All six were asked which line was the longest of four projected on a screen and labeled: A, B, C and D.

The first several times, the actors would all say that the correct line was the longest. Then, the actors would say the second-to-longest was the longest. The point of the experiment was to determine incidence of compliance and seek any commonalities. Among those people who complied erroneously with the group, meaning that they would agree with the group instead of saying that the correct line, was longer; about a third of this group had a mental breakdown in the next 12 months.

Damn. That is such a huge amount. Seeing something that you see as wrong, and not speaking out about it, is dangerous to your health, provided you aren't in a totalitarian government. That's why I'm working on a book. It's part of my path to sanity, to explain how I see world order, to not keep it all inside and feel conflicted. It could lead a man to something that looks like Alzheimer's disease.

Maybe that's why I'm doing this. To state my perspective. You're the first person who has listened to this much of my ideas, I mean somebody I wasn't paying to listen to me.

If you dislike what the government or a person is doing, you should be able to speak out without fear of reprisal, including being fired.

DR. WILLIAM FINK:

That's supposed to be the way it is, freedom of speech and all.

HOWARD CAMPBELL:

You can talk to The Hollywood Ten about freedom of speech.

DR. WILLIAM FINK:

I think it was The Hollywood Eight.

HOWARD CAMPBELL:

No matter. America has had outliers eliminated or squelched since our inception.

That's a primary reason I was let go of CCE&O.

DR. WILLIAM FINK:

You think you were wrongly fired?

HOWARD CAMPBELL:

Not in the least. I would have fired me if I was in their shoes. I spoke Truth. Truth is not always welcome when it's at odds with an agenda. I deserved to be fired. I just wish they had done it with more panache.

DR. WILLIAM FINK:

What did they do?

HOWARD CAMPBELL:

Legally, I'm not allowed to discuss it. I probably shouldn't have brought it up. Especially not here, with you recording this.

DR. WILLIAM FINK:

Nobody will hear these tapes but me.

[PAUSE]

HOWARD CAMPBELL:

Just because I'm paranoid, doesn't mean that there aren't real liabilities in discussing the details.

[PAUSE]

You know, the most frustrating part about living in America, is that most citizens are so fucking naïve as to the extent of our government's deceit and corruption.

DR. WILLIAM FINK:

You aren't just a tad jaded?

HOWARD CAMPBELL:

How about realistic and not naïve? The weekend after the movie *JFK* came out, I found myself at my uncle's house. He said, "You know, there really was a conspiracy." My cousins and I had the same basic reaction, "The government was involved. Of *course* there was a conspiracy." Are my cousin and I jaded or realistic? What makes me optimistic is that there appears to be chinks in the media armor. *Men in Black*, and *The Matrix*. Older movies lead the way like *Blade Runner*, *The Parallax View*, and *Manchurian Candidate*. Every medium has popular phases of self-analysis. However, I feel there is stronger listening now than there has been before. And, with the Internet and e-mail, we can find like-minded people more easily. Those who will think it's ridiculous how we spend more on military than the next eight largest military spending countries.

DR. WILLIAM FINK:

We need to defend ourselves. Besides, there is nothing conclusive to prove that JFK's killing was any more than the work of a lone gunman.

HOWARD CAMPBELL:

A rumor is not a rumor that doesn't die.

DR. WILLIAM FINK:

You said earlier that that phrase doesn't make any sense.

HOWARD CAMPBELL:

It makes sense if you listen to it differently. The phrase states that a story that is framed as a rumor, *that doesn't die*, is not a rumor. A rumor that doesn't dies has Truth. Maybe not literal truth, but emotional truth. A rumor that doesn't die becomes a legend, part of our cultural fabric.

DR. WILLIAM FINK:

Why would you present something one way and watch and see if I see it a different way? That seems sort of mean spirited.

[PAUSE]

HOWARD CAMPBELL:

Maybe we should discuss some of the exercises in your elementary school intelligence testing methods.

DR. WILLIAM FINK:

Point taken.

HOWARD CAMPBELL:

I didn't realize we were keeping score in points. Look, I'm just pissed and wigged-out. I don't feel like having this conversation.

DR. WILLIAM FINK:

Okay. I understand.

HOWARD CAMPBELL:

No, you don't.

[PAUSE]

I don't understand how you stayed at work today, having had a patient die.

DR. WILLIAM FINK:

I have patients who needed me. And, I didn't know how to reach you, and I wasn't exactly going to leave you a note.

[PAUSE]

How are you doing?

HOWARD CAMPBELL:

I'm angry. I never knew this guy who asked me to explain him, and before I do whatever it is that I am supposed to explain, he kills himself.

DR. WILLIAM FINK:

What would you want to tell him, if you could.

HOWARD CAMPBELL:

That the Finnegans are waking.

DR. WILLIAM FINK:

Which Finnegans?

HOWARD CAMPBELL:

Joyce's novel, doesn't have an apostrophe "s"? *Finnegans Wake* refers to when society wakes up. When we stop being such a herd. I like to think it'll happen, but stuff like war seems to head us in the wrong direction. I see so many people take war so seriously, instead of just as a power play like a bet or a raise in poker.

I've been alive for only thirty-five years. My entire life, media has been telling me I live in a tumultuous time. I'm getting tired of this. What I found is that just about any time, people were referring to their time as tumultuous times.

I brought with me a long quote that talks about this in greater detail. I was planning on ranting about sanity and insanity today. Maybe tomorrow.

I'm tired, and psychically reeling. If you can, let's meet up again tomorrow. Then, I'd better get back to Atlanta and get my life sorted out. I have to figure out how I'm going to support my mortgage.

This was written circa 1970 and appears in *Zen And The Art Of Motorcycle Maintenance*

[SOUND: PAPER BEING UNFOLDED]

Maybe you should read it.

DR. WILLIAM FINK:

Okay.

> "We're living in topsy-turvy times, and I think that what causes the topsy-turvy feeling is inadequacy of old forms of thought to deal with new experiences. I've heard it said that the only real

learning results from hang-ups, where instead of expanding the branches of what you already know; you have to stop and drift laterally for a while until you come across something that allows you to expand the roots of what you already know. Everyone's familiar with that. I think the same thing occurs with whole civilizations when expansion's needed at the roots.

"You look back at the last three thousand years and with hindsight you think you see neat patterns and chains of cause and effect that have made things the way they are. But if you go back to original sources, the literature of any particular era, you find that these causes were never apparent at the time they were supposed to be operating. During periods of root expansion things have always looked as confused and topsy-turvy and purposeless as they do now. The whole Renaissance is supposed to have resulted from the topsy-turvy feeling caused by Columbus' discovery of a New World. It just shook people up. The topsy-turviness of that time is recorded everywhere. There was nothing in the flat-earth views of the Old and New Testaments that predicted it. Yet people couldn't deny it. The only way they could assimilate it was to abandon the entire medieval outlook and enter into a new expansion of reason.

"Columbus has become such a schoolbook stereotype it's almost impossible to imagine him as a living human being anymore. But if you really try to hold back your present knowledge about the consequences of his trip and project yourself into his situation, then sometimes you can begin to see that our present moon exploration must be like a tea party compared to what he went through. Moon exploration doesn't involve real root expansions of thought. We've no reason to doubt that existing forms of thought are adequate to handle it. It's really just a branch extension of what Columbus did. A really new exploration, one that would look to us today the way the world looked to Columbus, would have to be an entirely new direction...Like into realms beyond reason. I think present-day reason is an analogue of the flat earth of the medieval period. If you go too far beyond it you're presumed to fall off, into insanity. And people are very much afraid of that. I think this fear of insanity is comparable to the fear people once had of falling off the edge of the world. Or the fear of heretics. There's a very close analogue there.

"But what's happening is that each year our old flat earth of conventional reason becomes less and less adequate to handle the experiences we have and this is creating widespread feelings of topsy-turviness. As a result we're getting more and more people in irrational areas of thought-occultism, mysticism, drug changes and the like–because they feel the inadequacy of classical reason to handle what they know are real experiences."

[PAUSE]

[SOUND: PAPER BEING FOLDED]

I'd need to really think about this.

HOWARD CAMPBELL:

Keep the paper. Take as long as you want on that. I'll give you all night on everything else we've discussed. Tomorrow will be our last session.

[PAUSE]

Can you write me a prescription for Kenelog in Orabase?

DR. WILLIAM FINK:

You have a chancre sore?

HOWARD CAMPBELL:

Yes. I did some fire eating last weekend, and I must have irritated something.

[SOUND: PEN WRITING. PRESCRIPTION BEING TORN FROM PAD]

DR. WILLIAM FINK:

Here. You can fill it on your way out.

HOWARD CAMPBELL:

Thank you. You are now my doctor.

DR. WILLIAM FINK:

I guess I am.

HOWARD CAMPBELL:

May I pay you or the hospital for this service?

DR. WILLIAM FINK:

It's on the house.

HOWARD CAMPBELL:

FTS.

DR. WILLIAM FINK:

FTS?

HOWARD CAMPBELL:

Fuck the system.

DR. WILLIAM FINK:

If I'd known you were going to say that, I may have charged you.

HOWARD CAMPBELL:

Actions speak louder than words.
[PAUSE]
And, I would like to welcome you into the brotherhood of the Illuminati.

DR. WILLIAM FINK:

Don't get weird on me.

HOWARD CAMPBELL:

Balking is the action of an illuminatus agent. Had more Germans balked, just a little, the Holocaust would have not been nearly as effective. Schindler was a master balker, making munitions that never ever worked. But most people didn't have the fortitude and confidence to balk at a system they knew was inhuman. That's what it is to be a patrist—you continue to inflict the pain, not because you are a sadist and get off on it, but because you are numb to the feelings of others. It's the moral of the story about the chimpanzees and the ladder. They beat up the newbie when he climbs the ladder because that's what the systems says they should do. That is being the matrix.

Those with the power, with the bigger stack of chips continue to press their advantage. To be a member of the Illuminati is to let somebody off easy just because you can. In the subtlest way, you are undermining the system by not having me pay for my services. Thank you. When we are undermining the inhumanity of the system, we are the illuminati.

DR. WILLIAM FINK:

I can't engage in this line of thinking.

HOWARD CAMPBELL:

We don't know what is real. Some of the greatest minds of our culture can't agree on if there is a single reality or a plurality. That's the difference between Universe and pluraverse. Einstein and Fuller hold to a pluraverse. If we can't agree on what's real, can we say what's sane? Can we say that somebody's experience is wrong? Ideologues can.

DR. WILLIAM FINK:

That's what phenomenology stems from, that since we don't know what's real, what realm we are truly in, then we must begin with what we experience.
[PAUSE]

HOWARD CAMPBELL:

You know, giving me the prescription makes you my doctor.

DR. WILLIAM FINK:

As you said already.

HOWARD CAMPBELL:

Which means that anything I tell you can not be disclosed.

DR. WILLIAM FINK:

It's not quite the same as lawyer/client privileges.

HOWARD CAMPBELL:

I know.

DR. WILLIAM FINK:

I'm sure you do.

[SOUND: RECORDER SWITCHING OFF]
(DISCUSSION OMITTED)
[SOUND: RECORDER SWITCHING ON]

SESSION 7

VOICE OF DR. WILLIAM FINK:

April 14, 2003, session seven with Howard Campbell.
[SOUND: FUMBLING OF PAPERS]

DR. WILLIAM FINK:

I was thinking about how you said fish swimming together is a meme.
[PAUSE]

HOWARD CAMPBELL:

Yes.

DR. WILLIAM FINK:

Well, I think that that attraction is the basis of all evolution and selection.

HOWARD CAMPBELL:

Go on.

DR. WILLIAM FINK:

It was attraction that created advantages in the primordial soup.

HOWARD CAMPBELL:

How so?

DR. WILLIAM FINK:

There were benefits to clustering. When like items clustered, they became a colony. But when items attracted non-like items, their union became a new organism. That was the first synergy. But attraction leads to systems.

Gravity is physical attraction. I'm contemplating whether DNA may be psychic attraction.

HOWARD CAMPBELL:

Tread carefully. You cautioned me about exploring psychic powers.

DR. WILLIAM FINK:

Attractions lead to new combinations. Some new systems were more stable than other systems. Evolution became when these couplings started replicating themselves. That was creation. Not creation like something from nothing, but creation like new from nowhere.

HOWARD CAMPBELL:

Okay.

DR. WILLIAM FINK:

Sometimes a self-replicating thing doesn't replicate itself exactly. Usually those non-accurate replications just die. But occasionally, the new thing has an advantage.

HOWARD CAMPBELL:

You figure all this out?

DR. WILLIAM FINK:

I found a website where this guy Richard Brodie talks about a level three of consciousness. He believes that while humans did evolve from monkeys, more importantly, we are just the culmination of trillions of mistakes that happen to have an advantage. Animals are the mistakes that seem to be able to communicate. Maybe not all animals, but many communicate or at least interpret their environment. Our mistakes have evolved to make us attracted to what is likely to further the replicating mechanism, our genes.

HOWARD CAMPBELL:

Our DNA.

DR. WILLIAM FINK:

Yes. But he goes on to say that attraction is often shaped by memes. He believes that memes are things. That memes are alive and live in minds. Just like physical adaptation, memes replicate and mistakes happen in replication. Some mistakes yield advantages. And, some memes have a better fit with other memes. Fit here means a competitive advantage towards sustainability. His hypothesis is that *belief systems are the culmination of replication mistakes.*

HOWARD CAMPBELL:

He's like Susan Blackmore, they disregard consciousness. At least Susan is an atheist and holds that when we die we are caput.

DR. WILLIAM FINK:

I don't know who Blackmore is, but I think you're wrong about Brodie disregarding consciousness.

HOWARD CAMPBELL:

Susan Blackmore wrote a lot of books about memetics, memes and memeplexes.

DR. WILLIAM FINK:

Okay. Well, Brodie believes that ideas survive not based on their Truth, but on their ability to replicate accurately and their fitness to survive the competition. Just like how a territory of land can only hold so many species, there are only so many minds, and ideas compete for replication. Idea wars are actually quite fierce. Religious wars are the most obvious example, but smaller ideas are warring all the time, right down to what shirt I chose to wear today.

[PAUSE]

HOWARD CAMPBELL:

Congratulations. You now understand memetics.

DR. WILLIAM FINK:

Thank you.

[PAUSE]

HOWARD CAMPBELL:

Most people never get to where you are right now.

DR. WILLIAM FINK:

Memetics has made me see things differently.

[PAUSE]

HOWARD CAMPBELL:

What else did you learn?

DR. WILLIAM FINK:

Well, Brodie goes on to explain that when we're born, our mind is courted by memes. These are just random thoughts. These memes that are geared towards infants are extraordinarily talented, from thousands of years of mistakes and trial and error.

HOWARD CAMPBELL:

It isn't trial and error. There is no intentionality in these mistakes.

DR. WILLIAM FINK:

Good point. We have our genes, which carry instincts that have successfully replicated for millions of years. But these memes, they are what shape a map of life, they form our cosmography.

HOWARD CAMPBELL:

Yes.

[PAUSE]

Why do you think Brodie includes consciousness in his model?

DR. WILLIAM FINK:

Well, because he talks about us having a purpose. When our memes are quiet, it's possible to *feel* when we are on purpose and when we are off.

HOWARD CAMPBELL:

Does he recommend meditation?

DR. WILLIAM FINK:

He doesn't say that exactly. But when we're quiet, and we find our purpose, we can influence the meme battle going on in our head.

HOWARD CAMPBELL:

So we develop intention, and our goal is to implement our intention?

DR. WILLIAM FINK:

Not exactly. A purpose is not a goal. Brodie says that a purpose does not feel like guilt, shame, or vengeance. Guilt, shame and vengeance are emotions used by memes to gain mastery over your life. By choosing memes consciously, we can eliminate the control that memes have over those emotions.

[PAUSE]

A purpose feels fulfilling, satisfying, joyful, and powerful.

HOWARD CAMPBELL:

How is that different from a goal?

DR. WILLIAM FINK:

I don't know. I think it has to do with needing to involve other people. So, it could be a goal, but only if the goal is a feeling and not an objective of domination. You see, domination feels bad. It feels good because of the addictive chemicals like adrenaline, but it's more like smoking—the good feeling isn't a real good feeling, it's actually an active agent that's killing you and was generated by a stagnate agenda.

HOWARD CAMPBELL:

You're beginning to sound like Buckminster Fuller.

DR. WILLIAM FINK:

Incomprehensible?

HOWARD CAMPBELL:

Using awkward words to make an exacting point. It's difficult to track sometimes.

DR. WILLIAM FINK:

So it is.

[PAUSE]

HOWARD CAMPBELL:

Tell me more about purpose.

DR. WILLIAM FINK:

A purpose is fluid, seeking balance. Craving sustainability. A purpose has to do with other people. Spreading memes fulfills a purpose. Every time we speak, write, create, or act we are spreading memes. To fulfill our purpose we must be conscious of which memes we are spreading.

HOWARD CAMPBELL:

Yes. Human life is largely composed of conversations. Conversations are composed of memes. The vast majority of people are unaware of this. I want to help more people reach this level of awareness.

DR. WILLIAM FINK:

How?

HOWARD CAMPBELL:

I don't know. I don't really have an agenda. I do hold that if this level of awareness is not reached, Earth as we know may not exist for much longer.

[SILENCE]

This is a vin-dit.

[SILENCE]

Thank you.

I don't know where this conversation will go, but whatever happens, I want to say thank you.

DR. WILLIAM FINK:

You're welcome.

I wouldn't have come upon this if I hadn't met you.

Richard Brodie invites people to take part in what he calls a *level three conversation* if they have an earnest interest.

HOWARD CAMPBELL:

How do I find it?

DR. WILLIAM FINK:

It finds you. The memes are seeking your mind.

[LAUGHTER]

HOWARD CAMPBELL:

Good point.

How do I find a level three conversation?

DR. WILLIAM FINK:

Just Google.

HOWARD CAMPBELL:

I will.

[PAUSE]

Where do you want to go with our last session?

DR. WILLIAM FINK:

What do you want?

HOWARD CAMPBELL:

I want to quit playing the game.

DR. WILLIAM FINK:

What game?

HOWARD CAMPBELL:

Exactly.

DR. WILLIAM FINK:

I hate it when I ask you a question, and you say something I'm not expecting.

HOWARD CAMPBELL:

You love your expectations.

DR. WILLIAM FINK:

Okay.

HOWARD CAMPBELL:

This game. This banter. I want to do something substantive. I want to stop wanting. I want to diminish consumerism as we know it. I want to come up with that one idea that will seed the healing of our planet. Maybe it's not one idea, but an idea that can help be a catalyst.

DR. WILLIAM FINK:

You sound like a hippie.

HOWARD CAMPBELL:

My middle name is Siddhartha.

DR. WILLIAM FINK:

Seriously?

HOWARD CAMPBELL:

Yes. I was born in the sixties. It was my mom's favorite book. She aspired to hippie values.

You use the term "hippie" like it's a tainted word. That's the type of speak that squelches. It is like the Republicans making the word "liberal" a bad word.

If enough people believe the seed idea exists, it will be found. Like the five minute mile. Once somebody ran it, it seems like now everybody can do it. Well, anybody with a modicum of talent that trains sixty hours a week.

Prognosis 2000 was my attempt to seed a healing meme. The book idea sprung from a Bucky saying that people were living in consumerism, disconnected from natural cycles, without being aware of the disconnection.

My goal with this almanac was to create a phenomenological connection within the reader, between consumer seasonality and the annual trip the earth makes around the sun.

This phenomenological connection was rooted in physical experience contained within the book. For instance, the right-hand side of the book worked as two flipbooks, like the cartoon books for kids where they can see a mini-movie. Except my mini-movies were of the earth with a solar perspective. One was of the earth revolving around the sun; the other was how the sun struck the Northern hemisphere. The movie showed how this changed over the course of the year and how the two were inter-related. Each page represented four days, and *Prognosis 2000* was 91 pages, creating a 364-day year, with a date on each page. The mini-movies were painstakingly accurate to each day.

DR. WILLIAM FINK:

How did you do that?

HOWARD CAMPBELL:

I hired a graphic artist who mathematically worked out the visuals.

Across the bottom of the pages were seasonal icons. These were snap shots of what might be seen in media around that day, corresponding with the mini-movie. So, that if you saw these icons you could figure out where you were in the annual trip around the sun. It was an idea that sprung from ancient man's seasonal baton. I chose many sporting events, not because I thought they were important, but because they tend to be predictable in their sequencing and prominent in the media. The purpose of the seasonal icons was to link the images we see in the media with where we are in our annual trip around the sun. I figured if people felt more connected by common cohabitation, we might start thinking like we are all connected. Maybe hokey, but I was being sincere.

DR. WILLIAM FINK:

I understand.

HOWARD CAMPBELL:

As a people, we are empowered to communicate with people we know, as many as we like, virtually instantaneously. Let's start talking. Let's find a way to organize as a large group, yet not demand group think. Let's stop playing the polite game, and let's pretend that the lives of our grandchildren depend on us garnering some consensus in our lifetimes. Let's talk about politics, religion and sex. Let's be real. Let's question ourselves. Let's talk about whatever keeps us from respecting ourselves enough to feel unified through diversity. Let's spend time listening. Let's spend enough time listening that we don't feel the need to get defensive. Let's find a way to respect nature. Let's find a way to respect different customs.

DR. WILLIAM FINK:

The last time large numbers of people began questioning the economic constructs binding this nation's laws, they were labeled as communists.

HOWARD CAMPBELL:

Many of these had no affinity towards the philosophy of Karl Marx.

DR. WILLIAM FINK:

America is a messaging delivery mechanism.

HOWARD CAMPBELL:

Yes.

Now ask yourself this, what is the message?

DR. WILLIAM FINK:

I don't know.

HOWARD CAMPBELL:

The message is, that the message is important and good.

DR. WILLIAM FINK:

But that doesn't make any sense. It's self-referential. It is Gödelian.

HOWARD CAMPBELL:

Sense? It makes sense because it affects our senses. One of the biggest crimes of mass idea pollution is that sense equals logic. No. Sense is any form of sense. Can we feel its impact? When we can feel an impact, something makes sense to us. Something makes sense when it spurs a sensation. There is only one sense, not five or six.

DR. WILLIAM FINK:

What sense is that?

HOWARD CAMPBELL:

Feeling.

DR. WILLIAM FINK:

Hearing isn't a sense?

HOWARD CAMPBELL:

When you hear something, you are sensing tiny, subtle vibrations. Our comprehensive sensibility incorporates all traditional sense. Sense does not equal logic. Sense equals gut.

[PAUSE]

Most people are not skilled enough at logic to discern good logic from bullshit. Mass media's biggest impact on America, aside from generating extended periods of sedation, is that TV watchers mistake themselves as apt Attacan thinkers.

[SILENCE]

You following me?

DR. WILLIAM FINK:

Yeah, I was just thinking of media more like how cigarettes are a nicotine delivery mechanism. Media is delivering addiction to the message. Nicotine and mass media each deliver the user with the substance of their addiction. Americans get prepackaged repartee, a sense of being a tribe of good guys, and smokers get their nicotine. I thought that the message was, "America equals enfranchisement."

[PAUSE]

HOWARD CAMPBELL:

Not quite. You're still equating thoughts with meaning. Think of the meme for fish that school. The meme is to stay together. That's the meme of mass media.

DR. WILLIAM FINK:

But media companies find it profitable to target audiences differently.

HOWARD CAMPBELL:

So *It* appears. The symbols are different against each target, but the overarching message is the same, "this message is important." This constant sense of heightened importance is neurasthenia. Neurasthenia is being on *It*. *It* is the corporate meme.

[PAUSE]

DR. WILLIAM FINK:

How do I displace *It*?

HOWARD CAMPBELL:

That attitude is *It*. That question is essentially competitive.

DR. WILLIAM FINK:

How do we dispel the corporate meme?

HOWARD CAMPBELL:

Nicely phrased.

First, we can understand the messaging mechanism better. This is being worked on. Media companies each seek to better understand how people consume media, better than their competition. The trick is to get experts in media to be passionate about promoting ideas that can heal our planet, physically and psychically. We are bombarded by 3,000 corporate memes a day. Where is my country that promised to protect me from intruders? I want my country to fend off some of these memes. I'm tired of being constantly barraged by synthetic ideas.

[PAUSE]

Do you think I'm founded in my anger?

DR. WILLIAM FINK:

Yes. But I'm confused about how understanding the mechanism is important.

HOWARD CAMPBELL:

How is critical. How is logic. *How* is the comprehension of the system. When you can see a structure of persuasion, then you can objectify the request as opposed to simply floating with the persuasive logic train that lets them depart at the desired destination. By seeing persuasion as a request, one is empowered, because you now have choices. Instead of being delivered to a mental destination, you can get off the logic train and go where you want to be. *How* is at the root of Attacan thought. *How* is important to those who are curious about technology. "Know how" became a noun for a reason, smart people like to know *how* something works.

DR. WILLIAM FINK:

But these people, those at the cutting edge of meme propagation research, work for corporations. Doesn't that lead to proprietary knowledge? If we need this technology, isn't it kept secret from us?

HOWARD CAMPBELL:

Not for long. The media companies have to share their strategies with their clients, which means that they are constantly striving to develop new insights to have another short-lived competitive advantage. Media companies compete for fitness just as genes or memes compete. Business is a physical manifestation of meme warfare. Media company choices do have tangible effects on shaping the structure of society. By creating targets, and crafting media delivery mechanisms for these predetermined audiences, we segregate the information they receive. Isolation breeds mutation.

DR. WILLIAM FINK:

Yes. So then this goes against the idea that there is only one message.

HOWARD CAMPBELL:

No. The division is imaginary. The message is still to take the system seriously. The imaginary division is like choosing between Republicans and Democrats. Do I want the capitalist puppet on the right or the capitalist puppet on the left?

The divisions are simply to create identity tribes. But all tribes pray to the message delivery system.

[PAUSE]

There is a constant dance with continual crafting of media devices and messages. The environment is constantly shifting. So, both the message and the media need to constantly evolve and adapt. This intentionality is often misconceived as a conspiracy.

DR. WILLIAM FINK:

How so?

HOWARD CAMPBELL:

It's like a mediocre poker player with a lot of money sitting down at a table with seven strong poker players. The mediocre player is the fish. The sharks need to eat. They want to eat the fish. There is less chance of being injured by biting into a fish than another shark. The mediocre player represents *easy money*. So the professional players are ganged up against you, not because they want to be familiar with each other, but because they have a common agenda: to make money.

The projection of a conspiracy happens when you can't see the forest for the trees. It's like a joke my grandmother told me about a border guard who worked at a station for 30 years. Every week, a known smuggler would come through. Every week, the guard would search the smuggler's mules and go through all his personal belongings. Nothing was ever, ever found. A few times they would kill a mule and search through its innards. Nothing found. After thirty years, the guard said to the smuggler, "I'm retiring." The smuggler replied, "I'm retiring, too." Then the guard asked, "Since we're both retiring, will you tell me how you've been able to sneak in whatever you're smuggling each week? I need to know." The smuggler says, "Okay, but let me get across first." So they go across and the smuggler says, "I'm smuggling the mules."

[LAUGHTER]

The guard thought of the mules as a contraband delivery mechanism. He couldn't see the mules as the contraband.

[PAUSE]

The media systems construct themselves the way they do because they sell *attention*. Their job is to hold an audience's attention, which allows their subscribers, the big brands, to become familiar with an audience. Media is structured as it is because it facilitates competition. *Our current media is state-of-the-art* at garnering and holding an audience's attention.

[PAUSE]

DR. WILLIAM FINK:

What's the most efficient way to hold attention?

HOWARD CAMPBELL:

Throw a war.

DR. WILLIAM FINK:

What?!

HOWARD CAMPBELL:

Throw a war. During intense events, people consume more media. When people consume more media, they are better consumers.

What keeps me optimistic is that the brands are fighting for our civil rights.

DR. WILLIAM FINK:

If brands are the avatars for corporations and corporations are sociopaths, then why should they care about our civil rights?

HOWARD CAMPBELL:

Because some of our civil rights are in their best interest. I am less concerned about corporations being sociopaths than governments being sociopaths. In part, because our government was established to ensure laze fare messaging—free speech and freedom of religion. That means we can say and think whatever we want. So long as that's true, companies are free to influence us. But our government has an agenda of growth. Our government has become the new church. The battle—of science dictates Truth versus church dictates Truth—is being replaced by the battle of American government versus free trade. Free trade will win or we will live in a totalitarian system.

DR. WILLIAM FINK:

How is big business defending our civil rights?

HOWARD CAMPBELL:

They put money into defending free speech. The government is trying to say that certain things cannot be said, like tobacco advertising aimed at children. The government won that one. But they're being fought hard on telemarketing. I say, "God bless them. Fight the government." Only big business has the resources to fight government.

What bugs me, what really sets me off, is the blatant hypocrisy. Marijuana is illegal but beer is fine. Which kills more people each year? Why is smoking cigarettes the cheapest way to ingest nicotine? Make gum cheaper and save some lungs.

DR. WILLIAM FINK:

That's a good idea.

HOWARD CAMPBELL:

Thank you. But what pisses me off is seeing the public service announcements that followed nine-eleven. I loved the first one that showed a person checking a book out from the library and being ambushed by secret service men. The ad was showing what the world would be like if America didn't exist. But the problem now is that the Patriot Act is making tracking library books part of their data set. We have become what the commercial said was un-American.

DR. WILLIAM FINK:

What do we do now?

HOWARD CAMPBELL:

I don't know. I need help.

[PAUSE]

If we quiet our memes, something might feel better.

[PAUSE]

We need to save what's left of the earth's ecological systems.

[PAUSE]

The movie *Almost Famous* starts with a vin dit, the lead character learns he is not the age he thinks he is. We need a societal vin-dit, where we learn that we are not as smart as we pride ourselves to be. Major reframing. We need to see that we have chosen our identities. In *Almost Famous*, writer/director Cameron Crowe had his maternal character say: "Adolescence is a marketing tool." It certainly is. Adolescence is contrived because it helps us make more money. Adolescence is yet another way to create a discrete audience.

[PAUSE]

How do we lessen media contrived identities and create a space for us to all see ourselves as one?

[SILENCE]

Can we teach Bill Hicks in elementary school? "All matter is merely energy condensed to a slow vibration, we are all one consciousness experiencing itself subjectively, life is only a dream, and we are the imaginations of ourselves."

[SILENCE]

What if we raised the cost of bulk mail? Wouldn't this save countless trees and help counter the greenhouse effect? Wouldn't this be a start? What if we charged large amounts of money for cutting down trees? Would this not encourage redevelopment in cities instead of the less expensive expansion model currently destroying our land? What if we charged a chemical tax for lawn fertilizers that are not biodegradable? How can we incentivize a better world for our grandchildren? Make it about the future. Teach that *now* is not that special.

[SILENCE]

DR. WILLIAM FINK:
Are you doing anything specific?
[PAUSE]

HOWARD CAMPBELL:
Good question. Buying *Ad Buster* and being pissed-off at SUV drivers isn't enough. I don't eat meat on Tuesdays and Thursdays.

DR. WILLIAM FINK:
What does that do?

HOWARD CAMPBELL:

One American carnivore becoming a vegetarian and not eating meat does more for the environment than 500 people buying alternative energy cars. With all the chemicals and land and waste associated with raising chickens or cows. Telling people facts like these, and acting on these facts, is what I'm doing. But I don't always act on the facts as well as I could. I rationalize that this book I'm working on is in some way doing my part. I try and spread my memes. I trust that by spreading my memes, my attitude will follow.

DR. WILLIAM FINK:

As a cynic?

HOWARD CAMPBELL:

I hope that isn't the case. Cynicism doesn't get much done. Righteous indignation at times. A teacher in Atlanta was fired for calling a student *black*. Not like a name, just referencing them as black. That is deplorable? Georgia law mandates that milk be given to students with their lunch. 70% of African Americans are lactose intolerant. Which seems more racist?

DR. WILLIAM FINK:

So racism is your focus?

HOWARD CAMPBELL:

Racism and headaches are the symptoms, not the problem.

DR. WILLIAM FINK:

What's the problem?

HOWARD CAMPBELL:

Very few people will actually work on identifying the problems. Most well intended people will feel content to help eases the symptoms. Just because we keep taking aspirin, doesn't mean we don't still have a headache. It just means we aren't conscious of the pain.

My real goal is to create a reality delivery mechanism.

DR. WILLIAM FINK:

A reality delivery mechanism?

HOWARD CAMPBELL:

A reality delivery mechanism.

DR. WILLIAM FINK:

Whose reality?

HOWARD CAMPBELL:

Good point. How about this, I'm trying to create words that help its consumers shake off some of their corporately sponsored memes. Antidotes.

DR. WILLIAM FINK:

Like an anti-meme.

[PAUSE]

How will you do that?

HOWARD CAMPBELL:

I'll create some sort of hook to make it compelling to read. Then, I'll explain the structure of attraction and, I'll show how corporations use this technology to generate and sustain attraction. Finally, I'll create a call to action.

[SILENCE]

William.

[SILENCE]

Dr. Fink?

DR. WILLIAM FINK:

Yes? Oh.

[PAUSE]

That sounds like you have it pretty well worked out.

HOWARD CAMPBELL:

I'm working on it. It's a start.

These notions are far from worked out. I think it fills an urgent need. The problem is that most Americans don't see a problem. I need the *ring-around-the-collar* of over-corporatized society. In many countries, they call it Americanization. In *Fast Food Nation*, it's called the Mc Donaldization of the world. I need a label that does not point a finger at any group of people.

DR. WILLIAM FINK:

People call it Americanization?

HOWARD CAMPBELL:

Yeah. In other countries, America's image is of being mean and untrustworthy. Most Americans never travel to places where their dollars are not so embraced as to make it worth it to hide this sentiment. But the perception is there, if you really listen or look outside the major tourist attractions. In many ways we've earned this image. I don't think this is the way we want to live as world citizens.

I need a word that doesn't point a finger at anybody.

DR. WILLIAM FINK:

I saw graffiti on a bathroom stall that said, "Don't be afraid to wake up."

HOWARD CAMPBELL:

That's closer. But, I don't want anything negative in this meme.

DR. WILLIAM FINK:

What do you mean?

HOWARD CAMPBELL:

Well, that phrase has the notion of being afraid within its core.

DR. WILLIAM FINK:

Yeah, but it says *not* to be afraid.

HOWARD CAMPBELL:

Neuro-linguistic programming holds that the mind doesn't really process the concept *not*. Try saying, "Don't smoke" to somebody who is quitting smoking. They won't really hear reinforcement. Instead, they'll probably visualize smoking. I was hoping *twisp* could be this shibboleth. But the word *wake* might work equally well. Except that wake is colloquial and has many other meanings already built around that meme.

I want something that is devoid of government references also. Making it about government leads back to Americanization. However, the root of America occurs to me as rather on-track. Let's look at what the founding fathers of this country stated were our ideals:

"We hold these truths to be self-evident, that all men are created equal, that they are endowed by their Creator with certain unalienable Rights, that among these are Life, Liberty and the pursuit of Happiness.--That to secure these rights, Governments are instituted among Men, deriving their just powers from the consent of the governed, --That whenever any Form of Government becomes destructive of these ends, it is the Right of the People to alter or to abolish it, and to institute new Government, laying its foundation on such principles and organizing its powers in such form, as to them shall seem most likely to effect their Safety and Happiness." I can live with that.

DR. WILLIAM FINK:

That doesn't sound like how we're organized, now. What should we do?

HOWARD CAMPBELL:

I don't know. Work on solutions. Figure out what can be done instead of just talking about how fucked we are.

[SILENCE]

The way I see it, cultural elites are defending their power and position against a less moneyed mass. The elites resent the mass for not respecting their place, as dictated by The Law. The lessers accuse the elites of creating the law. Both have morality on their side. Both manipulate the law to their own agendas; the elites are just better at it. This is a war for power that will be played out primarily on television. Those of us who oppose changing the foundation of our government to favor either group will have an additional burden placed on us. We have to find ways to influence public opinion that don't rely on the forms of manipulation we're trying to stop.

Tell me. What idea would help bring this to fruition?

DR. WILLIAM FINK:

I don't know.

[SILENCE]

Wait.

[SILENCE]

What the fuck are you doing to me? What the *fuck*? You're asking me to take responsibility for all the world's ills.

HOWARD CAMPBELL:

Yes.

[PAUSE]

DR. WILLIAM FINK:

Who the hell are you to tell me *I'm* responsible?

HOWARD CAMPBELL:

It's not me telling you to own your responsibility.

DR. WILLIAM FINK:

You most certainly *did*!

HOWARD CAMPBELL:

William, I asked you to take responsibility. I never told you to do anything. Your conscience turned my request into an imperative, and your Id is rebelling. Your conflict will begin to impair your faculties.

[PAUSE]

What you are about to experience is going to disrupt your way of life as you know it.

DR. WILLIAM FINK:

No, it won't. You are trying to hypnotize me.

HOWARD CAMPBELL:

I'm bringing your inner conflict to the surface.

DR. WILLIAM FINK:

I'm not conflicted.

HOWARD CAMPBELL:

If you aren't conflicted, then how come you feel compelled to heal people? You're okay with how they are without your healing? You aren't compelled to exert your will on others?

DR. WILLIAM FINK:

Exerting one's will is not evidence of being conflicted.

HOWARD CAMPBELL:

How come you cheat on your wife?

DR. WILLIAM FINK:

I'm not going to talk about myself again.

[SILENCE]

[SILENCE]

Maybe you should leave.

[SILENCE]

[SILENCE]

Leave.

[SILENCE]

I need you to leave right now.
[PAUSE]

HOWARD CAMPBELL:

For not being conflicted, you certainly are uncomfortable in silence.

[PAUSE]

Is that evidence?

[SILENCE]

DR. WILLIAM FINK:

Please leave.

[PAUSE]

I will kick you out of here, again.

HOWARD CAMPBELL:

The "again" is a stumbler. You'll appear even more foolish to your colleagues and superiors than you appeared the first time. No, calling security is not an option unless I threaten you.

[PAUSE]

DR. WILLIAM FINK:

I could say you threatened me.

[PAUSE]

HOWARD CAMPBELL:

I'm calm and collected. You're sweaty. Who do you think they will believe?

[PAUSE]

I will leave of my own volition in less than seven minutes.

[PAUSE]

DR. WILLIAM FINK:

Why seven minutes?

HOWARD CAMPBELL:

Keep resisting. The harder you resist, the harder you fall. Seven minutes? Because that's how long it will take me to destroy your corporate religion.

DR. WILLIAM FINK:

Why *seven* minutes?

HOWARD CAMPBELL:

Follow the structure. I taught you the first six structures of energy, now it's time for you to discover the seventh structure.

DR. WILLIAM FINK:

What structure?

HOWARD CAMPBELL:

One, an ambiguous answer. We explored existentialism. You can hang in ambiguity. You have begun to see the power structure and you can flip between seeing power as either a duplicitous thought with elites and lessers, or as one, meaning universe.

DR. WILLIAM FINK:

What lessers and elites? Yes, some people have more money than others, but we subsidize everybody. The poor are simply trying to extort money from the rich.

[PAUSE]

HOWARD CAMPBELL:

Keep resisting. The harder you maintain the division, and see the infraction, the more painful the unification will be.

[PAUSE]

Are you willing to destroy us all in order to keep making them wrong?

DR. WILLIAM FINK:

No.

HOWARD CAMPBELL:

Good.

[SILENCE]

DR. WILLIAM FINK:

But there isn't anything wrong with the system.

HOWARD CAMPBELL:

Two, a duplicitous thought.

DR. WILLIAM FINK:

What?

HOWARD CAMPBELL:

You graduated to the second grade. You are now grappling with duplicity.

DR. WILLIAM FINK:

What duplicity?

HOWARD CAMPBELL:

There isn't anything wrong with the system.

DR. WILLIAM FINK:

How is that duplicitous?

HOWARD CAMPBELL:

Because the universe is not a system.

DR. WILLIAM FINK:

I never said the universe was a system.

HOWARD CAMPBELL:

To which cosmography do you prescribe?

[PAUSE]

DR. WILLIAM FINK:

I'm a scientific Catholic, if that's what you mean. Evolution exists, and Jesus is the only begotten son of God.

HOWARD CAMPBELL:

A *scientific* Catholic?

DR. WILLIAM FINK:

Yes.

HOWARD CAMPBELL:

So, the Pope is not *divine*?

DR. WILLIAM FINK:

I never said that.

HOWARD CAMPBELL:

Yet you feel entitled to hold contrarian perspectives that the Pope says may lead you to eternal damnation?

DR. WILLIAM FINK:

I don't necessarily believe in hell.

HOWARD CAMPBELL:

And you don't call this duplicitous? The Pope is God on Earth. Not the only begotten son of God, but a man with divine connections who owns a throne of righteousness, upon which when he sits, he can say no wrong.

DR. WILLIAM FINK:

I'm not sure about that. Some of what has been said from that throne, latter Popes have recanted.

[SILENCE]

Okay, I have no firm cosmography.

HOWARD CAMPBELL:

Three, a solid thought.

DR. WILLIAM FINK:

What solid thought?

HOWARD CAMPBELL:

The world is not how you know it.

DR. WILLIAM FINK:

I'm a scientist. I grasp how the universe works.

HOWARD CAMPBELL:

This is pride speaking.

DR. WILLIAM FINK:

Fuck you!

HOWARD CAMPBELL:

Good.

[SILENCE]

DR. WILLIAM FINK:

What do you mean, *good*?

HOWARD CAMPBELL:

I mean you're getting in touch with your anger.

DR. WILLIAM FINK:

I'm not mad.

HOWARD CAMPBELL:

Denial.

DR. WILLIAM FINK:

Fuck you!

HOWARD CAMPBELL:

Good.

DR. WILLIAM FINK:

Fuck you!

HOWARD CAMPBELL:

Good.

DR. WILLIAM FINK:

Fuck you.

HOWARD CAMPBELL:

Better.

[PAUSE]

DR. WILLIAM FINK:

What are you getting at?

HOWARD CAMPBELL:

I'm getting at that you are letting go of your denial that you *are* getting in touch with your feelings.

DR. WILLIAM FINK:

I am in touch with my feelings; I completed psychotherapy in order to become a psychotherapist.

[PAUSE]

HOWARD CAMPBELL:

Completing psychotherapy is like getting to the end of the Internet. It can't be done. There is no completion. There is no end. We are always evolving our consciousness.

[PAUSE]

Your duplicities lay in the fact that you perceive your self as done. Static. You now only look at others through *objective* eyes. When you accept that everything is subjective, I will count the next number.

302

DR. WILLIAM FINK:

Four?

HOWARD CAMPBELL:

We're not there yet.

DR. WILLIAM FINK:

We can be if we label it so.

HOWARD CAMPBELL:

No, we can have the label. But, simply labeling something doesn't make it so without consensus. And, consensus without external validity is like history, a story agreed upon.

DR. WILLIAM FINK:

Napoleon.

HOWARD CAMPBELL:

Yes. You are a student of his thoughts.

DR. WILLIAM FINK:

He was an objective leader.

HOWARD CAMPBELL:

Yes, that he was. But, he also was a philosopher.

DR. WILLIAM FINK:

I'll give you that.

HOWARD CAMPBELL:

Good. He was literally a lover of language and a lover of knowledge.

DR. WILLIAM FINK:

We are agreeing already. Now, will you go?

HOWARD CAMPBELL:

No.

DR. WILLIAM FINK:

Are we at four?

HOWARD CAMPBELL:

No.

[SILENCE]

[SILENCE]

What are you thinking?

DR. WILLIAM FINK:

That all I have to do is wait another four minutes and you said you would promise to leave.

HOWARD CAMPBELL:

You are mistaken.

[PAUSE]

DR. WILLIAM FINK:

What?

HOWARD CAMPBELL:

Minute, as in seven divisions of time, and I am the umpire of counting.

[SILENCE]

DR. WILLIAM FINK:

Then how do I get through this?

HOWARD CAMPBELL:

We keep going.

DR. WILLIAM FINK:

Then let's keep going.

HOWARD CAMPBELL:

Four, a complete thought.

DR. WILLIAM FINK:

How is the notion of continuing a complete thought?

HOWARD CAMPBELL:

Because, time, change and continuity are the backbone of life.

DR. WILLIAM FINK:

Don't the concepts of continuity and change contradict each other?

HOWARD CAMPBELL:

Good.

[PAUSE]

DR. WILLIAM FINK:

Why good?

HOWARD CAMPBELL:

Because, you are beginning to call out *the longer line*.

DR. WILLIAM FINK:

Excuse me.

HOWARD CAMPBELL:

For what?

[PAUSE]

DR. WILLIAM FINK:

What longer line?

HOWARD CAMPBELL:

Dr. Ash's line length study. You are now reconciling that you've been entrained with the herd, into stating a false longer line.

DR. WILLIAM FINK:

No, I haven't.

HOWARD CAMPBELL:

Three.

DR. WILLIAM FINK:

What? Time can't go backwards.

HOWARD CAMPBELL:

Not to the best of our knowledge, but intelligence can regress.

DR. WILLIAM FINK:

Okay.

HOWARD CAMPBELL:

Good. Four.

DR. WILLIAM FINK:

Thank you.

HOWARD CAMPBELL:

You are welcome.
[PAUSE]
Do you get what that means?

DR. WILLIAM FINK:

What *what* means?

HOWARD CAMPBELL:

No. "*You* are welcome."
[PAUSE]
You are welcome is a standing invitation.

DR. WILLIAM FINK:

Huh?

HOWARD CAMPBELL:

Welcome is an assurance of hospitality.

[PAUSE]

DR. WILLIAM FINK:

You're counseling me to be okay with not knowing.

HOWARD CAMPBELL:

No.

DR. WILLIAM FINK:

What do you mean, *no?*

HOWARD CAMPBELL:

I mean, no.

DR. WILLIAM FINK:

Okay.

HOWARD CAMPBELL:

Five.

DR. WILLIAM FINK:

Why?

HOWARD CAMPBELL:

Because, you are beginning to understand.

DR. WILLIAM FINK:

What does Five mean?

HOWARD CAMPBELL:

A thought prone to persuasion.

[PAUSE]

You are accepting that there are frames of mind to which you do not have access.

DR. WILLIAM FINK:

Why was *okay* an indication of a susceptible mind?

HOWARD CAMPBELL:

Because, *okay* demonstrates compliance.

[PAUSE]

When money replaced the church as the unifying means of oppression, corporations became the new church. CEOs are the contemporary priests. As religious leaders used God to frighten their parishioners, CEOs and managers use the threat of discontinued dollar delivery to frighten their employees, or parishioners, if you want to keep the church metaphor going.

Priests say that if you didn't follow their religious doctrine, you won't enter the kingdom of God, and you'll suffer for eternity in hell. Media has become our modern priests, saying, *money is holy* and that if you do not follow the corporate structure, you will not reach the kingdom of financial well-being, and you will suffer in poverty.

They both use carrots and sticks to motivate herds of people.

[PAUSE]

What is a Church?

DR. WILLIAM FINK:

A place of worship?

HOWARD CAMPBELL:

No. Remember *Silence of the Lambs?*

DR. WILLIAM FINK:

Yes.

HOWARD CAMPBELL:

Hannibal Lecter asked the same question of the serial killer. Jodie Foster said that he killed. Lecter responded that that was incidental. It wasn't his essence. Lecter coaches, "Read Marcus Aurelius. Of each particular thing ask: What is it in itself?"

What is the essence of a church? What is a church in itself?

[PAUSE]

DR. WILLIAM FINK:

A place to build a community?

HOWARD CAMPBELL:

Closer, Fink.

[PAUSE]

DR. WILLIAM FINK:

I'm not getting it.

HOWARD CAMPBELL:

One.

DR. WILLIAM FINK:

What?

HOWARD CAMPBELL:

One. You regressed to our starting point, a duplicity hidden within a fallacy.

DR. WILLIAM FINK:

I'm confused.

HOWARD CAMPBELL:

Three. A solid thought.

DR. WILLIAM FINK:

I don't get it.

HOWARD CAMPBELL:

One.

DR. WILLIAM FINK:

Fuck you!

HOWARD CAMPBELL:

One, but a good *one*, because "fuck you" is pure energy, one-one.
[PAUSE]

DR. WILLIAM FINK:

I give up.

HOWARD CAMPBELL:

What's the difference between a solid thought and a complete thought?

DR. WILLIAM FINK:

I don't know.

HOWARD CAMPBELL:

It's the difference between three and four, the difference between a triangle and a tetrahedron, the difference between a platform and a structure.

DR. WILLIAM FINK:

Okay.

HOWARD CAMPBELL:

It.

DR. WILLIAM FINK:

What?

HOWARD CAMPBELL:

It.

[SILENCE]

Good. Concentrate.

[SILENCE]

DR. WILLIAM FINK:

What is *It*.

HOWARD CAMPBELL:

Six, a working system.

DR. WILLIAM FINK:

But we didn't resolve the essence of a church.

HOWARD CAMPBELL:

It's the same essence as a corporation.

[PAUSE]

DR. WILLIAM FINK:

Any clues here would be useful.

HOWARD CAMPBELL:

I cannot tell *It* to you. You must see *It* for yourself.

DR. WILLIAM FINK:

But, I don't see *It.*

HOWARD CAMPBELL:

One, a duplicity hidden in a fallacious truth.

[PAUSE]

DR. WILLIAM FINK:

What is *It?*

HOWARD CAMPBELL:

Excellent. *It* is objectivity.

[PAUSE]

The essence of a church, whether a government, a corporation, or a centrally organized religion, is a *power delivery mechanism*. When you harvest power, it's often called oppression. These organization's primary discipline is the redistribute of money. Money is energy. Energy is power.

DR. WILLIAM FINK:

America was founded to harness our collective power, to fend off England's religious oppression.

HOWARD CAMPBELL:

America was founded to harness the collective power of wealthy white men who were seeking to get out from under the oppression of England.

DR. WILLIAM FINK:

America stands for rising-up against oppression.
[PAUSE]

HOWARD CAMPBELL:

Really?

DR. WILLIAM FINK:

Yes, it does.

HOWARD CAMPBELL:

It must be nice to believe the newspaper.
[PAUSE]
Then we stand for freedom the same way a counterfeit bill stands for money, it's fake.

DR. WILLIAM FINK:

Are you a communist?

HOWARD CAMPBELL:

Communism stands for Un-Americanism? No. Communism stands for the applied theories of Karl Marx. Communism as applied in Europe tried to exclude Christianity. *That* was what instigated the religious zealots of this nation to rise up against communism emotionally, and the corporate sponsorship is what allowed America to rise up financially against communists. What in communism is so evil? Sharing the resources so nobody goes without?

[MOCKING VOICE]

That's a very *scary* idea.

[NORMAL VOICE]

Communism is scary in so far as it is threatening, to the fallacy of scarcity—a tenet necessary to perpetuate the ruthlessness of contemporary Capitalism.

[PAUSE]

Ameri-*ka* is a very scary idea, which is very threatening to many smaller countries.

DR. WILLIAM FINK:

What does this have to do with me? You're saying that because I'm an American, I'm responsible for the messed-up things our government does to other people around the world?

HOWARD CAMPBELL:

From that perspective, no more than any other civilian who supports the system.

But you are the system's sniper riffle. You oppress the minds with the greatest potential.

DR. WILLIAM FINK:

How do I do that?

HOWARD CAMPBELL:

You take aim on the unformed minds. You are the local strongman who brings the bright young minds before the king in order to keep the Pirate's trade routes free of obstruction.

DR. WILLIAM FINK:

How do you figure?

HOWARD CAMPBELL:

You prescribe Ritalin to kids who are not entitled to say "no" to your medication.

Did it ever occur to you that these kids that disrupt classes might not belong in a classroom setting? Maybe they're just over-stimulated introverts, blowing off excess stimulus. Introverts process stimulus differently from other people. When they get too much fluff or entrainment without content, they physically lash out, beyond their control or intent. But, they just can't handle the bullshit that is expected of them.

DR. WILLIAM FINK:

What *bullshit*?

HOWARD CAMPBELL:

Introverts find other people tiring; Extroverts are energized by people. Classrooms favor the extrovert, because a student is forced to be in a group for extended periods of time.

To an extrovert, introverts may seem antisocial. Well, that's because most extroverts bore them, most of the time. Introverts skew gifted and are more reflective. But it's difficult to be reflective in a room of chattering extroverts. In short, introverts are more sensitive and smarter than extroverts, yet, extroverts dominate most of society. So, they bulk up the bell curve, and being outgoing is considered normal and therefore healthy.

The DSMr4—written, no doubt, by a committee of extroverts—defines declining to banter as antisocial. Being an introvert is not a choice, or a lifestyle, but an *orientation*. But this is within your doctrine of abnormal psychology, which is what's fucked-up to begin with.

DR. WILLIAM FINK:

How do you see it that way?

HOWARD CAMPBELL:

As a course of study, abnormal psychology is like criminology, you only study failed endeavors. You've spent your whole life looking at what's wrong with people.

Self-help experts, such as Stephen R. Covey and the those like him, like Anthony Robbins, only study for "effectiveness" against a specific agenda, agenda thinking, attaccan thinking. This agenda promotes accumulation of money as good, keeping anything substantively qualitative from being accounted for. It's an arrogance that suggests that different people are wrong. It's arrogance that suggests that "not wanting to chat" is distasteful and abnormal. What gives you the right to be so righteous?

DR. WILLIAM FINK:

Perhaps it's that I think I can help them be happier.

HOWARD CAMPBELL:

Your version of happiness. Whatever happened to the right to pursue happiness? *Their* happiness. Kaiser's play *Emergency* depicts an arrogant psychologist. He can not let go of his pride, so his wife sends a psychologist to see him, posing as a patient who suffers from the symptoms of the arrogant psychologist.

Prudence isn't a discipline followed by extroverts who blab and blab about nothing, because they value the cadence of entrainment. To an introvert, self-deprecation is appreciated as a tool for not standing out. With extroverts, self-deprecation is tolerated, but not encouraged. Ever notice how there is no self-deprecation in chat rooms?

DR. WILLIAM FINK:

I've never been in an online chat room.

[PAUSE]

HOWARD CAMPBELL:

False modesty is self-deprecation with panache.

Name me one philosopher who was an extrovert. Can't be done. Introverts generally lack the social panache to tonally correct their grand ideas. Their grand ideas are forms of philosophy. Philosophy is a product of leisure time. We can't philosophize when we're being required to *pay* attention, constantly spending our time paying attention to the countless stimuli that bombards us.

When you give Ritalin to a child, you're cutting off our supply of new philosophy by drugging the minds of the exceptional youth. You are generating the objective of the elite, to maintain the status quo. You're like a psychologist in Nazi Germany, helping the system maintain itself.

DR. WILLIAM FINK:

Don't you think you're being a little harsh?

[PAUSE]

HOWARD CAMPBELL:

I forgive you.

DR. WILLIAM FINK:

What?

[PAUSE]

HOWARD CAMPBELL:

I forgive you.

DR. WILLIAM FINK:

For what?

HOWARD CAMPBELL:

For your transgressions against humanity.

DR. WILLIAM FINK:

Get out of here.

HOWARD CAMPBELL:

Five.

DR. WILLIAM FINK:

What?

HOWARD CAMPBELL:

Five. You went back a step.

DR. WILLIAM FINK:

I'm getting tired of your little game.

HOWARD CAMPBELL:

Four. We've been through this before. I'll leave on my own accord, when we get to seven.

DR. WILLIAM FINK:

Fuck you!

HOWARD CAMPBELL:

Very good. Five. We're back to anger and persuasion. Now, we just need to get acceptance of the system and seven.

[PAUSE]

I was offering you forgiveness.

DR. WILLIAM FINK:

I don't need your forgiveness.

[PAUSE]

HOWARD CAMPBELL:

This morning, I sent a letter to your wife outlining the details of your extramarital affairs.

[PAUSE]

I'm calling your bluff. You said you liked to see retribution. You just don't like to see it regarding yourself. Nobody likes to see themselves as the bad guys. Americans don't like to see themselves as well-armed thugs who destroy other financial constructs. You don't like to see yourself as an adulterer. You *are* an adulterer. I just thought it was fair if your wife saw you for what you are, so I sent her the letter.

[SILENCE]

DR. WILLIAM FINK:
You didn't.

HOWARD CAMPBELL:
Okay.
[PAUSE]

DR. WILLIAM FINK:
Shit.

HOWARD CAMPBELL:

Okay, I didn't.

DR. WILLIAM FINK:

Now, you're just fucking with me.

HOWARD CAMPBELL:

Yes, I am. But, you don't know if I did or not. And, it doesn't really matter. What does matter is that you are an asshole, and just about anybody you are mean to on this staff could write that letter, in spiteful retribution, any day they felt vindictive.

But my point is that you can't ascertain your position because you have huge exposed liabilities.

[PAUSE]

DR. WILLIAM FINK:

I'm not that vulnerable.

[PAUSE]

HOWARD CAMPBELL:

Let's take stock of the situation. You have chosen a lifestyle that could lead to your wife leaving you. You're at risk of having your medical license revoked. And you may burn for eternity because you aren't following all the laws the head of your church deems holy.

[PAUSE]

DR. WILLIAM FINK:

I am so fucked.

[PAUSE]

HOWARD CAMPBELL:

Six.

[PAUSE]

DR. WILLIAM FINK:

How am I now at six?

[SILENCE]

HOWARD CAMPBELL:

You are beginning to lose your arrogant perception of control and accept the precariousness of your situation.

DR. WILLIAM FINK:

It doesn't feel good. I am so fucked.
[PAUSE]

HOWARD CAMPBELL:

Yes.
[PAUSE]

DR. WILLIAM FINK:

How do I work through this? How do I get to the next level? How do I get to seven?
[PAUSE]

HOWARD CAMPBELL:

Own how this feels.
[PAUSE]

Be accountable for your sensation.
[PAUSE]

You chose this.

DR. WILLIAM FINK:

I didn't choose to feel like this, you lead me here.

[PAUSE]

HOWARD CAMPBELL:

Five. A position of manipulation.

DR. WILLIAM FINK:

Fuck you.

[PAUSE]

How did I choose this?

HOWARD CAMPBELL:

What you are feeling is the sum of your life choices. You have just slowed down enough to hear your feelings.

[SILENCE]

Good.

[SILENCE]

Six. Acceptance of the system.

[PAUSE]

DR. WILLIAM FINK:

When you taught me the number theory a couple months ago…

_____

[PAUSE]

HOWARD CAMPBELL:

Yes?

DR. WILLIAM FINK:

You only taught me up to six.

[SILENCE]

You didn't teach me seven.

[SILENCE]

Why didn't you teach me seven?
[PAUSE]

HOWARD CAMPBELL:

There is no seven.

DR. WILLIAM FINK:

What do you mean *there is no seven*?
[PAUSE]
There *has* to be a seven. You *said* there was a seven.
[PAUSE]

HOWARD CAMPBELL:

There is no seven.

[PAUSE]

DR. WILLIAM FINK:

If there is no seven, then, what are we doing here? When will you leave?

[PAUSE]

HOWARD CAMPBELL:

Life is perpetual motion. Life is a system we can never understand. Life is feeling precarious.

[PAUSE]

DR. WILLIAM FINK:

Fuck this. I'm going home and taking a hot shower.

HOWARD CAMPBELL:

I don't think you can do that.

DR. WILLIAM FINK:

Why not?

[PAUSE]

HOWARD CAMPBELL:

Call your wife.

[PAUSE]

[SOUND: CELL PHONE FLIP CASE OPENING. CELL PHONE BEEP]

DR. WILLIAM FINK:

Home.

[SOUND: FINK'S RECORDED VOICE]

"Home"

[SOUND: RINGING OF DIALED NUMBER]

Hi honey-bun. Hell…Hello?

That's odd.

[SOUND: CELL PHONE BEEP]

Home.

[SOUND: FINK'S RECORDED VOICE]

"Home"

[SOUND: RINGING OF DIALED NUMBER]

Melinda?

HOWARD CAMPBELL:

It won't work. I visited her this morning. I showed her pictures of you and Nurse Prynne showering together.

DR. WILLIAM FINK:

Where the fuck did you get those photos?

HOWARD CAMPBELL:

From the private investigator I hired.

DR. WILLIAM FINK:

I thought you figured that stuff out, about my affair, from how I called Prynn by her first name?

[PAUSE]

HOWARD CAMPBELL:

I'm not that good. I only made that observation after I knew you were having an affair with her. But a bigger point is that you believed me. You can't tell truth from lies. What I told you seemed plausible.

DR. WILLIAM FINK:

You intentionally tricked me.

[PAUSE]

HOWARD CAMPBELL:

How do you know that the forefathers of your church didn't do the same thing? People take for granted that during the Vietnam War, the government lied to them. Why should now be any different?

[SILENCE]

[SOUND: LETTER BEING UNFOLDED]

I also sent this letter to the American Medical Association, outlining the details of your treatment *system* at The Children's School, and how you write prescriptions for students, including your nephew, which is grounds to have your medical license suspended.

[SOUND: A CHAIR PULLING OUT AND FOOT STEPS]

HOWARD CAMPBELL:

You said you wanted to know everything. You said, *"Everything I can learn will help me."* Now, I've told you everything I can think of that feels relevant.

[PAUSE]

Deal with it.

[SILENCE]

DR. WILLIAM FINK:

Why are you doing this to me? You are my Satan incarnate.

HOWARD CAMPBELL:

[LAUGHTER]

I'm not Lucifer. Lucifer wants you to mindlessly continue the dumbing of our youth, to continue your infidelities, and your lack of integrity, your continued belief that Jesus is the only *begotten* son of god.

[LAUGHTER]

You slay me with your projections of evil.

[LAUGHTER]

I am Jesus. But, not like one of your delusional patients. I am a son of god. God is within me like he was within Jesus. God is within each of us, if we quiet our minds enough to listen, but busy minds can't listen.

[PAUSE]

All men are created equal, endowed by *our* Creator with unalienable rights, and whenever anything becomes destructive of these ends, it is the responsibility of individuals to alter or to abolish the source of destruction.

> *Blessed is he who in the name of charity and goodwill shepherds the weak through the valley of darkness, for he is truly his brother's keeper, and the finder of lost children.*

[RAISED VOICE AND INTENSITY]

> *And, I will strike down upon thee with great vengeance and furious anger those who attempt to poison and destroy his brothers. And you will know my name is The Lord when I lay my vengeance upon thee.*

[PAUSE]

Now sleep. Sleep my friend. Sleep is restorative. When you wake up, this will all be here. As long as you sleep, you are safe from reality. Sleep my friend. Sleep like you have never slept before. You are safe here. You are among friends. Here, they care for people who sleep with their eyes wide shut. You are feeling drowsy.

[PAUSE]

You can work it out another day. Right now it hurts to think. Go back to sleep. Embrace the comfort of a quiet mind. You are safe here. You are among friends. Your eyes are getting heavy.

[PAUSE]

Close your eyes. You are safe here. Dream a better dream. Flutter by, butter fly. Flutter bye.

[PAUSE]

Rest your head.

[PAUSE]

Sleep my angel.

[SILENCE]

Sleep my angel.

[PAUSE]

[SOFT VOICE]

Sleep my angel.

[PAUSE]

[SOUND: DEEP BREATHING]

Sleep my angel.

[PAUSE]

[SOUND: DEEP BREATHING]

going to go now.

[PAUSE]

[SOUND: DEEP BREATHING]

I'm running out of cigarettes.

[SOUND: BREATHING AND SNORING—SUSTAINED BREATHING AND SNORING]

I did this for Bucky.

[PAUSE]

May you both rest in peace.

[PAUSE]

Sleep my angel.

[SOUND: SNORT]

[SOUND: BREATHING AND SNORING—SUSTAINED BREATHING AND SNORING]

[SOUND: DOOR OPENS AND FOOT STEPS. DOOR CLOSES.]

[SOUND: AUDIO RECORDER CLICKING OFF]

[SILENCE]

[SOUND: COUGHING--UNIDENTIFIABLE VOICE]

PSYCHIATRIST 1:

Dr. William Fink became a patient in Ward 3 on April 15 when we found him, unresponsive, gazing out the conference room window. Apparently he hadn't moved since Howard Campbell left. Fink has not said an intelligible sentence that we have heard. Howard Campbell was not this guy's real name. Dr. Reid, what did you find out about his alias?

[PAUSE]

Art?

PSYCHIATRIST 2:

A Benjamin Garth won an *Award of Merit* from the Academy of Magical Arts in 1987, but Benjamin Garth was a stage name, it wasn't a real name, and there seems to be no forwarding address. The Magic Castle doesn't know his real name. Dr. Drake, See if you can find a Den, Dennis, Denny or Dan who worked for Cingular. Maybe a Ben. I want to talk with Nurse Prynne.

PSYCHIATRIST 3:

Nurse Prynne was let go two months ago.

[PAUSE]

Do we know if Melinda Fink received a letter from this guy? Art, you certainly have become close with her.

PSYCHIATRIST 2:

She didn't receive a letter. Howard Campbell visited her that morning and told her that her husband was cheating on her.

PSYCHIATRIST 1:

What did she do?

PSYCHIATRIST 2:

She called me.

PSYCHIATRIST 1:

Were you already close with her?

[COUGHING]

PSYCHIATRIST 2:

Her personal life is not relevant to these proceedings.

[PAUSE]

PSYCHIATRIST 1:

Well, I need you to check Fink's home office for the any files that relate to this—the bibliography and the pictures and whatever else you can find. You *do* have a relationship with Melinda Fink that will allow for this, don't you?

PSYCHIATRIST 2:

Um, yes.

PSYCHIATRIST 1:

Let's talk about how we're going to handle this with the press. Call our GM. We need to find out if there are legal ramifications to investigating this young man who calls himself Howard Campbell since, technically, Fink *was* his doctor. Please stop recording Dr. Maestrovsky.

PSYCHIATRIST 3:

I don't care about finding the kid. The best thing for the hospital is that nobody knows this ever happened. Dr. Fink had a breakdown. That's all anybody needs to know.

PSYCHIATRIST 1:

Dr. Maestrovsky! Stop the damn record... *[CUT OFF]*

[END TRANSCRIPT]

Media: WAV file 1 of 1
Source: PANELREVIEW062303.WAV

A SHORT INTRODUCTION TO THE FECUNDITY

THE PHENOMENA OF "OVERLAY"

Dear Reader,

I have, over the years, come to understand that I have had many experiences during the course of my life that many people do not have. I have consorted with a variety of people, from the plain and simple to the outlandish and the peculiar. During many of these liaisons, I have repeatedly witnessed a phenomena that I have since learned is known in psychological circles as "overlay". Many new age guru hacks have latched on to this syndrome, so be careful when and if you "Google" it.

In a nutshell, Overlay Syndrome is the tendency of a person to "take on" the beliefs or personality traits of real life people, characters in books, movies or other media sources that they come into contact with. You may have noticed this in a subtler fashion with people who will adopt your catch phrases and mannerisms after long-term exposure. You may have even caught yourself doing it from time to time. I have witnessed this phenomena manifesting itself with great ferocity among certain "unstable" types, hearing everything from accounts of alien abductions, to characters in comics books, *really being about" them".* After seeing the syndrome manifest many times over in a number of people, I've become quite adept at spotting it.

I only bring this up because the Fecundity and accompanying letter from Ben that you are about to read carries a lot of "Howardisms" inside of it. You can see that from exposure to the transcripts, Ben has not only begun to adopt a lot of Howard's thinking patterns but has also, quite frankly begun to write (and probably speak) like him. I include this little disclaimer as a warning. Howard did warn us that the "meme" was infectious, so you can now say that you were warned. Please, don't let me stop you. Read on.

That is all.

Joseph Matheny

FECUNDITY

A GLOSSARY OF PROPER NOUNS AND NON-STANDARD ENGLISH

Joseph,

First off, that committee hadn't really researched Howard Campbell. He is all over the place on the web. Once I found his email address, I found a ton of his postings. He was a kid magician, winning some award from The Academy of Magical Arts. He did go to Bennington College. He has worked in advertising. He helped launch Gundam in America. He also won a Silver Effie for his work on Yomega Yo-Yo's. Remember when yo-yos were the popular toy in the summers of 1998 and 1999? Well, apparently Howard was the strategist behind that. I say apparently because I found a blog saying the credit should have gone to someone at JWT Chicago. Since you have stopped replying to my emails, I've organized my thoughts below.

You accused me of making this all up, that the interviews never took place, that it is phantasmagoric for words to so utterly change a persons mind to the extent of insanity. I understand how you feel; I felt the same way too. I went through a period where I thought the interviews had been staged. But, I could not find a motive. Why would somebody make all this up and produce these tapes? I have good news for you. I went back to The Transcription Company to finish up some paperwork. I was jolly and they were unsuspicious. I found the tapes where I thought they would be. I'm sending these tapes to Dr. Hyatt. Listen to them. Judge for yourself. What I found is that the narrative is compelling. If it is a fake, I don't care. To quote Bokonon, "Anybody who can't see the value of a book based on lies won't see the value of this book either." That's what made me think this should be published. I trust you are a man of your word.

I'm kind of pissed. Dr. Hyatt said you would help me. He said you could help me get *The Transcription* published. You said you could, too, when you first read it. But, now I haven't heard back from you in so long that I'm beginning to doubt your integrity on this issue. Are you a man of your word? *The Transcription* hasn't changed. Maybe I shouldn't have been such a nudge. I guess you felt I was stalking you. That would be bad manners. However, stalking would mean that you are the object of my obsession. You are not. You are a conduit to this body of work reaching a larger audience. Fear of being perceived as a stalker is why I haven't corresponded in while, waiting to gather all my ideas together in a single correspondence. That, and I've been reading stuff I never read before. I'm hearing words differently. I read Jenny Holzer's Truisms, I never would have read something like that before, but now, each sentence resonates in me in a way I wouldn't have felt before. I felt I was being spoken to, or that I was a comrade in an ancient army, a force I figured long ago flickered-out.

Unlike most glossaries, this one is presented in order of usage in text, like movie credits that aren't alphabetized. Similarly, each proper noun or non-standard English word is only presented once.

Following this glossary, I've included GUERRILLA BRANDING, a book Howard Campbell was working on with Jay Levinson. At his invitation, I visited Mr. Levinson. His wife's art is quite good. Jay told me Howard had moved to Atlanta to work at DDBO. Howard never finished GUERRILLA BRANDING. Jay said *The Branding Gap* accomplished what they had set out do. Humbly, Jay added that it probably did a better job than they would have been able to pull-off.

I also found a PowerPoint presentation *Memetic Branding* that, while not attributed, I hold to be his pen—or PowerPoint as the case may be. Also, side note, Campbell never wrote *Perpetual Motion* or *The Longer Line*, his previous drafts were titled *Twisp* and *Manufacturing America*. How do I know that? Glad you asked. I met Howard Campbell.

He asked me why the liberals don't have a coordinated media plan. He suggests they read *The Republican Sound Machine*, not as an exposé but as a magick book of tricks.

He said that the biggest taboo of Western culture isn't being gay, but being a Wiccan. He said, "You have to give action to get action." Then he attributed it to *Swimming With Sharks*.

He said I should buy two copies of *Manufacturing Consent*. I asked why. Funny how it should be grammatically correct to end that declarative sentence with a period. Back on the train. I asked how that would work. He said that my mind had changed; I had obviously begun arming my mental defenses.

David Mamet did what Nobokov did in Lolita. They said it couldn't be done. He asked if I ever really read the preface of Lolita. I was having trouble tracking. He said that Mamet wrote a story about a sympathetic pedophile. I asked him where. He said in American Hero. Mamet wrote American Buffalo.

My notes aren't very clear. They are not clear at all. I'm not accustomed to taking down live information. I'm accustomed to taking down dead language, a set group of words that I can play and replay to ensure accuracy. It was overwhelming. Why didn't I think to bring a recorder? Obviously, I'm no Boswell. I don't have Boswellian tendancies.

Howard said that he wanted me to have something. I said okay. He asked if I would "stand under reciprocity." I said I was sure I didn't understand him. He said more than I knew. He gave me the Noam Chomsky video *Manufacturing Consent*. He showed me he had another in his bag. That Gihan had given him a copy. Gihan asked that if I didn't like it, to just pass it on to somebody else. If I did like it, to buy two copies and tell them the story of how they came to own their copy. He paused. Howard asked me if I would do the same. I said yes. He said he had to go but asked that we meet downstairs at noon for lunch. I said yes and he said he needed to work on an essay on how he thought he sounded to people who weren't tracking. I said, "what?" He mentioned something about Cartesian linguistics.

He said it was important for me to listen closely and not to interrupt him. Howard said it is in the interest of the conservatives to have the media appear as liberal. It would actually probably suit their needs if they gave airtime to the fringe because in 6 minutes an alternative thinker would appear Neptunian to the popular ken.

I apologized for interrupting. I said I wouldn't interrupt except that I needed to know why *Manufacturing Consent*. Why not another video? I would still be paying it forward. He shook his head and said that we were locked into Albania. Then, he explained to me that he had written *Manufacturing America*. That he changed the name of the manuscript for the sake of the doctor. That he had never read Chomsky. That Gihan was like a gift from God because he gave him his own perception back. He reflected his values. He thanked God for Gihan and prayed for Gihan's health. I felt quite awkward.

Anyway, He slowed down and told me the original title was *Twisp* but that he was trying out new material on the doctor. "New material?" I asked. He said he was refining his rebuttals and sharpening his arrows. He explained that since Dr. Fink, he had had three more mental kills. He said he wanted to tell me the story of convincing a girl he was Satan and she was damned and then fucking her. He suggested we grab a beer and he would tell me the story. I said, "Yeah, that would be nice." The he suggested lunch the following day. He said he had an appointment with Erik J. Hughes and had to go.

Before we said until then, meaning tomorrow for lunch, he asked me to see what I could find out about Thorn Tree in Africa that evening on the Internet and asked me if I could organize it for him, that that would be a huge help. He asked if I was prepared to really listen. I said yes. Howard reiterated that it is in the interest of the conservatives to have the media appear as liberal. It would actually probably suit there needs if they gave airtime to the fringe because in 6 minutes an alternative thinker would appear Neptunian to the popular ken. And, that that was the problem he was working on. He said that when he cracked this puzzle, it may be time to celebrate Bloom's Day and that the Finnegans would wake.

Howard said I should watch *Manufacturing Consent's* scenes 23 & 24 several times. He paused and said it might be too late. Then he shuddered and said it was doable. He said it is important to know that it is doable. He said actually that was probably the answer; to know it is doable and tell other people it is doable. That he didn't want to die like his paternal grandparents who saw the world as fucked. His words. Then he said he really had to go. He said we would have beers tomorrow and meet here at noon. We said, "Until then."

I said that I looked forward to hearing about how he made Yo-Yos so popular. He froze. He said, "Warning." He paused. "Successes have many fathers, failures are orphaned." And, he continued on to his car.

As he walked away, he told me I would make more money if I learned how to sell. I asked, "sell what?" He said, "If you learned how to sell your self."

Since coming in contact with this project, I have begun meditating. I've grown a stronger yearning to honor my mother and father and how I came into this world. My father and mother are brilliant people. My dad worked with the American Friends Service Committee during the Vietnam War. My mother has worked extensively to help Tibetan Buddhism for the past 30 years. We all do what we can; they have both certainly pulled their weight from a social perspective. My last parent is my stepmother. She seeds the minds of young women to continue a broader perspective. But this isn't about me: it is about the ideas.

Buckminster Fuller says he is an average man who has an average mind that he simply put in extraordinary situations. Haruki Murakami states something quite similarly in *Norwegian Wood*. I'm beginning to believe them. Joseph Campbell and Noam Chomsky both attribute their edge perspectives, edgy in terms of a bell curve of normality, to being raised literal devoutists, systemically raised to reproduce the memes of their grandparents with extraordinary fidelity, fecundity—raised among many little disciples. That breaking from these tribes was difficult and substantial. I'm ranting as you have accused me of.

Back to downstairs at DDBO. I left and went to Caribou Coffee to work on my assignment until they closed. I stayed up half the night and went to Kinko's at 3am to get the damn thing bound. I say damned because I was being played without my knowledge. I don't hold a grudge. It was the right thing for him to do. It was just painful when it happened. There is no ill will intentionally harbored. It wasn't an emotional choice of Howard's, but a structural choice. They both feel painful to the subject, but the motivation is very different,

The next day, I arrived downstairs and had a drink at Cirque De Something or Other restaurant and had a drink. I felt like I was in bullshit central and paying triple for the attitude of the clientele. History Connie. I didn't know Jim Bellushi was Albanian.

At 11:55 I went outside and waited. And, waited. He, as you may have speculated, wasn't coming. I called DDBO. They explained he didn't show up that day. Long story short, he never came back. I stayed in Atlanta, bought a recorder and was invited to go look for him when he missed his second day. Nobody at DDBO knew where he was or even that he had been taking trips to Hawaii.

His computer was scrubbed clean. Wouldn't even boot up. He had taken the hard drive. I went through his desk. I found empty drawers and a note addressed to me.

"Dear Ben,
You found me. It isn't nice to be stalked. It was bad form to approach me at work. I cannot afford your baggage of liabilities and indiscretion. I am safe. I just needed to evaporate. If you want to talk to me, or even ask about me to another, make sure you are not jeopardizing my livelihood, please. More importantly, you don't understand the grave consequences of getting this information into the wrong hands before proper forces of defense can be mounted. Fortunately, my defense fortresses were in place and I could evaporate safely. If you think this is a hyperbole, you haven't done your due diligence and probably don't know how.

*Get to know a coach or psychiatrist or in an est group before you are forced to see that you
need one. Do me that favor. Check out Landmark Education.*
*I'm heading to Ong's Hat, New Jersey. I'm hoping to join my love, Liz Boswell. Maybe
she will have me now. Maybe she doesn't love me. Maybe she's just scared. Her obsession
with Samuel Johnson is annoying.*
Best wishes,
Howard"

There is no Ong's Hat, New Jersey. I don't care what you can find
online. It doesn't exist. I'm ahead of myself. This note was handwritten,
but I transcribed it accurately, punctuation intact. I haven't spoken to
him since. His neighbors hadn't even known he had left. They said they
hadn't known him. He had kept to himself. He was cordial but avoided
any substantive exchanges. One neighbor said he felt like he had lived
next to the Judd Hirsch family in *Running on Empty*. It was from me that
he learned Howard wasn't there anymore.

I tracked Howard down in Madison Wisconsin. I interviewed Mr.
Hughes—arrogant S.O.B., Howard not Erik. Howard went and saw Erik
in Glenn Gary/ Glenn Ross. Then left, and Erik claims he hasn't spoken
with him since. Which is probably true. Erik did give me the book
Howard was reading, *A Cruel Passing of Innocence* by J. D. Jensen. I
thought it was pornography. Erik said that Howard said it was a
corollary to *From The Belly of the Beast*. He said I might check with
Stephan Fowlkes, Howard was heading to New York to see his show
Dialogues. I went, Howard wasn't there, and Stephan said he had no idea
where Howard would be, but that he wasn't worried about him.

When I didn't hear back from you, I called your cell number. It is
disconnected. My last email was returned with an auto-reply that you
aren't online at that email address anymore. I feel like a girl that got
stood up for the prom. I feel more than that. I don't know what to
make of anything. The postman knocked at my door and I was scared
they were coming from me. Now, I found a form saying they need my
signature for a registered lettered. I don't know if I should sign for it or
not.

I've gotten better at my investigative skills. I interviewed Carlo Vogel, a
schoolmate of Howard's that I found through Ginger Parker and Blaine
Graboise. Carlo went to Bennington as a theatre major when he
transferred from Julliard. He is an actor and a P.I. Different months
different gigs pay more, but any rate, he taught me about pretexts and
interviewing and suggested I read *Mindhunt* by John Douglas. He also
said that he was expecting me. Howard had visited and said that I should

have a copy of *Manufacturing America*. Howard used large segments from this book in his dialogue with Dr. Fink. This is the book Richard Wilson had read. It begins:

"In 1993, I was admitted into a mental hospital and initially diagnosed as being a paranoid schizophrenic. People had started appearing strange to me. In retrospect, I guess they were always strange; my newfound strangeness shifted my focus and each person I encountered seemed stranger than the next. The truth is, I was the stranger. I had manufactured an image of America that didn't jive with those around me.

"I hold this to be true: *We create that which we study*. I had been telling my closest friends that if I ever sent them the message, *'I'm running out of cigarettes.'* That I was in trouble and being held captive. That was Philip K. Dick's secret signal that he and his close friends would use if they were ever in serious trouble. I was focusing on the possibility of being held captive. Focus on anything submissive long enough and somebody will make you their bitch.

"What had thrown my spirits into the hospital was a mutated thought train. *Manufacturing America* is an attempt to reconstruct my perspective. In the first chapter, I start four days before my admittance to the care of Southern Vermont Hospital's mental ward for an eight-day stay. I track my experience preceding the admittance, through and out of their care. In the second chapter, I discuss what I was studying at Bennington College where I was an ontology major, in year seven of what turned out to be an eight-year undergraduate degree. Chapter Three illustrates the commercial applications of these ideas and I how I applied them as an account planner at Deutsch Advertising during the time that they won back-to-back 'Agency of the Year' awards from both *AdWeek* and *Ad Age*. Chapter Four is an analysis of relevant experiences that lead from incarceration through profiteering. Finally, Chapter Five is how I find peace of mind within this engineered society we call America.

"I know my recollections don't exactly mirror the events of the time. In addition, I have changed the names of everybody I mention in the medical profession. I'm sure they meant well. At the time, we just weren't connecting.

"As my pen trekked through this journey, I attempted to cite my influences. There are two notable influences from which I have drawn: Kurt Vonnegut presented Bokonon, a religion that seemed to have a psychology of humanity that I liked, and Mamet gave me the notion of Albanians, those people that you suddenly see as part of a program and not living like a human. What I strove to create was a Bokononist guide to living amongst Albanians."

I'm forwarding this manuscript to you. I asked him for a copy of TWISP. He said he didn't have one, and that even if he did, he might not give it to me since Howard had suggested I give him this other manuscript and that it had seemed like an inclusive sentiment. Howard had apparently asked him to help me with my investigative skills but not to give me facts about Howard's whereabouts. Carlo added, "Discretion is the better half of valor." Shit, that feels like an embedded clue to me. Am I becoming paranoid? Carlo also said that most things are as they appear.

This is similar to something another Howard friend said, asked only to be identified as Mullup Finger, "Women will tell you the symptom of their greatest neurosis at the first opportune time, men are just blinded by lust and usually choose to ignore it." Mullup said it works if you reverse the sexes. He called this his Red Flag theory.

Anyway, I'm becoming almost proficient at Googling. Carlo's tips have really helped me. I Googled Emily Kischell and found her listed at "anybody who's everybody in adult trade publishing" but she no longer worked at Writer's House. They were brusque and acted annoyed with every question I asked, reiterating that they had no forwarding information and that even if they did, they wouldn't tell me as company policy forbade it.

There are possibilities for change here in the United States that are not afforded elsewhere. Those of us who see the mass media as misdirecting the proper allocation of resources, have an obligation. We need to begin proposing media plans that leverage the new structure of appointment media. We need to create more of our own media and disseminate it as we can, as we see fit. There are a lot of reporters that do a very good job. Understanding pressures and barriers allows you to see the opportunities.

Most people just entrain with the masses. This binds the illusion of free will.

Joseph, what follows is the glossary I told you I would send. As I requested, please keep this to yourself. You wanted to know why I thought this interview was important. I saw it as self-evident. I imagine you were confused by much of the content. I have reorganized my journal notes to clarify concepts not within the popular ken. My goal is to decipher this over-weighted information, this web of Howard and Dr. Fink's conversation. Or, at minimum, instill confidence in others that it is decipherable.

I stand for the possibility that the myth of scarcity be washed away before it becomes a self-fulfilling prophecy with irreversible ramifications that will reframe our concept of substantial.

GLOSSARY

IN ORDER OF APPEARANCE, A HEURISTIC CHOICE

Fnord—word coined by Robert Anton Wilson in The Illuminatus! Trilogy. Fnord is the hypocrisy perpetuated by agendas. Seeing fnords is seeing the duplicity of a statement, action or situation. Boswell.

Bucky—The name "Bucky" is most often associated with R. Buckminster Fuller, the scientist who coined the word *synergy*. Howard Campbell was one of three children who interviewed this scientist in *Fuller's Earth: A Day With Bucky and the Children.*

Synergy—The title of a 3,000-page treatise in two parts, *Synergetics* and *Synergetics II*, on the metamorphoses of systems, where the change is not foreseeable by looking at the parts individually. When summarized into a sentence, it is often misunderstood and taken to mean an exponential increase in productivity or strength. Buckminster Fuller said that his greatest gift to humanity was the word, *synergy*. He also said the future of understanding lay in the field of topology.

Scarfed—To have eaten hastily or quickly.

Gödel—Mathematician who proved that some truths can not be proven. This was a seminal mathematical proof—no previous mathematical proof had attempted to prove the existence of things outside of mathematics. I don't know enough math to make sense out of most of what I have read about him. I also could not find articles that suggested he proved what Campbell said he proved. I think Campbell was bullshitting.

Einstein—Need I say more than relativity? How can I say more and not write a book. I found a post where Campbell was riffing on Einstein and memetics. He was criticizing physicist who was criticizing another for having relative values. Campbell was questioning the physicist's limited utilization of Einstein's theory of relativity.

Kuhn—Campbell states Kuhn's relevance. Nothing more really needs adding. Structure of Scientific Revolution was a seminal work, largely disregarded today. Why do I include Kuhn if I intend to add nothing, because I pulled all the words that were proper nouns or non-standard English and I will hold true to that system in this endeavor.

Patrist—This is a cosmographical slur. I don't how else to explain it. Patrist is overwhelmingly used in a pejorative context. It appears to be a memetic grouping.

Vonnegut, Kurt—Self proclaimed science fiction writer, he is usually classified under general fiction which suggests he has transcended his genre.

Pattern Integrity—"A pattern has an integrity independent of the medium by virtue of which you have received the information that it exists." -R. Buckminster Fuller. I found a blog of Howard Campbell's that reflects his integration of Bucky's ideas and branding. He wrote: "If we replace the word 'pattern' with the word 'brand,' we create the statement: 'A brand has an integrity independent of the medium by which you have received the information that it exists.'"

Google'd—Verb meaning to look something up at google.com

Giza—Further reading about Giza can be found in *Fingerprints of the Gods*, however, beyond the Giza section, the book spirals into stuff I just can't hold to be true. I found similar issues in *The Holographic Universe*. I don't know what to make of this. It is weird to have somethings seem so true and then to have the same source give me stuff that just seems like shenanigans.

Stickies—Generic word for Post-Its, those small and yellow (traditionally yellow but now available in a variety of colors) pads of paper with a sticky substance that allows it to stick to most surfaces. That sticky stuff is the marvel. How did they make it so tacky and yet not so tacky as to harm anything it sticks to? Then, the brilliance was in the application of this invention. They found a practical use for this magnificent tackiness. Sheer genius.

Voight Comm Test—Philip K. Dick. Ahhh PKD. Head fucker of them all. This test was to distinguish humans from machines. And, the premise that memories can trick a machine into believing it is human. We are living amongst an army of machines. The droid army in Star Wars II, this is the reality in which we live.

Dick, Philip K.—PKD. I feel humbled to write anything on this mad genius. Actually, he wasn't mad all the time. I just the movie Van Helsing. The "through the looking glass" scene near the end, he has read Dick as well as Alice in Wonderland.

Asimov, Isaac—While he could see insanity, it never consumed him. Reality and sanity were not as interwoven for Asimov as it was for Dick. Asimov presented alternative realities, but didn't focus on the power of perception as much as Dick did.

Maybe logic—Robert Anton Wilson's rational ambiguity. Speaking in E-Prime means always making subjective comments as opposed to definitive comments. This system of speaking/thinking would nullify Christianity. Don't you think? The woman who speaks in scene 24 of the video Manufacturing Consent, she doesn't see Robert Anton Wilson's concepts of structure. If she read *The Illuminatus! Trilogy!* she might see the structure within common values that deny connection. I hope that this is the structure of *Star Wars III*.

Spokesthing—There are some companies that have a spokesperson or a talking sock puppet as the primary speaker for the company. A spokesthing is when they personify an inanimate object. Turns out that Howard worked on Veringular.

Enlightenee—A person who becomes enlightened.

Hoffstadter, Douglas—The '90s master of self-referential material. Also, most popular author on media consumption theory—consumption as in the process, not as in quantity or variety of media, but more from a cosmographical perspective.

Oxford English Dictionary—The Shit. *The Professor and the Mad Man* details the depth of this undertaking. I've grown up with dictionaries. The idea of creating an all encompassing dictionary is not revolutionary to me. It was then a revolutionary idea. To have a single book, or at least 23 volumes of a single entity, that would encapsulate all written words—a project that would never end because they realized language was changing. No other language has as comprehensive and authoritative reference guide.

Propaganda—The antithesis of E-Prime. The speaker or source presents reality as if they know what reality is, objectively. Wait, that is only one type of propaganda. Propaganda is that which attempts to influence for the sake of an agenda. If that is true, what then is art? If art is as Hegel describes, that which catapults someone to an altered state of consciousness, then is art propaganda? Propaganda may be art. Is all art propaganda, trying to influence the viewer according to the artists agenda? Often, the craftsman is being hired by somebody. Art might be any object that can catapult a mind. Propaganda is that which is created with an end in mind. Commonly, propaganda is the intentional propagation of false facts. Like, "anything opposed to your church is bad." In short, propaganda is a fnord.

Sacra Congregatio de Propaganda Fide—A major advancement in human engineering grossly overlooked by most historians. Fuckers. Historians can't see that they are the blind craftsmen who are creating the mind catapulting art object for the agenda of their employer. The beauty of capitalism is the illusion of free will/free choice. If one creates the value system, the choices are easily influenced.

Pope Gregory XV—Fucker. Bad kind of pirate. Coined the term *propaganda*. Gave the military command to "Contain the productive." First memetic warrior with a mass media plan.

Internet—The greatest meme distribution system ever. The dissemination of ideas is the growth of civilization and isms. Isms are the great dividers of humans which keeps us animalistic. Like how rats can smell whether or not another rat is from their tribe, humans can intuit through memes whether somebody is of their tribe or grandfalloon or sometimes even karass. Back to rats. Rats will kill rats from alternative rat families; Humans will often kill humans from other isms.

It—A tool for objectification.

Intellishit—Something with internal validity but lacks relevance to the outside world. Is this Intellishit? Propaganda is intellishit. But when propaganda works, is it still intellishit? Intellishit is the stuff that if you erased, Nature could still function. Intellishit is the seed of culture. I'm beginning to see stickers that read "This is Intellishit" They tend to be on Bush/Cheney re-election posters and ads, but they are also on ads of all kinds. Re-election? When your brother is the umpire you usually win the contest. Nepotism is no reason to suspect a conflict of interest. This is intellishit, also.

Knights Templar—A group that fought the system.

Meme—An object or pattern of the mind. Anything a mind can replicate. However, just like how in physics the smallest particle is still made up of particles, every memes is made up of smaller memes, if you choose to seek them.

Memetic—That which propagates through mental replication/telepathy. Good example can be seen in a book by John Barnes called Candle, pg 58, talks about heroes as memes. Yet, Barnes, like so many, mistake memes for only ideas with significant impact, specifically those that seek to control a mind and subsequent body. Every entry in the OED is a meme, every song, every jesture or mannerism picked-up—even breating rates are meme because of entrainment. Memetics and entrainment are intertwined.

The basic idea though is to look at ideas as living organisms. I know you have seen *Wag the Dog*. The healthy idea is that the president is good for America, despite the fact that he is a pedophile. Any idea that threatens the vitality of this memeplex is a cancer. This is intended to be inferred, or deducted, when Anne Heche says, "They're all in remission. This is good Connie, its all war. They're only talking about war."

I could go on about this for an hour if you would ever invite me to talk about it. I would talk about the structure of arguments as revealed in this historic movie reveals and depicts. It is the Citizen Kane of our time.

Amped—Extra energy.

Pirate—Somebody living outside the dominant system, Or, a secret source of power controlling the system. Causa Latet Vis Est Notisima. A navigator of subtle power. Somebody with cunning and power whose very presence and existence challenges the power elites. Modern industrial life is controlled by convenient myths, Extraordinarily powerfully old memes.

The danger of pirates is that they have anticipatory skills in which they have confidence. This leads to a growing incredulity towards the Intellishit of pundits on TV, and mass media in general. Pirates perceive conditions of survival which are not often aligned with the immediate profit-motivated desires of the power elites.

Pirates see that Spaceship Earth is not an infinite resource. They have the capabilities to reorganize our allocation of resources to better serve humanity. The elites don't want to give up their positioning in this marketing premise. Reality is what is perpetuated through mass media— the power of consensus reality is truly under appraised.

Individual material gain may not be empirically good. No biological organism has sustained with this kind of parameter. Memes changed when they took on lives outside of the body, with the baton. In biological terms, 30,000 years is nothing. So, we Capitalists hold that we are doing god's work. Nature is god's work. She doesn't keep wasters around for long. She culls the portfolio in brutal ways. It is Utopia or Oblivion. When the RNC talks about destiny, I want to see the blue print. Quit distracting us with sports, especially this weird contest in Iraq.

> "As long as some specialized class is in a position of authority. It is going to set policy in the special interests that it serves. But the conditions of survival, let alone justice, require rational social planning in the interest of the community as a whole, and by now that means the global community.
>
> The question is whether privileged elites should dominate mass communication and should use this power as they tell us they must, namely to impose necessary illusions, to manipulate and deceive the stupid majority, and remove them from the public arena.
>
> The question in brief is whether democracy and freedom are values to be preserved or threats to be avoided. These may not only be values to be treasured, they may be essential to survival."
> --Noam Chomsky, *Manufacturing Consent* video, scene 23

Popular ken equates democracy with capitalism. Is this sustainable? Simply having a choice doesn't mean it reflects the will of the people. Most people can't conceive of a forced choice. Most people haven't studied influence.

Poker—The intentional application of power. Winners tend to raise more than they call, and fold more than they raise, but more importantly, prudence keeps them from entering very many hands to begin with. They have acquired more accurate maps than most. Playing poker has a psychic cost—excuse me, in a neutral tone—playing poker has an affect on one's physiology, their mental, physical and psychic composure. Yes, one develops the ability to concentrate with immediacy and for extended periods of time. There is a general dulling of empathy and excitement. Poker players are no longer pirates. The church has shifted from their position that poker players are vulgar to seeing them as "alternative businessmen." I suspect this is because the church now sees that poker players are basically benign because while they drop out of the primary work matrix, they are self-distracted by their worship of money.

Allan Carse—Modern Natural Philosopher.

Toole, John Kennedy—Tortured soul. He has his own bronze statue in New Orleans.

Ownership liability—What industrialists hope to do away with.

Sociopath— Non-humane entity imbued with the rights of a human. A corporation. A term no longer found in DSM. Low-grade sociopaths refer to themselves as *professionals*.

Pokemon—Proof the devil is real. A Christian mechanism to propagate their ideals to youngens.

Cosmic Wipeout—A recreational game.

Ganj—Pot. A recreational drug.

Justin Theroux—A failed cartoonist.

Sufi/Sufism—A group of idiots.

Sphinx. Geologist Robert Schoch—Author of Giza book.

Christian Huygen—Entrainment coiner.

Escher—Painter who illustrated that the map is not the terrain, showing how the rules of the map can be used to create shocking realities. Despite the Pope's efforts to destroy Escher, he had already caught on. Totally destroying him would make him a martyr and a bigger threat.

The Illuminatus! Trilogy—An object of catalyst. A popularizer of the psi repressed by the dark forces.

Wilson, Robert Anton—A pirate, but a poor financial navigator.

Crowley, Aleister—A prankster pirate.

Magick—Science that confronts the church's propaganda. Memetic Magic by Kirk Packwood is a great primer. Memetic Magic is a book Howard Campbell is sure to own. Memetic Magic should be spelled Memetic Magick. I went to Atlanta to find him. I met some people who knew him. Howard doesn't live there anymore. He was fired, then freelanced. Don't know where he went.

Magick is poker without cards.

Runaway Jury, the movie directed by Gary Fleder, is an inquiry into practical magick. Grisham is fascinated by magicians. He is Narcissistic that way. The first evidence of this is depicted when Gene Hackman is being driven by a cabbie who tells Gene he pegged him for a first time visitor to New Orleans. Gene Hackman plays a profiler working as a jury consultant. We are introduced to his skill-set by the cabbie's prodding of being able to "peg" somebody. Gary Fleder depicts Gene's perspective as he focuses on a cross hanging from the rearview mirror, then at a picture of an elderly woman, and finally at a parking stub for a memorial hospital. Gene asks, "How's your mother?... She feeling better?" The cabbie asks how Gene knew about his mother. Gene continues with his cold reading by saying that this cabbie had considered putting his mother in a home but that it didn't feel like the Christian thing to do and continues by recommending that cabbie "reconsider the home, because: better to have an unhappy mother than an unfriendly wife." I transcribed that accurately. How often does natural dialogue use a colon? Kudos to the screenwriters, Koppelman & Levien. But I digress. In the next seen we see the nebbish actor dude nobody remembers his name and does movies with John Cusak and Nicholas Cage, with Dustin Hoffman. Anyway, as Hoffman and Nebbish interact, we realize that these men are also magicians. Hoffman is feigning ignorance about Nebbish dude, or as we say colloquially, he is keeping his cards close to his chest. Or, is it vest? I don't know how that expression goes exactly. I'm getting ahead of myself if you haven't seen this movie. But, of course you have seen this movie. You're a profiler—if not trained or studied, at least by nature. You see. You see things most people don't see. You run scenarios in your head, revisiting how you might have better handled a scenario. Extraordinarily biting comments come out of your mouth when your filtering system is too stressed. This movie pits people like you against one another. This movie doesn't have a love triangle, it has a triangulation of manipulation, filled with overt intentions and clandestine tactics. This is competition at its best. Fuck football and auto racing, this is three-dimensional chess played with live bullets and for high stakes. A fundamental skill of the intentional magician is profiling. If you intend to persuade somebody, and you don't want to resort to brute force or threats thereof, an understanding of your target is the keyhole to subtle persuasion. *Mindhunt* articulates the craft of inductive insights. Similarly, *Zero Effect* summarizes the procedure; the art of research is to see through the facts to underlying passions. Most people are as they present themselves. A primary skill of a profiler, a magician, is to be able to identify when a person is lying; this is the skill to ascertain when things are not as they seem, when shenanigans are running amuck. Mike Caro, *Body Language of Poker* author, says that the first step in interpreting tells is to confidently ascertain when somebody is lying or not. Gene Hackman demonstrates this skill when he says to bounce a prospective juror who reveals himself to be an anti-gun advocate, trying to lie his way onto the jury. Following this scene, we learn that John Cusak is a player of poker without cards because we learn that he has previously presented a false front. Non-poker players think that the only time you lie in poker is when you bluff. Excellent poker players will sometimes muck premium hands if they know they are beat, and pretend they had rags to conceal their prowess in profiling. A poker player must concern himself with his table image. Many a well-quaffed dresser is as blind as a bat. Most "good dressers" are bound by societal standards inwardly projecting the meanings they ascribe to their surface symbols. Generally, magicians can dress well, but even if they can't, they understand how their presentation may frame the perception of those who view them. David Mamet once wrote in Men's Health that there are four levels of poker, you start by learning what you should do in a given situation. Next, you learn what other people are representing by interpreting the language of betting. Then, you learn to interpret how others see you. Finally, you learn to manipulate how others see you, to improve the likelihood of your effect. Our *tell* that Cusak is playing poker is when we learn that he was performing in an earlier scene when he pretended not to know his now obvious girlfriend. For the slow learners, Fleder has Cusak say, "Everybody has a button. We just got to find out where and push." Now, we know he not only hopes to persuade this jury, but that he has a clue as to how he might accomplish this. You see, Howard Campbell is a profiler. The work Howard does in advertising is the same technology FBI profilers and jury consultants use. If you think jury consultants are merely hired to find sympathetic jurors, your naïveté is painful to me. They are hired to be the account planners of their side's case. They don't make the speeches, just as an account planner doesn't make the ads, but jury consultants and account planners write the brief that say what should be communicate and in what tone to deliver the message. Jury consultants are like political consultants, their primary job is to frame the debate. Most bats, blind civilians, can't even pronounce the key words in important political issues, let alone truly know what they mean. Somebody has to explain this to the masses. The masses then go and talk amongst themselves. If you frame the debate correctly, they'll reach the conclusion of your intent. In *Runaway Jury*, the jury represents the masses. The courtroom is the media, the mechanism through which the meme wranglers disseminate their framings. This is theatre. The judge is the FCC. The battle is to be the stage manager. Since the masses are blind to subtleties, the primary weapon of the mass meme wranglers is stigma. If you can generate evil, people will avoid association. The primary story of Runaway Jury is over when Cusak asks, "Who's with Frank?" But, continuing to mirror life, Fleder ends the movie showing the media covering the trial blindly omitting the real players in the drama. Within good stories, the real players play poker.

Profiler—One who grasps how a person's values create their behavior, affecting their environment, simultaneously as their environment shapes their subtle values. Profilers are only profilers when they become predictive.

Mithras—An ancient temple.

Super-meme-plex—A religion not designated as an ism.

Goth—Where many wannabe pirates interact with struggling pirates. A big "F. You" to systemites.

Psi—Which came first--the chicken or the egg? 23=Illuminati or Psi=23?

Twisp—A tool to let go of an inappropriate thought, label or perspective.

Potemkin Village—Physical manifestation of intellishit.

Richard Brenneman—A Truth seeker. Which is a dangerous way to live if there is no Truth. The originator of the meme corporations are sociopaths.

Duprass—Mr. & Mrs. Fuller or any couple whose psyche is so intertwined they can think each other's thoughts and nod.

Attacca and Nacirema—Intellishit.

Proper Noun Anomia—Condition of not being able to use proper nouns as most do.

Sunsight—More accurate description of a sunrise than commonly used.

Sunclipse—More accurate description of a sunset.

Corporateland—Money-based environments.

Larry Beinhart—A brave writer.

Fuckupology—The study of failures including traditional crimonology. Also, can describe a perspective or background attitude such as the one many psychiatrists take when looking at patients or the category of abnormal psychology.

Twisp—Also can be used like fnord, to show when a system fails to do as it says. Did you say "dot com" in your head when you read the first page?

Gruntled—To be happy.

Ficial—Phantasmic word play.

Journaled—To write in one's journal.

Sortable—The precept that rubrics are functional.

Bokonon—As good as any metaphysical construct, better than some.

Priest—An officer in a corporation. Somebody whose job it is to bewilder consumers and blind them to seeing the word *God* as a metaphor.

hy-u-ook-kuh—A tool that keeps the church or state in place. Also, a tool to demonize. If you control that which is abhorrent, you control what is *good*.

Clipsed—As in e-clipsed.

vin-dit—A meme that re-orients your psychic navigational system.

Granfalloon—Human intellishit.

Wompeter—Foma and grandfalloon.

wookie—Those who it is generally best to let win. These beasts regularly play poker without cards because they are betting overt power.

Cialdini—Prominent author on persuasion, protected from church reprisal by academia.

Neurontin—Neuro blocker for the easily stimulated or overly stimulated.

Duchamp—Pirate & Poet. A poet is an artist with a business plan. Or, at least, I read that somewhere written by a great Sufi warrior.

Karass—Humans psychically directionally aligned. I'm beginning to suspect that Orson Scott Card is a member of my karass. Is "Card" his real name, or a play on words—Valentine was supposed to have written Ender's story. Is Ender's Game Orson's *Valentine Card*? Ender's Game introduces the concept of memetics. Speaker of the Dead—Is Jane not a conscious meme? Is memetics the recognition of an alien life form within us? What does it mean that I did a five-count like in *Xenocide*? Am I god-spoken without an adviser? Even if not my dupras, definitely part of my karass. I like her ass.

Alfred Binet—Bullshit artist, poet and scholar.

Cruelian—A corporation in human form.

Projectable—Pertaining to map-ability.

Melders—Those that can blend-in or those that actually adopt radically quickly. I'm searching for melders who share my perspective. I'm searching for the others—Timothy Leary's "others". I watched the movie, *The Others*. It is an indictment of a Fundamentalist Christian perspective, or maybe dogmatic perspectives in general. I read Dr. Hyatt's Dogma Days. That is helping me loosen my perceptions. The Black Book series is also good. I'm heading to Pangaea in North Bennington to meet Peter Vogel to discuss PortChicago.org. If you go there, tip well. I met Nina Diamond there. I showed her *The Transcription*. She said it should be called *The Longer Line*. She gave me great insight into Howard's writing and the confidence I could find him. Thank you Nina. I'm still tracking him. In fact, as I re-read The Transcription, that's its true name, back on the train—I'm tracking him better-and-better each day. Bill Hicks helps.

More at
http://www.pokerwithoutcards.com

Printed in the United States
41909LVS00004B/40